HIDE AND SEEK

HIDE AND SEEK

GAYLE ROPER

CHAPTER 1

Eight Years Ago

"What do you mean there's no account with my name on it?" Gabriella Francella stared at the bank teller on the opposite side of the marble counter. "You have my bank card in your hand." She pointed in case the woman didn't realize what she had.

The woman nodded and continued to study her computer screen. "There was such an account once, and your name was on it once, but it's marked closed."

Ellie's mouth went dry. "Closed?"

"Closed."

"That can't be right." Please don't let it be right! "There should be at least fifty thousand plus interest in it." She had to push the words out.

The teller, a chubby woman with puffy circles under her eyes, shook her head. "I'm sorry."

Ellie stood frozen, fighting panic. All her frantic plans depended on that fifty thousand. It *had* to be here. Her grandfather left it to her when he died ten years ago. She'd put it in the bank like he'd wanted her to where it would be safe as it accrued interest until she was ready to use it for something special.

"Like college, Ellie," he'd said as he patted her hand with his huge, gentle one.

Well, running away was special too.

She tried to think around the buzzing in her ears. What did she do now? A coherent thought finally surfaced, and she looked at the teller. "When was the last transaction on this account made?"

The teller read off a date nine years prior. Nine years. Just before Nicky was born. Just after she and Joey moved in together. Just after they made the account a joint account.

Joey had stolen her fifty thou even as he professed his undying love. She thought she might be sick right there on the shiny marble floor.

Blindly she turned away. The money was supposed to buy her a used car and let her and Nicky travel far, far from Philadelphia and Joey. It was supposed to feed them while they got settled and until she got a job.

The late morning sun struck her as she walked outside, and she squinted in the brightness. She pulled sunglasses from her purse and pushed them on. She felt hollow inside.

People hurried past, intent on their own problems. No one looked at her; no one understood that she had just been legally robbed of more than money. Joey'd also stolen that last bit of hope she'd struggled to hold on to over the years. It might be a warm day in late spring, but she was chilled to the bone.

Slowly she made her way to Ninth and Christian and the Italian Market. Somehow she had to put in her shift at Joey's deli/restaurant. No matter what happened in their private lives, Joey's deli came first. Heartache, physical pain, despair—none of it mattered. Joey's deli was everything.

Joey's deli, not hers, though she worked just as hard as he, though he'd told her when she was young and dumb that it would be theirs. Somehow she had to force herself to stand at the grill, shredding steak, cooking onions, slapping on slices of cheese, scooping it all into crusty Italian rolls as if nothing had changed.

But how could she squeeze past Joey, busy building the hoagies for which he was famous, without recoiling? Without grabbing the knife with which he split the rolls and jamming it in his back?

She shuddered. She was becoming as violent as him, and that scared her. She had to get away somehow. She had to before she lost herself completely.

When she reached Terafino's, she slipped in the back door. Joey was busy behind the counter, whipping out lunch orders for several businesses that had food sent in.

"You're late," he growled as she took her place at the grill. He gave no sign that he knew she and Nicky hadn't spent the night at home except for stepping on her foot as he passed, grinding his foot so it gave maximum discomfort.

Her breath caught at the biting pain, but she managed, "Only five minutes."

"Like I said, you're late. I need three cheese steaks."

She nodded as she tried to move her crushed toes. She slapped the meat on the grill beside the pile of onions already cooking, refusing to let the pulsing pain show in her expression.

"Antony got your work started." It was a verbal slap, something Joey was very good at.

Ellie glanced at Antony, all dark hair, dark eyes, and dark heart, Joey's best pal and minority partner in Terafino's Steaks and Hoagies. "Thanks." It choked her to say it. She hated being grateful to the man. There was something off about him, but Joey loved him like a brother.

Antony smirked at her and went back to slicing tomatoes.

Why had she ever worried about Joey sensing something was different in her attitude today? She could pass out from fear and loathing, and his only concern would be that she'd somehow compromised health regulations as she lay on the floor. He'd probably prod her with his toe and order her to her feet. No, he'd make a great show of helping her up, impressing the customers with his care and concern. Until later when they were alone.

To think that once she had seen him as thoughtful and romantic. When he had called her Angel Eyes, her pulse jumped and her heart swelled with love. These days he was Rocky Balboa and she was the side of beef hanging in the meat processing plant.

Well, she didn't have to worry about anything but the grill for the next few hours. Joey and Antony would be too busy with the customers or too caught up in ragging on each other to see her or her problems. The two of them wanted to be bigger and better known than Pat's or Gino's, Philadelphia's famous cheese steak places. And they wanted to be rich. One thing she couldn't deny: they worked hard to that end.

"I'm your sous chef," was Antony's latest attempt to make the customers laugh. He put on a tall chef's hat instead of the Phillies or Eagles, Sixers or Flyers cap he usually wore, depending on the season.

"Sandwich joints don't have sous chefs," Joey told him.

"If you said you had one, you'd sound classier."

"It'll take more than calling you a sous chef to make you one. Knowing how to ladle red sauce over meatballs doesn't qualify you for that title. And while we're the best at what we do—right, folks?"—this to the customers who answered with loud affirmatives—"shops like ours don't have sous chefs."

"Just because I didn't go to the Cordon Bleu...."

"You don't even know what the Cordon Bleu is," Joey taunted.

"Do too. It's chicken stuffed with ham and cheese, though how you *go* to it, I don't know."

The regulars laughed, loving the way the two teased each other. As far as they were concerned, Joey was the most charming and entertaining of men, Antony the most humorous.

If they only knew.

4

She checked the order slips and dropped a couple of burgers on the grill, made with freshly ground meat bought right here in the Italian Market this morning. Her mind ran wild as she inhaled the wonderful Italian smells that permeated the deli—garlic, olive oil, oregano, basil overlaid with onion and browning meat. And grease. What should she do about her missing money? Confront Joey? The thought made her dizzy with dread.

Maybe she could go to Nonna and ask for financial help. She cringed at the idea. Not that Nonna wouldn't help. She'd be delighted to get Ellie and Nicky away from Joey. She'd been praying for her to leave him for years.

It was pride and embarrassment that would keep her silent about the fifty thousand. She'd been stupid enough to believe that Joey would leave the money alone for no other reason than that it was hers. She'd already been foolish enough to get pregnant at sixteen, to leave Nonna and move in with Joey without benefit of marriage, foolish enough to drop out of school a year from graduation though she'd since gotten her GED.

And she'd been foolish enough to listen when he said, "Come on, El. All couples have joint accounts."

She slapped a fresh piece of steak on the grill. It lay, a red rectangle turning brown, sizzling, fragrant. She narrowed her eyes at it, and another brown rectangle superimposed itself over the steak. A desk drawer. A locked desk drawer. A locked desk drawer that Joey used as a safe of sorts. He kept several thousand dollars in it for emergencies.

"When you have a business, you never know when you'll need cash," he told her.

Or when you'll owe your bookie.

"Someday someone's going to rob you," she said. "Just wait and see."

Well. Today was going to be the day, and she was going to be the thief. Her skin prickled at the thought, and she suddenly felt renewed hope. She couldn't help her huge smile as she passed a pair of cheese steaks to a man in a dress shirt with his sleeves rolled up and his tie pulled loose.

"There you go," she said. He handed her a twenty, and their hands touched as she gave him his change.

Antony elbowed Joey, and Joey's eyes narrowed as he took in the slight contact. For once she didn't care. She merely smiled at Joey and turned back to the grill. If this were any other day, she'd be in an agony of distress from now until closing, worrying over how angry he'd be when he came home, how heavy his fists would be when he worked out that anger on her.

But tonight she wouldn't be there to be his punching bag.

There wouldn't be fifty thousand in the desk drawer safe—that would be too much to expect—but there'd be several thousand. Terafino's raked it in.

Today's business at Terafino's tapered off around two as usual and would stay soft until five or so. Joey and Antony could handle things without her help. She untied her apron.

"I'll be back by five." Not. She had to bite the inside of her mouth to keep from smiling. She could already taste her freedom.

"Bring Nicky," Joey said.

"I always bring him, Joey." He'd been a baby sleeping in his carry chair beneath the table in the corner, a toddler in a playpen by the soda coolers, a little boy sleeping in a Superman sleeping bag on the floor in the back room.

Joey grinned, as charming as if he hadn't hurt her last night. "He can bus tables tonight."

"Yeah," Antony said. "He's young enough to think it's fun."

Ellie glanced at Antony, a constant thorn in her side, but she had to admit that as much as he disliked her, he liked, maybe even loved, Nicky. Everyone loved Nicky. The boy was the very best of both her and Joey, handsome, charming, sweet, smart.

When she took him away, Joey would never forgive her. Neither would Antony. She shivered. If they ever found her .... She was more afraid of them than the police and possible kidnapping charges. She'd just have to make sure they never caught up with her.

Her desperate need to escape had solidified last night. She'd left Terafino's at eight to take Nicky home for bed. He was now too big to sleep in the back room with all the noise out front and too young to stay up until closing at eleven.

They met old Mr. Palumbo outside the deli. As usual he wore his slippers, his old work pants and his faded Hawaiian shirt. Missing were his sweet smile and jaunty manner.

"My Sophia, she's dying, Gabriella." Tears filled his rheumy eyes. "The doctors say they can't do no more."

"I'm so sorry, Mr. Palumbo. Mrs. Palumbo is such a wonderful lady." His despair and heartbreak moved Ellie, and she hugged him, never imagining Joey would find reason to be jealous about an old man of seventy. To her it was like hugging Nonno.

Antony made sure Joey saw. He also made sure that Joey had too much to drink at their stop at the Mona Lisa on their way home. Joey had finished off the evening with a quick visit with Vera Fachinetti.

The minute he walked in the door, she knew she was in trouble though she wasn't sure why. His gait was unsteady and his expression vicious. He reeked of Vera's perfume.

Not that she minded his attentions to Vera. She'd long ago turned cold to his touch. But his anger was another issue all together.

"It's a good thing that Antony is concerned about my happiness since you obviously aren't," he railed at her with slurred speech and bleary eyes. He grabbed her left arm in the tender area above the elbow and twisted. "Marco Palumbo? Give me a break."

Mr. Palumbo? "He's an old man, Joey!" She tried to pull free even though she knew it was hopeless. "An old man with a dying wife. I felt sorry for him!"

"A rich old man," Joey yelled. "You made a play for him because you want his money!" And he pushed her hard enough to knock her into an end table where the lamp fell with a crash, the bulb popping, and a piece of Lladro they had gotten last Christmas shattering.

Joey looked from the mess to her. "Look what you did! My mother gave us that glass thing!" And he hit her again, this time in the stomach. She doubled over, gasping for breath. When he shoved her, she lost her balance and fell. He kicked her in the ribs, and she gagged, sure she'd throw up.

Suddenly Nicky was there, standing between her and Joey. "Don't hurt her, Dad! Don't! She didn't do anything wrong!"

Joey went white with fury. "Are you telling me what to do?" His voice was low and terrible.

Ellie forced a smile as she tried to pick herself up. "It's okay, Nicky. I'm okay. I just tripped. You go back to bed."

"You're not okay. You're hurt." Nicky stared at his father. "Dad, you've got to stop. It's not right. She's littler than you. Please! Don't hit her again."

So Joey struck his son instead, a powerful slap across the face.

"No!" She was on her feet before she realized it. She rushed Joey, grabbing the nearest thing, a statue of the Virgin Mary. She swung it as hard as she could, catching him in the side of the head. He stared at her in surprise for a moment before his eyes rolled back and he went down. When he'd fallen, she'd grabbed Nicky, and they ran to Nonna.

The crack of that blow to Nicky's cheek changed something in Ellie. She might deserve Joey's violence, but Nicky did not. Ever.

Today when she left Terafino's after lunch, it was for the last time. She walked quickly toward home. When she was certain that Joey could no longer see her, she veered off and went directly to Nicky's school.

"We will be moving," she told the woman in the office, "and I need a copy of Nicky's records for his new school."

A half hour later she and Nicky left the school. They walked to Nonna's house, the one place they were loved unconditionally.

"Do your homework, Nicky." She ruffled his dark hair. As he tried to duck away, she was thankful that the red handprint from last night had faded from his face without leaving a bruise. "I need to talk to Nonna."

Nicky clearly didn't like being left out of the conversation, but he made his way to the kitchen. Ellie and Nonna sat on the plastic covered sofa in the living room.

Nonna, small, round, Italian, took Ellie's hand. "So tell me."

Ellie started to cry.

With her dark eyes full of sympathy, Nonna leaned toward Ellie in quiet support. She sat patiently until Ellie could pull in enough air to speak.

"I have to leave." Just saying it made Ellie's chest tight.

Nonna nodded. "Joey or Philadelphia?"

"It has to be Philadelphia because I'm afraid he'll come after Nicky and me if we left him but stayed local. I don't even want to think about what would happen then." She gripped Nonna's hand. "He'd end up with custody of Nicky. I know it. He'd convince the judge I wasn't a good mother." She thought of the many times he'd made her wonder about her own sanity with his petty manipulations and tricks.

"Where'd my keys go?" she'd say as she looked at the empty spot on the hall table where she always put them. "I've got to leave for my hair appointment."

"Where'd you have them last?" he'd ask.

"Right there." She pointed at the table.

"Well, obviously that's the wrong answer."

So she searched everywhere as he read the newspaper or watched TV. Finally defeated and late for her appointment, she walked into the front hall to find her keys sitting on the table in full view.

Joey would look at her. "I don't know, El. You must be losing it if you can't see something that obvious."

Even the memory made her shiver. "So I can't stay here, Nonna."

The lines in Nonna's face seemed to sag. "You're right, *cara*."

Ellie looked at Nonna, her short hair dark and shining from her weekly visit to the beauty shop, and teared up again. "I can't imagine living anywhere but South Philly. I can't imagine living anywhere without you."

Nonna leaned forward and kissed her cheek. "You have your money?"

Ellie hesitated. She didn't want to tell Nonna how foolish and naively trusting she'd been with Nonno's love gift.

"He took it, didn't he?" Nonna made a disgusted noise. "I knew he would as soon as I knew you got a joint account." There was only weary resignation in her words, not condemnation. "Well, wait here. I got something for you."

Ellie sat and waited, trying to imagine never sitting on this couch again, the plastic crackling under her in winter and her legs sticking to it in the summer, or never relaxing in Nonna's kitchen, never smelling her red sauce or homemade minestrone simmering on the stove or eating her chicken cacciatore. Never being held in the circle of Nonna's loving arms. Her stomach cramped.

"Here." Nonna placed a set of keys in Ellie's palm.

Ellie looked up. "What's this?"

"There's a car waiting for you."

Ellie blinked in astonishment.

"I been waiting three years to give you these keys, my Ellie, praying the day would come when you had the courage to leave."

"He'll go wild when I take Nicky."

"He will," Nonna agreed. "That's why you don't tell me where you are going or where you end up. I am not a good liar. We will use the email but that's it."

"You've thought about this a lot."

"I have." She pressed an envelope into Ellie's hand. "It's nowhere near the amount your nonno left you, but it will at least hold you until you get a job."

Ellie stared at the bills crowded together in the envelope. "Nonna, I can't take this."

"If you love me, you can and will."

Once again, Ellie wept. This time Nonna gathered her close and wept too.

A half hour later Ellie and Nicky walked into the home they shared with Joey. Their half of the double had the porch enclosed, and the bright sunny room mocked her dark desperation.

"Nicky, I want you to go upstairs and pack your favorite things in your father's black gym bag. Take at least four changes of clothes, and don't forget underwear."

He looked at her with a mix of curiosity and apprehension. "Where are we going?"

She decided to be honest. "I don't know."

"Are we coming back?"

She forced herself to look him in the eye. "No."

He swallowed hard and looked miserable. "It's my fault, isn't it?"

"Oh, Nicky!" She grabbed him by the shoulders. "Don't ever think that!"

"But I made him mad. That's why he hit me. That's why we have to go."

"Listen to me. You didn't do anything wrong, not one thing, but even if you did, he should never have hit you like that. He was wrong, not you."

Nicky's eyes took on a sheen that he blinked against furiously. "I thought he loved me."

If only Nicky were two years old again with a scraped knee she could kiss and make better. She brushed back the dark hair that fell over his forehead. "He loves you more than anything, Nicky."

"Then why'd he hit me?"

How could she explain what she couldn't understand? "It's like he's sick, honey, and he's getting worse."

"Can't a doctor make him better?"

"He'll never go."

"Can't we make him better?"

Ellie felt useless, powerless as she shook her head. "Only he can do that."

"But it's not fair!"

Ellie understood he meant life in general, and she had to agree. "That's why we're leaving."

He hung his head. "I used to pull the covers over me and stick my fingers in my ears so I wouldn't hear him yell or hear you cry. Or hear the slap or punch."

Her stomach dropped as she realized he was ashamed that he hadn't done anything before. She grabbed him in a quick, fierce hug. "Well, you were my hero last night." She kissed him on the cheek.

He returned the hug for a brief instant, then bolted for his bedroom, feet thudding on the steps.

She followed him upstairs, her heart filled with a combination of pride for the fine kid he was and regret for the guilt he'd been forced to endure. She threw jeans, tees and some underwear in a duffel. She hurried into the bathroom and grabbed her makeup and toothbrush. She stuffed in a fleece jacket and zipped the bag closed. Next she ran to the room she liked to call her studio though Joey called it the hobby center. She stuffed as many of her art supplies as she could into the oversized canvas bag she used when she did plein air painting in Fairmont Park while Joey and Antony played ball with Nicky. She glanced at the clock. It was already four. She had one hour in which to disappear. But first Joey's money.

She ran down to Joey's desk and the drawer safe.

"It's not really that secure," she'd told him time and again.

"It's secure enough. Besides, there's an alarm."

Well, the alarm would just have to sound. She was getting into that drawer.

She ran to the basement and grabbed a large screwdriver to use as a pry bar. Back at his desk, she inserted it between the top of the drawer and the desk. She put all her weight behind it as she pushed down. At first she thought there was no movement. Then there was a slight give, and she eased off. She slid the screwdriver more deeply into the opening. This time she pulled up on it with all her might. There was a terrible crunching sound, a rending of metal, and the drawer popped open.

Ellie waited for the alarm to sound, but there was nothing. Either Joey had lied about it or it was a silent one connected with some office somewhere. If it was a silent one, she didn't have much time.

She grabbed all the cash in the drawer and stuffed it in her purse with Nonna's envelope. *Oh, God, can You ever forgive me?*

Like God cared one way or the other about a stupid thief like her.

"Ready, Nicky?" she called.

He popped out of his room, his duffel bulging, and raced down the stairs. Just in case a silent alarm had sent the cops, they ran out the back door and into the alley. There they hurried three blocks to the garage where Nonna had had the car hidden for so long.

She rolled the door open and looked at the gray Civic.

Oh, Nonna, you did good. It was about as anonymous as a car got.

They threw their stuff in the back and climbed in. Ellie headed for the Walt Whitman Bridge and New Jersey, getting lost in the beginnings of rush hour traffic. Once in Jersey, she turned south on 295 and drove and drove and drove. She had no destination in mind. Since her sole goal was to put as much distance between her and Joey as she could, she headed west. Feeling frozen inside, she angled south. Maybe she could some-day feel safe and be warm.

They spent four nights in cheap motels, Nicky sleeping in one bed, Ellie staring wide awake and fearful at the cheap ceiling tiles or thrashing in nightmares. They ate fast food, going through drive-in windows, careful always to be in a line so the kid taking their money was too frayed to remember a specific lady and kid. They were just one of many.

On the fourth day they pulled into a small college town in Arizona. When she saw the For Rent sign in front of a little blue house across the street from a little white church, she sought out the Realtor.

"It's not in the best shape inside," the man said. "It's usually rented to a group of college kids. In fact this is the first year I can remember it being available. It usually just passes from group to group with no advertising."

Nonna would say that God had saved the little blue house for her. Whether He had or not, Ellie had no idea, but for now, she and Nicky had a home.

CHAPTER 2

Present Day

Ellie Loring walked into the small gray house in Lyndale, Pennsylvania that she and Nick would call home for how long? A month? Two months? A year? It depended on how sick Nonna was, how long she lingered. How long they could stay hidden from Joey.

"Don't come see me, Ellie," Nonna had written in her last email. "The risk is too great."

But how could she not?

So here she was in Lyndale, a mere thirty-five or so miles west of Philadelphia. Way too near Joey; still too far from Nonna.

Ellie looked at the pair of cats lying on the back of the slightly sagging sofa. Buddy, all gray and sleek, and Midnight, a ball of black fluff, stared back with blinking eyes. She'd obviously disturbed their sleep. How wonderful it must be to be so relaxed, to sleep all day. She gave the animals a tired smile.

In four steps she crossed the living room and scratched each behind the ears. They purred at her touch. She knew that as soon as she went into the tiny kitchen, they'd abandon their cushy seat and be up on the old Formica counter, pacing and whining until she fed them.

She reached past the cats and straightened the large painting on the wall. Swirls of color—sapphire, turquoise, gold, amber, bronze, cream, ecru, with a splash of crimson here and there—pleased her every time she looked at it. One of these days she'd have the funds to actually frame it instead of merely matting it.

Rarely did Ellie do abstract work, and when she did, it was usually very dissatisfying to her sense of balance and unity. This picture she loved. She'd painted it in Arizona not too long after they'd fled. In it she saw optimism, energy, possibilities, things she hadn't felt in longer than she'd realized. When she'd been able to afford her own furniture, gotten piece by piece over the years, she'd bought everything to go with the painting.

She walked to the kitchen, and sure enough, the cats jumped gracefully from the couch back and followed. With one effortless leap, they gained the counter. She grabbed the no name bag of cat food from the highest shelf and poured some into their empty dishes. She hadn't even set the dishes on the floor before the greedy beasts jumped down to shove her out of the way.

She ran a hand down each back and was totally ignored. Some things you could count on, and a cat's single-minded attention to his food was one.

Another was the magic of being near Nonna in spite of the circumstances that brought her here, in spite of the fear that sat on her shoulder like Snoopy's vulture. She couldn't believe she had found a house she could actually afford in Lyndale, not quite the prestigious address of the Main Line towns closer to Philadelphia but the address of choice for young upwardly mobile professionals. Granted she could stretch out her arms and almost touch the opposing walls, but she loved the home's coziness.

If only Joey didn't loom like a dark shadow over the gilded landscape.

Ellie sighed and walked three steps to the kitchen table and slumped in a scuffed chair. She was so tired. Bone weary. Soul weary. It wasn't that work had been any harder today than other days. She'd cleaned for a new client who had a very large house that hadn't been deep cleaned for months, if not years, and it took all her patience to ignore the lack of care for the lovely place. When she left, things gleamed that hadn't shone for far too long, and the house smelled of cleaning fluid and air freshener. She'd earned the right to be physically tired.

But her fatigue and frailty were more emotional than physical.

Nonna was dying.

Many times through the years, Ellie had thought she couldn't bear any more pain. Apparently she'd been wrong.

Oh, dear God, how can I lose this wonderful person who loves me like You do, warts and all?

Ellie wanted to put her head down on the table and cry. Instead she pushed herself up, opened the refrigerator and pulled out a bottle of green tea with honey. She rummaged in the snack cupboard, hoping Nick had left something for her. Surprise; he had. She grabbed the box of Social Teas.

She collapsed at the table again. She drank her tea right from the bottle, smiling slightly. Nick would approve, having a high school guy's distain for glasses. As she pulled a couple of her wimpy cookies from their sleeve, she absently opened the local newspaper.

The first thing she did every time she and Nick moved was order the local paper delivered daily. It was one of the fastest ways to learn a new locale. She checked out the coupons to help her pick their new grocery store. She turned to the church page and read the ads, trying to discern which church would be best for her and Nick.

Today she flipped through the pages, reading the obituaries of people she didn't know and the ads for movies she couldn't afford. Eventually she came to the sports section where she checked on how the rival high schools had done over the weekend. Lyndale High, for which Nick played tight end, was one of the smaller schools in an incredibly tough league.

And there above the fold was a picture of Nick, going up for the pass that he caught in the end zone to win the game Saturday in the final seconds. It was a great representation, his handsome young face a mask of fierce concentration, clearly visible in spite of the helmet and protective grill.

NICK LORING SCORES THREE TDS: Lyndale finally has a hero.

Ellie turned cold as fear stomped up her spine wearing football cleats. Nick looked so much like his father!

As she stared at the picture, anger arm-wrestled with her fear, temporarily overpowering it and rapping its knuckles firmly on the table. He'd promised! The coach had given his word. How dare he betray her.

With shaking hands she raised the tea and took a quick swig as she checked the clock. Practice was just finishing. No time like the present for a confrontation. Her adrenaline was flowing like the Mississippi at flood stage, overcoming her natural reticence, and she knew if she didn't act now, it'd be much, much harder later. And there was no question. She had to speak up. Nick's life might depend on it.

She grabbed her keys, purse and jacket and marched out the front door. She drove straight to the high school and strode inside by way of the door off the field where the team managers were carting in equipment for storage overnight.

Looking neither right nor left, she made straight for the coach's office.

"Hey, what are you doing here?" yelled an embarrassed teenage boy wearing only a towel. "This is the boys' area!"

"Stay in the shower room if you don't want to be seen," Ellie told him without batting an eye. Years of Nick had steeled her to towel-clad male youngsters.

"But I got to talk to the coach," the kid said, hugging the towel to his puny waist. "I got a problem."

Me, too, kid.

She studied him. He might be tall, but he was way too slight to be on a football team. Her anger spiked again as she mentally railed at a coach who would let a youngster built like this boy risk himself in a sport that demanded big and strong. "What's your name?"

"Kenny."

"Well, Kenny, you can see the coach later." Ellie jerked her head in the direction of the showers. "Go. It's my turn right now."

He frowned at her, but he went. She was glad she couldn't hear what he was muttering under his breath.

Ellie brought her fist up, gave a sharp rap on the glass paneled door of the coach's office, and opened it without waiting for an invitation.

Coach Gabe Hyland, blond, blue-eyed and startled, looked up at her abrupt entrance, his face surprised, then cautious. It didn't take any intelligence for Ellie to realize she was wearing what Nick called her Warpath Look. No wonder the kid had fled to the showers without further protest. She tried to smooth the scowl she knew puckered her forehead, but she couldn't. Her internal war drums were beating too loudly, and she was definitely on the warpath.

She slapped the sports section of the paper on the coach's desk. "How could you do that to him?" Her index finger skewered the picture of Nick. "How could you?"

To her horror her voice broke on the last word. She swallowed the sob trying to escape and cleared her throat. She wouldn't cry; she just wouldn't. She scowled even more fiercely.

"I thought the article was quite good." Coach Hyland eyed her like she was a bomb about to detonate.

Well, she had to give him marks for reading her correctly. She was a woman on the edge. All the years of circumspection, of caution, of paranoia, of moving every two summers, of lost nights' sleep when the fear rode her or nightmares woke her, all potentially wrecked by this man's carelessness.

"I especially liked my quote," he said.

She blinked. "What quote?" The picture had so unnerved her she hadn't even read the article. The words weren't the danger. The image was.

He laid his finger on the fourth paragraph and she read, "The joy of a player like Nick is that in spite of his singular and extraordinary talent, he is a team player and a young man of character."

"Uh, very nice." Maternal pride momentarily overrode her fear, and she almost smiled at the man. "And true."

He smiled at her, and she realized he thought he had chivied her out of her anger. She straightened her spine and listened again for the internal war drums. They began to thunder, keeping rhythm with her pounding heart.

"Nick told you he didn't want to be in the paper, didn't he?" She put her hands on the coach's desk and leaned in. His smile slipped a little. "He gave you my letter."

Since her son had developed into a player of unusual skill, she always told the coaches at whatever level he was competing that he couldn't be featured in the paper. She'd told them in Arizona, in Colorado, in Washington State. They'd all listened. They'd all cooperated when it probably didn't matter anyway. Nick was too young and they were too far from Philadelphia.

But now he was genuinely newsworthy, and they were less than fifty miles from the City of Brotherly Love.

"The first day of practice," Ellie prodded. "He told you he'd only play if you promised he'd never be in the paper. When I picked him up, he assured me you'd talked."

The coach blinked. "Sure, we talked."

"And he gave you my letter." She had put her request in writing because this time she couldn't be present to make the request in person. She had to be at Wexford College to make certain everything was in place for her transfer of credits and to sign up for a class on art, craft and design, grades K-3, required if she wanted to qualify for her art education internship. She also had to take a class on art history that she'd been putting off.

The coach studied her with contemplative eyes. "Ms. Loring, why can't he be in the paper?"

Because I've got to protect him. Because his father's abusive and lives nearby. "He just can't. If it happens again, I'll pull him from the team."

Gabe Hyland straightened, clearly indignant at her threat. "Your son is one of the most talented high school football players I've ever seen."

She nodded. "I know, but it doesn't matter."

He blinked. "Of course it matters. He's prime scholarship material. And with him this team is championship bound."

She closed her eyes, stricken anew at the high price both she and Nick were paying for her youthful stupidity.

"Championship teams get written about," he said.

"No."

"Game winning guys get photographed."

"Not Nick."

"College coaches need to know he's out there."

She shook her head. "No."

"Ms. Loring." Coach Hyland smiled a sweet smile which probably had brought him a lifetime of women swooning at his feet. If it weren't for the pensive look in his eyes, she'd believe he was what he appeared, a man trying to get her to agree with him and using his considerable charm to accomplish his ends. "Surely you don't want to jeopardize Nick's future."

Of course she didn't. She was his mother. And it was that very future she was trying to protect. "Surely you don't want to lose him as a player. And believe me, you will if he's ever in the paper again."

The coach rose, no longer smiling. Determination had replaced the charm. "I need to know why your son can't be in the paper if I'm to try to tell Jem Payne what he can or can't write."

She glanced at the paper and for the first time noticed the byline. Jem Payne, Sports Editor. She'd been so mad at the coach that she hadn't given the reporter a thought. Obviously she also should have written to him, asking for anonymity for Nick. How could she have been so careless?

"Do you know him?" Her fingernail dug into the name as if she were drilling a hole in the reporter's Adam's apple.

The coach nodded.

"Then tell him to leave Nick alone!"

They glared at each other. Who would have blinked first remained a mystery as Nick's surprised and concerned voice came from the doorway.

"Mom? What are you doing here? What's wrong? Is it Nonna?"

Ellie held out the paper, her heart breaking that he looked so worried. He was such a handsome kid, tall, with dark hair and eyes so deep a brown they were almost black. He might as well have Italian stamped across his forehead, and that's why they'd used Loring as their surname ever since they left Philadelphia. It was as un-ethnic as could be.

But it wouldn't protect him if his picture was in the paper.

Nick took the paper and turned thoughtful as he studied the photo. "Nice likeness. Don't let it worry you, Mom. I doubt he sees it."

"Nick!" Ellie stared. She wasn't certain which appalled her more, his casual attitude toward the picture or his off-hand mention of his father.

"Even if he does, it's no big deal."

"Did you have a letter for me from your mother, Nick?" Coach Hyland asked.

"We'll move," Ellie said, even though moving would mean leaving Nonna again. Not that Nonna knew they were near, but Ellie knew. Leaving a second time would be just as painful as the first time.

Oh. Lord, I can't deal with this!

She glared at the coach, a convenient target for all her frustrations and fears.

"Uh, Mom." Nick laid the paper on the desk. "Don't get mad at Coach."

"Why not? He ignored our request."

"Well...." Nick studied his Nikes where his untied laces pooled around his super-sized feet.

"Did you have a letter for me from your mother?" She suddenly heard what the coach had said. Ellie closed her eyes and her shoulders slumped. "Tell me."

"I-I never gave him your note."

"You never gave him—" She felt her stomach plummet all the way to her toes. "Nick!"

"It doesn't matter anymore, Mom. I'm too old. He can't do anything."

"Yeah, he can." He could take her son away from her.

"I'll be eighteen in just a couple of months."

"December 10. And it's only the second week in September." She sighed and looked at Coach Hyland who looked steadily back. It cost her, but she said, "I apologize. I jumped to the wrong conclusion. You weren't at fault."

His close scrutiny made her uncomfortable, but all he said was, "Apology accepted."

She nodded and wanted nothing more than to climb into bed and pull the covers over her head. She left the office, Nick trailing behind. How was she ever to work up the energy for the confrontation with Nick over his duplicity? She turned toward the door to the outside.

"Wait a minute," Nick said. "I left my things in the locker room. When Kenny said you were here, I ran out."

She just bet he did. "Take your time. There's no need to rush."

Nick disappeared, and Ellie looked around for a seat. Her legs felt curiously weak—the adrenaline draining away, she supposed—and she wanted to sit before she collapsed. There was nothing available, so she leaned against the wall and fought the shaking that rippled through her. She shut her eyes and leaned her head back against the wall. She pressed her lips tight to still their tremor.

The locker room door flew open and Ellie straightened. She forced a smile as Nick came toward her, followed by the skinny kid in the towel, though he now wore a faded tee and jeans that were too short for his long, skinny legs.

"This is Kenny," Nick said. "Can he come to dinner?"

Company. Just what she wanted. "Sure, if he doesn't mind Hamburger Helper."

Nick looked in question at Kenny who all but licked his lips. Obviously the kid's mother was no cook. "Good. You guys can make the salad."

"You got a bag one?" Nick asked.

She nodded.

He grinned. "Cool. We can manage that."

She followed the boys outside, her mind whirling. She'd thought in terms of hiding for so many years, she didn't know how to gauge the dangers in Nick's sudden decision to risk exposure. Was he right? Was Joey no longer a threat to him?

The scene in the coach's office replayed in her mind, and she wrestled with conflicting emotions.

Dear Lord, please tell me what's the right thing to do!

She glanced back over her shoulder and saw with a start that the coach stood in his office doorway, watching them. Watching her.

Something in his expression made her skin prickle.

CHAPTER 3

Nick rushed into the locker room, grabbed his sweaty practice clothes, and stuffed them into his gym bag. He knew his mother was very upset with him, and he understood why. Anything that might make it possible for his father to find them terrified her. The thing was, it didn't frighten him anymore, not like it used to. It used to seem like the worst thing ever if he discovered their hiding place. That was why Nick never complained about moving all the time or being called Nicholas Loring instead of Dominic Terafino.

But now he was six three, two hundred and five pounds and almost eighteen. His father didn't scare him anymore. Besides, Loring was easier for the papers to spell than Terafino.

He got that Mom was scared being so near Philadelphia, but she was willing to take the risk because she had to be near Nonna. It made him proud of her. Aside from him, Nonna was all Mom had.

And now he was so glad they'd come to Lyndale. Coach Hyland was great. He demanded discipline and obedience, but he was fair. And he knew what he was talking about. Nick felt he'd really grown as a player under him even in the short time they'd been here. There was no way he was willing to move again. He didn't want to get in a fight with Mom over it, but he would if he had to.

He'd been young when they left his father, but he remembered a lot. He remembered many nights when he heard Mom crying and begging, "Don't, Joey!" Even if he didn't hear the actual physical violence, he would know she'd been hit by the way she moved the next day, holding her ribs, favoring one arm. But when his dad was careless—read drunk—the marks showed.

He also remembered the way his father used to tease his mom, making her think she was dumb. At least he'd thought it was teasing back then. Now, looking back, he realized Dad had been deliberately nasty in what he'd come to think was just another way to hold power over her.

And he remembered the night his dad hit him.

All he'd wanted was to make Dad stop hitting Mom. He hadn't wanted to make him mad. But he had, and he'd paid the price. What always made him feel torn in two was that he loved his father even though he knew Dad was so very wrong, even though he'd slugged him, a kid. This loving made him feel disloyal to Mom.

She'd been through a lot, and she gave up everything to protect him. Nick knew he owed her his loyalty. But deep inside he wished his father could see him play ball. He wished his father would say, "Great job, Nick. I am so proud of you."

Talk about a fantasy!

But Nick was angry at his father too. It was Dad's fault that their family fell apart.

"I can't share you with him, Nick," Mom'd said back at the beginning. "I know you miss him, but I can't let him harm you or, worse yet, have you turn out like him."

He'd stared at her across the wobbly kitchen table in that little house in Arizona across from the white church with the slightly tilted steeple. "I'd never hit anyone," he said, insulted that she'd even think he'd do something like that. Beating up Tomas Hernandez at recess because he spoke with a funny accent didn't count.

Now that he was older, Nick knew slugging Tomas had been wrong and maybe the first step to becoming a violent person just like Dad.

The first time Nonna talked to him about the situation between his mother and father, he was eight. He was at her house without Mom or Dad.

"I was married to Vittorio Mancini for forty-five years, Nicky." She waved her wooden spoon dripping red sauce. "And he never once touched me in anger. Never once! And he didn't say mean things to me either. There is something broken in your father that he has to always be better than your mother."

"He doesn't do mean things to her," Nicky lied, trying to protect his father.

"We will always be honest, Nicky, you and me. I know, and you know."

"If he hits her, she should just hit him back." It bothered him a lot that she didn't. "She should stand up for herself."

"Is that what your papa tells you? That you should hit back? That you should stand up for yourself?"

Nicky nodded as he stuffed another bite of cannoli into his mouth. It sounded like good advice to him. Manly.

"Well, standing up for yourself when someone your own size bothers you may be okay, but your mama is much smaller than your papa. Only a bully hits someone so much smaller, and he does it precisely because he knows the smaller person can't stand up to him."

His father was a bully? Nicky knew about bullies. Giorgio Mastrantonio was a bully. He liked to find little kids and take their money, and if they wouldn't give it, he'd beat them up. Nicky always felt sorry for the little kids. In fact sometimes he told Giorgio to leave the little guys alone. Because Nicky was bigger than Giorgio, Giorgio listened.

"You're a big boy, Nicky," Nonna said. "You could be a bully if you wanted. But you have your mama's kind heart. Do not ever lose it. A real man, a man like your nonno, God rest his soul, is strong but has a kind heart too."

Then came the night his father came home and began yelling about Mom for talking to poor, sad Mr. Palumbo. Nick huddled in his bed and tried not to hear, but he couldn't help it.

The soft sound of fist on flesh made him feel sick. He heard his mother cry out.

"All she did was be nice!" Nick yelled in his dark room. The unfairness of what his father was saying upset him so much that he ran down the stairs and into the living room. He was just in time to see Dad knock Mom to the floor and then kick her in the side. His face was ugly and mean, and it scared Nick. Mom hugged her ribs and was crying.

"No!" Nick screamed, running to Mom. His heart raced, and he was so scared he thought he'd throw up. "Don't hurt her! She didn't do anything wrong. I was there. I know!" He knelt beside Mom as she lay curled up on the floor.

Dad's face went white with fury. "Get up, Dominic. Go to your room. This does not concern you."

"She was just being nice!"

Mom uncurled enough to smile at him, a very sad smile. She tried to pick herself up. "It's okay, Nicky. I'm okay. You go back to bed."

"You're not okay, Mom. You're hurt." He looked at his father. "She's hurt."

Nick was shaking with fear. He'd never defied his father before. Dad was big, and he had a temper though he didn't know anyone besides Mom that Dad actually hit.

Nick longed to do as his father said and run to his room because it would be safe there, but he protected kids he hardly knew from Giorgio Mastrantonio. How bad was it that he had never before tried to protect his mother. He was the opposite of a bully; he was a coward.

"Dad, you've got to stop. It's not right. She's littler than you are."

"I won't tell you again, Nicky. Go to your room." Dad's voice sounded like thunder.

Nick stayed beside Mom. What if Dad kicked him? He couldn't imagine how much that would hurt, and he wasn't big enough to make Dad stop. But why would his father hurt him? He always told Nick how much he loved him, and Nick believed him. At the deli he was always showing him off to customers.

Because of that, Nick was startled when his father grabbed him, pulled him to his feet, and shook him.

"You little—" Dad's hand moved so quickly that Nick didn't have time to duck. The blow caught him on the left side of his face and sent him flying across the room where he crashed into the wall.

He lay there, stunned. His father had hit him. Not a spanking that he had earned or anything. A punch like a boxer would give another boxer. Except he wasn't a boxer.

He used to wonder if maybe Mom deserved her beatings for something he didn't know about, but he knew she didn't deserve anything tonight, and neither did he. For an instant he wavered on the edge of tears.

But fury, hot and bubbly like the water before Nonna added the pasta, scalded him. He narrowed his eyes and glared at his father who glared back. That's why he saw the stunned look of disbelief on Dad's face when Mom hit him on the head as hard as she could with the statue of the Virgin Mary that Nonna had given them. Dad fell and was still.

Both he and Mom stood frozen, staring at the unmoving body.

"Is he dead?" Nick finally asked. What happened if your mom killed your dad?

"No. Of course not." But Mom dropped to her knees and felt for a pulse. She nodded when she found one, and Nick was flooded with relief. Mom said, "Just unconscious. Go to your room—"

He was ready to protest when she said the most amazing thing.

"—and grab the clothes you want to wear to school tomorrow."

"What?"

"We're spending the night at Nonna's. We can't be here when he wakes up."

Nick nodded. He ran and threw what he needed into his Nike bag and grabbed his Eagles green and silver backpack with his school stuff. When he came back into the living room, Mom was there with a duffel and her purse. She grabbed his hand and they ran.

One night hiding became eight years.

CHAPTER 4

Gabe Hyland frowned as he followed Ms. Loring out of his office. Pull Nick from the team? Move? Over his dead body. And what was this about Nick's picture never being in the paper?

Ellie Loring was leaning against the wall, her eyes closed, her shoulders slumped, her expression—sad? Where had the fierce warrior-mother protecting her child gone? Here was a weary woman, fragile even, with too much on her mind and heart. He felt the stirrings of concern.

Wait a minute. Mentally he hit himself upside the head. She had just threatened him, accused him wrongfully. Granted she'd apologized, but still, the last thing she deserved was his pity.

Gabe watched as the locker room door flew open, and Nick and Kenny Uplander came out. Ms. Loring straightened quickly and stuck a smile on her face. She didn't even blink when Nick asked if Kenny could come for dinner.

When Ms. Loring glanced back as they left the building and saw him watching, something like fear flashed across her face before she could stop it.

Gabe frowned thoughtfully. Her face was much too mobile for someone hiding secrets. And she was definitely hiding secrets.

Witness protection program?

Spiteful or abusive husband?

Legal problems? Outstanding warrants? Unpaid parking tickets?

GAYLE ROPER

Too bad those flashing dark eyes, that curly shoulder length black hair, and the curvy figure were matched with her thorny personality.

His cell fizzed against his waist, and he glanced at the read-out. The dispatcher down at the station.

"What's up, Dottie?"

"Domestic disturbance, Chief. Neighbors called it in."

"Who? Where?" Gabe hated domestic calls. You couldn't win, no matter what. You pulled the husband off, and the wife, dripping blood from his fists, yelled at you for being rough on the man. You carted him off to jail to protect her as much as because he'd broken the law, and the wife followed you to the cruiser, sobbing the whole way about how he didn't mean anything. She loved him, and she knew he'd never do it again. It especially irked him when she said this with her eye swelling shut and the bruises from his previous beating still purple and green about her face.

Of course they never pressed charges.

"Mitzi Uplander," Dottie said. "Eighteen—"

Gabe interrupted her with a long sigh. "I know the address." All too well. Which one of her clients had whaled on her this time?

"Hollis has responded to the call, but I figured practice was over and you'd want to know."

"Thanks. You did good." Gabe pressed off and slid the phone into its holder as he grabbed his fleece anorak. Sometimes he thought he was nuts trying to be both cop and football coach, but since he couldn't figure out which to give up, he kept on doing both. Even during football season, he put in eight hours plus each day as a cop, and each year he saved his vacation time for football camp. Everyone, by which he meant the town council, seemed happy, and his coaching staff understood that he'd run if there was an emergency.

32

Besides, with Robyn gone, he needed to do something to fill his time. It was that need to fill every second so he wouldn't grieve that started him writing mysteries in the lonely evenings in his empty house. Making up tales he could control was better than living his own sorry story.

He pulled the locker room door open. "Pete!"

"Yeah, Coach?" his assistant called back.

"I got a call. See everything's closed up tight for me."

"Will do, Super Cop. Go make Lyndale safe for democracy."

Gabe could trust Pete to take good care of things. He hurried to his car and took off for the ramshackle old house in the bad part of town. Not that Lyndale was big enough to have an authentic bad side of the tracks, but it did have a couple of blocks of old places going ever more rapidly downhill. Big early 20th century homes that had once housed well-to-do families were now broken into apartments with careless landlords and disadvantaged and/or lazy tenants. One of these withering old Victorians was where Mitzi lived.

Gabe pulled up to the curb behind Hollis's departmental car, its flashing lights reflecting red, blue and white off the dirty windows of the house. He clipped his gun in its holster to his belt at the small of his back, and pulled the anorak over it. He'd never had cause to use a weapon at Mitzi's, but you never knew. Some day one of her men was going to be lethal instead of merely abusive.

Gabe entered the house at a run and was startled to find the young couple from one of the downstairs apartments standing curiously at the bottom of the stairs as if waiting for something interesting to happen. The man from the other downstairs apartment stood by his door, a bag of groceries in his arms, looking startled at Gabe's abrupt entry.

"Go inside." He waved his arms and scowled, hoping to intimidate them into obeying.

The man pushed his door open and with a nod went inside. The couple stepped closer to their own door but didn't go in, no doubt thinking this was better than TV. Maybe they'd be so disappointed with the lack of action they wouldn't bother to come out next time someone called the cops on Mitzi. Unless they were the ones who called.

"She's a mess." The girl pointed upstairs.

"You who called about her?"

The girl nodded.

"Just stay out of my way."

He moved quickly up the front stairs to the second floor apartment where Mitzi lived in semi-squalor. Her door was open, and he entered slowly so he wouldn't surprise anyone.

"Hollis, it's Gabe."

"It's about time!" Hollis's voice came from the kitchen, and he was not happy.

"Don't hurt him!" Mitzi yelled.

Don't who hurt whom?

Gabe entered the kitchen and found Hollis, all one-hundred and fifty pounds of him, straddling a man lying on the floor on his back. The man had such a paunch that Hollis's knees didn't touch the dirty vinyl. The man beneath Hollis wore boxers and nothing else. He was blubbering like a baby, his nose running, drool sliding across his cheek into his hair, and his white belly undulated like little wavelets lapping the shore. He was not a pretty sight and sad evidence of how far Mitzi had fallen.

She stood beside Hollis, batting at him and trying to pull him off her gentleman caller.

"I didn't mean nothing, Mitzi," the man wheezed. "You know I didn't."

Hollis's weight must be making it hard for the man to breath. Of course, given his girth, he probably wheezed standing up.

"Tell him I didn't mean nothing." *Wheeze. Wheeze.* "Get him off me. I'm dying here."

Gabe swallowed a smile at the ridiculous scene and noted in passing that he was becoming way too cynical. He took a step forward to help Hollis by getting Mitzi off his back when suddenly the man tried to buck the officer off. Hollis lost his balance on the large mound of flesh and slid to one side. The man rolled, and Hollis's foot got pinned beneath him. Hollis gave a startled scream and pushed rather desperately against the man with both his hands and his free foot.

"Police brutality," Mitzi screamed, rushing Hollis with a frying pan raised high.

Gabe launched himself at her, catching her before she beaned Hollis whose thinning hair wouldn't have offered any protection. He saved Hollis but not himself. Her swing caught him on his right shoulder, and his arm went numb.

With his good hand he grabbed the pan and threw it across the room. It was a cheap, light weight pan and probably wouldn't have done lethal damage to Hollis, but it wouldn't have felt good bouncing off his skull either.

"Come on, Mitzi! Get a grip!" Gabe yelled in her face.

"Don't hurt her!" the man screamed. "Don't you dare hurt her!"

"I'm more worried about her hurting someone!" Gabe rubbed his shoulder.

Mitzi stared at him, her face a mix of disbelief and genuine horror at what she'd done. "I'm sorry, Gabe! I'm sorry!" She started to cry. "I never hit anyone before. You know I never did!"

Gabe studied her and decided her emotion was genuine, at least this time. He had a hard time reading Mitzi who was currently looking every one of her thirty-five years and about twenty more. Her blonde hair was tangled and her black roots showed. Her eye makeup was smeared from her tears, making her look like a blonde Goth if there was such a thing. Her short violent pink robe exposed thighs pocked with cellulite. Too much booze and too many drugs had given her a hard, ravaged, sad look.

Where had the pretty, peppy cheerleader with the sunny smile gone? Gabe remembered her from high school, just one year ahead of him, jumping on the sidelines as he and his team-mates limped from defeat to defeat. Lyndale's thirty game losing streak never dimmed her enthusiasm as she yelled, "Push 'em back, push 'em back, waaay back!"

He felt a profound sorrow as he thrust her into a chair. "Do not move."

She stayed where he put her, apparently still shocked by her attack on Hollis and the damage to his arm which started buzzing as the nerves decided to wake up. He rotated the shoulder and clenched and unclenched his fist to try and get normal feeling back.

In minutes Mitzi's caller, a man named Bobby Jones—yeah, right—was slumped in the kitchen's second chair. His nose continued to run, and Mitzi reached across the table and patted his hand. She smiled at him, and Gabe saw a glimpse of the old Mitzi.

"It's okay, Jonesy." She gave him a wobbly smile. "I'm not mad."

Gabe gave a mental shrug. Maybe his name was Jones. "Don't tell him it's okay before you look at yourself in the mirror. You're going to have quite a shiner."

Mitzi glared at Gabe with some of her old fire. "He didn't do it. I-I bumped my head on the door jamb."

"Mitzi." Gabe made no effort to keep the disgust and disbelief out of his voice.

She flushed but didn't back down. "Thanks for coming, Gabe." She stood and looked from him to Hollis. "I'm sorry about your arm. Really. And your foot, Hollis. Now go. I don't want you here."

"Mitzi, you've got to stop this." Gabe swept his hand around, indicating the bottle of booze on the counter, the cigarettes pluming smoke in the ashtray on the table, and the inebriated Jonesy.

She stuck out her chin. "I'm doing okay."

"You're doing okay?" Outrage tinged his voice. "Who are you kidding? You're killing yourself!"

She glared at him, and he wondered why he bothered. She wouldn't listen today any more than she had on other days.

"At least I'll die happy," she cooed, eying Jonesy.

Gabe looked at the obese man wiping his nose on a napkin and thought about differing definitions of happiness.

Mitzi turned her attention back to Gabe. "My life is none of your business, Gabe."

Still he tried one more time. "If you don't care about yourself, Mitz, think about Kenny. You want him turning out like you?"

She looked affronted, and he had to admit that he hadn't worded that too well.

"You leave Kenny out of it," she hissed. "He's a good boy."

"He is." No thanks to her.

She continued to glare at him, and Gabe realized he and Hollis might as well leave. Mitzi wasn't listening to advice tonight. He flicked a hand at Hollis who limped out the door, more than happy to flee this particular sinking ship. Gabe didn't fault him.

With a glance at Jonesy and a nod to Mitzi, he followed, muttering to himself about Mitzi throwing her life away. One of the most frustrating parts of his job was watching people make the same bad choices over and over. How many times had he been to Mitzi's about some altercation? Yet she continued to hang with men who used their hands violently.

It didn't make sense. No matter how often he reminded himself that logic didn't enter into these bad choices, he couldn't wrap his mind around inviting people who hurt you into your home a second time, let alone multiple times.

It was all his parents' fault that he didn't get it.

"I'm the victim of white collar abuse," he told them once when he was a kid.

"What are you talking about?" they asked.

"It's all love, love, love around here. How am I supposed to make my way in the real world without some dysfunctional experience?"

"Well, I guess I could beat you every night before bed if that's what you really want," Dad said. "I don't think it'll be good for my image as a family man, but if it'll make you happy...."

They all laughed, and Gabe went on being loved.

Had anyone ever loved, really loved Mitzi? Probably not, he thought sadly. Probably not.

Feeling weary and out of sorts, he drove home, calling Dottie on the way. "Hollis is on until midnight. Anything after that, call me."

"It's Monday," she said. "Nothing happens on Monday. Get a good night's sleep."

Gabe tried. He fell asleep easily enough, but he had dreams all night, wonderful dreams of Robyn, beautiful Robyn of the golden hair and the hearty laugh so at odds with her petite size, the from-the-toes laugh that always made him laugh in response.

He dreamed she stood in front of this house, his house, delighted with its size and their ownership.

"We'll fill it with kids, Gabe, lots of kids."

Then she came into this very bedroom, blue eyes shining with joy. "I'm pregnant, Gabe! Can you believe it?"

Even in the dream he understood that they'd still been living in the apartment when she discovered she was expecting. This house was still three years in the future, but the lack of an accurate timeline didn't seem the least bit illogical or incorrect.

"Our own baby," she crooned in the dream, putting his hand on her flat stomach. "A little Gabe."

"Or a little Robyn," he responded as he held her close in the very bed in which he was now sleeping alone.

Then the golden wash of the dream darkened, and panic gripped him as he realized what was coming. The baby had been a little Gabe, and he had died in utero when Robyn's car was struck by a drunk passing on a curve and a double yellow line.

He saw himself kneeling by her crushed car, his hand gripping hers through the shattered window as they worked to cut her free. "Stay with me, Rob. Come on, baby. One more breath. One more. Oh, God, please!" He felt again the slight flutter of her hand and then its awful stillness. He awoke drenched in sweat, his heart pounding, his chest aching with the agony of losing her.

He sat on the edge of the bed and lowered his head to his hands. He hadn't had this dream for more months than he could remember. Right after Robyn's death it had been so frequent that he dreaded the sun going down and feared going to bed. Gradually the frequency lessened until the dream stopped. Or so he'd thought before tonight.

Mister Thomas, his Royal Standard poodle, came to him, sitting on the floor beside him. He whined softly and pushed against Gabe's hands, offering comfort.

"It's okay, boy." Gabe buried his head in the animal's soft top-knot. "I'm okay. Or I will be in a bit."

They met in fourth grade when her family moved to Lyndale. She walked into the classroom, her red-gold hair a halo of curls around her freckled face. She looked straight at him and smiled, and there'd never been another girl. Even when his friends teased him mercilessly, he followed her around like an enamored puppy.

And wonder of wonders, she loved him in return.

They had married the week after they graduated from college, and Robyn became his, forever and always. Forever had been six short but wonderful years.

These days he didn't rail against the Lord as he had when the tragedy first happened. He accepted that bad things happened to good people, and he was but one of millions who lost someone they loved. It was part of being human. But he still regretted to his very soul that Robyn was one of those taken. The world was full of people who didn't deserve to live, and she did. Oh, she did. She had been light and life and love.

"Gabe," his mother often said these days, her eyes full of love and pity, "you've got to move on."

Well, he had. He'd bought this house, hadn't he? He was coaching, wasn't he?

Dad tried a different line. "You need someone to love, Gabe, someone to give you a reason to get up in the morning."

"I'm doing great, Dad. I have my work and the football team. I even find time to write my books. That's more purpose than most men."

What he didn't say was that he'd loved Robyn, the one and only. How could he love another?

With a sigh of painfilled resignation for what was no longer, he turned the light on and read for a half hour, then tried sleeping again. There were no more heart wrenching nightmares, and Robyn once again became only a memory.

There were no beautiful, golden dreams either.

CHAPTER 5

"She's dying." Joey Terafino set down the phone and rubbed his hands together in satisfaction.

Antony Morelli slouched in a leather chair in front of the big screen TV watching the Eagles play the Giants. "Who's dying?"

"Old Mrs. Mancini."

"Ellie's nonna?" Antony looked intrigued.

"Cancer. Down inside her somewhere." Joey gestured vaguely. "Some woman thing."

Antony laughed. "Serves her right. You know how they say: It couldn't happen to a nicer person."

Joey shrugged. It wasn't Sophia Mancini he was thinking about, but as usual Antony was ten steps behind. He and Antony had been friends ever since they lived down the block from each other as kids. Ellie had come and gone, but Antony had stayed true forever. Joey appreciated that, even if Antony wasn't the swiftest boat in the fleet. And he made a great hoagie.

"She's a terrible old lady." Antony actually shuddered. He smiled slyly at Joey. "She hates you."

"Yeah, she does." He spoke absently, his mind running ahead. He walked to the window of his apartment and looked down on South Street, only he didn't see the eclectic collection of people wandering from store to store, restaurant to restaurant, bar to bar. He saw a dark haired girl with big brown eyes who once upon a time looked at him with those eyes soft with love.

Even when the love died, there'd been fear and respect—for him, for his authority, for his domination. He liked the fear best of all.

She thought she'd pulled a fast one running out on him, but she had no idea how patient he was and how determined he was. He might have let her go, but she made the mistake of taking his Nicky. His boy. His son. He'd spent all these years waiting, knowing he was smarter, stronger, bigger. Knowing he'd have his chance. "The old lady's my link to Ellie."

He could almost hear Antony blink as he finally got it. "You think she knows where Ellie is?"

Joey smiled without humor. "Of course she does."

"She's always denied it."

"She's known ever since Ellie left. She knows where my Nick is. She's been lying through her teeth all these years, and I hope she suffers terrible pain for the pain she's put me through!"

Antony grinned. "Who do you hate more, her or Ellie?"

Joey didn't need to think. "Ellie. She took my son and she took my money. She made me look a fool. 'Where's Ellie, Joey? Did she leave you?' And they'd snicker behind their hands. No one uses me and gets away with it, Antony. No one." His voice shook with the intensity of his feelings.

Antony grunted and turned back to the TV. He watched with a stoic fatalism as the Eagles fumbled on their twenty yard line and New York recovered. The next play, the Giants scored. "There goes twenty thousand bucks."

"Serves you right for floating that much on the Birds."

"Yeah, but how can I bet against the Birds?"

"So you don't bet at all."

"What? Like you never do?" Antony sounded huffy.

"Sure, I bet." In memory he saw the broken desk drawer, his betting reserves gone, taken without permission by the woman he'd thought was his. In a fury he'd reported it to the cops. He'd reported the kidnapping, too, but he'd made the mistake of waiting until the next day. When Ellie hadn't come to work that evening and hadn't been at the house when he finally got home after a quick visit with Vera, he figured she was sulking at her nonna's again. By the time he noticed the broken drawer and realized she was truly gone, she had almost a day's head start.

The cops had debated issuing an AMBER alert for Nick, but they hadn't because, they said, Nick wasn't in physical danger, one of the criteria for issuing the alert. Also the critical time frame had passed. In stranger abductions, seventy-five percent of kids taken were murdered within the first three hours, and not only wasn't this a stranger abduction, a whole day had passed.

"But clearly he's in danger," Joey said, bewildered by their attitude. "He's been kidnapped!"

"He's with his mother, and we have no indication that she will endanger him. We'll issue a fugitive warrant against Gabriella Francella, and she'll be listed on all the crime data bases. Sooner or later she'll surface, and we'll get your son back."

"Sooner or later? Don't I have rights as a father?" he'd protested. "I want my kid! And my ten thousand!"

The cops had shrugged, and he knew the murder of a cop two days prior and the double homicide in Society Hill that morning as well as the multitude of others crimes in a city the size of Philadelphia were higher on their list than his Nick, especially after they talked to Sophia Mancini who'd filled their ears with lies about him. Next time he called the lady detective in charge of his case, he learned what the cops thought.

"You're lucky she's not here asking for a Protection from Abuse against you," the woman said, dislike dripping from her voice.

That was what happened when you got a woman in charge of your case. So Joey hired a private detective who found no trace.

"She didn't leave on any public transportation," the man said. "Not plane, train or bus. She hasn't used her credit cards."

"She doesn't have credit cards." Joey wasn't an idiot. You could borrow against credit cards. He gave her enough to keep her happy but not enough to be out of his control. Until she broke into his locked drawer.

It was a good thing he'd taken her fifty thousand or she'd have run with that. He smiled to himself when it occurred to him that she probably had tried to get that money.

Score one for me, Angel Eyes. I got fifty. You only got ten.

But it was his ten and he wanted it back.

"So break into the IRS data base," he'd demanded of the PI after she'd been gone two years. Nick was then eleven and Joey ached for him. "See if she's paying income tax."

The PI shook his head. "Not me. First I don't know how. Second I'm not risking federal charges for hacking into a data base that's off limits. I don't want to risk jail or, worse yet, an IRS audit if I'm found out."

"So find a hacker who can do it," Joey demanded.

The detective shook his head. "People may do stuff like that all the time on TV and in the movies, but in real life those files are so encrypted and protected, no one breaks in. Take my word. I've worked all the usual trace methods, some of them pretty sophisticated. Wherever she is, she's smart enough to keep her head down. Her file's open. If her name comes up, I got her. That's the best I can do." He gave Joey a hard look. "If I had her Social Security number it'd be much easier. Without it, this is the best anyone can do."

The mere mention of a Social Security number made Joey do a slow burn. How could he have lived with her so long and never noted it? Since he never paid her a salary, he'd never needed it, but still. They'd even shared a joint account for all of a month before he'd moved the assets to a more secure place and closed the account. He'd been young and dumb back then and hadn't known she'd turn on him in the future, so he hadn't noted her number.

When he went to the bank to get into the records not too long after she left, they told him they purged their system after seven years. The account had been closed more than nine years ago. Beyond the fact that the account had once existed, the information was no longer available. Sorry.

Ellie'd been gone eight years now. Nick was seventeen, a high school junior. What did he look like? Was he a good student? Did he play sports? Was he still an Eagles and Flyers fan even though he hadn't lived in Philly for years? What would he think of his old man's success?

Joey looked around his apartment. Everything was classy and expensive and impressed the ladies right out of their clothes.

"Yes!" Antony cheered as the Eagles kick-off receiver made it back to the forty-five yard line. "Maybe I'll win yet. This new QB can make things happen!"

"You should only bet on sure things, not QBs who maybe come through." Sure things like Ellie coming home.

An ad came and Antony wandered to the kitchen with its stainless steel appliances and marble slab counter. He grabbed another beer from the fridge. "You really think Ellie'll come to see her nonna before she dies? Or maybe to bury her?"

"A thousand says she does."

Antony hesitated, then shook his head. "If you're putting up that much, you're sure. So, no, no bet." He turned back to the game.

"And another thousand says she never leaves again."

Antony looked up, his eyes narrow. "What are you sayin'?"

Joey grinned. "Nothing, Antony. Relax. Just that Ellie will come home and be so happy here, she'll stay."

Antony frowned like he was trying to figure it all out. A burst of noise from the TV captured his attention. "Yes! We scored!"

Joey slumped onto the black leather couch, sinking into its warm embrace. Did Ellie know how good he was doing? Did she know him and Antony had a first class restaurant west of town, serving quality sit-down Italian cuisine with linen tablecloths and all? He'd hired a famous chef and a sous chef, a real one, not an Antony one. Did she know he was rolling in dough? If she did know, did she care? Did she tell Nicky his father was rich?

For all he knew, she was happily married to some guy and had lots of little kids, brothers and sisters for his Nicky.

He hoped not. He hoped she was poor and lonely. He hoped Nicky hated her for taking him away. He stared at the TV blindly. He had no doubt Ellie would come back. The bond between her and her nonna was too strong to resist. He wasn't exactly sure what he'd do when she came back, but he'd figure it out.

But one thing he knew: when she came, she'd never leave. Never. One way or another, he'd see to it.

CHAPTER 6

Eight-year-old Avery Mulholland peered through the hedge, waiting impatiently for a glimpse of her hero. She'd thought he was way cool even before she saw his picture in the newspaper today, jumping in the air and saving the day with his catch. Now she was in love.

She couldn't believe he was her neighbor. How lucky was that? Not that he even knew she was alive, but still, in her heart he was hers. Just thinking about him made her feel warm and happy. She watched him as much as she could manage, either from the hedge like now or from high up in the big maple tree that sat at the back of his yard.

What she liked best about him was that he was so nice. He smiled a lot and didn't yell, not even at his mother. When she grew up, she would marry someone like him, all tall and strong and smiley. And nice. Nice was most important.

Maybe if she prayed real hard, he'd wait for her. God answered prayers when you prayed hard, right? Not that she knew all that much about God. She heard stuff on TV when grumpy Mrs. Cotton, their housekeeper, watched. Mostly she just knew deep inside.

"Save him for me, okay, God? Please?" She whispered it because she wanted to be sure He heard. She thought He heard thoughts because after all, He was God, but she wasn't sure. She knew He heard stuff you said. "I'll even be willing to live in his tiny house."

It looked like it was very old, and it was a sort of sad gray with dirty white trim. It only had two bedrooms and one bathroom. One! And there was barely enough room in the kitchen for their little table. She knew these things because she'd peeked in their windows once. Well, maybe more than once. If she wanted God to answer her prayers, she'd better tell the truth, even to herself.

Mom said the little gray house was ugly in this upscale neighborhood, which to Avery seemed a very unfair comment. It wasn't as if it appeared one night without warning. It was already there behind its hedge when the developer bought the big marshy field next to it and built beautiful stone front houses and named his development Oakland Acres even though no one had an acre. Avery wasn't certain how big an acre was, but she felt sure it was bigger than the little patch of lawn that was theirs. At least the oak tree part of Oakland Acres was right, even if they were only about as big as a lamp post.

"It distresses me to look at that old place," Mom said about the little gray house. "It's a blight and an eyesore."

Avery always wanted to ask why they bought the house right next door if the little house was so terrible to look at, but she didn't. It was like she heard Daddy say once: Discretion is the better part of valor, which she thought meant that keeping quiet was better than being courageous enough to say what you were thinking.

So she watched. And watched. For just over a month now she'd been climbing her tree with its thick cover of leaves, watching Nick. From one special branch she could just see into his bedroom, and she waited for long stretches of time for a glimpse of him.

This evening she'd decided to hide behind the hedge that separated their properties rather than climb the tree. The advantage of the hedge over the tree was that she had a great view of the whole front yard. Since the gray car wasn't in the drive, she knew

Nick and his mom weren't home yet. That meant she could watch him get out of the car and walk to the house, much more satisfying than maybe catching a glimpse from the tree. For as long as necessary she would hide in the wild tangle that never got cut because no one seemed sure whose property the hedge was on.

"Look at how out of control that hedge is," Daddy would say as he stood on their deck and frowned. "She should get that kid of hers to cut it."

"Are you sure it's their hedge?" Mom asked.

"Of course. It was here before we were."

Maybe, but Avery still thought Daddy should get the lawn service to trim it because he could afford it. Of course if it got trimmed, it would be hard to hide in it, so she never suggested that idea.

She sighed as she thought of Nick and how wonderful it would be to be his. Not that he would ever notice her, let alone love her. She knew she'd never be good enough. He'd marry some pretty blonde lady like on TV or magazine covers. He could have anybody. He was like a-a-a god! Yes, that was it. She pictured him standing on top of a mountain, the wind whipping all around him. He was way beyond mere mortals like her. Especially her.

She was short and dumpy. She was ugly. She had crooked teeth and ugly braces to try and straighten them. The braces made her lisp. She had too much wild hair in spite of going to the beauty salon with Mom for "treatments". She wore thick glasses. She was an embarrassment. And she was dumb.

She knew all this was true not because of the mirror, which she avoided looking in as much as possible. She knew because while Daddy told Mom how beautiful she was all the time, he never, ever said anything nice about Avery.

It was hard, knowing you were a disappointment even when you tried your very best. She pressed into the hedge and blinked hard. That was another proof of her failure, the tendency to weep.

"Don't cry, Avery!" Mom would say. "It'll make your face blotchy."

"Mulhollands don't cry," Daddy would say. "You can at least try to be strong."

She tried, she tried so hard, but she stayed weak. Maybe when she was older, she could be stronger and hold in the tears. She hoped so, and she asked God to help her grow strong all the time.

A car pulled into the drive next door, and *he* climbed out. He had his gym bag and his backpack in his hand. She imagined the gym bag held his dirty clothes from practice, stuff like socks, maybe a sweat shirt, a tee shirt, maybe shorts or sweat pants. Tomorrow when he came out, it would be full of clean, sweet smelling clothes that his mother had washed for him.

Avery frowned. Had Mom ever washed her clothes? She didn't think so. It was Mrs. Cotton's job. Mrs. Cotton was old and cranky, but Mom liked her. Once when Avery complained about her, Mom said, "Mrs. Cotton has been with us forever. She stays."

It almost sounded as if Avery could go if she didn't get along with Mrs. Cotton. That was the way it was when you were an accident, a kid no one planned on and no one really wanted.

She blinked hard again. She had to be strong. She glanced over her shoulder at her house, half expecting Mrs. Cotton to be staring at her through the big window in the family room. Her shoulders relaxed when she saw only the black glass of a dark room.

She turned back and watched Nick through the little green leaves, pushing a branch aside for a better view. He was so strong. She wished she could borrow some of his toughness. She really needed it, and he'd never miss it.

His backpack bulged with his books. He always brought home a heavy load. That meant he was not only way cool but smart too. So that she wouldn't be embarrassed if she ever actually met him and he asked how she was doing in school—adults and older people like him asked that all the time—she'd been starting to work harder. She even did an extra credit report on horses. She loved horses.

Avery sighed, then almost died as he looked toward the hedge. He couldn't see her, could he? It was getting dark, she had on jeans and her navy jacket, and the hedge was the kind that never lost its leaves.

Oh, please, God, don't let him see me! I'll die if he does.

He turned away and she began to breathe again. It was one thing to spy and another thing all together to get caught.

He said something and someone laughed. For the first time, Avery noticed the other boy. He was almost as tall as Nick, but he wasn't nearly as strong looking. He had dark hair like Nick, but it was longer and shaggy, like it needed a cut. He had a full book bag too, but he looked like it was pulling him down on one side, like he wasn't strong enough to hold it.

Nick's mom was with the boys. She drove Nick everywhere unless one of the guys on the team picked him up. It puzzled Avery that Nick didn't drive. He was old enough. He had to be. At first she'd thought it was because he came from out of state and hadn't had time to take the Pennsylvania test for his license. Now she wondered if it was because there wasn't money for him to have a car. She heard Daddy muttering and cursing about how expensive it was to have cars. Gas, insurance, fees for leasing or monthly payments when you bought.

"It's a good thing you have a great job, isn't it?" Mom said whenever he complained. "Money to burn on a new Lexus every year."

Nick didn't have a job; his mother did. Nick didn't have a car; his mother did. It made perfect sense to Avery.

She burrowed deeper into the hedge and studied Nick's friend in the light that spilled out of the front door when Ms. Loring went in and turned on the living room light. He was skinny, too skinny to play football. Daddy had games on all weekend, and she knew only big guys played. This skinny boy would get creamed.

Unless he was the kicker. They were little guys lots of time. She studied him thoughtfully. Could a leg that skinny kick a ball very far?

When the front door closed and Nick disappeared from view, Avery crept out of the little hole in the hedge. Or she tried to. Her frizzy hair caught on a branch, and try as she would, she couldn't pull it free.

She started to sweat, and she was afraid she'd hurl. Daddy and Mom would be home any minute, and if they caught her spying, she'd be in for it.

In desperation she gave a mighty tug, and with a painful parting of hair from scalp, she came free. At the same time lights turned into their cul de sac. Daddy and Mom! Since they were partners in the same law firm, they often went to work together unless one had a court date.

Avery had to get inside before they turned into the drive. She raced across the back yard and in through the back door. When her parents came in the front door, she was watching TV in the family room, trying to control her breathing, hoping she looked like she'd been there for hours.

CHAPTER 7

Ellie looked at her reflection in the mirror attached to the back of the closet door in her little bedroom. Did she look different enough that no one would recognize her?

"What do you think, guys?" she asked the cats who lounged with total unconcern on the bed. Buddy blinked but Midnight didn't even bother with that minimal response.

She studied herself again. The cheap blonde wig drained her face of all color, and she looked anemic. The baggy jeans and old lady sweatshirt with three cats dancing on its front did nothing for her either. She wore a pair of oversized bifocals with lenses that darkened in the sun, so her eyes would be concealed. They gave her a headache when she tried to see clearly through them.

That's what happened when you got your specs at Goodwill. In fact she'd bought the entire outfit at Goodwill, and it would be worth every penny if it worked. If it worked.

She refused to consider what would happen if it didn't.

Oh, Lord, I'm terrified. She could feel her heart hammering. *You're going to have to keep me safe. I'm depending on You.*

The hardest part of the last eight years had been not seeing Nonna. Excitement at finally being with her again fought with the fear of being recognized by someone who would pass the news of her presence to Joey. Pressing her hand to her stomach to try and ease its nerve-induced distress, Ellie went out to her car. Memories swirled as she drove, and for once she let herself remember, something she usually fought because the memories always left her lonely and/or depressed at her colossal stupidity. Whoever said hindsight was twenty-twenty knew what he was talking about.

Nonna, in her wisdom, hadn't wanted Ellie to get involved with Joey. "He is not a good person, Gabriella," she'd said when Ellie was thirteen and Joey fifteen. "Stay away from him."

But as an alcoholic craves alcohol and an obese person food, so she craved the excitement of Joey. When he sneaked her into the movies, she felt alive. When he taught her how to smoke, she felt sophisticated. When he got her an illegal card and took her to clubs where he taught her to drink, she felt mature. When he taught her about sex, she felt loved.

Joey was eighteen when his father was beaten to death by an unknown person. Joey found the body behind Terafino's when he went to work one morning. No one missed Carlo Terafino, least of all his wife and son. He had been a violent man, and Joey and his mother Gina had felt his fists for years. His manner of death seemed somehow appropriate to the whole neighborhood.

Ellie had been so proud of the way Joey cared for his mother in the aftermath of his father's death. "See, Nonna? He is a good, kind man. A good son."

Nonna had said nothing at the time, but years later after Ellie left, Nonna had written her that she thought Joey had killed Carlo.

"Not that he didn't have provocation," Nonna wrote. "But murder is murder. When he started hitting you, can you imagine my fear?"

"But you never said anything!" Ellie wrote back.

"Because I didn't *know*."

Shortly after Carlo Terafino died, Gina married Vic Pascarelli, much to Joey's disgust. She moved into Vic's house and let Joey have hers about the same time Ellie discovered she was pregnant.

"Come live with me, Angel Eyes," Joey urged.

"Live with him?" Nonna said. "Why doesn't he ask you to marry him? That would be right."

"I'm too young to get married," Ellie said, repeating what Joey had said as if it made perfect sense.

"You're sixteen, Ellie. I agree that you're too young to get married. But you're also too young to live in sin. Why do you want to throw your life away?"

"Oh, Nonna, nobody feels that way about a couple living together anymore. I love him and he loves me. That's all that counts. We'll be fine. We'll be happy!"

What an idiot she'd been.

Nonna recognized a losing battle when she saw one. "If your nonno was still alive ..." she began and trailed off.

Ellie knew that if Nonno was still living, she wouldn't be leaving school and moving in with her boyfriend. But he was gone, and Nonna was afraid to make a scene.

"I don't want to lose you, Gabriella. Or the precious baby that's coming. You are all I have."

Nonna fell instantly in love with Nick and much was forgiven as he smiled and cooed and batted his big dark eyes so like Ellie's. A tenuous peace was established between Nonna and Joey and held until the day Ellie failed to hide the bruise on her cheek.

Nonna held Ellie's face to the sunlight streaming through her kitchen window. "Now I know why he gave you today off. He didn't want the customers to see you."

"I walked into the half open bedroom door in the dark," Ellie lied. "It's nothing."

Nonna made a skeptical noise. "Maybe it's good you didn't marry him. It will save the need for a divorce."

Divorce? How could Nonna even mention the word? In her mind Ellie was married. She lived with Joey. She had his child. She loved him. When troubles came, you worked through them. You didn't walk out. You didn't break up a family, even if the family was already broken.

"Just tell me when you're ready to leave him," Nonna said, "and I will help you."

"Nonna!"

Nonna gathered her close. "I will never stop loving you, my Gabriella. Never. No matter what, you are my girl and this is always your home. Come home to me any time you need to."

That was all so long ago, but the echoes still reverberated through all their lives. Now, as she took the Schuylkill Expressway into the city, her hands turned damp. She'd sworn she'd never come back to Philadelphia under any circumstance, but here she was, looking for a parking space as near Nonna's as possible. She didn't want to be on the street in the open any longer than necessary. She'd come over the lunch hour because she knew both Joey and Antony would be at the deli.

Still, as she climbed from the car, she thought she might throw up from anxiety. She stood for a moment, hand clutching the door to keep herself upright, while she waited for the nausea to pass. It didn't, but it lessened enough for her to make her way to Nonna's.

The neighborhood looked remarkably as she remembered. The Finellis had gotten rid of the bright green fake turf on their porch, thank goodness, and erected a shrine to the Virgin Mary that took up three quarters of the space. Ellie smiled through her nervousness as she remembered summer evenings with Mrs. Finelli sitting on the porch watching the neighborhood go by, her eagle eyes searching for any sign of drugs or hanky-panky of any kind. She and Joey must have made her evenings. Today's kids would be safe because there was no room for sitting any longer, thanks to the Virgin's grotto.

The Zinzarellas had enclosed their porch, making it a Florida room. Mrs. Z made wonderful pizzelles, the only ones that came close to Nonna's, all crisp and full of anise flavor. Ellie's mouth watered at the memory.

Aside from the shrine and the Florida room, everything else looked so familiar it was disconcerting. It was as if she had just gotten off the Septa bus coming home from school, not returned after eight years away.

As she started up the walk to Nonna's, she noted that Mr. Salerno, the man in the other half of Nonna's double, had his azaleas trimmed at exactly the height of his porch just as he had for as long as she could remember. Every spring his bushes flamed with brilliant color. As soon as the blooms disappeared, the electric shears came out.

Mr. Salerno'd had a crush on Nonna ever since Nonno died when Ellie was fifteen. Back then Mr. Salerno'd been a shrunken old man with a beak of a nose that overwhelmed his face. He must be a true gnome by now.

She rang Nonna's doorbell, a strange thing to do at the house she had been raised in. She still had a house key, but she couldn't risk using it in case someone was watching. *Hey, Joey! Strange lady with a key. Check her out.*

Tamping down her unease and feeling of exposure, she listened as the sound of the bell faded. She found herself waiting to hear Tipsy, the rambunctious terrier Nonna had loved so deeply. The little dog had welcomed Ellie home from school every day for years, but he had gone to his canine reward four years prior. The house sounded too silent.

For the first time Ellie wondered if there would be someone to let her in. She knew Nonna spent most of her time in bed, but for some reason, the issue of getting in hadn't occurred to her. She might have to use her key after all.

The door sprang open, startling her. She'd heard no one approach. Mr. Salerno himself stood before her, his skin draped over his skeleton with no fat or muscle to offer a softening contour. Was the man eating these days, or had he decided to let himself wither away? His nose appeared larger than ever and his eyes were cloudy with cataracts.

She waited for him to exclaim, "Gabriella!" Instead he looked at her blankly and said, "Whatcha want?"

Ever the charmer, Mr. Salerno. "I came to see my no—" She caught herself, "I'm here to see Sophia Mancini."

Mr. Salerno peered at her. "How d'ya know her?"

Hoping she wasn't doing deer-caught-in-the-headlights eyes at the unexpected question, she blurted, "Church," the first thing that popped into her mind.

"Huh. Women's stuff." He backed up and waved her in. "She's in there." He pointed to the living room. "Don't stay long. She gets tired real easy."

As she stepped inside, he stepped out. He pointed to his place.

"I live there if you need anything. Hospice will be here at one-thirty."

Hospice. The word had a finality to it that brought a wash of sorrow. How could the idea of losing someone you hadn't seen in eight years hurt so much?

Because it was the heart connection that mattered, not the physical proximity.

She mumbled goodbye to Mr. Salerno, but he was cutting across the small yard to his house and didn't hear in spite of the hearing aids in both ears.

Ellie shut the door and walked the few steps to the archway into the living room. Now her fear wasn't for discovery but for what she'd see. Nonna had been a strong woman, an active woman who was rarely still. She never sat when she could move. She never walked when she could stride. She had been the backbone of Ellie's life for as long as she could remember, the only one who didn't want something from her, the only one who just loved her. To see her frail and dying was going to be so hard.

Ellie stepped through the archway and stopped. The shock was so intense it felt as if she'd been struck. Nonna lay in a hospital bed, her eyes closed, her face lined, the gray pallor of the very ill leeching all her color. She was so thin her body made barely a rise in the covers. For a terrified moment Ellie thought she wasn't breathing, but as she looked carefully, her own breath stopped in her throat, she saw Nonna's chest rise ever so slightly. Her hands lay still, clasped on the outside of her covers, the tracery of veins obvious under the sagging, translucent flesh.

Ellie swallowed a fresh surge of tears. Nonna's hands were always busy. If she wasn't gesticulating, she was using them for cooking or cleaning or knitting, especially knitting. She made booties for any person she heard was having a baby, even Mrs. Facenda's second cousin's daughter-in-law in Jersey. Knitting bags sat all around the house so that whenever and wherever she did sit, she could knit. There was even a bag kept by the front door so that when she went out, she could grab it for the bus ride or in case she had to wait for an appointment. Ellie had been thirteen before she talked Nonna into letting her buy a ready-made sweater in a store.

Ellie moved as quietly as she could to the beige sofa, still covered in its heavy plastic. The armchair was gone from the room to make space for the bed.

The sofa crackled beneath her, and Nonna said without opening her eyes, "Louie? You still here?"

The weakness of Nonna's voice tore at Ellie's heart. She'd always thought that if Nonna were a man, she'd have been a very loud basso profundo.

"Mr. Salerno's gone, Nonna. It's me." Ellie could barely get the words out.

Nonna turned her head, and they stared at each other without moving for a long moment.

Then Noona held out her arms. "My Gabriella!"

Ellie fell into the embrace, emotions and memories tumbling over each other as indiscriminately as clothes in a dryer. She'd missed her grandmother with a physical ache she'd always thought akin to the phantom pain an amputee felt for the missing limb. She'd had no one to hold close, and no had held her close for eight long years.

"Oh, my girl." Nonna stroked a hand over Ellie's head, and Ellie felt five years old again, secure in her nonna's embrace. "Oh, my girl. I was so afraid I would never see you again."

Ellie kicked off her shoes and climbed onto Nonna's bed. She grabbed Nonna's frail hand between her two and lay down with her head nestled into the pillow in the crook between Nonna's neck and shoulder. Nonna rested her head against Ellie's. For a time they said nothing, just enjoyed the closeness, the delight of each other's presence.

"You shouldn't have come," Nonna finally said, her voice breathy, the words spaced from the effort talking and breathing took. "But I'm so glad you did."

"I'll come as often as I can."

"You mustn't. No more. Promise?"

"I'm safe here, Nonna."

"Which is why the disguise, right? By the way, you are not a pretty blonde."

Ellie shrugged. "I don't think Joey is looking for me anymore." Which was an outright lie but somehow seemed the thing to say. "I don't think he cares anymore."

"Of course he's looking for you." Nonna, ever the realist. "You are probably the only person who has ever defied him."

Ellie smiled without humor. It was strange, the welling of pride she felt because she'd had the courage necessary to take charge of her life and Nick's, and stranger still that it sat comfortably beside the fear of discovery. "Not just me. You, too."

She could feel Nonna smile. "Me, too. I don't think anything has ever given me such a sharp satisfaction as putting one over on that man."

Ellie raised her head, and she and Nonna grinned at each other.

"An old lady and a young woman." Nonna's smile broadened, then faded. "He'll never forgive us."

"No, he won't," Ellie acknowledged, "especially since I took his son."

Nonna kissed Ellie's cheek. "You saved his son."

Ellie nodded. "*We* saved him, you and me. And then God stepped in and cared for us when we were all alone and desperately needy and afraid."

Nonna frowned. "I don't understand how come you think God suddenly stepped in. He was there all the time."

"He was, but I wasn't seeing Him or seeking Him."

Nonna glared at Ellie with some of her old spirit. "We showed you, Nonno and me. We took you to church your whole life. Why were you so blind to truth?"

She had been blind to many things and blinded by many others. "But now I believe," she said. "That's what counts. Now I thank God for His presence in our lives."

"I still don't understand how you could hear and not hear."

Ellie shrugged. "We each find Jesus by our own route, like we each live our lives our own way. You trusted God always, loved Jesus always, followed God's ways always. You married Nonno and loved him as long as he lived, and he loved you. You went to church because you wanted to. It brought you comfort and made you feel close to God. It made you love Him more."

Nonna waited patiently for her to get beyond the obvious and to the point.

"I went to church because you took me, but I didn't listen. I didn't believe anything about God because I thought He didn't have anything to do with my life. He was out there somewhere, far away, not interested in me. And I didn't want Him to be. I wanted to figure it all out myself. I was so sure I knew all the answers." Ellie gave a rueful smile. "We both know what a disaster that was."

They were quiet a minute, thinking about the terrible mistakes Ellie had made.

"But you have Nicky," Nonna said. "Tell me about him."

Ellie pulled out a copy of the article that had been in the newspaper. "Look at him, Nonna. Isn't he handsome?"

Nonna's eyes flashed with some of their old life as she studied her great-grandson. "He is a fine boy. Too bad he looks so much like Joey."

"Don't hold that against him." Ellie traced his printed face. "It's not his fault. And he's so different in manner that you forget the resemblance. He's such a good kid, Nonna." If a bit too independent these days.

Nonna held the paper against her heart. "Do not bring him to see me, Gabriella. Joey knows I'm sick. He thinks it will bring you here."

Ellie grimaced. "Well, Joey was never stupid."

"But listen, cara. He and his men watch the house."

Ellie's blood chilled.

"Oh, not every moment, but they check with the neighbors, especially Louie."

"Mr. Salerno would tell on us?"

"He'd never tell willingly, but he's not as sharp as he used to be." Nonna touched her head. "If they get him confused or defensive, he might say something without meaning to, you know?"

Ellie knew.

"Did he see you just now?" Nonna asked.

"He did, but he thinks I'm from church. He thinks we work there on some women's things like the Altar Guild or the Shut-in Committee or something."

Nonna didn't seem terribly reassured.

"Besides I don't think he sees very well."

"That's true." Nonna looked a bit less distressed. "He needs cataract surgery, but he doesn't want it. I think he'll go blind first."

"Not good."

"Not good." Nonna's eyes slid shut. "Must rest a minute."

Ellie watched Nonna drift off, tears coming as she remembered Nonna's unquenchable energy. She put her head back on the pillow beside Nonna's and savored the closeness.

Nonna groaned, and Ellie sat up. "What?"

"The bottle," she said, and Ellie picked up what she pointed to. "Open it."

Ellie did, and Nonna took the lid with its attached dropper and squirted some liquid under her tongue. In a few minutes she relaxed. "Morphine. Wonderful stuff."

"Oh, Nonna!"

"Don't cry, my love. Shush, don't cry."

But Ellie couldn't help it.

"I have something for you," Nonna said.

"Something for me?"

"Go to the kitchen and open the big freezer. Take everything before Louie decides to."

Ellie imagined the little old gentleman stuffing Tupperware containers full of red sauce under his shirt to sneak it out.

Nonna gave a weak wave. "I have no more use for any of it. I kept telling myself that I'd get better and entertain the neighborhood at a big recovery party. I kept telling myself that I wasn't dying." Nonna gave a weak smile. "But I am."

Pain ripped through Ellie at that simple statement and had her wrapping her arms around her middle to keep from being sick.

"It's all right, Ellie." Nonna stroked her back. "It's just my time."

Ellie kissed her grandmother's withered cheek. "It's not all right," she said fiercely. "The Lord and I have had long talks about the unfairness of it all."

Nonna smiled. "Not my will but Yours be done."

Blinking and sniffing, knowing Nonna was right, Ellie climbed carefully off the bed and went to the kitchen. One of her favorite childhood memories was the fragrance of Nonna's red sauce wafting through the house, welcoming her home from school, or later, from Joey's house. Nonna and Nonno liked their spaghetti Italian style, the pasta prominent and the sauce barely wetting the noodles. Ellie drenched her pasta in the sauce, reveling in its wonderful combination of tomatoes and spices.

She opened the big freezer and saw the sauce, the lasagna, the ravioli, the chicken parmesan, the gnocchi, the stuffed shells. With her heart breaking, she pulled a pair of plastic grocery bags from the drawer where Nonna always stashed them and began transferring food.

She had just returned to the living room when the doorbell rang.

"Hospice," Nonna said. "You should go."

"I can stay until the nurse leaves."

Nonna shook her head. "Looks too suspicious. There might be watchers."

Ellie shut her eyes. *Lord, what if she's not here for me to come see next week?*

But Nonna was right. She had to leave.

"I'll let her in on my way out." Ellie slid her feet into her shoes and leaned over to kiss Nonna.

"Straighten the bed, Gabriella. I-I can't."

Ellie straightened the covers so no one would realize she had been in it with Nonna.

"I'll come back," she whispered, gently squeezing Nonna's hand.

"No, you mustn't. It's too dangerous."

Ellie just smiled. She would come back—that was why she had moved to Lyndale—but there was no reason to upset Nonna. Let her think she wouldn't.

Ellie went to the door and let in the hospice nurse who gave her an impersonal smile.

Ellie went down the walk, the plastic bags hanging from her hands. When she reached the sidewalk, she turned toward her car, keeping her head down.

A pair of men's shoes stepped into her line of vision. "How is Mrs. Mancini today?"

Ellie froze. She knew that voice. It was more mature than when she'd last heard it, but it still had the same unique raspy quality. Antony Morelli. Her stomach twisted, and sweat dampened her forehead. Why wasn't he at the deli where he belonged?

She kept her eyes down, afraid that if he saw her face, he'd recognize her in spite of the wig, which suddenly seemed a pathetic tactic against discovery. When she forced out words, her voice quavered with fear which she fervently prayed made her sound unlike herself. "Not so good."

"Good." She could hear the satisfaction in his voice, and shock ricocheted through her. Her instinct was to glare at him, to give him a piece of her mind, but she continued to study his shoes.

He stepped aside and let her go on. If he had any manners, he'd offer to carry the bags for her, but thankfully Antony had always been a bore.

Ellie shuffled on, her heart pounding. Antony! He'd never liked her. He saw her as competition for Joey's affection, maybe even for his position as second in command.

"Gabriella," he'd said once when he and Joey were about fifteen, she thirteen, hanging out after school. "That's a girl Gabriel."

She'd nodded. "Gabriel was an angel, so I'm a girl angel." She fluttered her arms like wings.

"An angel? Who you kidding?" He laughed.

She shrugged, stung.

"She's Angel Eyes," Joey said. "No one has eyes that big and beautiful but her."

Ellie stared at Joey, the undisputed leader of their little pack. No boy had ever said anything that nice about her before. Her heart melted.

Then she smirked at Antony, too immature to realize that enemies were made with such a simple show of favoritism. Until the day she left, Antony had tried to undermine her position in Joey's life.

Now as she stashed her bags in the back seat, she could only imagine Antony's delight in being able to unmask her and cement his position as the only one worthy of Joey's trust. Of course, her running away had probably done that long ago.

She climbed behind the wheel and fumbled the key into the ignition. Only then did she allow herself to look up and study the street. Antony stood in front of Nonna's house, Eagles ballcap pulled low over his eyes, talking to Mr. Salerno. He didn't give her a second glance.

CHAPTER 8

At six that same evening Nonna's marvelous red sauce filled Ellie's little kitchen with a mouth-watering fragrance, and Ellie thought how true it was that olfactory memories were among life's strongest.

She remembered being a little girl with dark, curly ponytails on both sides of her head, standing at the stove on a chair, a kitchen towel tucked into the waistband of her jeans, stirring the sauce under her grandmother's careful eye.

As Nonna added spices and olive oil, the young Ellie asked, "How do you know how much to add? You don't have a recipe."

"You just do," Nonna said. "You'll know when it's your turn."

Not true, she came to realize. No matter how hard she tried, her sauce never touched Nonna's.

Some of the sweetest moments growing up were dinners with Nonna and Nonno, even before she came to live with them. At Nonna's dinners, everyone relaxed and enjoyed each other under the spell of the plum tomatoes and olive oil, the basil and the garlic, the oregano and the onion. Dad told stories about some of his students he taught, making being a teacher sound like the most fun job going, and Mom regaled everyone with tales of her strange rich clients at Lord and Taylor where she sold more clothes than any other saleswoman.

Nonno would smile at Dad. "Dom, our favorite teacher, training our future leaders. I am so lucky to have such a wonderful son-in-law. And Rosa." His eyes glowed as he looked at Mom. "Our beautiful daughter is making the world even more beautiful one client at a time."

"Nonno and I love your daddy because he rescued you and your mama," Nonna told the young Ellie.

"How did he rescue us?" Ellie asked, looking across the dinner table at her daddy. She had visions of him running into a burning building and carrying them out or pulling them from a crushed automobile moments before it exploded, like some TV hero.

"The story starts with me," her mother said. "I met your birth father when I was at Penn State. His name was Mitchell Loring and while he was very nice, he was different from anyone I knew, very WASP. That was one of the things I liked about him."

"What's WASP?" Ellie asked and her mother explained about white Anglo-Saxon Protestants.

"We fell in love and married when I was a sophomore and he a junior and you were on the way." Here she reached out and tickled Ellie. "I was eight months pregnant when Mitch fell from the third story window at his fraternity house where he spent more time than he did with me. He broke his neck and died instantly." She smiled sadly. "We both knew getting married had been a mistake, and if he'd lived, I'd probably have been the first divorce in the Mancini family. As it was, I had you and named you Gabriella Sophia Loring."

"But where does Dad come into our lives?" Ellie demanded.

"We met him four years later and we fell for him big time."

"And we became Francellas!" Ellie said triumphantly. "I became Gabriella Francella, the girl with the rhyming names."

Life was good and Ellie felt safe and secure with her mother and father, so in love with each other and her. Then they were killed in an accident on I 95 when a driver cut in front of Dad and clipped his front bumper, sending the car spinning into a tractor trailer. A dazed Ellie, then twelve, came to live with her grandparents.

"Oh, my sweet girl." Nonna wrapped her arms around her when she came through the front door. She took her hand and led her to the kitchen. "Come cook with me, cara. When your mama was your age, we would create magic together. We knew it was magic because your nonno said so."

Ellie looked at Nonno leaning against the doorjamb watching them with tears in his eyes.

"Cook for me, Ellie," he said. "Help your nonna."

At the time Ellie thought he meant help her make dinner, but she now knew he meant help her survive the loss of her daughter and son-in-law. Not only did cooking with Nonna help heal her grandmother, but somehow the smell of red sauce helped Ellie climb out of her despair. Somehow the very fragrance gave her hope. Life could be good again, and when Joey came along, she thought she'd found her new yellow brick road.

Even after she'd gone to live with Joey, the two of them would come to Nonna's for dinner as often as they could manage. Each visit brought out Joey's good qualities as if the sauce were magic. He would be polite to her under Nonna's watchful eye, holding her chair, serving her first, making certain she had all she wanted, and she'd go back to their half a double certain that this time things would be different.

When Nick was a baby, a toddler, a little boy, Nonna's kitchen was a finely scented refuge as often as a place of sustenance. A plate of pasta drenched in red sauce always made the cruel words hurt less, the battering seem not so terrible, the threat to her life appear less real. Even Nonna's constant urging to leave Joey wasn't so bothersome when it was served with homemade pasta.

Now in her tiny kitchen in Lyndale, Ellie slid the wooden spoon through the simmering sauce on her stove. She lay the spoon down and pulled silver from the drawer and set the table for three. She had no doubt that Kenny would come home with Nick. That thought was confirmed when the front door opened and she heard Kenny say, "Wow! It smells good in here!"

"It does," said a deep voice, and Ellie frowned. The coach? Here? Why? Her heartbeat quickened. Had something happened to Nick?

She hurried into the living room and breathed easily only when she saw Nick tossing his book bag on the sofa. No casts, no neck braces. Her world steadied.

Coach Hyland stood just inside the door, looking bigger and more threatening in the small space than he had in his office. She decided it was because she didn't have any anger coursing through her to counter his strong presence.

"Hello," she said, voice cautious. She felt embarrassed when she thought of what he must see as her irrational behavior yesterday.

"Ms. Loring." He nodded as Nick and Kenny disappeared into the kitchen to check out the food. "I felt we left things unsettled yesterday."

"Oh." Ellie was surprised that, first, he thought they were unsettled, and second, he cared enough to come see her about it.

"I wanted to make certain you realized that Nick never gave me your letter. I would have done everything in my power to honor your request if I'd known."

"Thank you." She didn't know what else to say, but she had to give him full marks for understanding that such a request had a serious reason behind it.

"Do you still want him kept out of the paper? I'll talk to Jem Payne at the *Press* if you do." He gave a crooked grin. "He may claim freedom of the press and decide to buck my request, but I can certainly try if you still want me to."

"She doesn't," Nick said.

Ellie turned and found him leaning in the doorway between the living room and the kitchen. He was trying to appear relaxed, casual, but she could see the tension in him in the set of his shoulders.

Didn't he understand that this close to the city Joey might somehow see him? What if they put him on TV in the sports report about outstanding high school players or something? She blinked at a sudden and unwanted thought. Maybe that was what he wanted? His father seeing him play?

She felt the blood drain from her face and knew she was too pale when she turned back to the coach. She tried to smile. "It's all right. Don't say anything to that reporter."

"Are you sure?"

She managed to nod.

He looked at her with the intensity that had unnerved her last evening, but he didn't push. "If I can help you in any other way, just let me know."

"Thank you," she said again. "That's kind of you." She knew she'd never ask him for anything again, and she thought he knew it too.

He gave a half smile, another nod, and let himself out. She watched him walk to his car, a new SUV of some kind. When he pulled away, she gave a wave because she always waved people on their way. She didn't think he saw.

She turned to Nick who met her gaze with his chin high. Now she understood to some degree how Nonna must have felt when she had defied her all those years ago and moved in with Joey. All Nonna wanted for her, all she wanted for Nick, was what was best. She gave her son a wan smile and pushed past him into the kitchen.

Nick followed her, Midnight draped around his neck like an old fashioned tippet. Kenny leaned against a counter holding

Buddy cradled like a baby. Both boys wore sweat pants and had hair still damp from their after practice showers.

Kenny took a big sniff, then smiled with a sweet charm that touched Ellie. "Oh, Ms. Loring, I'm so glad Nick invited me for dinner again."

She smiled back as she studied the skinny boy. She suspected he wanted to become a regular at her table, which was okay with her, assuming his mother didn't mind. Maybe she worked four to midnight or something, and, sad thought, there was no dinner table at his house.

The kid's hair was too long, not in the rebellious way of some kids but in the hasn't-been-cut-in-way-too-long fashion of someone who rarely visits a barber. His sweater was full of pills and pulls, and his sneakers were literally falling apart, the toe of one flapping as he walked.

Clothes 2 Go, she thought. The church clothing give-away was scheduled for a Saturday in a couple of weeks, and she'd heard that if you went and helped set up on Thursday or Friday, you got first dibs on the clothes. Ninety percent help, then ten percent shopping if she had it right. She hadn't yet gotten a client for Thursday, so she'd go in and help. As a secondary benefit, she'd get to know some of the women from the church.

Kenny bent and rubbed his face in Buddy's furry warmth, and Buddy purred on cue, amazing for an animal who was usually as independent as a solitary hiker on the Appalachian Trail.

"I always wanted a pet." He stroked Buddy, and his delight at the simple pleasure of holding a cat made Ellie's heart break. Here was a lost child. She recognized the symptoms all too well.

"Two nights in a row for dinner, Kenny." She smiled at him, glad he was here to break the tension between her and Nick. "I'm going to fatten you up for the coach."

Kenny grinned. "You don't need to worry about me getting broken in half, Ms. Loring."

She blinked. How had he known?

"I don't play. I'm the team videographer. I record practices and games. I get why he wants me to record games, but I can't figure out why Coach wants film of practice scrimmages."

"To keep you off the mean streets." Nick lifted Midnight from around his neck and set him on the counter. The cat butted his hand and Nick scratched him behind the ears.

"Does Lyndale have mean streets?" Ellie dropped a fistful of spaghetti into the boiling water.

Kenny shrugged. "Like I ever spent time on the streets, mean or not. Anyway, Ms. L, don't worry. I never play, and I don't want to. I'm more a singing kind of a guy. A music man. And I make movies. Not of football games, but of stories, like real movies."

Ellie swallowed. The coach had made Kenny team videographer to keep him out of trouble. Another wrong assumption she'd made about the man. Well, at least she didn't have to be embarrassed about this mistake. He didn't know about it.

"I see you're a man of many interests," she said to Kenny. "I take it you're in the school choir?"

"Sure am. I love singing. I had a solo in the last concert." His skinny chest swelled with pride. "I'm trying to get Nick to join."

Nick rolled his eyes as he opened the cabinet over the stove and pulled out a box of Cheerios. "I told you I can't carry a tune for anything, Kenny. You do not want me in choir."

Ellie agreed. "You don't, Kenny. He sings just like me, and that's not pretty."

Kenny actually looked disappointed for a moment, then brightened. "I know. You can lip synch. You'd look good in the back row, and you'd make the other kids think choir was cool."

Ellie laughed. "Go wash your hands, you two."

"Or better yet, I can make a movie about a kid who wanted to be in the choir but couldn't sing, so he faked his audition. Lip synched to his iPod."

"How dumb is the teacher that he doesn't notice?" Nick asked.

Kenny brushed the comment aside. "I'll figure it out. Anyway, our hero stood happily in the back row lip synching until a guy who was jealous of his success with the babes told on him. He was kicked out in disgrace." He pointed at Nick. "You could star. It'd be cool."

Nick rolled his eyes.

"How does he redeem himself?" Ellie asked.

Kenny looked blank. "What?"

"The non-singer. You're not going to leave him in disgrace, are you?"

"Yeah," Nick said. "I don't want to be in a movie where I'm a loser."

Kenny frowned. "You two have no understanding of the artistic value of angst. No one puts hope and redemption in meaningful films."

"Which is probably why nobody goes to see them and they don't make any money," Nick said. "Give me a gun and let me blow things up, and you'll have a winner."

Kenny looked disconcerted as his vision of teen angst was suddenly transformed into a Bruce Willis/Tom Cruise action flick. "I don't like guns."

"But your audience will." Nick looked at Ellie. "How long until dinner?"

"Just until the pasta is finished. Not long."

Nick nodded, opened the cereal box, reached in and pulled out a handful of Cheerios. He offered the box to Kenny as he began munching. Kenny glanced at Ellie who smiled her assent. She'd long ago stopped telling Nick he'd ruin his appetite when he ate so close to dinner. Nothing could accomplish that.

"Uh, Mom." Nick studied the Cheerios in his hand instead of looking at her.

Ellie knew that "uh." She braced herself for what was to come. "Coach talked to me about not talking to you about the letter."

"Yeah? What did he say?"

"I should have told you. I could have saved you being so upset." He looked up and met her eyes. "But then you would have given it to him, and I didn't want that. I don't want that. I'm not going to hide anymore."

She turned and lifted the spaghetti from the stove and poured it into the colander so he wouldn't see her fear. "I don't know that I agree with you, Nick, but what's done is done. Let's just have dinner."

They took their places at the table, and after the blessing the boys inhaled their food like Hoovers inhaling dirt.

Kenny watched Nick twirl his pasta about his fork, using the plate to hold the noodles in place as he turned. "How do you do that? I always cut my pasta into bite sized pieces. Of course it's usually Chef Boy-ar-dee, not real stuff like this."

A lesson in spaghetti twirling followed, all three of them laughing at Kenny's less than stellar initial attempts, but by the time his plate was almost empty, he had the basic idea under control. He looked at Ellie with serious eyes.

"You just have to have me over for more spaghetti so I can practice," he said. "It's obvious this is a social skill I need to perfect if I'm to succeed in life."

"Right," Ellie said, her expression letting him know she wasn't that easily conned. "So's putting your napkin in your lap instead of on the table." She stared pointedly at both boys.

They grabbed their napkins and put them on their knees.

"It never stays put," Nick said. "Guys don't have laps."

"If it falls off your knee, pick it up and put it back."

Kenny looked from Nick to Ellie and grinned. "That's real mom stuff, isn't it?"

"Yeah," Nick agreed. "The kind that drives you nuts."

"Yeah," Kenny said on a happy sigh. "Nuts."

"Some more real mom stuff," Ellie said. "You guys are doing the dishes."

"Sure," Kenny said eagerly. "No problem."

Nick rolled his eyes, then turned to Ellie. "So how did your visit with Nonna go this morning, Mom? Any trouble?"

Ellie stared at him, appalled. They couldn't talk about Nonna in front of Kenny. She was an integral part of their secret.

Nick nodded toward Kenny, "He knows about Nonna. I told him we moved here to be near my sick great-grandmother."

Ellie pushed sauce around her plate with a piece of a crisped Amoroso roll. Was there any danger in Kenny knowing that Nick had a sick great-grandmother? Everything in her wanted to scream yes, but that was a conditioned response based on years of over-the-top caution. A realistic answer was probably not. Even if Nick said she lived in Philadelphia, it should be all right. There had to be hundreds of sick grandmothers in the city. How would Kenny ever come in contact with the right one and by extension Joey?

The real danger lay in Nick's sudden cavalier attitude toward what had been their secret all these years. How many others had he told and what had he said? People knew people, six degrees of separation and all, and one might know Joey.

Kenny picked up his empty plate and carried it to the sink. "I don't have a grandmother, let alone a great-grandmother, at least not one I know of. I'm sorry yours is sick though."

"Thank you," Ellie managed.

"I want to go see her," Nick said.

Ellie blinked. "You can't do that!" She hoped she didn't sound as panicky as she felt at the idea of him at Nonna's, mere blocks from Joey.

"Nothing's going to happen to me if I go, Mom. Nobody's going to hurt me."

It was hard to remember Nick wasn't a vulnerable nine-year-old anymore, but Joey somehow hurting Nick physically wasn't her biggest fear. It was influence. Joey could be charming and persuasive when he wanted to be, manipulative, and she had no doubt he'd do everything in his power to try and turn Nick against her. The very thought was enough to make fear bubble through her blood like a deadly virus.

"Let me think about it, Nick," she said, trying to buy time though her mind was firmly set on keeping him from going.

"I'll be eighteen in a couple of months, Mom."

She could see this was going to be his mantra. "But you aren't eighteen yet." That was going to be hers.

"I don't know who my father is," Kenny said as he carefully, too carefully, ran hot water in the sink and squirted in the soap.

There was a moment of silence while Ellie tried to assimilate the knowledge that Nick had not only told Kenny about Nonna; he'd told him about Joey too. Why else would Kenny have made the comment about his father? Her chest was so tight she could barely breathe while Nick just buttered another roll.

She knew their secrets had been a terrible burden for him to carry, but she hadn't expected him to throw them away without at least warning her. First the letter. Now Kenny. It felt like betrayal—which she knew was foolish.

Kenny took her empty plate and slid it into the dishwater.

She looked at him and somehow through her own distress she finally heard not only his words, but his tone of voice. Not knowing his father, not even his identity, hurt him deeply. Finally she said the only thing she could think of, given her own emotional confusion. "I'm very sorry, Kenny."

"Yeah," Kenny mumbled as he bent and picked up Buddy. "Who knows? Maybe between Nick and me I'm the lucky one."

CHAPTER 9

Kenny expected to walk home—nothing new there; it would be useless to call Mom—but Ms. Loring insisted on driving him.

"It's too far, Kenny. And it's too late to be wandering around alone."

Kenny checked his watch. "It's only ten-thirty. I've walked home much later and much farther many times."

"I insist." She put aside a yellow underliner and a huge book with the overwhelming title *Gardner's Art Through the Ages: the Western Perspective, 13th edition*. She saw him eying it and said, "For one of my college classes."

Kenny was fascinated. "What are you taking?"

"The class is an art history class. I'm an art major with a specialty in painting. I'd like to make my living with my art, but I'm also preparing to teach art in elementary school."

"She likes to eat," Nick said. "That's why the education courses."

"But I can dream." Ms. Loring smiled.

"You keep studying, Ms. Loring," Kenny said, wondering when was the last time his mom had opened a book, any book, let alone one as academic as Ms. Loring's. And painting? Forget it whether a picture or a wall. "I'll walk."

"Not on my watch." She grabbed her purse and keys.

He couldn't stop smiling as the three of them walked to the car. It was a wonderful feeling to have someone care enough to inconvenience herself for him. In fact he was amazed that Ms. Loring and Nick seemed to genuinely like him. He was used to being either ignored or the butt of jokes. He always smiled gamely like it didn't hurt, like it was fun to be mocked, even as the pain cut deep.

Somewhere he'd heard the phrase *outside the pale* and that was how he felt. Outside looking in. Never quite part of things. If it wasn't for singing and making movies, he'd probably find the nearest bridge and jump off. The trouble was that he didn't think anyone would notice he's jumped.

He knew he tried too hard and rubbed people the wrong way with his yearning to be liked, his desire to please. He just didn't know what to do about it. Being cool was beyond him, a holy grail he could never discover the secret to.

Nick was different. He was cool. Without even trying, he was liked and respected. Sure, being a football hero had something to do with it, but Kenny thought he'd be popular even if he never caught a ball. There was just something about him.

At first he'd been drawn to Nick to try and figure out what that nebulous people-magnet quality was so he could develop it in himself. Then Nick befriended him, and he'd been equal parts surprised and pleased though he tried not to show it too much. When Nick asked him home for dinner yesterday, he'd tried not to be over-eager or uncool. No one invited him for dinner. Not Kenny Uplander, son of Mitzi.

But Nick and Ms. Loring didn't seem to mind about his mom. Or maybe they didn't know yet. They hadn't lived in Lyndale all that long. The thought that they might pull back when they found out was enough to make the spaghetti with the delicious sauce twirl wildly in his stomach.

"That's my house," Kenny told Ms. Loring, and she pulled up to the curb. He looked at the dilapidated Victorian that must once have been lovely and tried to see it through Ms. Loring's eyes. It needed paint badly, and somebody'd better get a new sidewalk before someone broke an ankle or leg on the uneven paving. The porch sagged like a summer hammock, and the front steps looked too rickety for someone as sturdy as Nick. The house had been made into six apartments, two on each floor. He never saw the ground floor tenants, and the main floor people rotated in and out too fast to know.

"We live in the apartment on the top floor left," he said. "Crazy Achmed lives across the hall."

"Crazy Achmed?" Nick asked.

"Yeah. Some Middle Eastern guy who peers out his door any time there's noise in the hall. All you see is his eye reflecting the hall light." Kenny held up a hand blocking most of his face. He shivered. "Creepy."

"What is he?" Nick looked at the man's darkened windows. "The head of a sleeper cell of terrorists or something?"

Kenny thought about the strange collection of people who came to visit Achmed, all dark and distant, all talking a foreign language as they whispered in the hallway, all coming to the house only in the still of night. None of them, including Achmed, looked particularly dangerous, but then what did terrorists look like?

"Thanks for the ride, Ms. L, and for dinner."

"Come any time, Kenny. You're always welcome."

He couldn't believe his luck. "Thanks, Ms. L. Thanks a lot."

He climbed out of the car before he overdid the gratitude, hating to leave nice, normal people to go inside. Who knew how Mom would be tonight. She was a woe-is-me drunk, and he hated it when she was weepy. For just a moment he let himself wonder what it would be like to have someone like Ms. Loring for his mother. Then he'd never have to be ashamed. He'd never have to feel angry. Or overwhelmed. Or hungry.

Such thoughts filled him with guilt. Mom needed him. It wasn't her fault she was the way she was. Well, it was, but it wasn't.

As he climbed the inside steps that creaked ominously under his weight, he just knew that Ms. Loring wouldn't ruin Nick's credit before he even signed up for a credit card. No, that was his mother, the pathetic Mitzi.

One day just on a whim after hearing the creditreport.com guy singing about his financial woes because he never checked his credit, Kenny went to check his name. It was dumb, he knew. He didn't have credit, good or bad. He couldn't. He didn't have a credit card, and he never bought anything on credit.

To his great surprise, he did have credit and it was bad, bad, bad! According to the site he had lots of credit card bills he hadn't paid. Chadwicks.com. Speigel.com. Fredericks of Hollywood, for Pete's sake! And lots of cash withdrawals against the credit limit.

How could that be? He was a cardless kid.

It was Mom, of course. After ruining her own credit so she couldn't get any more cards to max out, she'd started sending in the applications in his name. Here he was, barely eighteen and his credit lay in ruins. How could he ever buy a car? How could he get loans to go to college?

Kenny heard the door across the hall creak as it was opened. He glanced up from his contemplation of the worn wood of the floor and there was Crazy Achmed, his eye peering out the narrow opening in his door.

"Hi," Kenny called, waving. "How are you?"

The eye went wide with surprise and something that might have been fear, except Kenny knew he was as non-threatening as they came. Still the eye disappeared, the door shut, and the lock clicked.

There was a man with worse problems than him. There weren't many such people, he was sure.

He blamed himself for Mom's hard life. She had him way too young. If he hadn't come along, she could have graduated, gotten a nice job as an administrative assistant or something, and married some nice guy. Instead she'd had him, and her parents kicked her out.

At least she'd had him. He was grateful for that. That was one of the reasons why he tried to be understanding when she went on one of her crying jags or did some of the terrible things she did. What would he have done in circumstances like hers?

Well, he wouldn't have ruined his kid's credit, that was for sure. And he wouldn't embarrass his kid by walking all tipsy down the street just as the school bus drove by. And he wouldn't spend money on booze when his kid's pant legs were almost to his knees.

Love/hate. He knew exactly what that meant. Some days he thought it would drive him nuts.

How old had Ms. Loring been when Nick was born?

And what made her so different from Mom?

Maybe if he could figure that out, he could figure life out.

———

"Is there a Mr. Uplander?" Ellie asked as they watched Kenny go up the stairs to his house.

Nick shook his head. "No Mr. Uplander."

"Ah." Another single mom, struggling too but apparently with less success if the house was any indication. At least Nick's and her little house was clean and had a yard and was in a nice neighborhood. Kenny's neighborhood was as close as Lyndale came to having slums.

Across the street an old man stumbled along, weaving his way in some kind of mental fog, reinforcing Ellie's opinion of the area. He stopped suddenly beneath the street light, held his hand in front of his face, and seemed to count his fingers. He spun abruptly and stumbled back the way he'd come.

"He lost a finger somewhere." Nick's voice was wry. "He's gone back to look for it."

"Poor man. And winter's not that far off." Ellie lost sight of him in her rearview mirror.

"He's probably got a home, Mom. He's just not there at the moment."

"I hope." But she wasn't convinced.

"You are such a softie. Now, home, James." He flicked his hand like a wealthy matron, and Ellie smiled.

"What does Ms. Uplander do?"

Nick didn't answer, and Ellie glanced at him. His face was screwed into a look of distress.

"You're not supposed to tell me?" she guessed.

Nick nodded. "Kenny asked me not to, but you can use your imagination."

Ellie could and her heart ached for both Kenny and his mother. "I take it from his reaction to something as simple as a ride home that she ignores him a lot?"

"All the time, Mom." Nick's outrage on his friend's behalf was evident. "You know how he said a couple of miles or so wasn't anything to walk? Well, he had a job last school year and over the summer at a grocery store all the way in Thorndale. He worked from four until eleven. His mom would forget to come and get him. He'd have to walk all the way home, even in the rain."

Poor Kenny.

"One of the guys on the team told me about the time early last spring when it was real rainy and cold for several days, and she forgot to come for Kenny. He couldn't walk home in that weather without getting sick, so he spent the night at the store, sleeping in the storeroom. Then the next day he had to walk to school in the rain anyway. School was closer than his house. Some of the kids gave him a hard time because he was all wet when he got there, and he was wearing the same wrinkled clothes as the day before."

No wonder the kid was so grateful for dinner and a lift.

"You know, I'm surprised he's not bitter," Ellie said. "In fact it's absolutely amazing."

"When he talks about her, it's more like he's really sad, not like he's mad."

"Well, bring him over as often as you want. We'll always find something for him to eat."

Nick nodded. "He wants to come to church with us."

"Yeah?" Ellie looked at Nick with surprise. "Wonderful."

"I invited him to stay over Saturday night."

"And all day Sunday, I suppose?"

Nick grinned. "Just reaching out to the lost, Mom."

"Good line, kid."

"I thought so. Knew it would get to you."

Ellie laughed, but she wasn't laughing Saturday at the game. That picture and article in the paper had brought college scouts out of the woodwork. She eyed a man with a Penn State logo on his cap sitting beside the guy in the Pitt jacket. There was even a man with a Florida State sweatshirt.

How did they even know about the article? The local paper was a nice paper and all, but it was a local paper, not the kind that was scanned for potential scholarship athletes.

When the game ended, the scouts along with two other men who weren't readily advertising their schools all made a beeline for Coach Hyland. Oh. Of course. How could she have been so stupid? The coach. When she'd told him not to muzzle the sports reporter, he'd apparently taken it as a sign to do whatever he wanted.

She'd love to give him a piece of her mind about turning her inch into a mile, but that would require talking to him, a thought that at the moment was as appealing as conversing with a skunk. The thing that irked her most was that as much as she mistrusted him, Nick and Kenny idolized him. It was, "Coach said this," and

"Coach said that." "Coach wants me to try this," and "Coach suggested I do that."

All she had to do was grit her teeth and hang on until Thanksgiving Day and the last game of the season. In two months his domination of her world would be over. In the meantime, she'd keep her eye on him, watch for any pressure he might exert on Nick.

But it wasn't that simple because pressures came from multiple sources. Every day the mail brought a fistful of letters from colleges beseeching Nick to consider them. The pile of flyers, pamphlets, and catalogues became so high it constantly slid to the floor, brought low by its own weight. And still they came.

As did the scouts. The only good thing was their inability to talk to Nick.

"It's an NCAA recruitment rule, Mom," Nick told her when she mentioned being glad they weren't bothering him. "College coaches or scouts can't talk to high school juniors."

"So when can they talk to you?"

He shrugged. "I'm not sure. I just know it's not now."

Lord, I'm so proud of him and his abilities, but why couldn't he have been average? She'd have been happy with good enough to play but not good enough to be sought after. Life would certainly have been easier.

With all the attention focused on Nick, Ellie's fear of discovery escalated, especially when there was a brief segment on the evening news about a boy from a nearby high school who gave a verbal declaration of intent to go to Notre Dame. There were sound bites from him and his mother and the high school coach. The same piece talked about other area players who were being courted diligently. Some reporter was bound to learn of Nick eventually, and then there he'd be, on TV.

She went online and looked at some of the recruiting sites, but the whole process was overwhelming. *You can do this; you* can't do that. You can talk to this person; you can't talk to that one. You can visit the colleges on these dates; you can't on those.

The issue was further complicated by the knowledge that she would never be able to send him to college without scholarship help. His future depended on the notoriety his skill generated while his safety depended on anonymity. She used to be able to convince herself that junior college would be fine for him for two years. Then he could transfer to a traditional university, preferably a state school. His outstanding athletic abilities combined with his love of football were slamming the door on what would otherwise have been an excellent and much more financially feasible plan.

So each week she went to his game and cheered for him and watched the scouts descend on Coach Hyland. Each week she sat in the gym reading as she waited for Nick to get dressed, and each week Coach Hyland stopped to talk with her.

"Nick did very well today," he'd say.

Or "How about that thirty-five yard run? He makes it look so easy."

"So what about all those scouts?" she wanted to ask. "Do you get a kickback if he signs with one?" But all she did was smile and say, "Thank you."

And fret about what was going to happen because the man was encouraging the attention on Nick. It was easier to be angry at him than to accept that Nick had changed the rules they lived by, and she was powerless to rewind the clock to the days when she felt he was safe.

Her stomach was in constant turmoil and her shoulders felt as tense and taut as an iron rod. When a hurricane churned its way up the Atlantic, sending strong winds and driving rain as far inland as Lyndale, the weather's chaos mirrored her own.

Nick and Kenny burst into the house the day of the storm, rain pouring off them to collect in puddles beneath them.

Ellie looked at them in surprise. "You're home early."

"Coach canceled practice because of the weather," Nick said.
A point for the coach, much as she hated to admit it.

Nick grabbed Midnight off the couch and gave him a belly rub
that had him batting his hands away and snarling in displeasure.

"You're all wet." Ellie reached for the cat.

Nick handed him over. "Kenny wants me to go to the reservoir with him to see the water storming over the dam."

Ellie glanced out the window at their maple tree whipping
like a mad thing in the strong winds. "Go out in this on purpose?
You're kidding."

"Oh, Ms. L, the water pours over the dam all white and wild
and the stream below it swells, and you get to feel the power!"
Kenny glowed with enthusiasm. "It's beautiful and exciting!"

She stared at the boy who was dancing in his excitement. "It
sounds scary."

"Sure, if you're caught in the current."

"It's raining. And it's cold."

Nick shrugged. "Chilly and it's only water. That's what jackets and caps are for. Besides we're already wet through."

"Baseball cap, bill backwards so it doesn't blow away and the
water doesn't run down your back as much." Kenny buried his
face in Buddy's soft fur and the cat purred in spite of rain dripping from Kenny's long hair onto his tummy.

"You're not planning to go in the water, are you?" She had
visions of the two of them being swept downstream, never to be
seen again.

"No way," Kenny said. "Moving water's too dangerous. But
it's great to watch. You'd love it."

The two stood, anticipation pouring off them like steam
from an about to blow geyser. She knew she was lucky that they'd
even bothered to ask her, but then she had the car that would
take them to the reservoir in minutes instead of a long walk in
the pouring rain.

Well, why not? That way she could keep an eye on them. Besides she and Nick had been in Lyndale going on two months, and she had yet to see the reservoir.

A half hour later she had to admit Kenny was right. She did love it. As she stood at the railing of the small bridge that crossed the normally placid stream below the dam, the wind whipped about her. She gripped the railing and felt an overwhelming sense of exhilaration as she stared at the water raging over the dam. Such power! Such beauty!

"Isn't it great?" Kenny yelled. "Come on, Nick!"

The boys charged toward the stream and its torrent of water.

For a minute Ellie thought they were going to keep right on running and rush into the water. She began to breathe again when they changed direction and began running parallel to the water, jumping and bucking like a pair of young mustangs.

God, keep them safe, both of them.

She leaned on the railing and listened to the roar of the water rushing over the dam, an angry white froth splashing down to become a cloud of mist. She looked down at the water surging beneath the bridge. The power and force were amazing, beautiful and frightening. She watched Nick and Kenny throw sticks into the stream, both of them laughing as the sticks were swept away.

She sighed. She had to let go of her need to protect Nick. He was strong and capable and smart, smart enough to make his own choices about his father. All mothers worked to get to the point where they were needed less and less as they ebbed in importance in their children's lives.

"But it's so hard, Lord!"

Tell Me about it.

Ellie had to grin at the thought. She pulled the hood of her pink slicker tighter. She didn't like the feel of the water trickling down her front where the rain blew past her protection or slid from her face down her throat. She hated to leave the fury and exhilaration of the raging wind and falling water, but it was time.

Just as it was time to give Nick his freedom.

She waved until she finally got the boys' attention, then signaled it was time to go. They started running toward her, hunching into their jackets.

She turned to go to the car, knowing they'd catch up with her, and found Coach Hyland standing behind her. He startled her, towering over her in a yellow slicker, and she gave a little yelp.

He grinned. "Sorry."

"I thought I was alone," she said in a combination of explanation and annoyance. She was afraid her Warpath Face was on display again, but she didn't care.

"Hey, Coach," yelled the boys as they came running. "What are you doing here?"

"Just checking to make sure everything's all right. I spotted your mom and wanted to be sure the car hadn't quit on her." He smiled at her and she managed a creditable smile in return. It was kind of him to stop even if it was unnecessary.

As the coach turned to walk with the boys, Ellie froze. Emblazoned across the back of his slicker were the words Lyndale Police in huge black letters.

Police? All the tension the storm had blown away returned three fold. What if he found out she was a kidnapper and a thief?

And she'd thought he was a danger as a coach.

CHAPTER 10

Joey Terafino walked aimlessly around the neighborhood as he thought about his business. Walking often helped him think. Maybe it was because Antony hated to walk so he didn't have his yammering to put up with. Sometimes Antony was almost enough to make him yearn for Ellie and her quiet and agreeable personality. Sometimes and almost.

Business. Nothing gave Joey more satisfaction, except plotting against Ellie, should he ever find her. Life's sweetness was the business. His father had started Terafino's and made a decent sandwich, but it was Joey who had made the deli legendary. It was Joey who created Antonio's, way out in the suburbs, the hottest dinner spot west of Philly.

When he selected the location for Antonio's, he'd gone far from Philadelphia, at least far from a city kid's perspective. He hated to admit it even to himself, but he'd been afraid he'd fail with a linen and crystal place. After all, most restaurants did fail. Far from the city, no one would know if the unthinkable happened. Possible failure was also one reason he'd named the place Antonio's. No sense attaching his name to a possible failure. And if it was a success, he'd see to that everyone knew who the mastermind was.

And he had. Business got better every day. Reviewers gave the place Best of ratings, and he made certain he was featured in the newspapers like *Main Line Times* and the *Daily Local News* as well as magazines like *Main Line Today* and *Chester County Life*. He had an interview scheduled for *The Philadelphia Inquirer* just after Thanksgiving. Local boy makes good and all that stuff.

The deli continued to do well, too, and the manager he'd hired was keeping things going nicely. The man didn't have the gift for making the customers laugh like the Joey and Antony Show with the shtick they'd developed through the years, but he didn't think that lack was a problem. The food was so good that the customers were committed.

Antonio's, though a success, was providing him with a different set of problems from Terafino's. The place might be named after Antony—which Joey let him think was a gesture of their undying friendship—but all the decisions fell on him. Sure he was the majority partner, but shouldn't Antony contribute something? All he wanted to do was strut around in his tux and play the charming host. Not that he wasn't good at it, and he certainly looked fine in his tux, but Antony was a hoagie man. A cheese steak man. A sandwich man. The scope of Antonio's was beyond him. Of course so was the day-to-day of Terafino's when you came right down to it.

Not that Joey thought there was anything wrong with being a sandwich man. He had hamburger grease and olive oil running through his veins too, but he also had vision. He'd been studying classy restaurants for years, planning to someday open his own. Now he had Antonio's, the challenges of running it, and Antony who was out of his depth.

Partnership was hard on friendship.

Joey sighed. Top of his must-do list for Antonio's was finding a new supplier for his linens. They were getting tablecloths with creases ironed in and stains remaining. Customers paying what he was asking would not return to eat on anything less than spotless cloths. Last week one had a hole right in the center. The diners had actually gotten up and left, a reaction he felt absurd.

The chef was still preparing the same meals. But if you wanted to be among the best, you had to be perfect.

He also had to think carefully about the contract with the florist supplying table flowers, something he'd never had to think about at Terafino's. There he replaced the silk flower on each table once a year. The real flowers at Antonio's were costing him a small fortune and weren't looking good for more than two days. Unacceptable, especially at the price he was paying.

Thank goodness his greengrocer and his seafood supplier were gold.

But there was the ever present problem of finding and keeping decent wait staff who knew how to be both efficient and polite. Kids today had no staying power and very few manners. You trained them—place the coffee cup with the handle at just the angle to be picked up; place the pie point toward the customer— they worked just long enough to earn some money, then they took off for some place warm for a few weeks, and you were left high and dry. Where were responsibility and pride in a job well done?

Snarling mentally, he looked up and realized he was walking past Sophia Mancini's house. He'd stopped thinking of her as Nonna years ago. She was the enemy, the one who helped Ellie and Nicky flee. They shared a mutual hatred, him and her, and wished each other nothing but grief. He hoped she looked out and saw him and hoped his presence spooked her.

"I'm watching you, old lady. I'm waiting."

It was driving him crazy that there had been no sign of Ellie visiting. He'd been so sure! If there was ever anything that would draw her back, it would be her nonna. Was she planning on waiting for the funeral?

The door to Sophia's opened, and old Louie Salerno walked out. Joey hadn't seen him in years, and he blinked at how stooped and frail the old guy looked. A good wind would blow him clear into Jersey, a fate no one should have to endure.

"Is she alone?" Joey called to Louie who jumped as if stung by a bee. He peered at Joey through thick glasses.

"Who's that?" His voice was old-guy quaky and querulous.

"Joey Terafino. Is she alone?" Joey pointed to Sophia's house. Louie nodded. "But she don't want to see you, Joseph. You will just upset her, and you give her enough heartache already."

"Yeah?" Joey smirked and started up the walk. "Then I think I'll visit."

Louie stopped his shuffle over to his half of the double and turned. "I think I left my house key over there. I gotta go back."

Joey scowled at the old man, making himself look as menacing as he could. "I don't think so, Louie. I think you can wait on your porch until I've paid my respects."

Louie narrowed his eyes, and Joey saw a flash of the strong, stubborn man he used to be.

"I'm waiting right here." Louie pointed to the spot in the lawn beneath his feet. "Don't you upset her. She's sick."

If he didn't upset her, why bother to visit? Joey climbed the front steps, grabbed the door handle and turned. The door opened, and he walked right in.

It was like stepping into a photo of the past, so much so that he hesitated in the front hall with its mirror and little table with the fancy glass dish for keys and the faded pink silk flowers in a brass bowl. Through the arch into the living room, he could see the plastic covered beige sofa. He'd always hated that plastic. He never felt like he was secure in the chair or on the couch. If he moved wrong, he'd slide right off. No wonder he loved the deep, enveloping leather furniture he had in his apartment.

A slightly hesitant voice called, "Is that you, Heather?"

Heather? Not hardly. Joey stepped into the living room where Sophia sat in her bed, a cluster of pillows behind her. She wore a fuzzy pink something over her nightgown. Her hair wasn't dark anymore, but it was combed. She didn't look nearly as bad as he'd hoped. "It's me, Sophia."

A flurry of emotions swept across the old lady's face as she looked at him—surprise, distress, anger, dislike. She ended with disbelief. "Joey? What are you doing here?"

"I wanted to see how you were doing."

"I bet. Do I look bad enough for you?"

Joey studied her. There was color in her cheeks. It could be rouge. Sophia always did like to look good. Or it could be stress or resentment or anger over his barging in.

He swallowed an evil grin. Maybe her blood pressure would go way high and she'd stroke out. Interesting possibility, that. And he wouldn't lift a hand to help her.

"Who's Heather?" he asked. Was that what Ellie was calling herself these days?

"My nurse. She's not due today, but I thought maybe I'd gotten my days confused when I heard the door open. I should have known better. She's always polite enough not to walk in unannounced."

Nice one, Joey thought. He'd forgotten how she was a master at the zinger, and she always said it with a bland face.

"Oh, Joey," she'd say in that infuriating way, poking her nose where it didn't belong, "you'd better get a door stop for that door Ellie keeps walking into."

Or "Make sure Nicky sees only love and support in your home, you two. Children need that, *Joey*." And she'd stare him down. Not many could make him squirm, but Sophia with her unblinking, critical eyes and bland expression was a past master.

Or "There's a sale down at the jewelry store this week, Joey. I bet Ellie'd like a nice glittery ring. Or even just a nice gold band." And she'd hum *Here Comes the Bride.*

The comments about rings, glittery or gold, stopped when she decided she had to get Ellie away from him. Then she'd say,

"Ellie, why not come home for a visit? Stay here with Nicky for a few days. Keep a lonely old lady company."

Since they lived only a block apart, *come home* was really code for *leave Joey*, and not a very clever code either. One of them Indian code talkers Sophia wasn't.

His purpose in this visit, aside from aggravating her, was to trick something about Ellie out of her. Or about Nicky. Joey sat on the edge of the sofa without an invitation and leaned forward, the better to intimidate her. He kept his feet firmly planted to minimize the plastic effect. "So, how you feeling?"

Sophia shrugged. "Okay."

"What's it feel like to be dying?"

She blinked at the purposely mean question.

"I only ask 'cause that's what I heard. How long you got?"

"I'm sorry to disappoint you, but I'm feeling better these days."

"Oh, well, one can't expect all one's wishes to come true."

They smiled at each other with teeth bared.

"How's Ellie?" he asked.

"I wish I knew," she lied with a straight face.

"Give me a break, Sophia. You know how she is and where she is. You've known all along."

"So you say, but what do you know? Nothing! You had a wonderful woman and you mistreated her."

"Who mistreated who?" He stood, so agitated his voice shook. "She took my son." He spit the words out slowly, one at a time.

"After you hit him." Sophia sat up straighter and pointed her arthritic finger at him. "After you hit your own boy."

Joey ignored her comments. A man had a right to control his home. Everyone knew that. Fathers passed that truth on to sons, like his father had to him. "So where is she hiding my son? Where's Nicky?"

She stared at him, her face set, her eyes cold. A brick wall of silence. She had no pity for him, only contempt. Well, he returned the favor.

He saw her laptop sitting on the far side of her bed. He reached out and grabbed it before she could stop him. Not that she could prevent him taking it even if she had all the warning in the world. It was her weakness against his strength.

"What's on here, Sophia?" He pulled up her email account. "Any word from Ellie?"

Her lack of distress warned him, and he wasn't surprised when all he found were letters from people he never heard of.

"What'd you do? Delete them?" He checked her deleted files. Nothing. "I bet there's a record in here somewhere. Maybe I'll just take it with me and have a geek check for me."

"And I'll report you for theft."

They glared at each other.

The front door opened and shut with a slam. Sophia jumped and looked at the archway with suddenly frightened eyes. Louie Salerno walked in, and Joey watched her fear drain away. Who was she expecting that upset her so? Certainly not Nurse Heather.

"Time to go, Joseph," Louie said. "She is too ill for someone like you to visit more than a moment."

"Someone like me?"

He nodded. "Someone like you. Someone who likes to upset people."

"Are you kicking me out?" Joey asked in amusement.

Louie puffed out his boney chest. "I am."

Joey glanced at the bed. "You got an admirer, Sophia."

"I got a friend," she said. "Call the cops, Louie. He's stealing my computer."

"No, he's not." Louie reached out and grabbed the machine, then took several steps back.

What was it with these old people? He could squash them with no more effort than it took to kill a spider. Not that he would. He needed Sophia, and the old biddy and Louie were smart enough to know it.

She slid down in her bed and shut her eyes. "Goodbye, Joseph. I'm too tired to talk any more. Please don't come back."

"Not a problem." He walked to Louie who was backed up against the archway. He towered over the little man, but Louie looked him defiantly in the eye.

"You are bad, Joseph. You have broken many hearts."

Joey glanced at Sophia who was pretending to be asleep. "Never forget, old man, that some people have gone out of their way to break mine."

CHAPTER 11

"Let me tell you, Nonna, it was a wonderful game!"

Nonna looked at the latest picture of Nick in the paper. "You must be so proud of him."

"I am, but not because he's great at football. Because he's a great kid."

"Just the reason I'm proud of you, cara mia."

Ellie soaked up the praise from her grandmother like a growing plant reveled in the sun. The power of encouragement was amazing.

"Now tell me about your cleaning people this week, Ellie. Who did what?"

Ellie made her clients sound as fascinating as she could, a stretch sometimes, but Nonna loved her stories. In fact Nonna seemed eager about everything these days. Her bed was frequently littered with the newspaper or her favorite gossip magazines, and she sat propped on pillows to read and work in her word jumble book. Then one week when Ellie arrived, she was sitting on the plastic covered sofa clad in her nightgown and pink robe, her feet in pink Deerfoams. The following week she sat dressed in a skirt, blouse and sweater, the clothes hanging on her thin frame.

"Nonna, you're looking better all the time!" Ellie cried as she hugged her grandmother.

"It's seeing you, Ellie," Nonna said. "For the first time, I want to beat this thing eating at me."

"We'll fight it together," Ellie assured her.

To be certain she wasn't somehow causing harm, Ellie called Nonna's doctor and spoke with him about her grandmother's renewed zest for life.

"Keep encouraging her, Ellie," the doctor said. "So much of handling any illness is attitude. Seeing you has given her something to live for. You make her happy. She now has a reason to fight."

"She told you she was seeing me?" The familiar shiver went through Ellie.

"I wanted to know why this sudden improvement, this sudden desire to fight. She swore me to secrecy." He laughed as if the need for such stealth was a big joke.

Ellie tried to be philosophical about the situation. It didn't matter if he thought Nonna was paranoid. If he honored doctor-patient confidentiality and HIPPA laws, they'd be safe. "Will she be cured?"

"No, but with her present spirit, she should have an undetermined season of good living. We can manage her cancer in a way that will give her minimal discomfort, now that she's willing to fight for her life."

On Ellie's most recent visit, Nonna had been standing at her stove wearing a pair of slacks that bagged about her with her weight loss, but she had been stirring freshly made red sauce. The house smelled so like Ellie's memories that she broke into tears. When she could speak, she asked, "How did you get to the store? I didn't realize you were feeling that strong already. I would have gone for you."

"I sent Louie Salerno with a list. He did good. I only had to send him back for three things he forgot. Considering the state of his memory, three things is good."

Ellie laughed. "How did you get him to go?" Mr. Salerno had never been very cooperative even when younger and sprightlier.

"Promised him some of my sauce." Nonna brought the spoon to her mouth and tasted. She grinned. "I still got it."

Ellie kissed her grandmother's cheek. "I can tell by the smell."

Nonna turned down the heat under the pot and began shuffling to a chair, obviously worn out from her stint at the stove. Ellie reached to take her arm.

"No, no." Nonna pulled from Ellie's grip. "I got to get my strength back."

"Well, at least let me get you a cup of coffee."

"That you can do."

When they were seated with their mugs of coffee and a plate of sugar cookies. "Nabisco," Nonna said in disgust. "I never let store bought cookies in my house before." She frowned into her coffee, then looked up. "I want to see Nick, Ellie."

"I know, and he wants to see you, but I can't bring him here."

"Of course you can't. You coming here in your wig is hard enough on my nerves." Nonna leaned back in her chair. "I will come to your house. I want to see him play."

Ellie reached across the table and took her grandmother's thin hand. "Are you strong enough?"

"I'm getting there."

"Thanksgiving? Will you be strong enough by Thanksgiving?"

"If it kills me," Nonna said.

If only that wasn't a real possibility.

Ellie didn't tell Nick about the coming visit because she didn't want to get him counting days in case Nonna wasn't feeling well enough after all. As it was, he reminded her several times a week that he wanted to go to South Philly with her.

"You have school, Nick."

"I can miss a day of school. Dad won't even know I'm there. He'll be at the deli."

Of course she didn't take him, wouldn't take him. His idea that he was immune to Joey due to his size and age seemed wishful thinking to her. He was still only seventeen. The authorities might make him spend time with Joey whether he wanted to or not. It wasn't that she didn't trust Nick or that she thought him weak and easily led. It was Joey's charisma. He'd manipulated her when she was just Nick's age, and the risk of history repeating was too great.

The Saturday before Halloween she sat in the gym waiting for Nick after his game.

"Hey, Mom!" The object of her concern and the joy of her heart came out of the locker room and skidded to a halt in front of her. "The guys are going for pizza to celebrate our win."

Your win, Ellie thought. The fourteen-point difference was all Nick's doing. "You going with them?"

He grinned.

"Are they drinkers?"

Nick feigned horror. "Mom, how could you suggest such a thing? They're underage."

"Like that ever stopped kids before," she said dryly.

"Don't worry, Mom. No drinking. Andy's license is new, and he's got a curfew. He says his dad's really strict."

"I like strict, but it's possible to drink before curfew, you know."

"We're not drinking, Mom."

"You may not be, but if any of those guys do, especially Andy-the-driver—whose mother is very nice, by the way—I want you to promise to call me to come get you. It's bad enough that he's a new driver. A new driver with alcohol zipping through his veins is way too lethal for this mother."

"Yes, ma'am. Whatever you say, ma'am."

She ignored his eye-roll attitude. "I'm serious, Nick. I don't want you wrapped around some tree somewhere because of a driver who's been drinking."

Nick studied her for a moment. "Mom, don't you think you might be over-reacting here?"

"Probably. But promise me, please. Promise me you'll call if this Andy drinks."

"I promise."

Kenny appeared in the doorway, saw them and waved. "Don't leave without me!" And he disappeared back into the locker room.

"What about Kenny? Does he know you're going out with the guys?"

"Oh, Kenny's coming, too," Nick said.

Ellie smiled. She doubted Kenny would have been invited if Nick hadn't been a two-for-one deal. She felt very proud of her son, more than she ever did about his football prowess. "Well done, Nick. Well done."

He brushed her praise aside. "They'll bring us home by midnight."

"Midnight." She nodded. "No later."

He studied her. "You don't really mind us leaving you alone, do you? We don't have to go."

What a kid! "Of course I don't mind, guy. I'm a big girl, you know."

"Well, no keg parties while we're gone." He pointed his index finger at her. "Promise you'll call if there's drinking."

Teenage boy humor. So clever. "I know my life has been wild lately, but I'll try to curtail the rowdiness until you're home to chaperone."

"Remember, I'm trusting you."

It was Ellie's turn for an eye roll. "Funny. What's Kenny going to use for pizza money?"

Nick shrugged and looked at her hopefully.

Kenny came running out, a great smile on his skinny face. "We're going for pizza," he said, trying to act like this going out with the guys was a common thing.

"So I hear." Ellie unzipped her jacket pocket and pulled out the cash she'd stuffed in there. She'd been planning on taking the guys for pizza herself, but this was better. Nick was making friends, a hard thing in the best of times, but as new kid on the block, even harder. She slapped a twenty in Nick's hand and another in Kenny's. "I want the change."

"I don't think there'll be any," Nick said with a grin. "Pizza's very expensive around here."

"Ms. Loring—" Kenny protested. Ellie could see his face flushing.

"Kenny, I'll get my money's worth out of you before we're done. This is an advance for all the leaves you're going to rake for me."

"That big tree the kid next door likes to climb?"

Ellie nodded. "She thinks it's a secret."

"She's got a crush on Nick." Kenny grinned wickedly. "He's got such a way with women."

Just then a pair of girls with their jeans painted on walked by. "Hi, Nick," they called, waving their fingers like they were practicing piano scales.

Nick gave them a glance and a nod. They started giggling.

"See?" Kenny said. "He doesn't even have to say anything!"

"Drop it, Kenny," Nick said mildly.

Ellie grinned. "Why don't you two invite the guys back to our place for dessert?"

"For ice cream and that chocolate cake with the caramel icing you made yesterday?" Kenny asked.

"We're all out of ice cream. Some people I know finished it off last night."

Nick and Kenny looked un-repentant.

"Be sure you get Rocky Road on your way home," Nick said.

"Rocky Road it is. Ken?"

"Vanilla."

"Vanilla?" Nick looked scandalized.

"And butterscotch topping. And chocolate chips, those little tiny ones. Not the jimmies, the chips."

"Got it."

"None of that low fat stuff either." Nick wagged a finger at her. "We're growing boys. We need all the calories to survive."

Two huge guys exploded from the locker room, laughing about something that Ellie imagined was off color as they both turned rosy when they saw her.

"Mom, this is Tyler Miller and Andy Rode."

The door flew open again and two more guys emerged.

"And Paul Jeffries and Nate Pike."

Noise, chaos, and testosterone filled the air, and Ellie wondered that they left enough oxygen for her to breathe. She walked outside with them and stood at the edge of the fence that rimmed the athletic field, watching as they drove off in a red SUV.

Oh, Lord, make Andy a safe driver!

"He'll be okay," said a voice at her shoulder, surprising her and making her jump.

She turned to find Coach Hyland looming next to her, his bulk back lit by the light from the school. What was it with him and sneaking up behind her? Not that he was really sneaking. It just felt that way.

He looked huge, as always, and she automatically tensed. Guilty conscience or her customary reaction when near a man, especially a big, powerful one, even after all these years?

Another sin to lay at Joey's door.

She cleared her throat and told herself to stop being foolish. She was perfectly safe with Coach Hyland. Besides there were people all around.

Only there weren't. The lights suddenly went out behind them, and the gym door slammed shut. A figure materialized out of the sudden darkness, waving and saying, "See you Monday, Gabe."

"Sure thing, Pete," the coach replied. "My best to Ginny."

And then it was just the two of them in the dark.

"Where's your car?" the coach asked.

She pointed down the street.

"I'll walk you."

He started to move, and she realized that short of stamping her foot and crying, "No!" like a two-year-old, she had no choice but to trot along beside him. She took a deep breath and waited for that irrational fear of men, especially big men, to overwhelm her.

It didn't. Their sleeves brushed, and though her heart accelerated a bit, it wasn't fear. He loomed over her, and it was all right. The fact that he didn't scare her frightened her in a different way.

He glanced at her, his face shadowed. "Nick gave me a few palpitations when he went down under that tackle.

"You? I thought I'd never draw another breath."

"It's got to be hard watching your son get tromped on and knocked around. My mom used to plead with me to take up baseball instead."

"Which you never did?"

"Of course not. Football is the love of my life."

A smart retort about how his social life must be as exciting as hers sprang to her lips, but she bit it back. Joking together was too much like becoming more than casual acquaintances. Too much like becoming friends.

He slowed and turned to her. "I wanted a chance to tell you that I'm not the one contacting all those college scouts who have been swarming the stadium lately."

She looked at him as they passed through a pool of light from a security lamp mounted to the side of the school. Her skepticism must have been obvious because he laughed ruefully. "Other people have seen Nick play, Ellie."

"Well, yes."

He grinned suddenly. "You don't know anything about recruiting, do you?"

She shook her head. "I went online and did some reading, but it's so complicated!"

"That it is."

"And it puts Nick in the spotlight." She hoped the shudder that passed through her at that thought wasn't visible. She'd run this creaky hamster wheel for years, especially in the depths of night, and always came to the same inarguable conclusion: Joey couldn't hurt Nick if he couldn't find him. That meant no publicity. That meant no college with a well-known athletic program, one where the team might play on TV. That meant denying Nick his best chances.

God, I hate this!

It'll be all right, He whispered back. *Trust Me.*

She blinked at how clear the words sounded in her head. *I'm trying!*

"The big schools are always looking," the coach said. "They have networks of high school coaches and alumni looking too. How many Penn State alums do you think sit in the stands every week watching Nick play? Enough of them contact the athletic department and a scout appears. It's that simple."

That made sense. "So who contacted Florida State?"

He shrugged. "Don't know. But Nick's going to be recruited, Ellie, whether you like it or not."

"I know." Resignation rang in her voice.

"He's going to play college ball, and he's going to excel."

They stopped by her car, and she stared at the ground, overwhelmed.

"If you'd like," he said in a voice that sounded as if he was unsure how she would respond, "I'd be happy to offer advice, to help you work your way through the maze of hype and promises people are going to make until Nick signs a letter of intent."

She told herself this was good. She needed the help he was offering. But what was his angle? He must expect to get something out of this "kindness." Who did things for nothing?

He studied her for a moment. "Look, I'm going to get a bite to eat. Come with me, and I can explain some of this to you."

Startled, Ellie was struck momentarily dumb.

"My car's there." Either not noticing or ignoring her silence, he indicated an SUV on the other side of street. "Why don't you just follow me? We'll go to my favorite place."

He jogged to his car without waiting for an answer, and Ellie stared after him. For the first time since she'd run, she was going to have dinner with a man. It wasn't a date. She knew that, but still....

And he was a cop.

It wasn't a date. He knew that, but still....

He was surprised to find he was looking forward to talking more with her despite the fact she obviously wasn't looking forward to talking with him. That reticence made her fascinating to him as a man and as a cop.

He was used to women wanting to be with him. Some were discreet in letting him know this, and others were nothing short of embarrassing. For some reason they seemed to see him as prime meat, and they were all too hungry. What they wanted with a small town cop and coach was beyond him.

But Ellie Loring—or whatever her name really was—gave off keep-away signals so strongly that he couldn't resist her. It must be that secrets thing. He loved solving mysteries whether in real life or in mystery novels. And she was the most interesting conundrum he'd come across in many a year.

Why she fascinated him so when she was the opposite of Robyn was also a puzzle. He was attracted to open, smiling faces, not wary, watchful ones. Exuberance, not reticence. Directness, not dissimulation.

As they were shown to a booth at Country Gardens, several people called, "Great game, Coach!" Gabe returned their comments with a wave, noticing that Ellie's tension ratcheted higher with every friendly comment.

They slid into opposite sides of the booth, and the hostess handed them menus. Ellie opened hers immediately, but she didn't appear to be reading it.

"Relax," he said as he shrugged out of his jacket and stuffed it down on the seat.

"I'm relaxed."

"Then why don't you take your coat off?"

She glanced up from the menu and gave him a tight smile. With a little nod, she put the menu down and let her black pea coat slip off her shoulders. She folded it neatly and laid it on the seat. She kept her red beret on. Gabe didn't think he'd ever known a woman who wore a beret except his younger sister. Berets were for arty people like Gracie. Was Ellie arty? Whatever, the beret looked wonderful on her black curly hair.

"They have great crab cakes here if you like crab," Gabe said.

"I don't think I've ever had crab cakes," she said.

Gabe was genuinely shocked.

"I'm used to Italian like linguine with clam sauce, but not crab," she explained, then clamped her mouth shut as if she regretted saying that much.

He let the comment go, tucking it away for later, though given her complexion and coloring, Italian did not require a great leap in logic.

"This place has comfort food, not chi-chi stuff. Meat loaf. Pork and sauerkraut. Chicken and dumplings. And great sea food."

A pretty blonde waitress appeared with her order pad in hand. "Hey, Mr. Hyland."

"Jenn, how are you?"

And Jenn proceeded to tell him in more detail than he needed, but it gave Ellie time to settle down. He could see her shoulders easing, her hands relaxing. Finally Jenn wound down enough for them to give their orders. "Crab cakes, baked potato, stewed tomatoes, and blue cheese on my salad."

Jenn turned to Ellie. "Hey, you're Nick's mom, aren't you? I've seen you at the games."

Ellie nodded.

"Nick's so cool." The girl blushed and gave a little fanning motion with her order pad over her flushed face.

Ellie actually grinned, and Gabe stared. Her usually tense or angry face was transformed into a work of art. The smile made her light up from within, her dark eyes glowing, her usually compressed mouth full and lovely.

When Jenn held out her hand for his menu, he blinked and handed it to her in a daze.

"I'll have what he's having except green beans instead of stewed tomatoes."

"Got it." Jenn hurried off to place their orders.

"If you steered me wrong and I waste my money, I'll—" She stopped and frowned, and Gabe thought, *Smile again. For me.* "Well, I'll think of something terrible." And she smiled.

He'd always thought her pretty, but wow! When she got a questioning look on her face, he realized he was staring like an idiot. "You have a beautiful smile."

It disappeared immediately, and she pulled into herself.

"That was a compliment," he said. "You were supposed to like it, to say something like 'Thank you, Gabe'. And now I'm going to change the subject. How's it going with Kenny as Nick's shadow?"

Ellie unwrapped her silver from the napkin it was bound in, laid it out neatly, and put her napkin in her lap, all with a serious expression. "Kenny's one of the Lost Boys."

"Too true."

She looked up. "Do you know his mother?"

"Oh, yeah. I do. She was a year ahead of me in high school. Cute perky cheerleader. Had Kenny too young."

Ellie nodded. "I know the difficulties of that."

Jenn showed with their beverages and a basket of crackers and cheese, and as he slathered cheese on a whole wheat cracker, he thought of how differently the two women had dealt with their challenges and the effect these differences had had on their sons.

"Where did you live before you moved here?" he asked.

"Washington state. A little town in the middle of nowhere."

He waited, but no more information came.

"I've lived in Lyndale my whole life," he said.

"That sounds wonderful, having roots that deep." Her voice was—wistful?

He shrugged. "It has its good points." He indicated the restaurant. "I know all the really good eateries."

"A valuable asset for a man living alone." Then as if struck by a sudden and unpleasant thought, she said, "You do live alone? I'm not having dinner with a married man, am I?"

He laughed as a faded picture of Robyn flashed through his mind. "I do live alone and I'm not married. I was, but she died."

Ellie's face showed her reaction to that piece of information, her distress.

"It was a long time ago," he said to take away the sting for both himself and her. "I've moved on. Of course, I go to my parents for dinner at least once a week, which some might say is a bad sign of overdependence. My mother says it's a good thing, or I'd forget all my manners." He offered her the last packet of crackers, relieved when she shook her head. He torn the package open and spread the last of the cheese. "But I think Thomas and I do very well, all things considered."

"Thomas? You have a son?"

"Royal Standard poodle about this big." He held his hand at the height of the table.

"He could probably swallow our cats in one bite."

"Nah. He's a sweetheart." He leaned back as Jenn set their salads down. "So you're Italian?"

She paused in the middle of pouring her ranch dressing over her greens, just the smallest of hesitations, but he'd been watching. He just wasn't certain what it meant. Probably that she wasn't used to talking about herself. All those secrets.

"Italian through and through," she said. "My grandmother is queen of the red sauce."

"Where's she live?" He made his voice casual as he forked up a mouthful of cucumber and lettuce.

"She's dying." Ellie blinked as tears filled her eyes.

Gabe jerked at the unexpected comment. "I'm so sorry." Grandma Hyland might be a bit of a trial at times with her push for him to remarry "before I die, Gabriel." Since she was the picture of health with more energy than he, he wasn't worried about her imminent demise. Still, when it came, he'd miss her terribly.

Ellie nodded, accepting his sympathy. "She and Nonno raised me after my parents died. I have wonderful memories of sitting in the kitchen talking while she cooked. Cooking was her way of showing her love. She kept a big freezer full because, 'You never know when you'll have company.'"

Gabe laughed as she spoke with an Italian accent.

"She's been feeling well enough to cook recently and has given me enough lasagna and stuffed shells and red sauce to open my own restaurant, except—" An impish look flashed across her face—"I'm not sharing!"

"That good, huh?"

"Better."

Their dinners arrived, and he watched as she took an experimental bite of her crab cake, her face a frown of concentration. When a smile of pleasure replaced the frown, he felt he'd scored a winning touchdown.

"So tell me what's going to happen with Nick," she said.

The rest of the meal they spoke of the pressures, the scholarship possibilities, and the many opportunities Nick would receive over the next year.

"There are very strict rules for recruiting laid down by the NCAA. Most coaches follow them scrupulously."

"How would I know the rule breakers?"

"The rules are easily found on the Internet. And I know them. I'll be in the loop as Nick's coach, and I'll be on the lookout for infractions."

Ellie nodded. "If I'd known how good he was going to be, I'd never have given my permission for him to play when he was little."

Gabe laughed though he thought she was more than half serious and that there was a reason he hadn't yet discovered behind the comment. "There are some basic things to think through before you get down to specific schools and offers. Does Nick want a large school with a pressure program but lots of exposure, or would he be happier at a smaller school with a good program but less pressure and exposure? Then too he's got to be comfortable with the coach and the program that he'll be part of for four years. Don't let money and prestige influence you too much when the big guns come to call."

"I'm for smaller," she said, "but I don't know how he'll feel. It's got to be exciting to know big schools want you. How does a seventeen or eighteen year old resist the allure of TV and fame and maybe a future in the NFL?"

"It seems to me Nick's got a good head on his shoulders."

Her face lit with pride. "Every day there are catalogues and materials in the mail, including personal letters from coaches. And there are those scouts at the games."

"Those scouts aren't allowed to speak to Nick. No one can until after July first at the completion of his junior year, and then only once a week on the phone. Nick can call them as much as he wants then, but the college is limited. Emails are unlimited on both sides."

Ellie nodded. "We've gone online and read lots of material about eligibility and recruitment, both on the NCAA site and on recruiting sites, but it's a confusing maze to me. Do this. Don't do that. Do it by a certain date." She made a face. "I used to consider myself reasonably intelligent."

"I can help Nick develop a plan to market himself, if you'd like," Gabe said.

"Market himself?" Ellie looked floored. "Kids really do that? It's not just online hype?"

"Well, you can hire a recruiting service to do all this for you if you prefer."

"A recruiting service?" Her voice was weak.

"The good ones take a lot of pressure off you."

"I'm feeding a teenage boy. I can't even afford the movies. I certainly can't hire a recruiting service."

"Then let me help Nick get ready. We'll go to beRecruited. com and get his profile up. We'll draft a letter to potential coaches. We'll create a highlights video of his big moments and his small ones during games and at practice. We'll work up both an academic and athletic profile. Does he play a second sport?"

"Baseball."

"That's good. A second sport is good. Colleges like that. And when it's time, we'll get him registered at the NCAA Eligibility Center. It's best to do that at the end of your junior year."

Ellie looked beleaguered.

"It determines if you're academically eligible to receive scholarships from Division I and Division II schools," he explained. "Division III schools don't give athletic scholarships."

"I know. I read about it and the core classes you have to have taken to qualify for scholarships."

"Does Nick have good grades?"

"He does. His GPA is a 3.8. He plans to take his SATs in the spring." She was quiet for a moment. "Can't he just decide where he wants to go and go?"

"Forgetting football? Sure, if he doesn't care whether he plays and if you can afford his tuition."

Ellie rubbed her forehead as if she was in pain, and she probably was. Weathering recruiting was an overwhelming process, and schools were getting serious with younger and younger athletes, getting verbal commitments from sophomores and juniors though official letters of intent couldn't be signed until school began for an athlete's senior year.

"Then too we'd like to get him invited to some camps next summer, maybe even the Nike camp."

"The Nike camp? It's big? It sounds big."

"The biggest."

"And they all cost money?"

"Sometimes."

"I think I'll lock him in his room from now until he's twenty-five."

Gabe grinned. "I'm already praying he'll make a wise choice."

Ellie's forkful of lemon chiffon pie froze in midair. "Really?"

Gabe told himself not to be offended that she was so taken aback by his praying. She didn't know him except as someone who made her nervous.

"And I'll keep praying," Gabe said. "Nick's a wonderful kid, but he's going to have a lot of pressure on him. Is his father anywhere in the picture to help him out?" He asked the question casually, hoping that it was so unexpected that he'd get a straight answer.

She shook her head as she chewed her piece of pie. He waited, but that was it.

Jenn reappeared with their bill, and he handed her his bank card before Ellie could protest. When she did, he waved her words aside.

"Please let me. You're feeding an extra kid on a pretty regular basis—"

"A very regular basis, at least for a while. He's moving in."

"He's moving in?"

"They double teamed me the other night."

Gabe listened in delight as she assumed each boy's lines as well as her own, recounting the conversation in its entirety.

"'Mom,' Nick says, 'can Kenny stay with us for a while? Like live here?'

"'Live here?' I say like my hearing's gone bad. Our house is so small the two of us are crowded. A third will definitely stretch the seams.

"Nick leans against the kitchen counter oh-so-casually. 'He can stay in my room with me.'

"'But there's only a single bed in there,' I say.

"'He can use my sleeping bag.'

"'I don't mind the floor.' Kenny says, all earnest and sincere.

"So I'm wishing Nick hadn't asked in front of Kenny. How can I say no without hurting the kid deeply? Then I get it. I can't and they both know it. Setup City."

"What can you expect?" Gabe asked. "A 3.8 GPA."

"That plus a soft-hearted mother. Well, it isn't as if Kenny's much trouble. If anything he's too little trouble. He wants so to be liked and accepted that he tries too hard."

Gabe nodded. He knew exactly what she meant.

"'Besides,' Nick says with the air of a salesman presenting his deal-clinching argument, 'his mom's moving around Thanksgiving and things are going to be chaotic at his house.'"

"Yeah." Gabe grabbed his jacket. "Mitzi told me she was moving. New boyfriend."

Ellie slipped her coat on. "Kenny hasn't officially moved in yet, but he's spending the night tonight so he can go to church with us again tomorrow. That's become Saturday night SOP."

"Then all the more reason to let me be the generous one tonight." Gabe paused, then took the plunge. "Maybe you could repay me with some of your nonno's great food."

"Not *nonno*. That's *grandfather*. *Nonna* is *grandmother*. *A*, not *O*."

"Ah. Got it."

What he didn't get was a dinner invitation.

CHAPTER 12

Nick was on his third giant soda when he decided it was time to visit the men's room. "Back in a minute."

Andy nodded and the rest of the guys were so busy eating and eyeing the girls that they didn't even notice—except for Kenny.

"We'll save your seat." Kenny smiled like he thought someone might actually try to take it. "And stay away from *them*."

Nick glanced at *them* as he left the room, players from Coatestown, the team Lyndale had just beaten. Sitting at the head of their table was the guy who had flattened him during the game. Nick bit back a smile as he passed them. They were not enjoying themselves while he and his guys were just the polite side of rowdy in their euphoria over the game.

When he came out of the men's room, Nick noticed a commotion at the far end of the hall where the ladies' room was.

"In you go, Kenny. The girls are just waiting for you. Not." And the guy cackled.

Nick's stomach plunged to his knees. Kenny had followed him, and now the kid was in trouble.

"Let me alone!" Kenny's voice was both angry and scared. Nick didn't blame him for either. No one wanted to be pushed around, especially when the pusher was the guy who had put the nasty hit on him. Given the force and fury of that tackle, there for a moment he'd feared his football career was over before it really began.

And now this beast was manhandling skinny, undersized Kenny.

Nick's blood began to boil. "Yo!" He made his voice as loud and drill sergeant-ish as he could.

The beast glanced over his shoulder to see who had yelled, sneered when he saw Nick, and doubled down on his grip on Kenny. The beast had him trapped between the women's room door and his huge body. Kenny wasn't going anywhere.

Hands fisted, Nick was halfway to Kenny when a pair of girls wearing Coatestown colors entered the little hallway, intent on the ladies' room.

Nick blocked them. "Not now, ladies." He smiled his best even as he kept an ear tuned to the beast. "Come back later."

The girls stared at him as if he was crazy.

From the corner of his eye Nick saw Kenny try to kick back and get the beast in the shins. Good. Kenny wasn't crumbling.

The scraping and grunting caught the girls' attention. They looked at the source of the commotion, then each other, then at Nick.

"Are you with Jeremy?" One girl spoke, but the scathing expressions on both faces told Nick that every bad thought he'd had about the beast was accurate and then some.

"No, I'm with the other guy." He spoke loudly in another attempt to make the beast back off.

"Right." The girl pointed. "That's why you're here instead of there where the fight is. I hate bullies!" She screamed the last three words.

"Yeah, yeah. Like I care," the beast named Jeremy snarled. He pulled Kenny away from the door a few inches, then slammed him into the wood. Kenny hit with a thud that made Nick wince. He stepped back, ready to slam Kenny again.

"Stop it!" Nick ran toward the beast, hand out to pull him off Kenny, just as the girls' room door was pushed open from inside. The beast stepped back some more but kept his hold on his prisoner.

Three girls wearing Coatestown cheerleader uniforms exited. They saw Kenny, his face undoubtedly looking scared and embarrassed and bruised. Nick's guts twisted. It was bad enough the kid was helpless in the grip of the much bigger guy, but to look like a wuss in front of the girls had to hurt as much, if not more, than the hit on the door.

"Hey, ladies." The beast smiled at the girls. "Meet Kenny, the weinie from Lyndale who's about to use the ladies' room." He grabbed for the door handle to hold it open.

Two of the cheerleaders stepped back into the ladies' room, but one who reminded Nick of a young Taylor Swift glared at the beast, hands on hips. Anger and disgust rolled off her in waves.

"Geez, Jeremy, can't you act like a decent human being for once?" She pushed past him and Kenny, the other two right behind her, using her as a shield.

"Now what kind of an attitude is that, sweet Stephanie?" Jeremy let go of the door and tried to grab Stephanie as she passed.

She whirled. "Do not touch me, Jeremy Calder. I mean it. You do and I'll get you thrown off the team and out of school so fast you won't know what hit you. One touch is all it'll take."

Nick blinked. Impressive! He and Stephanie passed each other, and he couldn't help looking. And smiling. That was when Kenny screamed.

The beast—Jeremy—had Kenny's arm bent behind his back. He was using the pain of the move to control Kenny as he groped for the handle of the now closed door.

"Let go of him!" Nick roared.

Jeremy didn't even bother to turn his head. "Butt out or I'll break his arm!" He gave an extra tug on Kenny's arm.

Time seemed to stretch. It felt like forever since he'd exited the men's room, but he knew it was only a couple of minutes.

"I warned you!" Nick grabbed Jeremy by the shoulder and spun him around. Eyes wide with surprise, Jeremy released Kenny who ducked under Nick's arm to stand with Nick between him and his tormentor. Jeremy swung at Nick.

Nick dodged the swing and laughed. "That's the best you've got?" He pushed Jeremy in the chest with both hands so his back came up against the bathroom door.

Jeremy narrowed his eyes, and Nick knew another swing was coming. Somebody should inform the beast about tells. Narrowed eyes was a big one.

Before Jeremy could act, Nick punched him in the stomach. He pulled his punch at the last moment, but there was still plenty of anger left in it.

Jeremy gasped, grabbed his middle, and went to his knees. He bent over, trying to breathe.

The hallway was suddenly full of guys as Andy, Tyler, Paul and Nate came rushing to the rescue. "Those girls said you were in trouble."

Kenny waved his arm like he held the checkered flag at Indianapolis on Memorial Day. "You missed it! He finished it!"

Andy looked at Nick, then at the beached whale on his knees. "Hey, he's the guy who flattened you this afternoon. That'll show him to mess with you."

"No, it wasn't like th—"

"You should have seen him!" Kenny was dancing about like some soon-to-be-voted-off dancer on *Dancing with the Stars*. "One shot! Boom!" He gave his version of the punch.

Nick rolled his eyes and poked Jeremy with his toe. "You okay down there?"

The only answer was a wheeze.

"He's fine." Andy reached down and took Jeremy by his arm. Nate grabbed the other arm, and they pulled him to his feet.

Jeremy tried to straighten, then bent again. "I'm gonna be sick."

"Not here you're not." Andy pushed him down the hall. With Nate's help he perp-walked Jeremy into the dining room. As they passed the girls clustered at the entrance to the hall, the girls cheered.

"Time you got some of your own back," called the one who'd yelled she hated bullies.

"Took six to get me," Jeremy croaked. "Six."

Nick shook his head in disgust. Jeremy was already on his knees when the guys showed up. Some people never learned.

"Six, my eye," Stephanie called. "One, you idiot."

As Nick passed her, Stephanie stepped to his side and held out her hand. "Very nice. Someone needed to stand up to him. Thank you."

Embarrassed, he managed to shake her hand and give her his best smile. He pointed to her cheerleader's outfit. "Coatestown? Really?"

She grinned back. "Someone's got to live there."

"He won the game for us." Kenny pointed to Nick as he bounced past with the guys.

Stephanie cocked her head. "Lyndale's hero, huh? The enemy. You know what the Bible says about our enemies."

Nick stared at her, unsure what she meant but hoping like crazy it was *love your enemies.*

Kenny and the guys escorted Jeremy, still slightly green, to his table. Nick fell in behind. To his surprised delight, Stephanie walked beside him.

"I want to hear how Jeremy explains this." She grinned at Nick again with her special sass and sparkle.

He was a goner.

The Coatestown guys watched the Lyndale guys approach, uncertain what was coming. Andy pushed the still hunched Jeremy forward. "He yours?"

"We sure don't want him!" Perhaps Kenny was enjoying Jeremy's humiliation a bit too much. "Take him, please!"

The astonishment on the faces of the Coatestown guys gave way to sly smiles. "Why, Jeremy," their quarterback said. "Looks like you ran into a little problem. What a shame."

He answered by vomiting all over the table.

———

Nick lay in bed listening to Kenny snore as he lay on his back on the air mattress on the floor. Nick picked up one of the collection of socks he now brought to bed nightly. Clean, dirty, he didn't care. He took aim and lobbed it. It hit Kenny in the face.

The kid snorted and brushed it away. "Direct hit."

"Hooray for me."

"She's cute."

"Go to sleep."

"I was. Now I'm not. You woke me."

"Go back."

"Yeah. Any minute now." Kenny yawned and turned on his side. "Real cute."

Nick grinned to himself. She was. And he had her cell number. He'd already texted to make sure she got home all right. "Good night, Kenny."

No answer, just wonderful silence.

Except it gave Nick time to think.

He was as bad as his father.

Sure Jeremy had asked for it, but wasn't that the reason Dad always gave for his violence? She asked for it?

But what else could he have done? The beast wasn't the kind of person who listened to, "Stop it, Jeremy. You're hurting him." He enjoyed hurting and humiliating people too much.

Sometimes force was necessary to right a wrong. It was the only language bullies understood.

But it hurt him more than it ever hurt Jeremy.

CHAPTER 13

"Hello, up there."

Avery's heart gave a big thump. She'd been seen! She'd been so busy trying to peek into Nick's window that she hadn't even noticed his mother come outside, hadn't seen her walk right up to the tree.

"Is it hard to climb so high?"

Avery looked down through the wrinkled brown leaves at Ms. Loring. She was a pretty lady with curly black hair. She usually had it pulled into a ponytail, probably because of work. Avery knew she cleaned houses, and who would want hair hanging in the soapy water?

She frowned. Did cleaning ladies use soapy water or just those squirt bottles like she saw Mrs. Cotton use when she cleaned for Mommy? She shrugged. Who knew? Who cared?

But today was the first Sunday in November, and Ms. Loring had her hair long, resting all around her shoulders like black, curly angel's hair—if angels had black, curly hair.

Ms. Loring smiled up at Avery. "I grew up in the city, and we didn't have many trees like this to climb."

Avery frowned. How sad was that? A sudden thought struck her. This tree was on Ms. Loring's property. Would Ms. Loring think she was trespassing? Okay, she was trespassing. Would Ms. Loring make a big deal of it? She knew Daddy would raise the roof if some kid came into his yard and made herself at home in one of his trees, if he had a tree big enough to climb.

"I always thought it looked like such fun to climb up into the sky. I always wanted to try." Ms. Loring stood on tiptoe and reached up. The tips of her fingers just brushed the lowest branch.

Avery could see she meant it when she said she wanted to climb a tree. The thought of a grown up lady climbing made her giggle.

"If you take hold of that rope with the knots," Avery called down, "you can climb it until you can reach the lowest branch. Then you can swing one leg over. If you brace your foot against the trunk, you can pull yourself up until you're sitting. Then it's easy."

Ms. Loring walked around the tree until she came to the knotted rope. It was the water skiing rope Avery had taken from the garage when her parents were out and Mrs. Cotton napping. She'd looped it over the branch. Tying the knots had been one hard job, but she'd finally managed.

Ms. Loring studied the rope and the branch it hung from with a frown. She didn't think it was all that easy. Well, she was starting to get old. Maybe she even had a bad back like older people sometimes did. Mrs. Cotton complained about her back all the time. Of course Ms. Loring wasn't that old. Still Avery thought it was brave that she wanted to try to climb.

"Come on," she called down in an encouraging voice. "If I can do it, and I can't do anything, you can do it."

Ms. Loring reached out and wrapped her hands around the rope.

"Grab just above a knot," Avery called. "So you won't get rope burns from your hands sliding."

"Rope burns? Sounds painful. I didn't realize climbing trees was so dangerous.

"What do I do after I grab the rope?"

"You sort of jump and put your feet just above a knot. Then you straighten, move your hands to a higher knot, then bring your feet up."

"You're kidding."

"Unh-unh. It's easy."

Ms. Loring grabbed the knot just above her head and let her weight fall as she tried to bring her feet up.

"You got to jump, not just sag," Avery called.

"Huh?" Ms. Loring looked up, her feet off the ground but not yet on the knot. Just that fast her hands lost their grip. She gave a little yelp as she fell and landed on her back with a dull thud and a little puff of dirt.

Avery was caught between giggling at the surprised expression on Ms. Loring's face, and fear she was hurt. "Are you all right?"

Ms. Loring just lay there, staring up through the branches. Dead guys on TV stared like that. Avery bit her lower lip, suddenly very worried. What did they do to you if your suggestion killed someone?

"Solitary confinement for life, young woman. To your room!" She imagined a prison guard who looked a lot like Daddy pointing the way.

Finally Ms. Loring blinked and Avery felt she could breathe again. The vision of bars on her bedroom windows fell away. She watched as the lady climbed to her feet and brushed off her seat. Now if she didn't raise her voice when she yelled, Mom and Daddy might never know.

"I didn't know climbing trees was so hard," she said. "You are obviously very clever and very strong."

Avery looked at her closely, wishing she'd taken time to clean the smudges off her glasses, but she couldn't see any evidence that Ms. Loring was making fun of her. Clever and strong? Had anyone ever said that about her before? She felt awkward because she wasn't sure what to do with a real compliment.

Mrs. Harbison, her third grade teacher, told her she was clever too, but teachers were supposed to say stuff like that to build you up. Ms. Loring didn't have to be nice. In fact she could have been really mad. When she thought of how Mom or Daddy would react to a fall like that, she couldn't believe Ms. Loring. In Avery's experience, adults were never that easy about things.

"Well, since I'm not going to be able to climb up to you today, why don't you come down to me? I don't know many of my neighbors, so it'd be nice to meet you without getting a crink in my neck."

Still very uncertain, Avery slowly worked her way down. When she made the final swing and dropped to the ground, she half expected a slap.

"Okay, show me." Ms. Loring stood beside the tree. "I want to see how you do it."

When Avery hesitated, unable to believe the woman actually wanted a lesson, Ms. Loring added, "Please."

Please. Wow! An adult saying please. To her! Feeling like she could float up to the branch, Avery jumped, arms raised. She caught the rope just above a knot and quickly rested her feet on another knot. She reached for a higher knot and moved her feet up. When she reached the branch with her hands, she swung her right leg over it real close to the trunk and tucked the toe of her sneaker against the trunk. She gave a great swing, using her leg as an anchor, and grabbed the branch just above the one she ended up sitting on. She settled on the branch and looked down at Ms. Loring.

"I forgot to tell you about grabbing the second branch. I'm sorry."

Ms. Loring actually laughed. "Since I never got as far as the first branch, it's no big deal. But at least I now know how to get started."

"You're going to try again?" Avery couldn't believe it.

"Not right now. I have a one fall a day rule."

Avery laughed, then slapped her hand over her mouth. Adults didn't like being laughed at.

But Ms. Loring just grinned at her. "Ah, a girl who gets my jokes."

Overcome by Ms. Loring's niceness, Avery blurted, "I like Nick." She heard herself and turned bright red. Who cared that a fat little kid with pink glasses liked a handsome guy like Nick?

Ms. Loring nodded, but she didn't laugh and make Avery feel ridiculous. "Me too."

Avery felt brave enough to continue sharing her heart. "He's very handsome."

"He is."

"And he's nice." Then thinking she should be more inclusive and not so dumb-kid-with-a-crush, she added, "His friend's nice too. That's what I like best about them."

"That proves you are a clever girl. Nice is always very important."

"It's most important," Avery insisted, her legs swinging. "Don't you think?"

Ms. Loring considered her question. She felt a curious sensation inside. It was as if Ms. Loring actually thought she was important. Well, not exactly important. Avery knew better than that. No, not important exactly, but not unimportant either. Somewhere in that gray space between.

"I think the most important is loving God," Ms. Loring said. "Then being nice comes right after."

Avery was shocked. "Loving God?"

Ms. Loring nodded. "Oh, yes. Don't you think so?"

Avery was so excited that she bounced on her limb, and the wrinkly leaves made a shushing sound as they rubbed against each other. "I do! I do! I never met anyone before who thought so too and said it out loud."

"A-ver-y! A-ve-ry! Where are you?"

Avery looked toward her house, a big stone one with lots of roof angles and big windows and five bedrooms and six bathrooms and a hot tub and a huge kitchen that no one but Mrs. Cotton ever used. "My mom. I've got to go see what she wants."

"Of course you do," Ms. Loring agreed.

Avery slid out onto her branch and wrapping her hands firmly around it, fell backwards, swung her legs over her head and dropped to the ground.

"Now that was impressive," Ms. Loring said. "When I finally climb up there, I don't have to get down that way, do I?"

Avery had a mental picture of Ms. Loring trying to flip over the branch, losing her grip, and falling right on her head. "Oh, no. You can just jump or shinny down the rope."

Ms. Loring studied the rope like she was trying to picture herself not only going up it but also coming down. "Huh," was all she said.

Avery ran along the hedge and started to go around it, then stopped and waved at Ms. Loring.

"Come visit me again, Avery," Ms. Loring called. "Come be my neighbor."

Avery stared. Did she mean it or was she just saying it, like Mom or Daddy when they said they'd take her to the store to get a new video game and never did.

"I mean it," Ms. Loring said as if she could read Avery's mind.

Wow! Avery ran home, thinking maybe God was listening to her after all.

CHAPTER 14

When Ellie walked into Lyndale Chapel's all-purpose room on the first Thursday in November, she couldn't believe her eyes. The room was full of tables, round ones and rectangular ones, even a couple of small ones borrowed from the little kids' Sunday school rooms. That in itself wasn't enough to make her mouth drop open. It was the sheer volume of clothes that took her breath.

Garments in a rainbow of colors sat on tables and hung from racks like in a store. Blues, greens, browns, reds, yellows. Patterns, plaids, stripes. Children's, women's, men's.

More garments lay in piles waiting to be sorted and put in the right place. A score or more of huge plastic trash bags brimming with sweaters, shirts, and pants waited to be sorted. There were even shoes arranged neatly under the tables.

"Amazing, isn't it?"

Ellie turned to the woman about the age her own mother would have been had she lived. The woman was pretty with blond hair curled back from her smiling face. She held a group of hangers tied together with a twistie. She began unwinding the tie to free the hangers.

Ellie let her amazement show. "I expected a few tables of stuff people could go through, hoping to find something they could use. This is a department store."

"It is, isn't it? I'm Maris, by the way."

"Hi, Maris. I'm Ellie."

"You've come to help, I assume?" Maris indicated the room.

Ellie nodded. "But where do I start? Everyone seems to know what they're doing."

"That's because I gave them all a job. Come on, let me show you how things are set up, and then I'll give you a job too."

Ellie followed Maris around as she showed her table after table of clothes sorted by gender and size. Clearly the woman had the set-up highly organized.

"There are thousands of dollars worth of clothes here." Ellie still couldn't believe it.

Maris beamed. "Happens twice a year, spring and fall. When the door opens Saturday morning at nine, there will be a line of people from the community and nearby towns stretching well into the parking lot. Some will be young moms who can stay home with their kids because they clothe them here. Some are migrant workers' wives. We even have Muslim women new to the country who need to get decent American clothes for their kids. We give everyone who comes a black plastic bag to fill, a hand selecting what they need, and a Bible and an invitation to services."

"And no one pays?"

"Not one penny." Maris pointed to several women busy arranging clothes. "Those are women from the community who don't go to our church, but they volunteer to help so they feel they've earned the clothes. We appreciate their willing hands immensely."

As they passed the table with large men's things, Ellie saw a black sweater with small gray slubs that would be just right for Nick. At least she thought so. Could you return things to a give-away program if your kid didn't like them?

Maris followed her gaze. "See something you like?"

Ellie pointed to the sweater, and Maris pulled it free of the pile. A tag hung from the back of the neck.

"It's never been worn!" Ellie couldn't believe it.

"It'll fit your husband?"

"My son."

"It's yours." Maris pushed it into her hands. "See anything else there you want?"

She did, but she was afraid of sounding greedy. "But don't I have to earn the right to take things like those ladies are doing?"

Maris grinned. "Don't you worry about that. You'll earn the right before I'm done with you."

And earn the right she did. Maris set her to emptying the garbage bags full of garments of all kinds. "You sort them," Maris said. "Angie over there—" she pointed—"will take them to the right tables. As you sort, if you find something you can use, just set it aside. If you find something stained or with inappropriate language or pictures on it, put it in a pile to get thrown away."

Ellie dragged a fat bag to one of the empty tables, swung it up, and began pulling the contents out. She found some boys jeans that had obviously belonged to a kid who never walked when he could crawl. She could picture him with little cars or Legos or Transformers, crawling across the floor in some battle or race, like Nick used to do. She sighed. Sometimes she missed that little guy with the engaging grin and ready supply of hugs and kisses for his mother.

Not that she was complaining about the big guy he'd become. He was any mother's joy.

Beneath the jeans and the seen-better-days tee shirts was a little gray suit that would look adorable on some four or five-year-old who had to get dressed up for an occasion. There was a white shirt and a regimental striped tie to complete the outfit.

Ellie thought of the little white church across the street from their house in Arizona. No one there would have gotten their boy a suit this fine. A shirt with a collar was as dressy as it got.

Lyndale Chapel was in size and people far different from that church. Back then she'd never have come to a place this big and obviously well-to-do. It would have overwhelmed her, made her feel a traitor to everything Nonna and Nonno had taught her.

But God knew her need, and back then as now He placed her right where He wanted her.

It was gratitude to God for their safe escape that caused Ellie to go to that little church one Sunday shortly after their arrival in Arizona. The service was like nothing she'd ever known. Raised with liturgy and ritual, she was appalled and uncomfortable at the amens that sometimes rang out and the hand clapping during the much too enthusiastic singing. Church was supposed to be stiff, formal and uninvolving, but someone had forgotten to tell these people.

Still, she tried to talk to God while she was there.

I know You're probably mad at me for living with Joey, and I'm sorry about that. You were right, and I was wrong.

That one sentence covered a multitude of sins—her rebellion against her grandparents, her having sex out of curiosity and outside marriage resulting in pregnancy, her moving in with Joey against Nonna's advice, her not attending church because she knew God was unhappy with her.

But I do thank You for getting us here safely. Please don't let my mistakes ruin Nick's life. And please, please, don't let Joey find us.

When they left that morning after shaking hands with what seemed like the whole congregation, she planned to never return. She'd voiced her gratitude to God, and that was all she felt the need to do.

Nick had a different idea.

"You don't want to go back there," she told him the next Saturday night when he said he was going to Sunday school in the morning.

"Yeah, I do," he said. "You don't have to come if you don't want to. I can walk across the street by myself." There was a bit of sarcasm in that last because he had been managing the streets of Philadelphia for years. Nick's getting around this little town was like Lewis and Clark traveling from Washington to Baltimore after their return from Oregon and the Northwest Passage. Elementary. And wasn't sarcasm a sign that he wasn't psychologically ruined by their move?

"Okay," she said. "Go ahead." After all, how could learning about God be bad even if it wasn't the way she was used to? It might help him cope with the disruption she'd put him through.

So go he did, every Sunday for several weeks. During those weeks the pastor came to see her four times. She thought she'd hyperventilate when she opened the door and found him on the porch the first time. He was surely going to yell at her for all her sins and tell her she was going to Hell. That's what the TV preachers did a lot, or so it seemed in the brief flashes as she flicked through the channels.

Instead they talked about the differences between living in big city Philadelphia and small town Arizona. It was only as he was leaving, after he'd told her what a good kid Nick was, that he invited her back to church. Each time he came, they talked about something different—the weather variations in different parts of Arizona, the local flora and fauna, places she and Nick should visit. Once he did ask her what she thought of God, and she'd given him some vague answer laced with comments she remembered Nonna making. She knew he realized it was a whole lot of nothing, but he didn't call her on it.

"Come try us again, Ellie," he'd say as he crossed the porch and started down the walk. "It'd make Nick so happy."

She hadn't gone, but the pastor didn't take offense. He waved whenever he saw her, and when she and Nick were trying to paint the front porch with paint their landlord had provided, he and his fifteen-year-old son came across the street with their brushes and helped.

Then came Christmas, and the little church had a live Nativity in their parking lot for two nights. Nick played a shepherd both nights, and Ellie crossed the street to see him. It reminded her of going to a school play, except that several of the players were adults. The sight of a real baby squirming in the manger made her smile, especially when he began crying.

"Getting stuck by the hay," said the man standing next to her.

"Nope," the woman with him said. "He's hungry."

And for the first time, Ellie thought about Jesus not as a sweet-faced infant in the Madonna's arms, his and her halos shining gold, but as a real baby who got hungry and felt hay pricks and wore a diaper. Not those distant and mysterious swaddling clothes, whatever they were, but diapers like Nick and all babies. God become human. She crossed the street again for the Christmas Eve service and every Sunday thereafter. Jesus became real to her, the Center of her life, and the Giver of the strength needed to continue whenever life became overwhelming.

It was the same Jesus who lived in the hearts of the people of Lyndale Chapel. They might dress better, have better jobs, be more upwardly mobile, and give away fantastic clothes, but it was the same Lord. And Ellie found the same joy in serving Him as she pulled things from her garbage bag.

Beneath the boy's suit were several women's things, all beautiful, all in wonderful condition.

"If she's giving this stuff away, what must the stuff she's keeping be like?" Ellie muttered. She was staring with longing at a crimson ribbed turtleneck sweater when Maris stopped to see how she was doing.

"Oh," the older woman said, "that's perfect for you. With your dark hair and eyes, it'll look wonderful! Put it in your pile. And I bet this will look great too." She held out a quilted jacket in a lovely soft yellow. "I saw it on one of the tables and thought of you."

Ellie blinked. She wasn't used to people thinking about her like this.

"We'll have to see if we can't find a yellow top to go under it," Maris said. "Something with sleeves since winter's almost here. It'll be perfect for church. Or work."

Ellie ran a hand over the lovely jacket as Maris pushed it into her hand. She hadn't owned anything so fine since she left Philadelphia. "Not my work," she said absently. "I clean houses."

She folded the jacket carefully and put it and the crimson sweater on top of the black sweater for Nick and the bright blue one she'd picked for Kenny because it would make his eyes even bluer. And it didn't have a single pull or pill.

"You clean houses?" Maris asked.

"I do." How much sorting did she have to do to earn the boys another sweater each?

"Do you have a full client list?"

Ellie finally heard the interest in Maris's voice, realized that she had a potential customer here, and started paying attention.

"What days are free?" Maris asked. "My cleaning lady of several years just retired, and I'm desperate! I'll pay whatever you ask."

Ellie grinned. It looked like she was going to get more than clothes today. "Mondays and Thursdays are still free."

"Mondays. Can I have you Mondays? That way, if we entertain over the weekend, you can help me clean up the mess and get ready for the next weekend." Maris beamed at her. "There's only my husband and me at home most of the time. Our younger daughter comes home from college sometimes, but not often, and our boys and older daughter drop in for meals periodically. I try to have everyone at least once a month. But it's the entertaining for my husband that's what trashes the house—but don't you ever tell him I said that."

Ellie laughed. "Never." She pulled a red fleece anorak from her bag.

"It's yours." Maris folded it and added it to Ellie's growing pile. "When you empty that bag, put your things in it and put your name on it. Fill it up."

"Fill it up?" Surely she hadn't meant that.

"Sure." Maris swept her hand across the room. "You think we're going to run out if you fill it?"

Ellie had to laugh. Her bag wouldn't even make a dent.

"Mrs. Hyland," a young woman called. "There's a guy here who wants to know if you want all his store's leftover Halloween candy. Free."

Ellie blinked. Had she heard correctly? Mrs. Hyland? As in Gabe Hyland, football coach?

"Oh, my," Maris said, frowning. "Do we want to get into food? I don't think so."

"The high school youth group is meeting tonight," Ellie said, glad she could contribute. "I know because my son's coming. I'm sure they'd take care of the candy for you."

Maris laughed. "I'm sure they would." She turned to the woman. "Tell him we'll take his candy. He can put it on the information desk in the lobby."

Ellie pulled a pea green women's shirt from her bag and studied it. Somehow it didn't seem the right color shirt for the woman who had worn the crimson sweater.

"Who's your son, Ellie?" Maris asked as she took the shirt and added it to the pile of women's clothes on Ellie's worktable. "Would I know him?"

"Nick Loring, but I'm sure you wouldn't know him." Though if she was the coach's mother . . . .

"Oh, but I do! He's the football player, right?"

Ellie nodded. "Are you Coach Hyland's mother?"

Maris nodded, looking proud. "That's my boy, or one of them. He loves your Nick. It's been good to see him so enthusiastic. He's had a hard time since he lost Robyn." Seeing Ellie's blank look, she said, "Robyn was his wife. Lovely girl. She died several years ago now, and while Gabe does well, your boy has really perked him up."

Of course he has. Nick wins games for him. Ellie heard herself and was ashamed of the nasty thought. The man was a widower. He was allowed to be sour. She forced a smile. "Nick thinks he's a great coach." That was the truth.

"Mrs. Hyland." Another woman waved from across the room. "We've got a problem over here."

"Be right there," Maris called. "Give me your phone number, Ellie. I need to call and give you directions to our house. Can you come this Monday?"

Ellie nodded and gave her number which Maris wrote on a tablet she pulled from the pocket of her jeans.

"Now I want you to fill that bag with clothes for you and your sons," she said. "Promise me."

"I only have one son," Ellie said.

"Well, you're collecting for someone smaller than your Nick then. Or is that blue sweater for you?"

"Kenny Uplander. He just about lives with us these days."

"Poor Kenny," Maris said. "Gabe's so concerned about him. I'm glad to see someone else coming along side to help too. Remember, fill that bag!"

And she was gone. Ellie stared after her, bemused. Now there was a take-charge woman. She wondered what Mr. Hyland did, and how he dealt with that strong personality.

Ellie pulled the rest of the clothes from her bag, finding a pair of jeans that she thought would fit Kenny. She began unloading a second bag, her mind still trying to get around the fact that she was going to be working for Gabe Hyland's mother. Life could be so strange.

CHAPTER 15

The first Saturday in November Gabe headed home, a tired but happy man. Today's game had gone well, and Nick had performed at the top of his form for the various scouts. Gabe and Nick had talked about getting his recruitment information together, and Kenny had focused his filming on Nick during today's game.

He saw Ellie Loring standing with a collection can for Football Parents during the first half—she was hard to miss with her red beret. He hadn't had much contact with her after their dinner together, and he chalked it up to the long hours he was putting in, trying to discern where the explosion of drugs in his territory was coming from. Every moment he wasn't on the football field, he was at the station. Poor Mister Thomas was going to start barking at him as an intruder if he didn't start coming home more. Spending time with a fascinating woman was somehow lost in the crush, and he was sorry about that.

And she was fascinating as well as frustrating and feisty, but he appreciated people with spirit even when they drove him crazy or made him wary. He frowned. He realized that he liked her—respected her even for raising a fine kid like Nick—but he also distrusted her. Or maybe he distrusted his response to her. As a man who liked life to be black and white, right and wrong, he felt itchy over the many shades of gray that made up Ellie Loring.

He pulled into the drive of his two-story Colonial, eyed the leaf-covered lawn, and wondered again why he'd bought a house with four bedrooms and more trees than Sherwood Forest. Then the sensor light over the garage came on, and as the yard was illuminated, he caught a glimpse of the golds, oranges, and crimsons still clinging to his three giant maples, the pale gold of his oak, and the graceful drape of his purple beech with its leaves going from bronze to crunchy brown, and he remembered. His beautiful acre lot with its mature trees afforded him dogwoods blooming in the spring, cooling shade in the summer, glorious beauty in the fall, and privacy all year long.

And none of it was gray.

Feeling somewhat better, he pulled into the garage. Matt pulled into the drive behind him. Gabe opened the door into the mud room, eager for a night vegging in front of the TV with his brother. There were several great games on.

Thomas jumped him before the door was even all the way open. Gabe couldn't help but grin. What was it about the wiggling enthusiasm and unconditional love of an animal that lifted the spirits? He rubbed the ecstatic dog's ears. "Thomas, old man. Want to go out?"

Stupid question. He and Matt stood in the back yard as Thomas watered the shriveling marigolds his mother had planted for him in the spring.

"Even you can't kill these," she'd told him.

Maybe not, but Thomas was certainly trying.

He patted the dog's head as, nature's call heeded, Thomas's attention turned to the bag of takeout Gabe held. Large Philly cheese steaks and salads. It was one of his favorite dinners, the healthful salad allowing him to enjoy the cholesterol and calorie laden steak. Thomas had no such nutritional qualms. His interest was all for the steak.

"Sorry, big guy. It's ours."

Gabe went through to the kitchen, Matt on his heels. He had a bag too, and it contained several pint containers of various Ben and Jerry's ice cream. "Didn't know what you'd want, so I got lots." He stuck them in the freezer. "With luck you'll forget them when you leave, and I'll be set for the week." Gabe pulled out large paper plates, forks, and napkins.

"Napkins!" Matt grabbed a couple of liter bottles of Coke and a bottle of tomato bacon salad dressing from the fridge. "Mom would be so proud."

They carried everything into the living room where Gabe kept a TV tray set up in front of his fifty-six-inch flat screen TV. Matt grabbed another tray they kept stashed behind the couch for evenings like this one.

With contented sighs, the men sat in the pair of recliners and unwrapped their sandwiches. Gabe flicked through the channels and found three college games to choose from. The perfect Saturday night.

Halfway through his sandwich, Matt turned to Gabe with a frown. "I just noticed Robyn's picture's gone. It was always on the end table." He flicked a hand in that direction.

Gabe looked, expecting to see her photo in its black and gold frame where it always sat, but it wasn't there. Her laughing face, looking back over her shoulder at him as she walked along the beach one bright summer day, was his favorite picture of her. Her hair was windblown and her freckles obvious, but it was the love of life and him in her eyes that made him prize the picture. Where had it gone? He hadn't moved it.

"Don't let Thomas finish my sandwich." He stood and roamed the house looking for her. He found her on his bureau in his bedroom. His mother must have done it on one of her stealth visits, and he hadn't even noticed.

GAYLE ROPER

He returned to his dinner, aggrieved at her presumption and his lack of awareness. "Mom. She put it on my bureau. Part of her Move On, Gabe campaign."

Matt gave a facial shrug. "If you think about it, that's a pretty good place. Now you can say good morning and good night to her."

He grunted, took his seat, and took a bite. One day, he knew, he'd put her in a drawer beside his wedding ring, though that day hadn't yet come. When a woman with dark curls and a red beret came to mind, he blinked her away.

Matt dumped half the bag of chips on his tray. "Maybe Mom's right, Gabe. You should move on. Date. Live more."

"Says the man who's spending Saturday night with his brother and a dog."

Matt gave a bark of laughter. "Dinah keeps telling me I should try an online dating service."

"So you can meet interesting people like she did? Yeah. I get the same line."

"I noticed she didn't marry one of the online guys."

"She did not. She married the one she met the old-fashioned way, face to face." Like he'd met Ellie Loring. He smiled to himself as he thought of that first meeting.

When she roared into his office waving that newspaper picture of Nick, she hadn't known the coach was also the police. She'd probably have done things differently if she'd realized her little tantrum would waken his cop's curiosity.

And he was certainly curious. Here she had this great kid with hands so soft and sure on the pigskin that Gabe broke into a sweat just watching him play. And she had threatened to pull him!

What were her secrets and why was keeping them so important that she'd risk her son's future? He felt a strange ambivalence about searching them out. What if he found things he didn't like? What if he found things he had to deal with as an officer of the law?

142

And what if he was obsessing about nothing?

"Go! Go, go, go!" Matt rose halfway out of his seat, jarring Gabe back to the game. He watched the replay so he'd know what Matt was screaming about.

"Nice run."

"Nice run? Nice run?" Matt looked at him incredulously. "It was smokin' great!"

"Okay. Great run."

"That's better." Matt settled back on his chair.

Concentrate, Hyland. On the game, not on wanting to see another of Ellie's glorious smiles. He squirmed, afraid doing his duty might sweep away any possibility of that smile as surely as today's rain washed away yesterday's pollen.

He arrived at the last two bites of his steak, mostly bread. He glanced at Thomas, staring unwaveringly at the sandwich. Gabe flipped the bread in the air, and Thom caught it with unbecoming greed but impressive speed.

"Subtlety's never going to be your style, is it, boy?"

Thomas grinned happily and after checking that Matt had nothing to offer, went to find his bowl of dog food.

During halftime Gabe and Matt wandered to the kitchen and pulled the Ben and Jerry's from the freezer. They ate one each leaning against the counter, then grabbed another and returned to watch the second half.

"Your Loring kid's as good as that guy." Matt pointed to the replay of a nice catch.

Gabe nodded. "Pretty much. You see all those scouts checking him out?"

"Free ride to college for sure." Matt looked at him. "You think the pros?"

"Way too soon to tell." But sometimes he allowed himself to imagine the intense satisfaction of watching one of the kids he'd coached make it to the NFL.

When the game finally ended, Matt pulled on his jacket and headed toward the door. "Don't let Mom get to you, Gabe. She's just worried."

"I know." He gave Matt a brotherly slap on the back and watched him disappear down the street.

He wandered back to the living room, his laptop in hand. He opened it and logged onto YouTube. Next he skipped over to Facebook, Instagram and Vine. Ever since the Philadelphia police caught a quartet of serial convenience store robbers because one of them was stupid enough to post a picture of himself with his gun on his Facebook page, Gabe had been checking daily for any local rumblings. Eventually some kid was going to be thoughtless enough to post that first lead in solving this flood of drugs. He hadn't noticed anything posted that seemed significant thus far, but you never knew. He paid special attention to the pages of his players and the school's troublemakers, looking for situations where he could step in before things got to the break-the-law stage.

He shook his head at some of the posts he read. Didn't these kids realize that once they posted, it was there forever for anyone and everyone to read? What was it with the need to share every thought? What about personal privacy or self-respect? Did a girl really need to share what color underwear she was wearing? Or a guy use the crudest language he could manage? What about good taste? What about keeping one's counsel? Between the cell phone and the social networking sites, every thought, appropriate or un, was blabbed to the world.

And he was turning into an old-before-his-time curmudgeon.

He typed in *Nick Loring* but wasn't surprised when he came up empty. Not a single post or picture. Previously he hadn't thought much about Nick's lack of a presence where everyone else his age was all too present, but after thinking more about him and his mother, this absence now assumed significant import. Exactly what that import was, he wasn't certain, but he'd find out. It was just a matter of time.

He typed in *Kenny Uplander*. Nothing there either, but that didn't surprise him. On his many calls to Mitzi's apartment he'd never seen a computer though he supposed there could be one in a bedroom. He just didn't think so. This probable lack made Kenny's academic success all the more astounding.

He thought of his parents and the time and love they'd poured into his life and those of his sisters and brother. Still did. Kenny on the other hand was clawing his way out of the gutter without much help and little fanfare. There was a lot more to the kid than most people gave him credit for. The thing that would make the difference for him would be college, but how was he to manage that? He was going to need a free ride but he hadn't the automatic ticket Nick had.

Gabe signed off, tucked the laptop into the space between his recliner and the side table and settled back to watch another game. When his phone sounded, he grabbed it with a sigh.

"Mitzi Uplander's again," said a weary Dottie.

He wished he didn't feel so responsible for Mitzi, but there was no one else to care. He was it. It was as if there was an election on who should be Mitzi's caretaker, and he won by acclamation. He pushed himself out of the recliner. "Thanks, Dottie."

He pulled up to the curb in front of Mitzi's and walked to the front door of the old Victorian. As soon as he entered, he was assaulted by several voices all screaming at once, each ignoring the others. He quickly identified two screamers as the young couple he'd seen last time he was here. They were standing at the bottom of the steps looking up toward Mitzi's. A glance showed the other downstairs apartment door was closed. One person was smart enough not to be a public nuisance.

"Out! Get out!" the boy yelled at Jonesy, who was clothed and upright tonight, a vast improvement.

"I called the cops," the girl yelled up the stairs. "They're going to haul you off and throw you in jail."

"Shut up! This is none of your business!" Jonesy was so red in the face that he matched his scarlet sweater stretched over his ample tummy. He turned to Mitzi's door and began banging. "Let me in, Mitzi. Come on, baby. Let me in."

Whining was ugly on anyone but on Jonesy, it was appallingly demeaning.

The door to Mitzi's apartment flew open, and a pretty blonde stood with feet planted and arms crossed. "I told you, Jonesy! Go away! I mean it."

Gabe blinked. Mitzi? He hadn't seen her looking that good since her cheerleading days.

Gabe turned to the young couple. "Why don't you two go back into your apartment? I'll take it from here."

"It's about time!" the girl said ungraciously. "I called hours ago."

Gabe smiled politely. "I'm sorry we took so long, but I thank you for calling."

"He won't go away." The boy, who looked too young to shave let alone either be married or have a live-in girlfriend, pointed at Jonesy. "He's been here forever, banging and banging, yelling her name. It's enough to drive you nuts! He's nuts!"

"Don't worry. He won't be here much longer."

"I hope not." The girl gave a disgusted glance up the stairs, turned and went toward their apartment. The boy followed. They stopped in their doorway and waited to see what would happen next, but at least they waited silently. There was still no movement from apartment #2.

Gabe climbed the stairs. "Mitzi, how you doing? Good to see you, Mr. Jones. What seems to be the trouble?"

"She won't let me in," Jonesy whined.

"Is this your residence?" Gabe asked him.

Jonesy blinked. "It's Mitzi's."

"Then she doesn't have to let you in if she doesn't want to."

"Hah!" Mitzi glared.

"But—" Jonesy seemed bewildered by that thought. "She always lets me in."

"Not anymore," she snapped. "Just go away and leave me alone!"

"Uh, Mitz." Gabe still couldn't believe how good she looked. "Maybe you should be a bit more gracious. After all, you've got the law on your side here. You can afford to be nice to the man."

"I may be able to *afford* to be nice, but I don't *have* to any longer." She gave Jonesy a look to curdle mother's milk. "Get lost. And you!" She pointed at the door across the hall where a sliver of a swarthy, dark haired man could be seen in the partially open door. "Get lost, too!" And she slammed her door.

Gabe nodded briefly at the man across the hall who hurriedly shut his door but without the dramatic crash of Mitzi's.

Jonesy raised his hand to knock again.

"Unh-unh," Gabe said. "I wouldn't if I were you. Unless, of course, you don't mind being run in for disturbing the peace and stalking." He reached back and rattled his cuffs.

"Stalking?" Jonesy looked aghast. "I'm not stalking her. Stalkers are crazy people."

Gabe shook his head. "Could have fooled me. Anyone who won't leave another alone, especially a man who bothers a woman, could be said to be stalking." He reached in his inner pocket and pulled out a laminated card.

Jonesy stared at the card, eyes wide. "What's that? Is that the Miranda warning thing? I watch TV. I know all about it. You can't read me my rights. I haven't done nothing wrong. I just wanted to talk to her."

Gabe looked thoughtfully at Jonesy, then stuck the card back in his pocket. "Why don't you go quietly down the stairs and out of the building, Mr. Jones? Why don't you go home?" Gabe glanced at the ring on the third finger of Jonesy's left hand. "To your lucky wife."

Jonesy took a deep breath and let it out. His shoulders slumped. "I love her, you know."

"Mitzi or your wife?"

Mr. Jones suddenly looked as if life was too much for him, and maybe it was. He turned and walked slowly down the stairs and out into the night.

Gabe glanced at the closed door across the hall, then slowly descended the stairs himself. He smiled perfunctorily at the young couple still avidly watching. "Thanks again for calling."

The boy shrugged. "Can't say life's not interesting around here. Between Mitzi, Crazy Achmed, and the silent guy next door, we never run out of stuff to talk about."

"Crazy Achmed?"

"The guy above us. Scurries around like he's scared of the world. Only comes out at night. Has weird friends who come see him after dark like a bunch of vampires. Kenny says he's always peering out his door. Kenny's the one who named him. Personally I think he's a terrorist hiding out here until he gets his chance to blow up Independence Hall or something." With a small smile, he followed the girl inside.

At the last moment he stuck his head back out. "We're gonna report him to Homeland Security."

Gabe sighed. "You do that." But the boy was gone.

Gabe went back up the stairs and gave a sharp rap on Mitzi's door. "It's me. Open up."

The door opened immediately, and Gabe saw he hadn't hallucinated. Her messy hair had been tended to by a professional who knew what she was doing. It hung soft and shining, dark roots gone, the color expertly applied. She wore jeans and a V-neck sweater in a soft peach that made her skin glow. She'd had her nails done, and they were painted to match the sweater.

"Looking good, Mitzi," he said.

"Thank you." Her eyes sparkled like the old Mitzi.

"Do you think you could cultivate a new demeanor to go with the new look?"

She laughed. "Is that your way of asking me not to scream at idiots like Jonesy?"

"Arresting you for disturbing the peace would be hard on both of us."

"He stays away, I'm as sweet as a Hershey bar."

"Nice simile."

"Is that what it is?" She patted his arm. "You're a nice guy, Gabe. But don't worry. Soon you won't be seeing me here anymore. I'm leaving this hole."

"Yeah? Where you going?"

"Those new condos just west of town? Soon as mine's finished, I'm out of here."

"That's quite a jump in housing."

She grinned. "Yeah."

Gabe shook his head at her appalling ignorance. "What's his name, Mitzi? Where'd you meet him? Does he work you over too?"

She narrowed her eyes. "I take back what I said about you being a nice guy. And it's none of your business."

"You're an old friend, Mitzi. I don't want you getting hurt."

"I'm not going to get hurt. This guy's got class. Be glad for me, Gabe. Something good has finally happened."

"I sincerely hope so." But he doubted it. "So what about Kenny? The new guy met him yet?"

Mitzi's look made Antarctica seem cozy. "Not your concern."

"Point taken. Take care." With a wave he started down the steps, then stopped. "Who's your neighbor?" He pointed to the closed door across the hall.

"Crazy Achmed?" She shrugged. "He doesn't talk to anyone. He has guys come visit him sometimes, and I've seen him bringing up groceries, but otherwise he stays in there all day. Only goes out at night. No job that I can see." She came out into the hall and leaned toward Gabe to whisper, "I don't think he likes women. He won't even look at me."

If his name really was Achmed and he was a Middle-Eastern Muslim, she probably offended him deeply with all her gentlemen callers and skimpy clothes. "Takes all kinds," Gabe said, and went on down the stairs. He pushed the front door open just as a man came up the sagging front steps. Gabe stood aside to let him enter.

"Thanks." The man started up the stairs.

Gabe watched him for a minute, curiosity piqued. The guy was wearing good threads, black dress slacks, black silk shirt, and black tasseled loafers. What was he doing hanging around this place? Was he Mitzi's mysterious new man? Or one of the men who visited her neighbor?

The man rapped softly on Mitzi's door.

Question answered, Gabe walked to his car.

The sleek black BMW parked in front of his own Rav4 made him blink. How had Mitzi made contact with money? And who was the guy?

He pulled out his phone and took a picture of the Pennsy plate. Might as well discover who he was so that when he beat up Mitzi in her new condo, Gabe would know who to go after.

He drove home where Thomas greeted him as if he'd been gone for weeks. The two of them settled in the living room to watch a rerun of one of the *Die Hard* movies. Gabe wasn't sure which number it was, but it didn't matter. John McClane saved the day, and that was what counted. Yippee-ki-yay.

It was after one when Gabe's phone jarred him awake.

CHAPTER 16

"Mitzi's," Dottie said, "but it's not Mitzi. Drug overdose."

"Got it." He pushed himself from the recliner where he'd fallen asleep. "EMTs on the way?"

"On their way."

He grabbed his gun and ran to the car. Not Mitzi, thank You, God. Her new guy? Not Crazy Achmed. If Mitzi offended him, so would drugs. The couple? It wouldn't take much to put that skinny kid under. Or the girl who looked like an extra from a vampire movie, no makeup required. Or maybe the silent guy in #2?

He stuck the revolving light on his roof and tore out of his drive and into town. Most of Lyndale was tucked up for the night, so he made good time. He ran every light and pulled behind the ambulance as the EMTs raced up the stairs. He reached into the glove compartment and grabbed his naloxone kit just in case and ran into the house after them.

The door to the front downstairs apartment gaped open and Gabe had part of his answer. One of the kids. He glanced up the stairs. Mitzi's door was closed, so she and her guy were either in for the night or still out somewhere. To his surprise Achmed was in the hall, peering over the railing at the commotion downstairs. When he saw Gabe looking up, he scurried back to his room, closing the door except for his little slit. Strange guy.

So all the action was downstairs tonight. Gabe entered the room. The boy or the girl?

The girl. She lay on the couch like a pale, skinny Sleeping Beauty. Toby Brightman, the best in the business, was on his knees beside her, checking her vitals.

"She breathing?" he asked Toby's partner, Alicia Marlowe.

Alicia gave a little shrug as she pulled a naloxone box out of her magic medical case and tore it open. She held it toward Toby.

Relief raced through Gabe. He won't have to administer the meds. He'd gone to classes, gotten certified, made certain Lyndale PD was a Certified Purchaser, but having someone's life depending on him made him sweaty all over. He'd happily stare down a rabid dog or arrest any gun-toting bad guy, but give meds? What if he did something wrong? The time he'd used an Epi-Pen to stave off a kid's death by anaphylactic shock, he'd felt clammy for hours afterwards. He happily stuffed his naloxone in his jacket pocket.

"Give her that stuff!" Wild-eyed, the skinny boy stared at the unresponsive girl, then at Toby. "Give her that stuff!"

"What did she take?" Toby asked.

"How should I know?"

"You found her like this?"

The kid screwed up his face like he was trying to think. "Yeah. That's right. I came home and found her like this."

Gabe had to admire Toby for not rolling his eyes at the obvious lie.

"Give her that shot!" The kid poked Toby in the back.

Gabe moved to the boy and pulled him away from Toby and Alicia. "Stay out of the way. Let the man do his job."

The kid turned on Gabe. "Get your hands off me!"

Gabe released him, hands held out to show he wasn't restraining him, but he blocked his path to Toby.

"She's not breathing!" Unable to stand still, the kid danced in place. "He needs to give her that stuff!"

"What did she take?"

"I already told him." The kid indicated Toby. "I don't know. But if he gives her that stuff, she'll be all right."

"You thinking she can take anything she wants, and a shot of naloxone will save her?"

"That's not the stuff! That's not the stuff!" He frowned as he jittered in place. "It's something else."

"NARCAN?"

"Yeah, NARCAN!"

"Same thing. This happen before?"

"No!"

"Then how do you know about naloxone?"

"TV. I seen it on TV!"

"And you believe everything you see on TV?"

"Huh?"

Gabe mentally shook his head. The kid probably believed reality TV was real. "What if it's too late?"

The kid was about to jump out of his skin. He couldn't focus, he couldn't think clearly, he twitched all over. "It's not too late. It's soon enough! I called right away. She went to sleep, and I called."

"What did she take?"

"How many times I gotta say? I don't know!"

"You're her boyfriend. You live with her. Aren't you supposed to take care of her?"

"I am taking care. I called 911."

"You didn't think of stopping her from taking—" Gabe flapped his hand. "—whatever?"

"You ever tried to stop her from doing anything?"

Sometimes the little skinny ones had wills of iron that'd make a general seem indecisive. "She a runaway?"

"She's my lady." He said it with an amazing amount of pride.

"And you let her overdose." The kid was probably too busy enjoying his own high to notice anything she did until she collapsed.

The boy tried to see around Gabe's bulk. "Did he give her the stuff? Is she all right yet?"

"Where did the drugs come from?"

"I don't know. She just had them."

"They magically appeared?"

"Yeah!"

A young man walked into the room and, careful to stay out of Toby's and Alicia's way, came straight to the kid. He put an arm around the kid's shoulders. "Easy, Rock."

"Mel!" Relief washed over the kid. "They won't give her the stuff!"

"They're using the nasal spray." The man patted the kid's back. "It takes a few minutes to have its desired result."

"But it'll work?"

The man nodded. "She'll be fine."

Gabe eyed the young man. He spoke with more confidence than Gabe felt. "Apartment #2?"

He nodded.

"Chief Hyland, Lyndale PD."

"Mel Vining. I recognize you from the other day." He kept a hand on the kid's arm.

Gabe eyed the kid, much calmed by Mel's presence. Rock? Really?

The boy leaned around Gabe to get a look at the couch. The girl's hand moved and her face contorted. "Look! She's better!" He'd have rushed to her if Mel hadn't kept his hand on him.

"They're still working on her," Mel said. "You don't want to get in the way."

"She's going to be okay." Rock was dancing again, this time with relief. "I knew it!"

"Come on, Rock." Mel put a hand on the boy's back. "Why don't you come to my place while the kind people do their job?" He gave a gentle push toward the door.

"Yeah. Your place. That's good."

"Wait a minute, Rock." Gabe forced the ridiculous name out. "We're not quite finished."

Rock looked from Mel to Gabe and back to Mel.

"It's okay, Rock. You finish with Chief Hyland. I'll wait for you right over there." He pointed to a corner of the room. He gave Rock a final pat and stepped back out of the way.

Gabe clapped his hands to get Rock's attention. "So where are they?"

"What? Where are what?" Rock looked to Mel for help with the answer.

"Mel can't help you here, Rock. Where is what she took?"

"Uh, it's gone."

"She took the last?"

"Yeah. The last."

"Then you don't mind me taking that baggie of pills on the end table."

"What? You can't take them! They're ours."

"Without a prescription, they're illegal."

"You don't got a warrant." He looked proud of himself for having this thought.

"You called 911. I responded. You let me in. I don't need a warrant."

"I didn't ask for the cops. I just wanted the emergency guys."

"Well, lucky you, you got us both." Gabe picked up the bag, noting several kinds of pills inside. "Which one did you take?"

"Me?" He blinked and tried to look innocent. His pupils were so dilated the irises didn't even show. His fingers moved constantly as if he was playing piano scales, and he bounced, a boxer shadow boxing. Mixed metaphors for a mixed-up kid.

There was a gasp and a woman's voice filled the room. "What's wrong? What happened?"

Gabe turned to the door. Mitzi and her boyfriend stared in at the chaos.

"It's her fault!" Rock rushed toward Mitzi. "All that noise! All that yelling! It's her fault. Made Bette so nervous!"

Gabe grabbed the boy around the waist and lifted him off the ground. The kid weighed next to nothing. He looked at Mel. "Take him. He's yours."

Mel led Rock from the room and past Mitzi and her friend. As Rock passed, he stuck out his finger. "Your fault! I oughta sue!"

Mitzi leaned into her guy, and he pulled her close with an arm around her shoulders.

"I oughta sue," Rock yelled as Mel pulled him into his apartment.

"Yeah? Just try." Mitzi's scorn should have shredded Rock, but Mel's door closing cut off the conversation.

"Mitz, come on." She might look upscale tonight, but personality didn't change just because of pretty clothes and clean hair.

"He's an idiot. She's a skank."

Gabe sighed. "Did you ever think that God looks on the heart?"

"What?"

Gabe shook his head. Just because the verse about man looking on outward appearances but God looking on the heart crossed his mind didn't mean he should say anything.

But Mitzi was no mental slouch. "If God looks on their hearts, He'd probably find them missing."

Gabe didn't tell her he had been thinking of her, not the kids. "Good night, Mitzi."

"Yeah, yeah." She and her guy backed out of the way as Toby and Alicia wheeled Bette out of the apartment.

"She going to be okay?" She was so emaciated her body barely raised the blanket covering her.

Toby shrugged. "She'll survive tonight."

Gabe nodded. He understood what Toby wasn't saying. He shut the door behind them and looked around. He'd take the baggie of drugs to the state police lab for analysis. He recognized some of the pills—oxi, fentanyl—and figured the others were forms of knocked together methamphetamines or hallucinogens. The lab nerds would tell him for sure.

He fell into bed close to three. By 9:30 he sat, freshly showered, shaved, and dressed in Dockers and a plaid sport shirt and sweater. In front of him were ten fifth grade boys, his Sunday school class. The kids were a bunch of scalawags. There was no other word for it. He prayed each week that he could teach them one new thing about God. They seemed to counter his prayers with prayers of their own that they remain ignorant.

An hour later he slid into a pew next to Matt just in time for the worship service. He thought he might have taught them something this morning, but he'd probably have to wait about ten to fifteen years until a bit of maturity surfaced to know if he was correct.

"Hey." Matt elbowed him. "Isn't that your star player, the Loring kid?"

Gabe looked where Matt pointed, and there was Nick with Kenny right behind. Both boys were following Ellie down the aisle. They slipped into a pew, and in one of those strange things that happens sometimes in a crowd, he could see Ellie clearly, straight line of sight. Nick, taller than she, was lost behind the heads of others as was Kenny.

The service began, and Gabe did his best to concentrate on the singing and the message, but his eyes kept slewing to Ellie.

When she shrugged out of her black pea coat, she had on a pretty yellow jacket that looked great on her. Sitting relaxed and unaware of him, she sang with her eyes closed, concentrating on the words. Her black hair sat about her shoulders in a dark cloud, and he suddenly wondered what it would feel like to have one of her curls wind itself around his finger. He pictured her beautiful smile and remembered his gut-wrenching reaction to it. He hadn't responded to a girl or woman like this since he fell in love with Robyn.

Think gray. Think complicating secrets. Think bad for you. He forced his attention to the pulpit only to find the pastor leading in the closing prayer.

He was still thinking about how idiotically he was behaving when he crossed paths with Ellie on the sidewalk outside.

Smile, Ellie. Come on. Smile for me. You can do it.

"Hey, Coach." Nick grinned. "I thought I saw you here a couple of weeks ago, but then I didn't see you again, so I wasn't sure."

"Do you work some Sundays and not others?" Kenny pulled up the collar on his good looking faux leather jacket and slid his hands in the pockets.

"I'm on call Sundays. You know, if you zip that jacket up, it'll do you more good."

"Probably, Chief. I'm just trying to look cool." He leaned close and whispered. "I never had such a nice jacket before."

"Chief?" Was it his imagination or did the color drain from Ellie's face?

"Of Police," Kenny added.

Gabe nodded, reminding himself again how bad she was for him and his peace of mind. *Gray. She's gray.* "Just this year. Chief Gordon retired, and I got the job. But I rarely arrest people at church."

Somehow he didn't think Ellie found the comment funny.

"Gabe, introduce me." Matt walked up, unaware of the sudden tension pouring off Ellie like heat shimmers off a July sidewalk.

"My brother Matt," Gabe said. "Ellie and Nick Loring. And you know Kenny."

"Everybody knows Kenny," Matt said, shaking Kenny's hand.

"That's me, Mr. Popularity."

Matt grinned at Nick. "I wanted to tell you how much I enjoy watching you play."

Nick flushed with pleasure, and Ellie lit up with a mother's special pride. She never lit up like that for him, Gabe thought, suddenly grumpy.

Matt turned to Gabe. "Dad said we're to pick up the order Mom's calling in to Applebee's."

"She's too worn out from Clothes 2 Go to cook?" Gabe's grump deepened. He loved his mother's cooking.

"Hey, this is a Clothes 2 Go sweater." Kenny indicated his blue sweater as if they couldn't see it without help. "The jacket too. Ms. Loring got them for me."

"I met your mother." Ellie took her red beret from a pocket and pulled it on. "She's very nice."

"That she is," Matt agreed.

"I'm going—" Ellie began as two teenage girls walked by, their eyes on Nick. They were so determinedly casual that it was obvious they had planned their route very carefully. Gabe bit back a grin as they feigned surprise and said, "Nick! How are you?"

Nick smiled without interest. "Good."

"How you doing, Cheryl? Andrea?" Kenny asked the girls.

They ignored him as they waited for more from Nick. If Gabe gauged the kid correctly, they'd still be waiting at midnight.

Kenny made a face and said without rancor and to no one in particular, "Story of my life."

Ellie took advantage of the disruption, shooing the boys toward their car.

As the two men walked toward Gabe's car, Matt said, "She is very pretty,"

"Who?" As if he didn't know.

"Ellie, of course."

"Really? I didn't notice."

Matt laughed so hard Gabe thought his brother might never again catch his breath.

CHAPTER 17

"Mom, can we get the rest of Kenny's stuff now?"

"Like right this very moment?" Another week of Kenny living with them had passed, and if they hadn't needed it this past week, would they need it the coming week? Ellie put the last of the pans from their meal in the dish water. "Aren't you too tired from a hard game?"

Both boys frowned. Obviously they weren't tired. She was the one who was wiped out. All that breath holding and hand wringing as the kid got knocked around by guys eager for the glory of taking down Nick Loring was hard on a mother. But the season was almost over, only the Thanksgiving game left, and she'd have a respite of several months. She needed it.

She glanced at Kenny's hopeful face. "Why not?" She grinned at Kenny, and he grinned back. "Just let me finish here."

The drive across town took only a few minutes in spite of the rain that had begun to fall during dinner. They pulled up in front of the old Victorian and Kenny climbed out. "It won't take me long."

"I'll come with you and help carry stuff." Nick opened his door and climbed out, hunching against the rain.

"Uh, no thanks. I can manage." Kenny shot onto the porch stairs before Nick could argue.

That bad, eh? Ellie settled into the bend between the seat and the door, studying the house and the neighborhood as

Kenny disappeared inside. After hesitating a moment, Nick followed.

Ellie almost called him back, but she decided to let him do what he thought best.

As she scanned the area, she saw the same old man she'd seen other nights they dropped Kenny off. Tonight he was shambling along the pavement across the street. If he'd been female, she'd have called him a bag lady. His clothes were raggedy and looked much too light for the chill rain that was falling. He had an old newspaper wrapped around his shoulders as if it would protect him from the wet, and he wore a dark watch cap that he had pulled to his eyebrows.

He stumbled and went down on one knee, then seemed unable to rise.

Pulling her collar up and her beret down over her ears, Ellie climbed into the weather and crossed to him. She bent and looked into his bleary eyes. She had to blink against the alcohol fumes that hung in an invisible fog about him. She held out her hand. "Let me help you up."

He batted her hand away.

"Can I take you to your home or a shelter or something? Get you out of the weather?"

He stared bleakly at her and belched.

She kept her face carefully neutral and took his arm. "Come on. Up you go."

"Go 'way. Lea' me alone."

"I can't just leave you out here in the rain. You'll get sick. Pneumonia maybe or at the very least a terrible cold."

"Lady, go 'way." He pulled his arm from her grasp and climbed to his feet where he swayed like a windblown willow, amazingly supple in his movements. "I don' wan' help. I'm real happy as I am." Belch.

"Maybe you don't want it, but you need it."

"Ain't you the do-gooder." He curled his lip. "I hate goo-dooders."

"Let me take you to the mission. I bet they could take care of you. Give you something hot to eat and dry to wear."

"Lady, lea' me alone!" He gave her a little push.

Ellie took a step back, suddenly wary.

"Go 'way!" He took a threatening step toward her, one hand raised. "Ge' out before you ruin everything."

She raised her hands in a protective movement. "I'm sorry. I meant—" She didn't know what she meant. Feeling foolish, she turned and hurried to her car. Before she ruined everything? What did that mean?

And who was the man? She'd seen him here several times before. She went still as a thought hit her. Was he watching Kenny's house? She knew that Gabe was here frequently on police business. Maybe the drunk was watching to see when Gabe wasn't here. Maybe he was watching the house for some nefarious reason. But what?

She studied the house. Who lived here besides Kenny's mother? Or was he watching Kenny's mom, hoping for a time to talk with her? Was Kenny's mom a dealer? She knew the girl who lived here had overdosed last week. She'd seen it in the paper. Had Kenny's mom supplied her?

Or maybe the drunk was a dealer. Maybe he acted the fool so the police wouldn't suspect him, and he could make his drug deals. Maybe he had targeted Kenny, thought him vulnerable, and was waiting for a chance to get to him. Now that Kenny had come to their house, would the pusher come too?

Or was the man watching her? Ellie's breath rushed out on a whoosh as that thought rocked her. Had Joey somehow found her? Hired a private investigator? There were ten thousand reasons why she might be under scrutiny, and all of them were green and read In God We Trust.

She leaned her head back and looked toward the heavens. *Oh, Lord, can't life ever be simple?*

———

Only one more game, the big Thanksgiving one. Gabe took another bite of his Chinese takeout as he thought back over today's game with satisfaction. Another win. His phone rang and he quickly swallowed.

"Trouble, Hollis?"

"Nah. Just that black BMW is in front of Mitzi Uplander's again. What do you want me to do?"

"Nothing. Just keep an eye out. I'll be along in a couple of minutes." Mitzi and BMWs made his neck itch. He'd run the license when the guy was here last time, and there was no way a man like that should be interested in someone like Mitzi. Opposites might attract, but this was a case of poles apart. Jonesy was her style, not this guy. And he was here again.

He rubbed the back of his neck and took one last forkful. He'd just reheat the food whenever he got home. In the interest of making sure it still existed then, he picked up the dish, carried it to the kitchen, and shoved it into the fridge. Thomas looked at him with grave disappointment.

Gabe ruffled the dog's ears. "Sorry, chum. That's mine."

Thomas collapsed in a huff, his chin resting on his paws, his eyes sad as he watched Gabe grab a warm jacket. Gabe's conscience pricked as he watched the unhappy dog. "Want to ride along?" It wasn't like he was going on an official call.

The dog was on his feet in an instant, alert and eager. They walked to the car. Gabe opened the back door and Thomas jumped in. Gabe slid Thomas's seat restraint over his head and buckled him in. Then he got in and buckled his own restraint.

He sighed as he started downtown. He hated it when his instincts acted up.

Not that there was anything wrong with the car being parked on Main Street outside Mitzi's. It was more a matter of what was it—or more to the point its driver—doing there. Well, he had a good idea about that. Same as most of Mitzi's callers.

If it weren't for her history of execrable taste in men, Gabe wouldn't pay him any attention. It was the man's interest in Mitzi that made his spidey senses tingle with threat.

His hands-free phone buzzed as he turned onto Main. Hollis.

"Kenny Uplander and some kid just went inside the house," reported Hollis. "Their driver, some lady, is waiting for them at the curb."

Geez Louise. "Describe the kid."

"Big. Dark hair. Broad shoulders."

Gabe frowned. Nick Loring, ten to one. And the driver was Ellie.

He'd also spent a lot of time this week searching the internet for any indication of who Ellie Loring might be beyond Super Mom and Very Pretty Lady. There wasn't much information to be found, suspicious in itself. After trying Eleanor Loring, Ella Loring, Ellis Loring, Elaine Loring, Elena Loring, he'd tried Gabriella Loring at Dottie's suggestion and found a Sophia Gabriella Loring born thirty-three years ago, her Social Security number issued shortly after birth.

That was his Ellie, he was certain, but that was about all he found. Driver's licenses in Arizona, Colorado, and Washington. A new one issued a couple of months ago in Pennsylvania. No employment records, not terribly surprising since she was self-employed, but had she never worked for anyone but herself? She paid her taxes on time, always nice to know, and there were no outstanding warrants in her name in any law enforcement data bases.

Her landlord for the little two-bedroom house she was renting told him that she paid cash for her first month's rent and the two months he required against damages, and she made her continuing payments electronically from a recently opened account at the local credit union.

But no one could be quite that invisible without trying. Instincts again, the same ones that brought him out on this rainy Saturday night.

"Any special orders, Chief?" Hollis's voice over the phone sounded eager. "Should I question the lady in the car?"

Wouldn't Ellie love that. "Keep watching but be careful you aren't seen. I'm almost there."

Gabe ended the call and in a few minutes pulled his car behind Hollis's which was parked around the corner from Mitzi's in the shadows of the First Presbyterian Church.

"Back in a minute, boy," he told Thomas who sat at attention as he studied the street for someone or something suspicious to bark at. Gabe stepped in the chill air and the intensifying rain. He slid into the passenger seat of his patrolman's car.

"What's happening?"

"Nothing much." Hollis looked disappointed. "I was driving around, keeping my eye out for any trouble, when boom! This BMW pulls up in front of Mitzi's. So I called you 'cause I know you keep an eye on Mitzi and wanted to know if he showed up again. Then the kids arrived. Probably interrupted Mitzi's fun."

Gabe ignored Hollis's leer. "Thanks for the call. I'll take it from here." He reached for the handle, ready to climb out.

"The woman in the gray car?" Hollis asked. "Any idea?"

"Ellie Loring."

"Yeah, that's what I thought. Well, she got out of the car and crossed the street to help some old guy walking in the rain. I don't know what he said, but he sent her scurrying."

Gabe shook his head. What did she think she was doing? Trying to help a street person could be potentially dangerous and almost always thankless. He knew that from experience. Not that Lyndale had many street people, but the few who made the town their home liked to be left alone and didn't want help, not even shelter on a rainy night. And they didn't hesitate to tell you so in explicit and colorful terms.

Ellie the Tenderhearted probably got an earful. The woman seemed drawn to the needy. Kenny. The homeless man. Who else that he didn't know about?

He climbed out into the drizzle, and Hollis rolled quietly away into the night.

Gabe walked to the corner and looked toward Mitzi's. Ellie's gray car was parked behind the BMW. He had run her plates in his search for her identity and learned the old car she drove was registered to a Sophia Mancini of Philadelphia. Mrs. Mancini paid the registration yearly and had for several years. She had no presence on the internet, but since she was eighty-three, that wasn't surprising.

The coincidence that intrigued him most was the shared name. Sophia Mancini. Sophia Gabriella Loring.

One day soon he planned to visit Mrs. Mancini to see what he could learn about Ellie and her secrets. The thing was, there was no legal reason for this visit. Mrs. Mancini had done nothing wrong, nor had Ellie—that he knew of. Still he wanted to know who this old woman was and why Ellie was driving her car. The shades of gray around Ellie's life were driving him crazy. Give him trustworthy black and white. Or Robyn's sunshine yellow.

As Gabe watched from the shadows, Kenny came out of the house followed by Nick. Both carried plastic grocery bags stuffed fat with who knew what. Ellie hit the remote and popped the trunk. The boys dropped the bags inside and Nick slammed the lid.

Kenny said something, then ran back into the house. Nick climbed into the back seat. He and Ellie sat and waited.

———

Nick frowned in the silence of the car.

"It must look better than usual, Mom. Kenny just stood there in the living room, staring all surprised like. When his mom walked into the room, he grabbed her and hugged her and told her how pretty she looked."

"Did she?"

"She did. Her hair's all soft and shiny, and she was dressed nice and pretty too."

"Well, that's good, right?" Mom turned and looked over the seat at him. "Maybe she's finally getting her act together."

Nick shrugged. "Maybe. There's a guy up there visiting her. I didn't see him because he was in the bedroom or the bathroom. I think they're going out for dinner. That's his car, I think."

"Pretty slick car."

"Very slick car."

"Did you see Crazy Achmed?" Mom asked. "Was he peering out at you?"

"Yeah." Nick grinned. "Just like Kenny says. I raised my hand and waved and said, 'Hi, Mr. Achmed.' I thought it was best to leave off the *crazy* part."

"A show of good manners if ever I heard one. I'm so proud of you."

Nick grinned. He loved it when his mother was sarcastic. "Well, my good manners paid off. He opened the door wide enough to see all of him. He's slight and not very tall."

"Does his nationality match his name?"

"Yeah. He stared at me. 'How you know my name?' he demanded with this real heavy accent. Kenny was right behind me and we both started to laugh. He'd actually guessed the guy's name. So Kenny starts singing that line from the old *Cheers* reruns, 'Where everybody knows your na-a-ame.'" Nick tried to sing it, and the noise that came out made him doubly certain he wasn't going to let Kenny talk him into joining the choir. "And Achmed got this funny look on his face and slammed the door. Bang!"

"Did he think you were laughing at him, not the name coincidence?"

"Oops. I never thought of that."

"It's got to be scary coming to another country by yourself." Mom gave a little laugh. "It was hard enough going to Arizona, and they spoke the same language."

Kenny came running out of the house followed by a tall man dressed all in black. He even had a black fedora pulled low over his face to keep the rain off. Sort of like Indiana Jones meets the Caped Crusader, only without the cape or pointy-eared head piece.

Mom popped the trunk again.

Kenny, shoulders hunched against the weather, lifted the trunk lid. As he tossed his things in, Coach Hyland walked around the corner and started down the street toward them.

"Wonder what he's doing here?" Nick eyed him curiously.

Mom saw him and muttered something under her breath that sounded like, "Leader of the local Lollipop Guild."

It made Nick smile. She and the coach were like two people in some movie, driving each other crazy up until the big I-love-you scene. Matthew McConaughey and Kate Hudson or something. Now wouldn't that be a trip.

"I need to ask him about that man across the street." Mom pointed, but the man was gone. "See if he knows why he's here."

Kenny slammed the trunk. "Hey, Coach!"

Coach, his collar turned up against the rain, waved. "Kenny."

Nick buzzed his window down and Coach bent to peer in. "Ellie, Nick."

The man in black spun to see who Coach was talking to. "Ellie? Nick?"

Kenny pulled the car door open to climb in, and the interior light came on, shining down on Mom.

A car drove past, its lights illuminating the tall man in black.

Mom gave a soft cry and turned her head away.

Nick jerked and his breath caught in his suddenly dry throat. "Mom," he hissed. "It's Antony!"

CHAPTER 18

Antony! Here! Ellie thought she'd be sick and slapped a hand over her mouth.

Oh, Lord, no! Please, no!

She reached for the ignition. She had to get away. She had to save Nick.

Before she could even turn the key, Antony was standing beside her, looking down at her. Only a pane of glass separated her from Joey's best friend and her enemy.

Antony knocked on the window. "Come on, Ellie. Open up."

Ellie closed her eyes. *Lord, make him go away!* If he'd just disappear in a puff of smoke....

Antony knocked again, and she jumped as a hand closed over her shoulder. It was Nick, leaning forward, offering her comfort.

"Mom, it's okay. He can't hurt us anymore."

Did he mean Antony or his father? His father. While Antony would be happy to be the tattletale, he would never touch her or Nick. That privilege was reserved for Joey, and Antony knew it. "You aren't eighteen yet, Nick."

"But I'm not nine either. He can't hurt me. Or you."

She wished she believed him. With a heavy sigh and a feeling of inevitability, she lowered the window. The wind whipped rain into her face. Gabe had rounded the car and stood behind and beside Antony which made her feel a tiny bit less fearful. At least they were safe for the moment.

"Hello, Antony."

"Joey said you'd come back to see your nonna." Antony laughed. "The man is never wrong."

Ellie didn't say anything. Her eyes bumped into Gabe's alert ones, and she looked quickly away. If there was anyone on the face of the earth she didn't want to witness this confrontation, he would be the one. What little respect she had earned in his eyes was bound to disappear like smoke in the wind when he learned her history.

"Where you been all these years, Angel Eyes?" Antony demanded.

At the intimate-sounding nickname, Gabe seemed to go extra still and watchful.

"Wait until I tell Joey where you are." Antony laughed. "He's been going nuts looking for you for years."

Of course he had. She'd bested him, stood up to him and won, at least until tonight. Now she was found out. Fine shudders shook her, and she clutched the steering wheel so her shaking hands wouldn't give away her terror.

Antony bent down and peered over Ellie into the back seat, looking at the boys. "Which one's Nicky?"

She didn't answer.

Antony reached through the window as if to grab her and make her answer. Gabe's hand clamped on his wrist.

"I wouldn't touch her if I were you." Gabe's voice was steely.

"And who are you?" Antony demanded.

"Chief Gabriel Hyland, Lyndale PD."

"And that's supposed to scare me?"

"If you've got any smarts."

Antony studied Gabe who stared right back. Gabe was taller than Antony and broader in the shoulders. Since he often did drills with the team, he was in better physical condition. Antony looked like he'd been eating too many Terafino's hoagies, a little paunch pulling his black shirt taut beneath his unbuttoned jacket.

"Leave us alone, Antony," Ellie pleaded. "Forget you saw us. Please."

"You kidding? Joey wants his kid."

"He can't have him."

Up until now Antony had treated seeing her like winning the lottery. Big score for Antony! At her defiant words, his expression turned mean, the real Antony emerging. "You've had him all these years, lady. Now it's Joey's turn."

Every Mama Bear bone in Ellie's body stiffened. "Over my dead body."

Antony shrugged, a sneer curling his lip. "That can be arranged, I'm sure. Now which kid's Nicky?"

"I'm Nick," her son said from the back seat, his voice firm and so mature.

"No, I'm Nick," Kenny insisted, his voice weaker but adamant.

Ellie looked at Kenny in surprise. What was he doing?

"Well, you both can't be Nick." Antony squinted to see the boys better. "And this isn't *Truth or Dare.* Which one's Joey's kid?"

"Yoohoo, Tony." A pretty blonde woman stood on the porch, waving.

"Tony?" Ellie bit back a nervous laugh. No one called him Tony.

He gave Ellie an insolent look. "Some people are privileged." He turned toward the blonde. "Right here, Mitzi." He started toward the house, opening his umbrella as he went.

Leave! Now! But her hands were shaking too hard to grab the key, and she'd have to run over Gabe who stood beside her, rain dripping from the beak of his baseball cap.

Mitzi hurried down the steps and under the umbrella. She huddled close to avoid the rain, and Antony pulled her closer.

At the curb, he opened the passenger door and Mitzi slipped inside. He slammed the door and walked around the rear of the car. Just before he pulled the driver's door open, he turned to Ellie. Looking at her through the watery windshield, he raised his hand like a gun.

"Bang," he mouthed and smiled as Ellie flinched.

———

Gabe watched Ellie jerk at Morelli's parting shot. What was her history with the man? Whatever it was, it was obviously unpleasant.

He called her Angel Eyes, all in all not a bad nickname. Her dark eyes were gorgeous, large and luminous. Now they were wide with fear.

"Can you drive?" Gabe asked her.

She blinked and looked at him. It took a beat for her to focus. "Of course I can drive."

He nodded. "I'll follow you home."

"That's not necessary." All the barriers that had slowly come down over the three months he'd known her were being re-erected before his eyes. He wanted to tell her that he wasn't the enemy, but at the moment he suspected that anyone male was suspect.

"I'll follow you home," he repeated and walked away before she could object again.

Thomas gave a *woof* of welcome when he climbed in his car.

"We're going visiting," he told the animal. "You're going to love this crowd."

He'd thought the comment would be sarcastic, he'd planned it to be sarcastic, but somehow between his brain and his mouth it became all warm and toasty. He realized he did think Thomas would enjoy Ellie, Nick, and Kenny. Nicer people were hard to find, even if two of them were living—well, not exactly a lie, but not the whole truth either. Chances were Thomas would even love her cats though that affection might not be returned.

He pulled into the short drive of her tiny house and parked behind her gray Civic. He climbed out, and unhooked Thomas from his restraint. Before he could grab the dog's collar, he swept past Gabe and raced happily across the lawn to greet his new friends. He was a big animal and Gabe held his breath as he walked toward Ellie, Nick and Kenny, each holding a plastic bag of Kenny's belongings. He didn't expect the boys to be intimidated by Thomas, but he worried about Ellie. He watched as she rubbed the wriggling dog behind the ears. Upset as she was, she still paid attention to his dog. It said things about her that he liked.

"Well, Thomas, how nice to meet you," she said as she took the paw he offered.

Thomas obviously returned the thought, his tongue lolling happily as he stared at her with love-at-first-sight.

Nick squatted beside the dog who proceeded to wash his face. He said around a laugh, "He's great!"

"Big," Kenny said, not quite as enthusiastic as Nick. He patted Thomas's back tentatively. "Our cats are going to love him."

Kenny's ownership of the cats wasn't lost on Gabe. Ellie caught it too because she flicked the boy a quick, sad look, but when she turned to him, her face was wiped of all expression. Gone was the fear she'd shown when she recognized Morelli as well as the pleasure she'd shown when she loved on Thomas. It irritated him and he had to force himself not to scowl his displeasure.

"You didn't have to see us home," she said, voice cool and distant. "We're fine."

"Right, Angel Eyes."

She stiffened. "Don't call me that! Ever!"

Definitely a story here. He held up his hands. "Sorry. But I do want—need to talk to you about— " He twirled his hand vaguely. "—stuff."

She shook her head. "I want to be alone."

He took a step forward, but she did not move from her doorway.

"You can't force your way into a house without a warrant," she said quietly.

He blinked. Where had that come from? "Why would I want a warrant? You haven't done anything wrong."

She gave a half-hearted nod that made his stomach cramp with implications.

"But something *is* wrong."

"Go home, Gabe," she said quietly. "Please."

She tried to stare him down, but years of dealing with kids and crooks had made him a master of the stare down. After a minute she gave a little sigh and stepped inside without inviting him in but without slamming the door in his face. Taking that as permission to enter, he did. Thomas and the boys followed.

They stepped into a homey living room that he immediately felt comfortable in. He'd liked it the time he stopped to talk about that non-existent letter Nick hadn't shown him, but this time he looked around carefully. Now he knew her, and seeing her home gave him clues.

A gigantic leafy something sat on the edge of an end table, threatening to eat the brass lamp that had seen better days, its leaves looking as if they had been nibbled on frequently. A flat screen TV of modest size sat beside a bookshelf stuffed with books, a combination of colorful paperbacks and what appeared to be academic tomes. A wildly colored painting hung over the sofa. Straight back through an arch was the kitchen and to the side a short hall with three doors. He assumed two bedrooms and a bath. Compact but complete.

Two cats, one black, one gray, lay bonelessly on the back of the sofa. They raised lazy lids to see who was disturbing their rest, and decided to ignore Ellie, Gabe and the boys. Then Thomas, fresh from heeding nature's call, burst into the room, all good will and unbridled energy. He paused to shake off the rain.

The cats leaped to their feet, backs arched. Thomas spotted them and saw two new friends-to-be. He rushed to meet them, planting his front feet on the sofa seat and leaning close so they'd all be eye to eye. With a cry of outrage the black cat fled by way of the end table, almost upending the ragged plant. The gray one, trapped with Thomas inadvertently between it and the escape route, swatted at the dog, hissing and snarling. Thunderstruck, Thomas froze. The cat went up on its back legs and began punching with all the innate skill of a naturally talented boxer.

With each blow to his nose, Thomas was more stunned. Finally he looked to Gabe with a help-me-he's-picking-on-me expression, and the cat took advantage of the moment to leap past Thomas to safety. He followed the other into a bedroom.

"Shut the door, Nick," Ellie tipped her head in the direction the cats had fled.

Nick took the five steps necessary to reach the bedroom and pulled the door shut. Thomas, deeply shaken by the hostile encounter, went to Gabe for comfort.

"What a baby." Gabe checked the dog's nose for scratches. "You could have eaten him in one bite." He gave the dog a comforting head rub.

"In his dreams," Ellie said. "My money's on the cats."

"And rightly so," Gabe conceded as Thomas collapsed forlornly beside him.

"Give me your coat," Ellie said, holding out her hand. "And hat."

He felt a bolt of satisfaction. He was in and she wasn't hostile. Progress.

GAYLE ROPER

She took them and disappeared into the second bedroom. When she came back, she gestured toward the couch. "Have a seat while I get you something to drink."

"That'd be nice, thanks." He became aware of the quiet. "Where'd the guys go?"

"To the kitchen. They haven't eaten for at least an hour."

"Awful," Gabe said agreeably. "Who is Sophia Mancini?"

"My nonna." She spoke automatically, then assimilated the question. Her head spun toward him, her scowl fierce. "She's my grandmother. How do you know her name?"

"Your car registration."

"You've been checking on me?" She looked appalled and afraid. She studied the wild painting for a minute, turned and went to the kitchen.

The boys passed her, bags of snack food and glasses of lemonade in hand.

"We're going to watch some TV," Nick announced.

"Keep the volume down, okay?" Ellie called.

Gabe wandered to the kitchen archway and watched as, her back straight and her expression tight, Ellie opened the refrigerator and pulled out a pitcher half full of lemonade. It had real lemons floating in it. He wished he knew what she was thinking.

He stepped into the room and leaned against the counter. She refused to look at him. She put the pitcher down and opened the top cabinet. Neat rows of glasses sat on the second shelf. Gabe reached over her to retrieve two.

When he lifted his arm, Ellie cringed and put up a hand as if to ward off a blow.

Both of them froze.

Then Ellie's eyes filled with tears and she pressed a shaking hand to her mouth. "I'm—I'm sorry," she whispered. "I never thought...."

His heart hammered. Some of the answers at last? He waved a hand to ease her worry and embarrassment. "I know."

"I haven't flinched like that for years."

But she used to. "That guy tonight? Is he the one who hit you?" It was all he could do to ask the question in a calm voice. He wanted to strike something himself, preferably the man who had struck her.

She shook her head and reached for one of the glasses he held. Her hand was still shaking.

"Ellie." Gabe put the glasses on the counter. "Look at me."

"Would you like some pretzels?" she asked as if he hadn't spoken. "If the boys left any, that is."

"Look at me, El," he repeated, his voice soft.

She stopped in the process of pulling a crinkling bag from a cabinet, eyes fixed firmly on the Sourdough Specials label.

He took the bag and laid it on the counter. He turned her to him. He put a hand under her chin and watched her work up the courage to meet his gaze.

"It was seeing Antony tonight, right?" He knew that was the catalyst. "It brought back—what? Memories of some kind. Bad memories."

Her expression was bleak. "Very bad memories."

"Sit." He pushed her gently into a kitchen chair. With a resigned sigh, she let him. Gabe put the glasses and the bag of pretzels on the table and sat across from her. He purposely took a long drink of the cold tangy liquid to give her time to gather herself. He opened the pretzel bag and pulled out a couple he had no desire to eat.

"I feel like such an idiot." She grabbed a napkin from the holder and passed it to him, then took one for herself.

"Don't waste the energy," Gabe said. "Tell me who Antony is."

"A guy I knew growing up." She began shredding her napkin.

"Since Antony's got South Philly written all over him and I know he still lives there—"

"You know who he is?"

"I ran his plates the first time he showed. BMWs and Mitzi?" He shook his head. "Anyway I can assume you grew up there too?"

Ellie nodded. "I....used to work with Antony."

Gabe watched her closely. What she said was true, but it wasn't the whole truth. "You're not very good at dissimulation, El. I'd suggest you never go into a life of crime."

Her hands stilled and she glanced at him, then away. He studied her bent head, all too familiar with a guilty look from a normally innocent person. She went back to shredding while he pondered what was behind that expression.

"Antony is a tale bearer," she said. "He's going to tell people that he's seen me."

"People you don't want to know?"

She nodded.

"And you think they'll come after you."

"I know he will."

He. "Who? And why?"

Before she could answer, the thump of large boy feet sounded, and Nick and Kenny spilled into the room. Thomas, who had been lying beside Gabe, greeted them with a happy dance.

"They got the pretzels." Nick stated the obvious, either not sensing or ignoring his mother's distress. He reached over Ellie's shoulder and grabbed the bag. Kenny pulled out the pitcher of lemonade and refilled their glasses, leaving the pitcher on the counter.

Ellie got up and went to another cabinet. "Nick," she said and pointed to a top shelf. Nick sighed, reached up and pulled out a basket. Ellie lined it with a napkin and poured the bag of pretzels in it.

She set it on the table in front of Gabe. "I'm sorry. I should have done this sooner."

Gabe must have been wearing a bemused expression because Nick nodded like he understood. "It's a girl thing," he explained. "No matter how many times I say the bag is fine, she insists on the basket."

"Someday some girl is going to thank me for teaching you the finer points of life," Ellie said.

"Yeah, yeah. Come on, Thomas." Nick took his lemonade and a handful of pretzels and went into the living room, the dog trailing happily, eyes on the pretzels. Kenny threaded several pretzels onto his fingers, took his glass, and followed.

Gabe could hear Nick slapping the sofa cushion. "Come on, Thomas. Up you go. Good dog. You like pretzels?"

"At least poodles don't shed," Gabe said.

Ellie shrugged. "Not a problem if he did. Cats do."

Gabe grabbed a pretzel from the now nearly empty basket, surprised to realize he'd eaten the ones he'd taken earlier. "Ellie, we have to talk." He kept his voice gentle.

She sighed. Her face was pale.

"What was his name?" Gabe asked.

"Antony Morelli."

"Not Antony. I already know that. The other guy."

She sighed. "Joey Terafino."

"Ex-husband? Ex-boyfriend?"

"Boyfriend. Nick's father." She shook her head. "It's so hard to believe that part of my life ever really happened. It's embarrassing to think I was that stupid."

"Nick's how old? Seventeen? And you're what? Early thirties? You were only a kid when you got involved."

"Younger than Nick is now, and I thought I knew so much." She studied her pile of shredded napkin. "You know, it's a wonder any of us grow up, given how stupid we were when we were young."

He ached for her, so clearly hurting from the consequences of bad choices made long ago. Her beautiful eyes were full of pain and regret. They were also full of experience and resilience.

"I started dating Joey when I was thirteen and he was fifteen. I got pregnant at sixteen, and we moved in together against my grandmother's wishes. My parents were already dead. My grandfather too. Had they lived, things would have been different, I'm sure. But I knew what I was doing. Isn't that what all kids who make bad choices think at the time?"

"When did he start to hit you?"

"He came from an abusive family. He used to have terrible marks on his back from his father's belt." She got a distant look. "Mr. Terafino was murdered, beaten to death. Joey found him behind their deli." She paused. "Nonna thinks he did it."

"Ellie!" Not that he was scandalized at a murder. But she'd lived with a murderer?

Ellie shrugged. "Nonna may be right. He hated his father enough." She studied her hands. "And now he hates me."

"For taking Nick."

She nodded. "And for besting him. No one bests Joey Terafino."

"Except you."

"Nonna and me. I sometimes wonder how long I'd have stayed if he hadn't hit Nick. Nick was nine the first and only time, and the moment that happened, I knew I was out of there."

"How did you get away?"

"That night I hit Joey over the head to keep him from hitting Nick again. I knocked him out and we ran to Nonna's."

"I'd say it served him right."

She snorted her surprise and slapped a hand over her mouth to smother the noise.

He gave her a wry grin. "Not very law and order of me. Sorry. What did you hit him with? It's not easy to knock someone unconscious."

"A statue of the Virgin Mary Nonna had given us."

In spite of himself, Gabe had to smile.

She glared at him. "It's not funny."

"Have you ever run that scenario in your mind like a movie trailer?"

"Okay, maybe it is sort of funny, but it's not like I planned it. She was just handy. After that, I knew I could never be alone with Joey again. We left the next day."

"How did you manage? Did you go to the police? Report the abuse?"

She shook her head. "It was too embarrassing, and he didn't hit me that often."

She put up a hand when he started to speak. "I know. One time is too many. I'm talking about how I thought back then."

Gabe's heart twisted at the thought of this woman being yelled at, ordered about, struck. "You know these guys rarely change. They think they have the right to assert their authority by any means they deem necessary."

"He used to tell me how stupid I was, especially with numbers."

"You are not stupid."

She nodded. "I know that now, but I do have dyscalculia issues. Number inversion problems and sequencing. It happens if I'm not careful and even when I am."

"I never heard of dyscalculia."

"It's the numbers equivalent to dyslexia. He used my disability to control the money. It wasn't until I'd been on my own for several years that it dawned on me that I was managing my money and doing fine. I paid our bills. I kept my budget. I had to double and triple check everything and make certain I used a calculator, but I was doing fine. And I saw another sign of Joey's manipulation for what it was. But when I was in the middle of it …."

"My experience as a cop has been that most women don't have the emotional or financial resources to escape. There's no one to help them because the guy isolates her. There's no place to go and no funds to get there even if she had a place. Money's a big control thing for these men."

"Are all these guys charming to everyone but their woman? Everyone at the deli thought Joey was the greatest guy going."

"It's a characteristic many of them have. As a result everyone thinks the woman has problems. Even she thinks it's somehow her fault."

"Nonna believed me and she helped. She bought me a car. I didn't even know it until I told her I was leaving. She'd bought it three years previous so it'd be there when I got smart. Nick and I climbed in, and we drove and drove and ended up in a little town in Arizona across the street from a little church that changed my life."

Her eyes lit up as she talked about the church and the pastor and the Nativity scene that led her to Jesus.

"We still deal with the consequences of my choices every day, and I regret that, especially for Nick's sake, but the worst of the guilt is gone. The Great Burden Bearer has taken it from me."

Gabe took one of her hands and enfolded it in his. "You are a remarkable woman, Ellie Loring."

She flushed and tried to withdraw her hand. He held on.

"What's your real name, by the way?"

"Ellie Loring is my real name, my birth name. Sophia Gabriella Loring. I went by Gabriella Francella for years, from when I was four on when my mom married my stepfather, but nothing was changed legally. Gabriella Francella is how everyone in the neighborhood knew me."

"Including Joey?"

"Including Joey."

"No wonder he couldn't trace you. What's Nick's real name?"

"Dominic Vittorio Terafino."

Nick appeared in the doorway to the kitchen. "You told him our names?"

Ellie shrugged. "Why not after tonight?"

Nick gave her a huge smile. "Why not?"

CHAPTER 19

Joey lay comfortably on the black leather sofa watching the third of the Godfather movies. He liked this one because everyone got what they deserved. It was just like Sister Maria Angelica used to say in school, "Be sure your sins will find you out."

He smiled. No matter how many times he watched it, there was a great satisfaction in the lonely Michael Corleone falling off that chair at the end. But the story wasn't there yet. He had to be patient.

"You like the massage, Joey?"

Joey blinked and looked at the young thing kneading his feet. He'd all but forgotten she was there. Thoughts of revenge and just desserts were so much more satisfying than bimbos.

"Wonderful, baby." He grinned as he tried to remember her name. "You got great hands."

She simpered and he went back to the debacle at the opera house, bodies falling left and right, including Michael's beloved daughter.

The door flew open and Antony came rushing in trailing his latest babe, a bottle blonde named Mitzi.

"Have I got news for you!" Antony announced, so excited he was bouncing on the balls of his feet.

"At one in the morning you got news? It couldn't wait until tomorrow? I got company." He flicked a hand at Harper who got off the floor and climbed onto the sofa beside him, wrapping her arms around him like a skinny octopus.

Antony stopped in front of him, waves of self-satisfaction flowing from him. "I found her."

Joey felt his whole body suspend animation for a moment. His heart forgot to beat. His blood stilled in his veins. His nerve synapses stopped jumping and sending signals. His brain went blank.

Then everything kicked into overdrive. His heart pounded, his vision sharpened, his mind raced. It was like thoughts of revenge and just desserts had conjured her up. Joey pulled his feet from Hayley—that was her name—and stood.

"Where?"

"Lyndale."

"Where?"

"Lyndale. You know, out in Chester County not too far from Antonio's. It's where Mitzi lives."

"Lyndale." Joey became thoughtful. Small town. Small police force. Small time cops.

"I went to pick Mitzi up tonight and guess who's there, right outside Mitzi's house sitting in an old beat-up Civic? Ellie. And Nick."

"And Kenny," Mitzi added.

Joey didn't care in the least about Kenny, whoever he was— unless he was Ellie's new man. "Who's Kenny?"

"My son."

"Ah." Joey brushed Kenny aside and focused on Antony. "She was just sitting there? Waiting for you?" He couldn't believe it. After all these years! Had she been this close all the time?

"Waiting for Kenny," Antony said. "He lives with Ellie."

Joey eyed Mitzi. Why didn't the kid live with his own mother? But that was a puzzle for another day. Tonight he was concentrating on what counted: Nick.

"How's he look? Is he a big kid? Is he smart? Is he—" Joey couldn't think of anything else to ask because the most important question filled his mind. "Where can I find him?"

"Where does he live, Mitz?" Antony asked.

Her face went blank. "I don't know. Somewhere in Lyndale."

"You don't know where your kid is?" Joey couldn't believe it. Antony'd picked another winner.

Mitzi looked affronted. "Of course I do. He's in Lyndale."

"With Ellie." Joey shook off Hadley and walked over to the window. He looked down on South Street where clubs and restaurants were making the most of the last hour before closing. The street teemed with people enjoying their version of Saturday night sin.

Eight years and he finally had her. Eight long years and he was mere hours from seeing Nicky.

"Mitzi says he calls himself Nick Loring."

Joey turned from the window. "Loring? What kind of a name is that?"

"Not Italian," Antony said. "That's all I know."

Joey had to grin. Antony looked so proud of himself, like a little kid who'd beaten everyone else in a foot race.

"You did good, Antony. Who'd have believed it, huh?" Joey indicated Mitzi. "You better hold onto her. She's obviously good luck." Dumb broad.

Mitzi beamed, and Harley—Harper—Hayley, yeah, that was it, looked confused. That was the trouble with liking them young. They never understood about history. "Go home, Harper."

"Hayley." How come he never noticed how squeaky her voice was before?

"Right. Go home, Hayley."

"It's raining." And whiney.

"You melt? Go home." The last was a roar, and Hayley couldn't run away fast enough. He glared at Antony and Mitzi.

He wanted them to go too. He wanted to be alone to plan. To dream of seeing his Nicky.

He'd bring him here. That second bedroom, sitting empty as a constant reminder of what was missing in his life and who was to blame, was about to get some use.

Anticipation unfurled in his chest. *I'm coming, Nicky!*

On a snarl, he added, *I'm coming, Ellie.*

CHAPTER 20

"Hi, up there."

Avery looked down and saw Ms. Loring looking up.

"Hi," she called back. Sunday afternoon was her favorite time to tree sit. Nick was home and Mom and Daddy went to the Country Club to golf and Mrs. Cotton took a long nap. Nobody cared what she did. Unless Ms. Loring did. Avery frowned, trying to read her expression.

It was very distressing that the leaves were almost all gone. Even though she'd worn her camo shirt and pants, she was way too obvious. It was her white face. She'd picked a branch to sit on that let the trunk come between her and her own house, but that made her face easy to see from the Lorings'. She needed camo face paint, but the chances of getting someone to buy that for her were zero, zip, zilch.

"Not ladylike, Avery," Mom would say.

"You look bad enough already, Avery," Daddy would say.

Of course her parents would want to know why she needed it.

"So I can sit in the tree and spy without being seen." Yeah, they'd love that.

Avery peered at Ms. Loring who was carrying a small step ladder like Mrs. Cotton used in the kitchen to reach the top shelves.

"Look what I've got." Ms. Loring set it against the tree and Avery realized she was going to climb right up! She couldn't believe it. She'd thought that failed attempt last Sunday was just that, a failure she'd walk away from.

But no. Ms. Loring climbed the little ladder, easily reached the lower limbs, and began very carefully picking her way up.

"Don't look down," Avery called. "Look up so you can pick your hand holds."

"I've got to look down to see where to step," came a muffled answer as Ms. Loring looked down to see where to put her foot. In a short time she was sitting one branch below Avery, her arm wound tightly around the trunk.

"It doesn't look this high from the ground." She didn't look very happy to be so high.

"Don't be scared," Avery told her. "I come up here all the time, and nothing's ever happened."

"Yeah, but you don't weight quite as much as I do."

Did she think her branch was going to break under her? Avery giggled. Her tree would never do something as thoughtless as give way.

"Hello, up there!"

Avery looked down and saw a man wearing a baseball cap that read Lyndale staring up at them.

"Yikes!" Ms. Loring said and made a funny face.

"Who's he?" Avery whispered.

"Mr. Hyland," Ms. Loring whispered back.

"What's he doing here?"

"I don't know. Maybe he wants to see Nick."

"Why?"

"He's the football coach."

The tree began to shake, and Avery couldn't believe her eyes. The man was climbing the tree.

Ms. Loring gasped and hugged the trunk as if she'd fall if she didn't. "Wh-what are you doing?" she called down. "The tree's going to topple over!"

Mr. Hyland laughed as he quickly and easily scrambled to a large branch halfway between Avery and Ms. Loring. He sat with his leg dangling and smiled at them both.

"Ladies, so good to see you."

"You've climbed lots of trees," Avery said, admiring the way he was so easy up here.

"Lots back in the day," he agreed. "My brother Matt and me, sometimes my sister Dinah and even Gracie though she never went very high."

"You got brothers and sisters?" As an only, Avery couldn't think of anything cooler.

"One brother and two sisters. You?"

"I'm a singleton." That's what Daddy called her.

"Sorry about that. What's your name?"

"Avery."

"Nice to meet you, Avery. That's a neat name."

"What's yours?"

"Gabriel."

"Like the angel?" She'd heard about the angel on TV. "Is he real?"

"The angel? Yep, he is. But people usually call me Gabe."

"Avery calls you Mr. Hyland," Ms. Loring scowled at him. "And hold on. You've got to hold on."

Instead of holding on, he turned on his branch and leaned his back against the trunk and stretched a leg along the limb.

"Show-off," Ms. Loring said through gritted teeth.

"Hey, up there!"

Avery looked down, and this time it was Nick and Kenny staring up at them.

"Mom?" Nick started to laugh. "Coach?"

"Hi, Avery." Kenny waved at her.

Next thing Avery knew, Nick and Kenny were climbing the tree. Nick was a lot better at it than Kenny. Ms. Loring made a funny noise and closed her eyes.

"We're all going to die," she muttered. "The tree's going to fall over and squish us all."

Mr. Hyland laughed at her. "Not us, right, Avery?" He looked at her with a huge grin. "You picked a very sturdy tree. At least I assume you're the one who picked it, not Ms. Loring."

Avery nodded. "I picked it."

"I knew it. I know a smart kid when I see one."

A smart kid? Avery's heart hammered. He liked her name and he thought she was a smart kid! He was way too old for her, and she planned to marry Nick if she could manage it, but her heart tumbled at Mr. Hyland's feet.

The tree finally stopped shaking, and Ms. Loring opened her eyes. She looked down at Nick and Kenny sitting on branches just below her. A loud crack made her scream.

Avery didn't roll her eyes because that would be impolite, and Ms. Loring had been nice enough to climb up even though she was scared. But then Avery'd seen Nick reach behind him and snap a small branch.

Mr. Hyland reached to Ms. Loring and pulled one of her hands from its death grip on the trunk. He wrapped his large hand around hers. "It's okay, Ellie," he said in a kind voice. "It's just your son having his version of fun."

"What?" Ms. Loring glared down at Nick who grinned up at her.

"Sorry, Mom. Couldn't resist."

"Yeah, right." Then she seemed to realize Mr. Hyland was holding her hand. She blushed, something that fascinated Avery because she didn't realize that adults turned red like that. She thought it was only kids like her. With a tug Ms.

Loring pulled her hand free. But she didn't hug the tree so hard after that.

"What are you doing here, Coach?" Nick asked.

"I just thought I'd join a pair of beautiful ladies for a relaxing afternoon," he said, smiling first at Ms. Loring, then at Avery.

He smiled at me! And he called her beautiful.

Avery knew he was just teasing, at least about her because she wasn't beautiful even though Ms. Loring was. Still a warm glow slid through her.

God, this is so much fun! I think maybe You are hearing me when I talk to You after all.

CHAPTER 21

Somehow Ellie found herself playing football with Nick, Kenny, Avery, and Gabe.

"You're on my team, Ellie." Gabe said as he grabbed her hand.

"What?" she said, trying to ignore how warm his grasp was, how good it felt. "You want a guarantee that you'll lose?"

He grinned as he led her across the back yard. "I don't think winning or losing is going to be an issue here. Look at our opponents."

She looked at the triple threat of Nick, Kenny, and Avery. "Point taken."

Kenny handed the football to the little girl. "Avery, you're our quarterback."

"Me?" the little girl squeaked. "No way. I see football on TV. The plan is always to kill the quarterback. I'll be a cheerleader even though I'm not a pink girl."

"What do you mean, you're not a pink girl?" he asked.

She looked embarrassed and studied the ground. "You know. Pink girls are thin and pretty. Pink girls are popular. Pink girls are cheerleaders."

"Well, we don't want pink girls or cheerleaders in our game," Nick said. "We want you."

"We like cammie girls in cool cammo clothes," Kenny said.

Ellie's heart swelled with pride at the guys and their kindness to a sad little girl.

She looked at Gabe to see if he realized how special those two were. He was smiling, so she knew he got it. "I can't decide whether Nick knows that Avery spies on him or not."

Gabe barked a laugh. "She spies on him?"

"Why do you think she's up in the tree all the time? And she hides in the hedge sometimes too."

"Poor kid," Gabe said.

"I know. I don't think she has much of a life."

"I meant Nick. Having all the girls chasing him must be so terrible."

Ellie heard the tongue firmly in his cheek. "You should know. I bet that was you in your day."

"Hardly. I was a one-woman man, and everyone knew it."

A one-woman man. She tried to imagine what it would be like to have a man like Gabe Hyland be your one-woman man. She doubted she'd ever be so lucky.

"I hear there's a cheerleader named Stephanie in Nick's life these days."

Ellie studied him. "And just how do you know this?"

"The locker room is an interesting place."

She nodded. "My source is Kenny."

"Here we come, ready or not," Nick called.

"I came to ask you a question." Gabe talked to her over his shoulder as he assumed a football stance.

"Yeah?" She bent at the waist, but that was as football-y as she got.

"You busy—"

"Go, Avery, go!" Kenny yelled as Avery tucked the football close and ran. Nick blazed a path for her, running as slowly as he could. Ellie giggled at what looked like slow motion, especially compared to Avery's churning legs. Gabe artfully missed a tackle and Ellie didn't even try.

"Go, Avery," she yelled. "Yay for the girls!"

Avery started giggling so hard she could barely run. Nick finally picked her up and carried her over the goal line.

Everyone cheered as Avery scored. Nick held her high, spinning with her in a victory dance. The little girl smiled so broadly it was a wonder her face didn't split.

A voice barked, "Avery Mulholland!" Everyone froze.

Avery's parents stood at the edge of the hedge, frowns of disapproval on their faces. Ellie's heart broke as the girl's smile vanished and she looked hounded. Nick lowered her to the ground, and without a backward glance, she ran for home.

"We had a great time with her," Ellie called, waving. "She's a wonderful kid."

"Inside, Avery," her father ordered, not bothering to lower his voice, not bothering to acknowledge Ellie.

"Mrs. Cotton was worried about you," her mother said. "That wasn't very nice of you to upset her."

"I was just playing."

Ellie couldn't fault Avery the whine. She'd whine too if people spoke to her like that.

Gabe muttered, "Talk about killjoys. I see what you mean about her not having much of a life."

"Smile and wave," Ellie instructed him, and to her surprise he did.

"Have fun storming the castle," he called, and Ellie rolled her eyes.

Suddenly Avery stopped and turned. "As you wish," she quoted back.

Nick and Kenny started laughing while Mr. Mulholland pointed a stern finger to the house. Avery raced inside, but Ellie loved the girl's mini declaration of independence.

"You're a nice person, Ellie Loring, giving that little girl such a fun time," he said.

"We all played with her."

"Yeah, but you started it by climbing that tree. Like I said, nice. Can't say that was my first impression—"

"I wonder why." Ellie shook her head as she remembered the shrew who had rushed into his office ready to draw and quarter him.

He grinned. "—but my opinion's slowly changed."

He really had lovely blue eyes.

Gabe's mouth turned up on one side, and Ellie realized she'd been staring. She looked quickly away, flustered and embarrassed.

As Kenny and Nick raced up, Gabe leaned in and said for her ears alone, "It's okay. I like looking at you too."

She had time to shoot him a quick startled glance before Nick demanded, "When's dinner?"

Ellie looked at her watch. "Soon." Which, as Nick knew, was code for anywhere in the next two hours.

"Want to stay, Coach?" Nick asked. "We're having Nonna's baked ziti."

"It's ambrosia," Kenny said, kissing his fingertips.

"What are you doing?" Nick asked Kenny. "Practicing to be Italian?"

Kenny shrugged and flicked his fingers over his cheek ala *The Godfather* movies. "Why not? I wanna be an honorary goombah."

"So can you stay, Coach?" Nick asked again.

"I wish I could."

Ellie felt a shaft of disappointment, startling in its intensity.

He looked at Ellie. "I think—I hope—I have an alternative dinner date tonight."

Ellie's breath caught. Did he mean—?

"Do I, Ellie?"

As she nodded and tried not to grin too broadly, she felt Nick's eyes flick from her to Gabe and back.

"Okay," Nick said, the speculation in his narrowed eyes as thick as old Mr. Palermo's accent. "Maybe another time."

"Another time," Gabe said firmly, his eyes never leaving Ellie.

"Late game should still be on, Kenny," Nick said.

"Yeah, I can study camera angles."

"Who watches football to study camera angles?" Gabe muttered.

"You're the guy who made him the videographer," Ellie reminded him.

The boys disappeared into the house, and silence descended on the yard. Ellie pulled her beret down over her ears and waited. She was afraid to say anything for fear she had misunderstood Gabe. And if she hadn't, how could she leave Nick now that Joey knew their location?

"Will you go out for dinner with me tonight?" Gabe stepped closer. "Much as I like Nick and Kenny, I'd rather talk with you. Only you."

Warmth spiraled through her. He wanted to spend time with her, just her. But her past reached out to ruin this evening as it had ruined so many things over the years.

"I'm worried about Joey," she said. "What if he shows up now that he knows where we live?"

Well, he didn't know their address specifically, and since they weren't in the phone book because they didn't have a land line, he couldn't find her that way. But the ever-handy internet would cough up the information in way less than a minute now that he had the name Loring.

"Do you honestly think anyone is going to make Nick do something he doesn't want to do or go someplace he doesn't want to go?" Gabe asked.

She shrugged, wanting to be convinced but not quite there.

"Talk with him about it. Tell him what concerns you. And remember Kenny's here."

"A witness to whatever happens." That thought eased some of her tension.

"*If* anything happens, which I strongly doubt." Gabe smiled reassuringly. "And we won't be gone that long."

She still hesitated.

"He's got a cell phone, doesn't he? He can call you if Joey shows up. He can call the station if there's a problem. Hollis will come out and Dottie will call me. He'll be all right, El."

"You probably think I'm over-reacting, that I'm being over-protective."

"I don't. But I do think things aren't as they were. Nick makes a valid point when he talks about his size and age changing things."

She bit her lower lip as she tried to think through the twin antitheses of responsibility and yearning, then slowly nodded. "Okay."

He grinned. "Six-thirty?" He looked down at himself. "I have to go home and get cleaned up a bit."

"Six-thirty sounds fine." She tried to remember the last time she'd had a date—and this had to be classified as a date unlike the other dinner the night they talked about recruitment. That was just a casual I'm-going-to-eat-want-to-come-along thing.

"Wear something nice. I'd like to try the new restaurant everyone's talking about."

"Anywhere's fine with me. All I ask to make it a great night is someone else doing the cooking."

You mean we could have done Chick-fil-a?"

"Not open on Sundays. Besides I've got a new skirt I've been dying to wear." Gotten at Clothes 2 Go, but he didn't need to know that.

As he drove away, she hugged herself and held close the memory of his hand on hers. As she fed the ravening beasts who lived with her, feline and human, she recalled his confession of liking to look at her.

Lord, is this really happening? It seems too good to be true.

As the boys ate, she hurried into her room and shut the door. She pulled on her new skirt, smoothing it over her hips, adjusting it even though it didn't need adjusting. It was just a repurposed black knit with a flip at the knee length hem, but it was new to her.

She slipped her arms into the red faux suede blazer she'd also found at Clothes 2 Go. When she checked herself in the mirror, she didn't think Gabe would be embarrassed to be seen with her. At least her hair looked good. She never knew from shampoo to shampoo exactly what it would do, but tonight it cooperated and fell in soft curls about her shoulders.

She added silver-toned hoops and a silvery bangle to match the silver buttons on the blazer and did another slow turn in front of the mirror. Did her shoes look as bad as she thought? The only good thing that could be said for them was that they looked better than the sneakers she wore for work.

Her stomach was a mass of nerves. She sat on the edge of the bed and took several deep breaths to calm herself. In spite of her growing attraction to Gabe, he scared her. Not that she thought he would physically harm her in any way like Joey, but he was a cop. He enforced the law, and the bottom line was, she was a thief. A thief who might be able to justify her actions, but still someone who took what wasn't hers.

As if Gabe's profession wasn't enough, he himself was more than enough. The thought of spending the evening with just him made her shiver with anticipation even as she told herself he was dangerous.

Don't get too swoony, girl. It's just dinner.

The doorbell rang and she jumped. She heard the boys rush to answer.

"Hey, Coach," they said, practically in unison. She could hear the laughter in their voices. To them this date thing might be funny, but to her it was terrifying. Wonderful but terrifying.

Ellie walked into the small living room, stepping over the cats who sat in the bedroom doorway eyeing Gabe warily, ready to run if his dog followed him in. Gabe, Nick and Kenny turned toward her and stared. She gave a smile, trying to project serenity and confidence, two commodities she felt sadly lacking. Maybe she needed to get dressed up a bit more often if this was the surprised response.

"You've got legs, Mom," Nick said.

Yep, she definitely needed to. "I find them handy to have around."

"And quite attractive too," Gabe said gallantly. He looked wonderful in a navy blazer and gray slacks, his open collared blue dress shirt making his blue eyes even lovelier than usual.

He pointed to the swirl of color hanging over the couch. "That's a great picture. I meant to tell you last night, but I got sidetracked."

"Mom did it," Nick said. "She's really talented. She's a great cook and a great housekeeper too."

Ellie stared at her son. He sounded like a seller at a horse auction, reading off a mare's strengths with the hope of a sale. Next thing she knew, he'd have Gabe checking her teeth.

Ellie pulled her coat from the closet, but before she could put it on, Gabe took it. He held it for her, and swallowing her delight, she slipped her arms in the sleeves. She hadn't realized she was such a sucker for a man with manners.

"This is how a gentleman does it, guys." Gabe settled the coat on her shoulders.

"Huh," was the boys' underwhelmed response. Apparently she had a bit more work to do in the etiquette department.

Nick made a big show of pointing to his watch. "Make sure you have her home by curfew," he said sternly.

Ellie shook her head at her son who grinned back.

"No problem," Gabe said. "I'll take good care of her."

Ellie felt a fizz along her nerve endings at Gabe's casually spoken words. No one had taken care of her in years. She was the care giver, the worrier, the problem solver. Someone being concerned for her wellbeing sounded absolutely intoxicating even if it was only for an evening.

But, she wondered as they walked to the door, while he was busy looking out for her, what in the world would they talk about? She had nearly hyperventilated over this thought as she dressed. Her knowledge of football only went so far, and certainly he didn't want to debate the merits of one cleaning solution over another. Or Van Gogh vs. Matisse vs. Monet vs. Pollock. Did she know anything else?

Her step faltered. Forget this dating. It was too loaded with stress. Besides Nick needed her.

Maybe Gabe sensed her wavering because he took her elbow and hurried her out the door. Rain again. So her hair had looked good for five minutes. It was anyone's guess what it would look like by the time they reached the restaurant.

He had an umbrella waiting on the stoop. As he ushered her to the car and into her seat, he kept her dry beneath it. Once in her seat she looked back at the house and saw the boys watching avidly.

"This is so weird!"

Gabe slipped into his seat and inserted the key. "What is?"

She pointed from herself to him, then to the boys. "Isn't it?"

"Only if you let it be."

"You don't mind a pair of grinning kids who can't wait to tell your team anything they can glean?"

"Ellie, after years of dealing with kids and criminals, there's very little that shakes me."

"Lucky you."

He laughed. "Relax. You just need some good food."

When they pulled into the restaurant's lot, the rain was coming down so hard it was like trying to see thorough frosted glass. Indistinct images loomed up suddenly and became cars or in one case a man loping toward the eatery's front door.

Gabe pulled under the restaurant's awning. "I'll let you out here and go park." He handed her the umbrella.

"You keep it," she said. "You're the one who's going to need it." She climbed out and waited for him just inside the door. He walked in, looking too handsome for her peace of mind with moisture gleaming on his blonde head and his smile aimed directly at her.

"You're getting curlier by the moment." She had to grin.

He reached up and ran a hand through his hair. "Tell me about it. My sisters have straight hair. So does Matt. Why I got the curls, I'll never know, but I'd be happy to be rid of them."

"Not manly enough?"

"We have pictures of me with my hair in ringlets that Mom says she used to brush around her finger like it was a curling wand. Do you have any idea what that does to my macho sensibilities?"

"Well, give it time and you might be fortunate enough to go bald."

He laughed. "Now there's a thought."

Ellie relaxed a little. She'd made him laugh. Maybe she could manage this dating after all.

They followed the hostess to their table set with ecru linen, fine stemware and silver. In its center was a round vase of mixed roses and a low faceted glass container holding a flame. The restaurant was softly lit, not so dark you couldn't see the menus and your dinner companions, but not garish and bright like bistros.

Soft classical music flowed in and around the muted conversations at each table.

"This is wonderful!" Ellie hugged the elegance tightly. Had she ever eaten in so fine a place?

The hostess handed them leather bound menus and stepped away. A silent young man in black pants, white shirt, black tie, and a white apron appeared, poured water, and left a dish of pita chips and another of a black olive pesto.

"My nonna used to make a pesto like this." Ellie ignored the menu and scooped a bit onto a piece of pita. The first taste brought a rush of memories. "It's like being in Nonna's kitchen."

Gabe took a pita and scraped on some pesto.

"Not too much. It's a strong taste, especially first time out."

He let some fall back into the dish, then bit. He chewed slowly. "You grew up with things like this? You are one fortunate person. It's delicious."

"I can't get over how much it's like Nonna's. But maybe it's faulty memory. I haven't tasted hers in years."

"She didn't give you the recipe?"

"I never thought to ask for it. I must before—" Ellie stopped and swallowed. She forced a smile. "I can't imagine why I never thought to make it myself."

Gabe slipped his hand over hers and gently squeezed. She looked up, surprised at his sympathy.

"Losing someone you love is very painful," he said simply.

"Robyn."

He nodded. "How do you know about Robyn?" He spoke with curiosity, not like he thought she was invading his privacy.

"Your mother told me, and I saw a picture of the two of you at your mother's." Ellie took another piece of pita and pesto for something to do with her hands. "She was very beautiful."

Gabe smiled. "She was. If she was a color, she'd have been yellow, all sunshine and joy."

Ellie wondered what color he'd think her. He was a strong sturdy sapphire blue, not as garish as a royal blue or as muted as a navy. Color #1974D2. Sort of what Crayola called Bright Navy Blue but not as dark as we think navy. "You must miss her dreadfully."

He gave a little shrug. "Five years is a long time to get used to the hole in your heart."

Ellie swallowed. Even in her wildest daydreams, she knew she'd never fill a hole of that magnitude. On a deep internal sigh she turned to the young woman with an order pad standing at the table. "I haven't even opened the menu."

"Nor have I," Gabe said. "Do you like calamari?"

Ellie nodded and Gabe ordered some.

"I have a grandmother too," Gabe said, and Ellie was happy to leave the ghost of sunshine-y Robyn. "Her goal in life is to live long enough to marry all four of us kids off. My parents seem content to wait for nature to take its course, but Grandma has made our marital happiness her crusade. 'Gabe, forget the bad guys and the football guys and go find yourself a nice girl. Someone Interesting.' Capital S, capital I."

Ellie had to grin at his miming an older lady's voice. "What does your grandfather say about her match making?"

"Would that he was still around to restrain her, but Grandma's been a widow for ten years."

"Maybe you need to distract her by finding *her* Someone Interesting."

Gabe blinked. "Now that is an outstanding idea. Why didn't any of us think of it?"

"Is this your dad's mom or your mother's mom?"

"My dad's."

Ellie nodded. "I met your dad once when he came home for some papers he'd forgotten. Handsome man." An older version of Gabe.

When the waitress returned, Ellie chose spaghetti carbonara and Gabe eggplant parmigiana. The food, when it arrived, was delicious.

"This place is authentic Italian," Ellie said. "The way these things taste, I could be in Nonna's kitchen."

She was enjoying tiramisu like Joey's mother used to make and laughing at something Gabe said when a shadow fell across the table. She looked up and froze.

"Well, well, it is you, Angel Eyes," Joey said. "It really is you."

CHAPTER 22

Joey grinned down at Ellie, satisfaction flowing like a drug through his veins. The look on her face almost made the torment of the past eight years worthwhile.

When he first saw her while she stood waiting at the door for her date to come in from parking his car, he had the strangest feeling, sort of like walking into a brick wall and bouncing off, which was ridiculous because he already knew she was in the area.

Still he hadn't expected her to walk into Antonio's, and he hadn't expected her to look so good. He'd always thought her beautiful with her great dark eyes and hair and flawless skin, but the years since he last laid eyes on her had matured her beauty. No wonder the big blonde guy couldn't take his eyes off her.

He couldn't keep his hands off her either. Joey stood behind some plantings and watched them go to their table. Ellie's date had his hand resting at the small of her back as they walked, guiding her as if she couldn't follow the hostess on her own. When he finished holding her chair for her, he squeezed her shoulder. She looked up at him and smiled, her face open and guileless.

Joey started to shake. Those smiles belonged to him! Seeing her all happy and flirty made him want to grab her around the neck and squeeze until she begged his forgiveness. Or maybe just squeeze until she couldn't even manage that. His handprints could be like a lovely purple scarf marking ownership.

He went to his office and closed the door. He rested his forehead against the cool wooden panel and realized he was gritting his teeth and clenching his fists. He forced himself to relax. He could not allow his reaction to her make him lose control. Not here. Not now.

His hand went to the back of his head, and he rubbed where she'd cracked him with that statue of the Virgin. Through a red haze he remembered waking up in the dark living room, cold and dizzy. At first he couldn't remember why he was lying on the floor. Had he had too much to drink and passed out? Then he'd put his hand to his aching head, and it had come away sticky with blood. At the same time his blurry vision rested on the Virgin, broken in two, lying a few feet from him.

Ellie'd hit him! Him!

He forced himself to his feet where he swayed so much from dizziness that he had to grab the wall to keep from going down. When the vertigo eased, he stumbled from the room and up the stairs. He had to stop halfway and swallow several times or he'd have thrown up all over himself. His head felt bigger than one of Terafino's Sicilian pizzas and twice as hot. He suddenly knew what a volcano felt like. He couldn't wait to erupt all over her.

He threw open the closed door of their bedroom. She deserved to feel his fists, his feet, his words. By the time he was finished with her, she'd be in bed for a week.

"Ellie!"

But the room was empty. Even today he remembered the frustration, the fury. He'd punched the wall with both fists, imagining it was her. The pain that shot across his knuckles and up his arms brought a red haze that pulsed in time with his heartbeat. He railed and swore as he stormed to Nick's room. If she thought hiding behind the kid would protect her, she was greatly mistaken. And if Nick thought he could take his mother's side again, he needed a lesson in who was in charge around here.

But Nick's room was empty too.

For a minute Joey went cold all over. She'd taken Nicky. His Nicky.

Immediately he rejected that idea. This was Ellie the Meek and Mild, Ellie the Pleaser. Ellie the Easily Led. She'd never run away. She didn't have the courage or the smarts. Or the money. He'd seen to that.

Then he realized what she must have done. She'd gone to Nonna's, afraid of what would happen when he woke up.

Well, she was right to be afraid. And he would teach her a whole new level of fear when he got his hands on her. But first he had to lure her back home.

He returned to his bedroom, fell onto the bed, and passed what was left of the night plotting his revenge, imagining her face white with fear and pain, her eyes black and blue, her bones cracking under his strong and righteous hands.

Dosed with multiple aspirin, he went to Terafino's the next day like nothing had happened. When Ellie walked in, confident he wouldn't do anything to hurt her at the deli, he acted as if he wasn't seething inside. Truth was the concussion she'd given him made him feel like throwing up every time he turned his head, but he refused to let her know even for one minute that she'd gotten the best of him. He dealt with the dizziness by imagining her cringing and crying, pledging her love while pleading for her life.

Then she hadn't come to Terafino's for dinner. Alarm bells went off immediately. He couldn't leave because of a heavy dinner crowd, so he sent Lenny, the dishwasher, to the house to check on her. He'd come back saying neither she nor Nicky was there.

"Was her painting stuff there?"

Lenny looked even dumber than usual. "What painting stuff?"

"Go back and see if her painting stuff is in the third bedroom."

Lenny returned to say the room was a mess. "I don't know what should be there, Joey, but I do know she ain't neat."

But she was, especially about her precious supplies. He sent Lenny to Nonna's but she wasn't there either. Or so Nonna said.

Did the old lady really expect Joey to believe that? He knew she was there. Where else could she be? He decided to let her sulk for another night, not because he couldn't figure out how to get her away from Nonna but because he didn't want to have a nasty fight in front of the old lady. He needed her alone for what he had in mind.

To remind himself that he was the one calling the shots, he spent the night with Vera, a woman who appreciated a manly man. The next morning when he went home to change, he found the cash drawer broken into and about ten thousand dollars missing.

She had run. And taken his Nicky and his money!

If he could have laid hands on her at that moment, he'd have killed her.

And now, eight years later, she just walked into his restaurant, pretty as you please. He made himself uncurl his fists. Not here. Here he was a gentleman, a gracious host. He would deal with her later. When and where were the only questions.

He stayed in his office, gauging his time. When she was just about finished her tiramisu, made from his mother's recipe, he walked casually to her table.

"Well, well, it is you, Angel Eyes. It really is you." He smiled at her, Mr. Joe Charming, pulled up a chair, and sat. No sense waiting for an invitation that would never come. "Heard you were back in the area."

He watched with a deep sense of fulfillment as the blood drained from her face. Even her lips went white.

The blond bozo with her blinked at her pallor and reached under the table where she was no doubt wringing her hands. He must have taken a hand because she looked at him and managed a pathetic smile.

Joey gave her his most predatory smirk. "I've been wondering where you went to, Angel Eyes. I've got about ten thousand reasons for wanting to spend time with you again."

——

She couldn't breathe. The edges of her vision turned gray, and she thought she'd pass out.

She felt Gabe's hand grasp hers beneath the table, something stable and solid in her tilting world. She looked at him, so handsome and *nice,* and tried to smile.

Joey! With ten thousand reasons for wanting to spend time with her again. Ten thousand!

"I have to go," she said as much to herself as to Gabe. She pushed back her chair and stood. "I-I have to go!"

Out of Antonio's. Out of Lyndale. Out of Pennsylvania.

Before the law showed up and took her away.

The law. Her eyes slewed to Gabe. He was the law. Her heart tripped.

He stood too and pulled his wallet from his pocket.

Joey waved a hand, all charm and bonhomie. "No, no. The dinner's on the house." He looked at Ellie, his stare as sharp as an icepick and as deadly. "For old time's sake."

Ellie bolted. How could she have been so foolish as to think things were fine just because Nick decided he was safe? All Joey had to do was talk, and they'd come for her—if there was anything left to collect after Joey was finished with her.

She had to leave Gabe. Her heart wept at the thought. He knew a lot, but he didn't know the worst. He didn't know she was a thief. A kidnapper. He'd have to arrest her.

Sure, she could say she was entitled to the money she took and much more, but she had still stolen it, taken it without permission. Joey's theft of Nonno's money had been legal. Not ethical or moral, but legal, account to account, right there in the bank. Her actions might seem justified, but they were still wrong. Illegal.

And she'd stolen Nicky. Again with good reason, but still she'd taken him from his father and fled and hidden him for years

What was it Scripture said? God would bring to light things hidden in darkness?

Lord, I don't think I can stand so much light.

It also said something about revealing motives of the heart. At least her motives had been pure. Sort of. She wanted to protect Nick, which was as good as it got. But her motives were tainted, if she were honest, with a good-sized dollop of get back at Joey. He took her money; she'd take his. And his son.

Now she had to get away. From Joey. From Gabe. She had to escape. Joey could ruin her life, ruin Nick's. Gabe could break her heart when he turned away from her in disgust. She and Nick had run before with only clothes hastily packed. They could do it again. And Nonna was feeling better. She could come too.

She ran out into the rain without any idea where she was going. She only knew she had to run. A horn blared. She stopped long enough to realize she dashed right into the path of a car. Only the fact that the driver was going slowly in the parking lot prevented her from being knocked to the ground.

Who cared? She couldn't hurt any worse.

The thought of leaving Gabe tore at her. And how could she ask Nick to miss the Thanksgiving game and next season and his scholarships? And they'd have to leave their little house and Avery and Kenny and Maris.

"Ellie!" Gabe grabbed her by the arm and pulled her under the umbrella he held. He wrapped an arm around her, holding her against his side. "The car's over here."

She let him lead her, uncertain whether the wetness on her face was rain or tears or both. They stopped beside the passenger door, and Gabe turned her until she was facing him. Then he pulled her close and just held her, one strong arm around her even as he held the umbrella over her to protect her.

She stood rigid for a few seconds. She didn't deserve comfort. She had made her own messes, and she deserved all the pain she got.

"It'll be okay," Gabe said. "We'll figure it out."

It was the *we* that did it, that turned her into a sobbing limpet who clutched him like a frightened child gripped her mother, though there was nothing remotely parental about the feelings he invoked. It hit her that she was falling in love with this man, and she began crying harder.

Lord, is this some kind of heavenly irony that You let me meet and fall for a cop?

"Ellie," Gabe said softly. "Look at me."

She burrowed ever more deeply into his damp sports coat.

"Ellie."

She looked up and waited for whatever wisdom he had to offer her. Instead he gently brushed damp curls from her cheeks. Then he kissed her, softly at first, in comfort and support, then deeply, with genuine passion. She kissed him back with all the doomed love in her heart.

"I can't get involved with you," she said when they pulled apart.

"I didn't want to get involved with you either."

"I didn't say I don't want to. I said I can't." She wanted to; oh, how she wanted to.

He pulled her close again. "Why not?"

She laughed without humor. "I've about ten thousand reasons."

"I'm not that bad, you know. I leave my socks on the floor. I'm grumpy in the morning until I get my coffee. I've a great hairy dog I treat like a child. I've a tendency to work too hard. And I can't decide whether I want to be a cop or a coach. See? That's only five. Nowhere near ten thousand."

"It's the last one that scares me."

"What I want to be?"

"What you are."

"A coach? A cop?"

"Door number two."

"Being a cop." His voice went flat, and his eyes searched hers.

She grabbed his blazer lapels, whether to keep him close or to hold herself upright, she wasn't sure. She couldn't stop shaking. "I haven't always been a very nice person, Gabe."

"I don't know all you were, but I know what you've become, what you are. And I like it. A lot."

She shook her head. How could a man be this wonderful? She went up on tiptoe and kissed his cheek. "You're exactly the kind of man I prayed for, yearned for, and never thought I'd find."

"That's good, I think, unless a *but* is coming."

"But—" She gave a quick, sad smile. "All I can say is that I wasn't a Christian at the time, but I knew what I was doing." With that she turned to the car.

He spun her back to him. "Not so fast, El."

She stared at him, letting her love show because he'd never again be this pleased with her. She was trying to memorize his face for the lonely nights ahead when he kissed her again.

———

He hadn't meant to kiss her. It was just she looked so sad, so lovely, even with her face streaked with tears. He tasted the salt of her weeping, and her sorrow broke his heart.

Somehow the umbrella handle, caught between them, shifted, and he became aware of a steady stream of cold water running straight down his back. He gave her mouth a final swift caress and stepped away, straightening the umbrella as he did. They stared at each other for a minute, she with a look of great sorrow, he probably looking an infatuated fool.

He opened the door and she slid in. He closed the door and walked slowly and thoughtfully to his side.

He had no doubt that he'd just met Nick's father. The physical resemblance was amazing, but that was where the similarities ended. There was a slyness to Joey Terafino that, thank God, did not come out in Nick. Joey wanted to hurt, at least hurt Ellie. Nick wanted to help as evidenced by his attention to Kenny.

Gabe's experience with guys like Joey had shown him they liked to project a good guy image to their friends and extended family. Everyone but the one they abused, whether psychologically, physically or sexually, thought the abusers were wonderful, salt of the earth. This careful manipulation of people's opinion made it incredibly hard for anyone to believe the stories of the abused women, even when they stood there with his marks on their bodies.

"She fell," the abuser would say, looking so sad. "Please forgive her ramblings. She's not usually like this." Choke back a tear.

And based on the charming image he had created, he was believed and she was marked as unstable.

But there was nothing unstable about Ellie. Gabriella Francella, the girl with the rhyming name. Gabriella to his Gabriel. It made him smile in spite of the tense situation.

He had resisted the urge to look in the law enforcement data bases when he finally had the name Francella to work with. He wanted Ellie to tell him her story herself. He'd come this afternoon to give her that chance only to be waylaid by multiple kids and a wild game of football. He'd asked her out tonight, and Joey appeared.

He sighed as he pulled his door open and collapsed the umbrella. Whatever was going on, he and Ellie had to talk about Joey.

When he climbed into the car, he was immediately aware that talking wasn't going to happen easily. Ellie was staring straight ahead, and her arms were wrapped protectively around herself. Emotionally there was a great Keep Away sign hanging from her neck.

So what was his next step? If he was to help her, he needed her to tell him her secrets no matter how bad she thought they were, all ten thousand of them.

The question was whether she'd trust him with them.

CHAPTER 23

"Good night, Gabe, and thanks." Ellie was out of the car and running for the house before he even had the gear shift in park.

Good night, my eye. Gabe climbed out and stalked after her. He was not leaving until they talked things out. She wanted to disappear again—he could all but hear her brain evaluating escape plans and possibilities—but she wasn't going anywhere if he could help it.

Ellie vanished into the little house, either unaware he was following or hoping if she ignored him, he'd go away. Not a chance. He was a cop with all the doggedness that meant. He was also a man falling in love, and he had to help.

The front door was swinging closed when he reached it. He simply held out a hand and prevented it from shutting. He stepped into the living room where the TV flickered its way through Iron Man III. Robert Downey was flying through the air in his magic suit, his steely eyes fixed on his target. The noise of the movie covered the sounds of his entry.

Ellie, Nick and Kenny were in the darkened kitchen where the only light was the flickering wash from the TV. The boys had large bowls of ice cream in their hands. Nick also held what was left of the bag of pretzels from last night.

"What's wrong, Mom?" he asked.

"We have to leave, Nick. Now. Grab a few things. Kenny, we'll just drop you at your house."

"What?" Nick put the pretzels down with a slap that shattered the remaining whole ones. "Why? Did you see Antony again?"

"Worse."

"You saw Dad?" Gabe heard more interest than fear in the kid's voice.

Ellie nodded. "We went to eat at this place called Antonio's. Guess who's the Antonio it's named for?"

"Our Antony?"

"He's not our Antony." Ellie practically spit the words.

Nick ignored her. "Antony has a fine dining restaurant? Somehow I never expected that of him."

Ellie snorted, a clear indication of her opinion of Antony. "It might be named after him, but your dad's the brains behind the operation. Oh, Nick, he's practically in our back yard. We need to go while we can."

There was a short silence. Then Nick said, "No," politely but very firmly.

"What do you mean, no?" There was shock and disbelief in Ellie's voice.

"I'm not running any more, Mom."

"But, Nick—"

"Kenny and Stephanie agree with me."

Ellie glared at Kenny who tried not to look like a turncoat. "Sorry," he mumbled.

Both anger and hurt flashed across Ellie's face at the thought that Nick was paying more attention to a girlfriend and a guy than her. "I don't think they get to make this choice."

"No, I do. He's not going to hit me, Mom. I'm as big as he is. Maybe bigger. And you can be sure he's not going to hit you either. I won't let him."

"But, Nick—" The anguish in her voice made Gabe ache for her.

"Mom, we had to run before. You did the right thing then. We don't have to run anymore."

"You're not eighteen yet."

"As good as. No court's going to make me live with him if I don't want to."

Ellie didn't say anything, but her shoulders slumped.

"You're worried about the money, aren't you?" Nick asked.

Gabe stilled. Here it was. Money. *Oh, Ellie, what did you do?*

"What if he presses charges?"

"Then we'll press charges back." Nick sounded so assured. "Assault and battery. Terroristic threats. Endangering the life of a minor."

"He said he had ten thousand reasons for wanting to see me." Her voice was full of despair.

She'd taken ten thousand dollars? Gabe closed his eyes as pain shot through him. No wonder she hated that he was a cop.

"He took fifty thousand from you," Nick said.

"But he did it legally."

Gabe stepped into the crowded kitchen. Nick stood in front of the counter, his ice cream melting in his hand. Kenny sat at the table, eyes wide as he followed the conversation. Ellie stood beside the refrigerator, her arms wrapped around herself as if to hold body and soul together.

"How did he rob you legally, Ellie?" Gabe asked. "And where did you get fifty thousand in the first place?"

Ellie spun, her hand flying to her mouth, her eyes wide. "What are you doing here?"

She looked so frail, so overwhelmed. He wanted to gather her to him, but he couldn't. He was chief of police and he needed answers.

"I followed you inside to make certain you were all right," he said.

"You met my father?" Nick asked.

Gabe nodded. "You look very much like him."

"Then he must be handsome," Nick said, but no one laughed. Nick sighed. "Coach, tell her we can't leave Lyndale. Tell her it's time to stop running."

———

Ellie felt as if she stood paralyzed in the middle of roaring traffic, a great truck bearing down on her, and she couldn't get out of its way. She felt drenched in despair and fear.

Nick wouldn't leave, and one look at Gabe showed body language that meant he would try and stop her if she bolted. Maybe he'd even come after her—as police chief, not friend.

Which meant she'd have to run alone and in secret.

And she couldn't.

She couldn't leave Nick. She couldn't leave Nonna. She didn't want to leave Gabe.

But how could she stay?

If only the spaghetti carbonara didn't feel so heavy in her stomach. She swallowed again, but the rich sauce and her stomach acid had joined forces in revolt against digestion.

"Ellie, come with me." Gabe reached for her, encircled her wrist gently, and pulled her toward the door.

"You're going to arrest me?" She couldn't believe it.

He stared at her as if she'd lost her mind. "I want to talk to you."

"Oh. Well, we can talk here." She grabbed the refrigerator handle to keep herself moored to the kitchen, the boys, and safety. Her grip merely had the effect of opening the door. The light cut across the shadowed room, illuminating Gabe's determined face.

He gave another tug on her wrist. "We need to talk alone. We're going for a walk."

"It's raining!"

"So we take the umbrella."

"Tell her, Coach." Nick took a spoonful of his soupy ice cream, proof he had no concept of how scary things were. "Make her see that the days of running are over."

Ellie felt that speeding truck plow into her. She felt flattened, smooshed, hopeless. She pushed the fridge door closed with resignation. She'd just have to get used to wearing orange jump suits.

"So it was probably me the drunk guy was watching," she said as she followed Gabe outside, her hand still softly manacled in his. "For Joey."

"What drunk guy?" Gabe reached into the back of his SUV and pulled out the oversized umbrella. He flicked it open and held it over their heads, but Ellie didn't care. What was freezing rain when your life was washing away as fast as the water flowing in the gutters? In fact, freezing rain might be good. She could catch a cold which could become pneumonia which could turn into one of those viruses that ran rampant, and she could die by Thanksgiving, four days away. Heavenly robes beat orange jump suits any day.

Gabe slid an arm around her shoulders and pulled her close. Ellie couldn't resist and slid her arm around his waist. After all, if she didn't, they'd keep bumping into each other, and that would be awkward. Also one of them would be out in the rain.

"Now tell me what drunk guy you're talking about," he said. "Someone I missed at the restaurant?"

"The man at Kenny's." The one who said she'd ruin everything.

"A man at Kenny's?"

"Across the street. The one who acts like he's a drunk."

Gabe stared down at her, brow furrowed. "There's a man at Kenny's pretending he's a drunk?"

She nodded. "I tried to help him last night, and he told me to get lost. I'd ruin everything."

"What does that mean?"

"I don't know, but that's what he said. Maybe he's your drug guy. Or maybe he's a cop looking for your drug guy, but you'd know about him then, right? He's probably a PI spying on me."

"That's quite a range of options."

She shrugged. "All I know is something's not right. I don't think he's a drunk. Mitzi's not a dealer, is she? I thought maybe he was spying on her."

Gabe gave a short laugh. "Mitzi? A dealer? Not a chance. Now the non-drunk drunk? I'll check into him tomorrow. In the meantime, talk to me." He started to walk, and she kept step. "I know Joey was abusive to you for years and Nick once. I know you've been hiding in Washington."

"And Arizona and Colorado. We moved every two years."

He nodded. "Tell me about the money, the fifty thousand and the ten thousand."

So she did, knowing she had no choice, knowing he'd take his arm away when he heard, yet still feeling the weight of the long-held secret lift as she talked.

"Joey took your fifty thousand your grandfather left you," he clarified.

"Yes. It was supposed to be my college fund."

"And he knew this?"

"Sure. He got me to make my account a joint one, and the money disappeared."

"You didn't call him on it?"

"I didn't know until the day we ran."

If his expression of disbelief—not of what she said but of what she'd let happen—was any indication, Gabe would never lose fifty thousand dollars. It was a strangely comforting thought.

"And you took ten thousand of his."

"Yes. His betting money. To finance our escape."

"And you're afraid he'll press charges?"

"Yes."

"The statute of limitations on theft is five years in Pennsylvania."

She stopped and stared at him. She could feel her mouth hanging open. "It can't be that simple."

Gabe shrugged and with a tug started her walking again. "It may be. If you look at it a certain way, he still owes you forty thousand."

She felt lightheaded. "It can't be that simple," she said again.

He gave her a squeeze.

"I don't have to go to jail? Not even about Nick?"

"I think you can make a good case for fleeing to protect him as well as yourself."

"Yeah, but Joey won't give up. He'll make my life a living hell if he can."

"Statute of limitations again. It's five years for kidnapping."

"But I crossed state lines with him. All I wanted was distance, but I committed a federal crime, didn't I?"

"The statute of limitations, *if* this was kidnapping, would be seven years."

"Civil suit?"

"Not possible because of the time limits. Remember that if he accuses you, you would testify to his actions, and Nick would corroborate your testimony. Joey would be opening himself up to his true nature being revealed." He kissed the top of her head. "I doubt he'd take the chance."

She basked in this wonderful news for a few minutes as they walked in the quiet night. Then she asked the question that tied her stomach in knots. "Am I supposed to just let him back in Nick's life?"

"I think you can't make that choice for Nick anymore."

Not the answer she wanted.

"You've raised a good kid, El, a smart kid, a kid with values. You've got to let him decide about Joey for himself."

She shivered and not from the chill. "The very thought scares me to death."

"I bet." He fell silent, and there was something in his manner that made her stomach pitch. She doubted she'd ever be able to eat spaghetti carbonara again.

"There's something else. What?" she asked.

"Do you know if he went to the police when you and Nick left?"

"He did. Nonna wrote that a detective came to talk with her."

Gabe sighed. "I'll check tomorrow to see if there's a fugitive warrant out there in your name."

"A fugitive warrant?" The words caught in her throat. They made her sound like some lowlife Dog the Bounty Hunter was chasing.

That orange jumpsuit looked like her future wardrobe after all.

CHAPTER 24

Avery sat high in her tree Monday night, resting her head against the trunk. It was sort of scary being up here in the dark when she was supposed to be in bed, but it was better than being in the empty house. Well, not completely empty. Mrs. Cotton was there, but she wasn't any comfort. And she snored. Loud.

They'd left her again. She wiped at a tear and told herself not to be such a baby. After all, they'd left her before. She should be used to it by now. And she was pretty certain they'd leave her again unless she somehow became a princess over night. She snorted. Like that would happen.

She'd almost felt like one yesterday when Ms. Loring and Mr. Hyland and Nick and Kenny climbed the tree with her. It had been so much fun! And then they'd played football, even Ms. Loring though she wasn't very good.

Of course Avery knew she wasn't very good either, but she'd been on Nick and Kenny's team, and they made her quarterback. Quarterback! Kenny threw her the ball, and miraculously she caught it. Then she couldn't stop giggling as she followed Nick as he zigzagged across the yard. Mr. Hyland purposely missed his tackle and Ms. Loring yelled, "Go, Avery!" even though she wasn't on her team.

By this time, Avery was laughing so hard she was afraid she'd wet her pants and she could hardly run.

Nick solved that last problem. He scooped her up and ran for the goal line. It wasn't the most comfortable ride in her life, bouncing like some bobble head doll, but they'd scored. *She'd* scored.

Then Nick said, "Victory dance, Avery!" He put his hands over his head and strutted across the lawn. "Come on!"

So she'd put her hands over her head and tried to strut too. Kenny, Ms. Loring and Mr. Hyland clapped like she'd done something really special. She didn't think she'd ever had so much fun.

Then she'd turned around, and there was Daddy, staring at her, open-mouthed. Mom stood beside him, her face full of disbelief.

They'd made her come home so they could say good-bye. Mrs. Cotton made her stay inside for the rest of the day.

And now she was all alone.

Maybe if Daddy had remembered to give her a kiss good-bye or if Mom hadn't been so happy about going without her, it wouldn't hurt so much. She thought about that for a few minutes and decided that she'd be sad even with a kiss and a tear. Left behind was left behind.

As she thought about how lousy her life was, she watched Nick's room. If she could see him, things wouldn't seem quite so terrible. Not good, of course, but not jump-out-a-window bad either. She thought about the good time yesterday and almost smiled in spite being weepy.

The light came on in Nick's room, and she saw someone moving around. Her glasses were so fogged from her tears that she couldn't tell who it was. She stuffed her new pink cell phone, her parents' guilt gift, into her heavy new pink fleece jacket pocket. She'd had the phone out so she could take a secret picture of Nick. She pulled her metallic pink framed glasses off. She wiped them with the edge of her jacket, expecting that all she was doing was smearing the dirt and tears around. To her surprise, the lenses were clearer when she put the glasses back on.

So maybe the pink fleece wasn't so bad after all. Well, the fleece wasn't. The pink was a big mistake. She kept telling Mom she wasn't a pink kind of girl, but Mom kept trying to make her one.

She blinked hard. She'd never be a pink girl and grow up to marry a handsome guy like Nick. No wonder Mom was so disappointed in her and Daddy didn't even kiss her goodbye. She was going to cry again if she wasn't careful and fog her glasses all over again.

She sighed and stared at the lighted rectangle, willing the person to walk by the window again so she could take his picture. He did, and she recognized Kenny. Once she'd heard the phrase kindred soul on TV. She thought it meant someone just like you, someone you felt close to because you were alike.

Kenny was her kindred soul. If he was a girl, he wouldn't be a popular pink girl either. Nick was the guy equivalent of pink because he was handsome and big and popular, a great athlete, but skinny Kenny was the wrong color just like her.

Kenny disappeared from view, and Nick appeared. He was laughing at something, and he looked so handsome.

The wind blew suddenly, fluttering the few leaves still left on the tree. Her branch moved, and she jumped and hugged the trunk until it stopped. If she fell, she'd lie there in a heap until morning before anyone noticed her. Maybe she'd lie there all day. Mrs. Cotton would never miss her. If Ms. Loring or Nick or Kenny didn't look out the right window, they'd never see her either.

Yikes! She could die right there on the ground by the tree.

She imagined Mom and Daddy having to come home early from their vacation to bury her. Would they cry? Would they tell each other what a mistake they'd made leaving their darling girl, their princess, at home? Or would they be mad because they lost their days in the sun?

Mad, she decided, and sighed again.

The wind died down, and she relaxed against the trunk. She reached in her pocket and pulled out her new phone.

"It's got a camera," Daddy had said, showing her how to use it so fast she could barely follow him. It was a case of get it done and get away from Chubby Girl. "Here. Take my picture."

He handed her the phone and posed. Obediently she did as he said, but her heart was screaming, *I don't want the phone or your picture. I want you!*

Then he showed her how to put the picture with the phone number of the person so that if you called them or they called you, the picture popped up. "You can call me every other day if you want."

He smiled like this was a big deal. She didn't tell him that Trina and Alana at school could call their moms or dads whenever they wanted. Well, every other day was better than never.

After Mom and Daddy left, she programmed in Ms. Loring's land line and her cell. What if Mrs. Cotton fell down and broke something? She was old, like sixty or something. Maybe eighty. Avery needed someone she could call who was close by right after she called 911.

She looked at the lighted window. Some day if she got up the nerve, she'd ask Nick for his number. And Kenny. If they had cell phones.

Maybe she could tell Mom and Daddy she'd lost her phone and ask for another one. She could give it to Nick. Then she'd "lose" the second one and give it to Kenny.

She shook her head. Two problems there. Daddy was bound to notice that he was paying for two phones that were lost and cancel the service. And Nick and Kenny probably didn't want a pink phone. Talk about the wrong guy color.

God, I was just trying to be nice. Nice is good, right?

"I think the most important is loving God. Then being nice comes right after."

Avery had to look all around to be certain Ms. Loring wasn't up in the tree with her. That's how strong the remembered words sounded to her.

As she settled back against the trunk again, she wished she had brought a blanket with her. She was starting to shiver. A few more minutes and she'd sneak back inside, maybe get a blanket or the quilt from her bed and come back out. She didn't feel sleepy yet.

She made a face as the light in the boys' room went off. The living room light was already on, but that room was on the other side of the house and she couldn't see in from here. If they decided to watch TV, she might as well go home and be warm.

The kitchen light came on and Avery perked up. She could see the boys moving around in there almost as well as in the bedroom. They were getting something to eat. She saw Nick collapse in one of the chairs at the kitchen table. Avery held out her camera and snapped.

The glow of the kitchen light fell out on the lawn through the back door, and Avery knew it was a good thing she was up in her tree. The light didn't reach this far. What if she'd been hanging upside down from that bottom branch or running across the lawn to go home? They might have seen her, and that would be very embarrassing.

She heard a hissing noise. She squinted into the night. Had that shadow by the side of Ms. Loring's house moved?

It had! It turned into a man, skulking around the side of the house, staring in the kitchen. She grabbed her phone. She had to warn Nick!

She depressed the quick dial number and waited as the land line rang.

"Hello?" Nick said.

"Nick, it's Avery." She tried to keep her voice soft so the man couldn't hear her but loud enough that Nick could.

"Hey, kid. How you doing?"

"Listen! There's a man sneaking around your house. He's peering in the windows."

"What?"

"I'm up in my tree—"

"Avery! It's ten o'clock at night! You should be in bed."

"Yeah, but listen. There's a peeping Tom or something hanging around your house. Want me to call 911?"

"Nooo." Nick drew the word out like he was thinking about something. "I have an idea who it might be. You just come down from that tree and go home to bed!"

"Right. But what if he's dangerous?"

"He isn't. You just go home. Promise?"

"Sure." Eventually. She hunkered down and started taking pictures.

CHAPTER 25

Nick put down the phone and stared out the kitchen window into the night. He thought he knew who was out there, and he thought he knew why.

Taking a deep breath, he slipped out the back door and stood under the light on the back porch.

A man stepped from the shadow of the forsythia. "Nick?"

"Yes?"

"It's me. Dad." The man stepped to the edge of the porch.

Nick studied his father and saw no devil's horns, just a big man dressed all in black.

"Nicky!" The man rushed up the steps and grabbed him in a bear hug, taking him completely by surprise. "I've missed you, buddy!"

Just because the man didn't appear to be the evil creature he expected, Nick wasn't prepared to hug him or anything. Not yet. He patted his dad awkwardly on the back and tried to keep the daydreaming half of his mind in check, the half that yearned for everything to be just a misunderstanding. Dad hadn't meant to hurt him, to hit him that night. He had regretted the action every day Nick'd been gone, and he had repented and changed his ways. He was now a wonderful man who would love him and Mom, and they would do wonderful things together. Be a family.

Stay skeptical! But it was so hard with Dad right here.

"Let me look at you." Dad stepped back and studied Nick. He turned him so the porch light fell on his face. He grinned. "It's like looking in a mirror!"

"That's what Mom says."

Dad laughed. "Bet it drives her nuts."

Nick shrugged. "She doesn't say."

Dad threw a companionable arm about Nick's shoulders. "Come on. Let's go."

"Go where?"

"Home."

Considering that he lived in this little house, Nick thought he already was home. "You mean your place?"

"I live on South Street in Philly now. Lots of color and lots of action. You're going to love it there."

"Why don't you come in here?" Nick countered. "We can sit and talk. I've got so much to tell you."

"And I want to hear it all." Dad gave him a squeeze and stepped away. "Just not here."

"I can't just leave, Dad. Mom would be upset to find me gone. And I've got school tomorrow."

"Run in and pack a few things." He flicked a hand toward the house. "We can get you everything else you need later."

Nick blinked. "Dad, I can't go with you. Not tonight. School. Another night? There's the long weekend coming up."

"Tonight'll be fine." Dad smiled encouragingly. "I've been waiting eight years to see you, Nicky. I deserve to have you."

Nick nodded. "But—"

Dad took a step closer. He was still smiling, but it looked a bit strained. "No buts. You're coming with me, Nicky."

With real regret Nick shook his head. "I can't. Not tonight."

"Tonight." Dad stepped closer still, and the smile completely disappeared. "Or you will so regret it."

Nick blinked. What?

"And so will your mother."

Nick stared at his father as totally unexpected feelings of panic fluttered through him. That tone of voice. He'd heard it too many times though only once before had it been directed at him.

But he was seventeen now, not nine, every bit as big as his father. He wasn't in any danger. He breathed deeply and forced the fear away, sort of like he did before a big game.

So should he stay or go? Well, he should stay, no question. School and practice. But then again, maybe he should go. Maybe going was the least dangerous to Mom because—he glanced at his father's angry face—there might be a real threat there. He couldn't be the reason she got hurt. He hadn't been able to protect her when he was a kid, but he could do his best now.

Lord, show me!

He glanced at his watch. She'd be home from class soon, and she couldn't find Dad here. She'd had a terrible meltdown last night after seeing him at the restaurant. He couldn't imagine her reaction to finding him at her house.

"I'm not leaving without you, Nicky," Dad said quietly, the intimidation gone as if it had never been. Now he was all loving father.

Nick nodded. He'd go with Dad tonight to save a confrontation. Tomorrow they could figure out how the three of them would make this situation work.

"Let me at least tell Kenny. We don't want Mom calling the cops."

Dad gave an easy smile. "I'll just wait here."

"I'll be back in a minute."

Nick hurried to his bedroom and grabbed a duffle. Into it he shoved whatever his hand happened to touch. He stopped in the living room where Kenny was watching TV.

"Tell Mom not to worry. I'll be back soon."

"Where you going? It's late."

"Yeah. Take care."

"Where you going?" hung in the air as Nick followed his father down the drive to a slinky, silver sports car. Dad beeped the trunk open and Nick threw his things in. Then he climbed into the low slung leather seat and smiled.

"Very cool car." In fact, the coolest he'd ever been in by far.

"Bet it's nicer than your mom's."

Nick ignored the score-one-for-me tone and laughed. "You could say that."

Dad glanced at him as he stepped on the accelerator and took the corner with careless ease. "Have you lived in Lyndale long?"

"Nope. Just since the middle of August. We got here in time for football camp. And Mom wanted to be able to go see Nonna before she got any worse."

"I knew it." There was satisfaction in Dad's voice. "I told Antony she'd come."

"The visits have been hard on her. She comes home and cries."

"She's been already?" Dad was surprised.

"She's been a few times." Nick decided it was prudent to downplay the real number. "She brought back lots of great food."

Dad nodded. "The old lady always was a great cook."

"Mom's a great cook too."

Dad didn't actually hoot, but his attitude shrieked I-don't-believe-it. "Then she must have learned in the last eight years. She was no good before."

"She was too busy working at the deli to learn," Nick defended.

Dad shrugged. "So tell me where you been all these years."

"Arizona, Colorado, Washington."

"State or D.C.?"

"State."

"She sure dragged you around, didn't she? What'd she do for money?"

"She worked. She cleans houses."

Dad laughed. "I should have known. What else is a high school dropout to do?"

"What's wrong with cleaning houses?"

"Nothing if you've got limited smarts."

"Mom's very smart."

Dad's condescending smile was caught in the lights of an approaching car. "If you say so, but you don't have to defend her. We both know she's no mental giant."

"She's almost got her college degree. She's taken classes everywhere we've lived."

"Right."

Dad didn't believe him. It was a new and disconcerting feeling to have his word doubted. Well, Dad would learn the truth in time.

"What have you been doing, Dad? You still have the deli?"

"We do, me and Antony, and we got a classy linen and crystal place too. It's called Antonio's. But then you probably know that. It's where I saw your mother last night."

Nick translated linen and crystal to mean table clothes that weren't plastic coated and glasses that didn't have lids. "Congratulations. That's great. I read somewhere that most restaurants fail."

"Not mine." Dad talked the rest of the way to Philadelphia, telling Nick all about his deli and restaurant and how happy he was that Nick was back to learn the business. Nick thought of all the times he and Kenny and the guys talked about what they'd like to be when they grew up, and running restaurants wasn't on his personal list even once.

———

Ellie pulled into the drive, glad there were lights on in the house and the boys were there. It was ridiculous when your son and his friend were your security, but she didn't trust Joey not to come after her. Somehow, sometime, somewhere, he'd get her—if she wasn't careful.

She grabbed her laptop and purse, tucking Joey to the back of her mind. Class tonight had been so exciting. There was no other word for it. She'd been working with watercolors, a medium that usually gave her difficulties. Tonight her strokes were easy, fluid in a way she hadn't known before. As a result the paint obeyed her instead of running all over the place.

It was the lifting of guilt. It had to be. Nothing else had changed. If anything her fear was greater now that she'd seen Joey, but her guilt over the money and taking Nick were relieved. The fact that the primary color in her work tonight had been Blue #1974D2 was coincidence.

She grinned. Right.

As she hurried to the house, it wasn't a big mental leap from sapphire blue to Maris Hyland who just today had asked her and the boys to have Thanksgiving dinner with their family. She'd tried to be casual as she accepted the invitation but was afraid Maris knew she was jumping up and down inside, clicking her heels. Even now she felt like turning cartwheels.

She hung her coat in the tiny closet just inside the door, thinking how typical it was that all the lights in the house were on except those in her bedroom.

"Hello," she called. "Anyone still up?"

She reached to turn off the light by the sofa when a loud banging at the back door made her jump. Ellie glanced at her watch. It was about twenty minutes before eleven. She started for the kitchen.

The boys' bedroom door popped open, and Kenny stuck his head out. "Maybe it's Nick. Maybe he left so quickly he forgot his key."

"Nick? I didn't know he was going out tonight. Where'd he go?"

"I don't know. He didn't say. He just took off."

"When?"

"About ten."

Frowning, Ellie crossed the little kitchen to the door. She flicked on the light and looked out through the panes.

"Avery!" She threw the door open, and the little girl fell into the room.

"What are you doing here at this hour, sweetheart? What's wrong?" Ellie went to her knees and took the obviously distraught child in her arms. "Oh, honey! You're freezing to the touch. Have you been in the tree?"

"They left me, so I climbed up."

"Who left you?"

"Mom and Daddy. They went on a cruise."

"You're all alone?" Ellie was scandalized.

"Mrs. Cotton's here to babysit."

"Well, she doesn't do a very good job if you've been up in the tree at this hour." Kenny declared. He grabbed a bag of chips and began chomping his outrage.

Avery shrugged. Obviously Mrs. Cotton wasn't important at the moment. "He went with that man!" she said as she tried to clear the condensate off her glasses.

Ellie took the lenses, stood, and dried them on a dish towel. "Who and what man?"

"Nick and someone he called Dad."

Ellie grabbed the counter as her knees went weak. *Dad.*

Avery slid her glasses on and swiped at her nose. "I got a picture." She held out her pink phone and Ellie saw a dark, blurry picture.

"See?" Avery pointed. "That's Nick."

"Okay." Ellie nodded though she couldn't tell by the photo.

"And that's the man."

"And Nick called him Dad?" And he went with him?

Avery wasn't finished nodding before Ellie had the phone in her hand. Her hand was shaking so hard she had trouble hitting Gabe's number.

"Gabe, it's—" The works stuck in her throat.

"Ellie! What's wrong?"

"It's Nick! Joey has him."

———

Nick studied what was visible in the light cast by the bare bulb over the back door of an old building that held apartments. He was not impressed.

"I know it doesn't look like much on the outside, especially back here," Dad said, "but it's a great place. You'll see. I moved here about a year after your mom took you. The old place was filled with too many painful memories."

His voice actually caught on the word painful, and Nick thought not for the first time that he must have imagined that threat. *You will so regret it. And so will your mother.* It must have been just regret like an opportunity missed, nothing more.

Dad had been all that was kind and charming the whole trip. Granted he was a bit obsessive on one topic, but all that meant was that he loved his work. Nick was the one who was a nervous wreck, his stomach doing somersaults all around his middle. He'd dreamed of being with his father so many times. That it was actually happening was beyond believable.

They climbed out of the car and Dad popped the trunk. Nick grabbed his things and followed his father inside. They took an elevator up two levels and Dad opened the door of his apartment.

"Whoa!" Nick stared at the modern black leather furniture and the fancy electronics. Everything looked very expensive, very sleek, very contemporary. The Bowflex in the corner made his palms itch with the urge to try it out.

Dad smiled at his reaction. "Welcome home, Nick." He walked down a short hall. "This is your room." Dad indicated a bedroom that was a guy's dream.

"Whoa!" Nick said again. Every electronic gadget he'd ever heard of was there. He stepped through the door and tossed his duffle on the bed. He began a slow circle of the room, stopping before the collection of video games. He could play for the next ten years and not use them all.

"I went shopping after Antony told me he'd seen you. I knew you'd want to come home if you had the chance, and I wanted you to have the best."

With a flash of insight Nick understood that his father was trying to buy him away from his mother. He shrugged mentally. He might as well enjoy it while he could.

"Your clothes are a disgrace," Dad suddenly said.

Nick looked down at the jeans and tee he was wearing. Sure they'd come from Clothes 2 Go, but they were okay, what every other kid at school was wearing. Then he looked at Dad in his black silk shirt and black dress slacks. Very Mob, at least the Hollywood and TV version.

The thought crawled over his skin like a swarm of fire ants. Was he Mob? Was he a don or something, maybe part of some-body's family, the Philadelphia version of the Sopranos? Was that why Mom took him and ran? Had she just never told him because it was so ugly?

In reality she talked very little about his father. He always knew why they left Philadelphia originally—that slug in his face—and why they moved every two years, or he thought he did. After the I-don't-want-you-to-be-like-him talk when they sat at the rickety table in Arizona, Dad's name rarely came up. It was like don't mention him and he's doesn't exist.

But he did, and Nick had wondered about him for years. Not all the time, not even a lot of time because he had a busy life.

Besides, it made him feel like a traitor to his mom. But he did wonder, especially since they'd moved so close.

"We'll go shopping tomorrow," Dad said.

Tomorrow he needed to get back to Lyndale, but he didn't want to provoke a confrontation now. "Just no silk shirts. I'd get laughed out of school."

"We'll have to figure out where you should go, won't we?"

"Go?"

"To school. Maybe a fancy school like Penn Charter? It's only $39,000 a year if you don't mind Quakers. Or an all boys school like St. Joe's Prep? It's only $25,000 a year, but the Jesuits know what they're doing."

And the Quakers don't? Nick stared at his dad. He could afford to pay tuition like that? It was as expensive as going to college!

"What are your grades like?"

"My grades are fine, but I don't want to go to another school."

"Sure you do."

"I like Lyndale."

"No, you don't. You just don't know it yet." Dad's grin was charming.

"Dad, I'm not nine. I'm almost eighteen. I know what I like." With a strong personality like Dad's, it was important to establish yourself before you got swept away.

"Of course you do. I didn't mean to imply you didn't. It's just that now you're living with me, you won't be able to go to school there."

"I'm living with you?"

"Sure. Us guys against the world." Dad gave him a little punch in the arm.

Another topic for discussion tomorrow. Nick glanced at his watch. Oops. Today. It was well after midnight. He yawned.

Dad saw and smiled. He gave Nick a hug and walked to the door. "I'll see you tomorrow morning."

"Thanks. I would like to get some sleep. This is all a bit strange, being here after not seeing you for all those years."

Dad's face turned ugly. "And I'll make sure she pays for that."

"Dad, don't."

Dad immediately turned conciliatory. He reached for Nick and hugged him. "I'm sorry. I don't want to ruin the evening. We're together again, Nicky, you and me. That's what counts."

"Right, Dad. That's what counts."

CHAPTER 26

As soon as Dad left the bedroom, Nick reached for his cell phone clipped to his waist. He needed to call Mom. Kenny would have told her he'd be back in a little while, but since it wouldn't be until tomorrow, he had to let her know he was fine. He also needed a ride home. Somehow he didn't think Dad would be willing to take him.

His phone wasn't in its holder.

How could that be? He pulled the holder free and stared. Had the phone somehow fallen out? But how could it with the velcroed lid to hold it in place?

Well, Dad must have a phone he could use. He opened his door only to find the apartment completely dark. In the spill of light from his room, he found the switch for the hall light. After he flicked that on, he went to the living room. No phone visible here. He tried the kitchen. None there either. Dad must be the kind who didn't have a land line, only a cell phone.

He made his way back to the hall and stopped outside Dad's room. Should he knock? Ask to use his cell?

Nah. It was okay. Kenny would tell her, and she'd be fine. Definitely not happy, but fine.

He went back to his room, fell into bed, and slept soundly until Dad knocked on his door in the morning.

"Seven o'clock. Up and at 'em. We got to get to the deli by eight. It's my manager's day off and my day on."

Nick took a quick shower in the bathroom that connected to his bedroom, a feature he could get used to in a hurry, and was ready in under ten minutes.

"Have you seen my cell phone?" he asked his father.

Dad shook his head. "Did you lose it somewhere in your room?"

"I don't think so. I looked all over. Do you have a phone I could use?"

Dad pulled a cell from his belt. "Here you go." He glanced at the phone, then made a face. "Oops, I'm all out of juice. I've got the recharger at the deli." He slipped his phone back in its holder.

Nick frowned. The dad he remembered wasn't the kind to run out of juice, and if for some reason he did, he wouldn't be so cool about it. But then he barely knew his father anymore.

Dad opened a white bag lying on the kitchen counter and pulled out some fresh bagels from the bakery down the street. He poured himself and Nick cups of coffee. They sat sharing *The Philadelphia Inquirer* as they ate in what Nick thought a very guy moment.

When they finished and walked through the living room, Nick noticed his father's laptop on the desk. "Can I use that to show you something?" he asked. And send Mom an email or IM while he was at it.

At Dad's nod, he quickly logged into *The Press*'s web site and went right to the sports pages. He pulled up an article about himself complete with picture. He spun the laptop to face his dad.

Dad looked at the photo. "That's you!"

Nick nodded and Dad grinned. He began reading the article. A frown replaced the grin.

"What's this Nick Loring stuff?"

"That's me," Nick said, suddenly wary. He tried for the light touch. "Present and future football star."

"Loring?" Dad's voice was sharp. "Your name is Dominic Terafino. Nick Terafino."

Nick swallowed. "I go by Nick Loring." He should have known this would be a sore spot with Dad. He just wasn't thinking. He'd been so excited to share what was going on that he hadn't thought what Dad would say or what he would feel.

"What? Terafino isn't good enough for you?"

Nick couldn't meet Dad's gaze, and his tongue felt glued to the roof of his mouth.

"No, wait." Dad looked chagrinned and held up a hand. "I'm sorry, Nicky. I should have realized immediately. It isn't you having the trouble with your name. It's your mother."

Nick ignored the slight negative emphasis on *mother*. "It's her last name, Loring. The one she got when she was born. We started using it when we—" When we what? He couldn't say ran away. Dad was too tender on the topic. "—when we moved."

"Her last name?" Dad looked confused. "Francella's her last name."

"It was her stepdad's name."

"Dom Francella was her stepfather?"

"Her real dad died before she was born."

Dad swore. "No wonder I couldn't find you. I looked, Nicky. For years."

A happy warmth filled Nick's chest, and he realized he was grinning like an idiot.

"Well, we'll just change your name back to Terafino."

"I don't know, Dad." How could he do that without Mom seeing it as a slap in the face? But if he didn't, Dad would be upset. What he needed was a third neutral name. Of course, then they'd both be mad at him. "The scouts are used to looking at Nick Loring. We wouldn't want to confuse them, would we? There's a lot of money at stake here."

Dad grunted, clearly not happy. "We'll talk about it later. Now let me read these articles, and you can tell me all about your season."

For the next few minutes the only sounds in the apartment were the muted city noises that seeped through the closed windows.

"Very impressive, Nicky!" Dad looked up when he finished reading. "I knew you'd be a son to be proud of."

Nick felt his chest expand three sizes. Apparently sometimes fantasies did become real. "You can see why I don't want to leave Lyndale. We've got an undefeated season on the line. Thursday's our last game of the season."

"You need your old man, Nick. To help with the recruitment stuff. To coach you. If you're this good without me, imagine what you can become with me at your side." Dad's eyes sparkled with excitement.

Dad wanted to coach him? Nick swallowed a gulp. Did he know anything about football? About recruiting? And why replace Coach who was so very good?

Dad glanced at his watch. "Oops. We got to go. We can talk more about it at the deli." Dad flipped the lid down on his laptop and stuffed it in a black leather case. "Lots of prep work to be done before the place opens at eleven. How are you at slicing tomatoes and chopping onions?"

"Don't know. Never tried." He followed Dad out, unhappy he hadn't had a chance to contact Mom. It was almost as if Dad was keeping him from all means of contact. His hand went to his empty phone holder. No way.

At the deli, Dad immediately had him behind the counter slicing tomatoes and chopping onions. The work area of the deli was open to the customers who watched their sandwiches, pizzas, and salads being made. Nick remembered Dad and Antony using that visibility to joke with their regulars, to build client loyalty. It had been fun at the deli when he was a kid. It was only at home that things could be rough.

Nick's eyes were soon stinging and running from the onions as Dad kept up a running commentary on the deli business and the restaurant business, all of which held no interest to Nick.

"So someday it'll all be yours." Dad draped an arm around Nick's shoulders.

"I don't know, Dad."

"Sure you do. Terafino men run Terafino's. I took over from my father, and you'll take over from me. You can get your degree in business and marketing, and we can bust this place into a national chain. Antonio's too."

Nick didn't want to hurt his dad's feelings, but the idea of working in the deli left him cold. And who wanted the headaches of running a national chain? There were only so many onions a man could face in a lifetime. "I've been thinking about being a Park Ranger at a place like Yosemite or Yellowstone or something. If I don't make it to the NFL, that is. I want to get my degree in environmental engineering."

Dad took a step back, and the chill in his manner was enough to give Nick frostbite. "She turned you against it, just like she turned you against me."

"She didn't, Dad! Believe me. This is me talking, not her. If I wanted to run a deli, she wouldn't care." Just not this deli.

But Dad wasn't listening. He turned his back on Nick and started for the storeroom without a word.

Nick felt confused. How had they gone from all cozy hugs to this chilly manner? Sure, a father wanting his son to go onto the family business was sort of natural. It certainly wasn't a bad plan, like evil or anything. Lots of men seemed to want to add "and Son" to their signs, and that was great if the son liked the family business. If not.... He straightened his shoulders. Each son in each generation should be able to pick whatever interested him.

Still, he didn't want a rift between him and his dad after less than twenty-four hours together.

"Okay, I'll think about it," Nick said to his father's back.

Dad swung around, a huge smile lighting his face. "Good man!"

More to change the subject than anything, Nick said, "I'd like to go visit my great-grandmother while I'm here."

"What?" Winter iced the atmosphere again.

"I'd like to see Nonna." But he said it apologetically which made him mad at himself. "I haven't seen her yet because Mom wouldn't let me come into the city."

"We have nothing to do with that old woman, Nick. Nothing!" Dad spit the words, he was so angry. "Do you hear me?"

"But Dad—"

"Nothing, Nick. It is not open for discussion."

Nick turned back to the onions, his vision blurred not only from the fumes but from his own anger. According to his father, he didn't want to live in Lyndale, he had to take over the deli, he couldn't visit Nonna, and he couldn't contact Mom.

And while he was at it, he could learn to roll over and play dead.

———

Joey studied Nick as he chopped. The kid's back was rigid, a sure sign of his displeasure. She'd done more harm than Joey had imagined possible. He'd expected Nicky to welcome him, even view him as his savior. They'd laugh together, maybe even plot together.

Joey sighed. He could see now that such an expectation was naïve. She'd had eight years to turn Nick against him. It would take more than one night to undo the damage. He thought of his relationship with his father at that age. He should have known better than to project that unrealistic rosy picture.

He smiled wryly to himself. It would all come right eventually. He had the rest of Nick's life, and he'd learned to be a patient man. All he needed was to keep Nick close.

"I'm going to the bathroom," Nick announced and walked to the back of the deli without looking at Joey. He shut the door with more umph than necessary.

Smiling at the kid's petulance, Joey went to the storeroom, grabbed several packs of rolls delivered fresh that morning and carried them into the deli. He had returned for another load when he heard the beeps of phone keys being depressed.

Joey bolted for his office. Nick stood there, back to the door, the land line phone at his ear. Furious at the kid's sneakiness, Joey reached around him and depressed the button that broke the connection.

Nick spun, face a thundercloud. "Dad!"

Swallowing his anger, Joey smiled as if interfering with a private call was a normal, acceptable thing. "It's us, Nick. You and me. We don't need or want her."

Nick's eyes narrowed, and with a jolt Joey realized he was looking up at his son. His stomach did a queer flip.

"I need to let her know I'm all right." Nick spoke through clenched teeth.

"She's unstable, Nicky. I hate to say it, but you know I'm right." Joey carefully made his voice the epitome of rationality and concern. "Look at what she did. She ran away. She changed her name. She changed your name. Why, she's guilty of fraud for having an assumed identity and could go to jail."

"There was no assumed identity. Her real name is Gabriella Loring. It's on her birth certificate."

"All right." Joey kept his voice even though he was boiling inside over the boy challenging him. "Forget the identity thing. Just consider the rest. Those aren't normal actions, Nicky."

"And slugging your kid is?"

"Slugging—?" Joey feigned confusion. He'd known this was bound to come up, and he was ready. "You think I hit you? Nicky! How could you?" Adopting an abject expression wasn't easy, but Joey managed. "She must have told you I did. She did, didn't she?"

Nick shook his head in disbelief. "Dad, I was nine. Nine-year-olds remember."

"She's convinced you. Oh, Nicky. No wonder you're cautious around me. But know I'd never hurt you. Never! You're my son. I love you."

"I'm your son." Nick nodded. "And I guess in your own way you love me. But I remember what I remember, and I'm going to call Mom." He reached for the phone.

Joey grabbed Nick's wrist. "Don't," he said quietly.

Nicky stared first at Joey, then at the hand clamped around his wrist, then back at Joey.

Joey let go though he wanted to squeeze until the kid went to his knees. Teaching respect to the arrogant prick was going to be lesson number one. But not now. He had a scenario he wanted to play out sometime this morning, and he needed to keep Nick in a good mood until it happened. If he had to fake it, he'd gladly do so.

He forced a smile. "Come on, kiddo. It's just us guys for the day." He gave Nick a pat on the shoulder. "We need to get back to work."

Any minute now Ellie would come looking for her baby and begin banging on the door, all weepy and distressed. She'd see Nick behind the counter helping with the prep work and go crazy. She'd cry and plead for him to come back to her. Her eyes'd be wild with fear—fear of losing Nicky and fear of Joey. She'd beg Nicky not to leave her, and the boy'd see her for the pathetic, unbalanced witch she was.

He, on the other hand, would be gracious, charming even, to show Nick what a reasonable person he was compared to his maniac mother. He'd speak kindly to her, offering her a chair and a cup of coffee. He'd ask Nick to go back to the apartment for a while so he and his mother could talk. Then—well, then he wasn't quite sure. It would depend on Ellie. But violence of some sort was definitely a much-anticipated possibility.

———

Nick studied his father, pleased to note that he was a couple of inches taller and a few pounds heavier. There was no way this man would hit him again. In that area he'd been right. He could handle his father.

What surprised him was the man's absolute need to control. In spite of all he'd remembered about Dad's actions, especially toward Mom, he hadn't understood the domination thing. Now he realized that the hitting and the swearing and the nasty games like the one with her keys were all about power, control, dominance. Dad had obviously never grasped the concept that you held people closest when you held them with a loving, open hand.

Well, he wasn't going to be dominated.

"Dad, I have to call Mom. I know she's got to be worried."

Dad managed to look sad. "And how do you think I've felt these past eight years?"

Probably furious that you didn't have us to lord it over. Nick looked away, and his eyes fell on his father's open black leather computer case. Sitting in it was a cell phone with a scratch in the black surface.

"My phone!" He reached for it.

Dad stepped between him and the desk. "That's not your phone," he said. "Why would I have your phone?"

"Good question." Before Dad realized what he was doing, he reached down and grabbed his father's cell from its holder on his belt. He flicked it on even as his dad reached for it, and surprise, surprise. The little icon in the upper corner had all the bars in place.

He handed the phone back with a sad, sinking feeling in his stomach. So much for fantasies. "You can't force me to stay here, Dad. And you can't keep me from talking to Mom."

A loud knocking sounded on the steel door that opened onto the back alley. When Dad automatically glanced at the door, Nick grabbed his own phone from the briefcase. He hit his mother's quick dial number.

Dad reached for the phone. "No, Nick! Not yet!"

Nick caught his father's wrist and was hit with the desire to crush it until something cracked. Horrified and ashamed that he'd have such a thought, he flung his father's hand aside.

The knocking continued, louder and more insistent.

"Today's meat," Dad muttered and, rubbing his wrist, went into the little hallway to open the door.

"Where is he, Joey?" a woman demanded even as Nick heard Mom's ring tone in his ear and in the hall.

"Mom?" Grinning with relief that he didn't have to fight with his father any longer, Nick went into the hall. Mom rushed him and wrapped him in a hug. He hugged her back. When had she gotten so tiny?

"Are you all right?" she demanded.

"I'm fine," he said both to her and to Coach who stood just inside the door.

She stepped back and studied his face. She looked pale and had huge sleepless circles under her eyes. "Really?"

He nodded.

"Want to go home?"

He nodded again. A brief vision of his room at his father's apartment flashed, bright and tempting with all its gadgets and that attached bathroom, only to dim and die as abruptly as a TV whose plug was pulled. The cost was just too great.

Mom smiled and started for the door, carefully not looking at Dad.

Nick slipped his cell phone back into the holder on his belt. He followed Mom, pausing to shake hands with Coach who pushed the heavy door open for them all.

"Nicky! Stay!" Dad shouted the order as if he was a general telling a soldier what to do or a trainer giving obedience lessons to a dog.

Nick stopped mid-stride. He looked at his mother, then over his shoulder at his father. If only he'd asked instead of commanded.

Mom took a deep breath. "You can't stay today, sweetheart. School and all. If you want to come back the day after Thanksgiving, I guess we could arrange it."

Nick knew how hard it was for her to say those words.

"I'd rather you didn't," she continued, her voice soft and sad, "but I won't try and stop you. He is your father, and you're old enough to make your own choices."

Nick smiled at his mom. "Thanks. I'll think about it."

Dad rushed forward and grabbed at Nick. "Forget about her, Nicky! Forget her! Stay here. She's a thief and a kidnapper."

Nick's stomach pitched at the hatred twisting his father's face and dripping from his voice. "Don't, Dad."

His father tried to pull him back into the deli. "We don't want her. You don't want her! Stay here, and it'll be just you and me like we ought to be. We'll cut her from our lives like she's dead, like she doesn't even exist."

Nick's head snapped back as if he'd been slapped. He stared at the man who was his father. "Wrong thing to say, Dad. Wrong thing." And he walked out the door.

CHAPTER 27

As they walked down the alley and onto the street, Ellie could see her son shaking in reaction to the rage pouring off Joey. "You handled yourself well in there, Nick. I'm very proud of you."

He didn't look convinced. "I must have been a very dumb kid to have missed all his craziness."

"No, no! He was careful to keep it hidden from everyone but me, and he had me convinced I was the crazy one."

Nick looked at her with an expression so sad it broke her heart. "I thought he'd be different, you know? Nice. I had this idea he'd come see me play, maybe want to be with us."

She wrapped her arms around him. It didn't matter how big he was; he was her baby. "He is what he is, sweetheart."

"There was a minute there when I wanted to hurt him." Self-loathing laced Nick's words. "I'm as bad as he is."

She shook her head. "Did you hurt him?"

"No!"

"That's the difference." Gabe spoke for the first time. "I know you, Nick. You are not your father. You are your own man, and I respect you for who you are."

Nick turned his head to hide the tears that appeared in his eyes. Ellie looked at Gabe and mouthed, "Thank you!"

In silence they walked to Gabe's car, parked halfway down the block. He depressed the lock fob. "Where to? Home?"

"Nonna's," she said.

Nick managed a slight grin. "Yeah, Nonna's."

Mr. Salerno was standing on his front porch as they came up the walk.

"It's the real Ellie," he called as he waved at them.

She crossed the lawn and gave him a hug. "I never fooled you with that wig, did I?"

He patted her on the cheek. "Not for a moment."

"Thanks for not giving me away."

"I would never give Joseph anything, especially not you."

Her eyes pricked. "You are a good friend, Mr. Salerno."

He grinned. "This is your Nick?"

Ellie nodded.

The old man looked him up and down. "He's big."

Nick smiled at the little man. "I play football."

"So Sophia tells me." Mr. Salerno studied Gabe and looked at her in question.

"This is Nick's coach, Gabe Hyland."

The men shook hands.

"Is he good?" Mr. Salerno pointed at Nick.

"Very," Gabe said.

Mr. Salerno nodded. "Just had to ask. Sometimes grand-mothers are prejudiced, you know. You should hear her talk about you, Ellie."

A warm flush of pleasure spread through Ellie.

Mr. Salerno looked toward Nonna's. "She is so much better since you started coming." He blinked at the sudden wetness behind his thick lenses. "I was very worried for her, but now she has a reason to live. It's you, Ellie. You and Nick. You are so good for her."

"Thank you for being her friend all these years when I wasn't here." Ellie patted his arm. "They don't come any better."

Mr. Salerno glowed. "Her door's locked," he said, "but I got a key."

"Thanks, but I've got mine." Ellie waved hers in the air. As she inserted it in the front door lock, ribbons of emotion unfurled in her chest, bright swirls of gold and crimson, emerald and vibrant blue, #1974D2, happy shades, the-world-is-a-wonderful-place hues. She was coming home. Gabriella Loring Francella was coming home.

"Surprise," she called as they entered. "I've brought you some visitors."

Nonna started to cry the moment she saw Nick. She was sitting on the plastic covered sofa, and he went to her, going down on his knees beside her. He wrapped his strong arms around her frail body, and Ellie began to weep at the beautiful sight. Gabe slipped his arm around her shoulders and pulled her close. He gave her a gentle kiss on the top of her head.

Soon they were all seated, Ellie beside Nonna on the sofa and Nick and Gabe on the edge of the bed.

"So tell me all about you," Nonna said to Nick who proceeded to tell more than she probably wanted to know about his season. Nonna listened with rapt attention.

"And you, Mr. Coach," she said when Nick ran down. "Tell me about you."

Ellie sat quietly listening to the men she loved share their thoughts and lives and felt full to bursting. She still wasn't certain why Nick had gone with Joey in the first place, but it wasn't something to make an issue of now. Maybe later. Maybe Nick would tell her voluntarily. But she finally understood that the only way to keep Nick close, given his age and personality, was to hold him with an open hand.

They didn't stay too long because Nonna's strength was still limited. When they left, she walked to the door with them. She moved slowly, but the difference in her health and spirits between Ellie's first visit and this one was nothing short of a miracle. She was still too weak to come to Lyndale for Thanksgiving as they'd hoped, but they'd come see her after the game and before dinner at the Hylands.

At the last minute Nonna grabbed Ellie's arm and pulled her close.

"This one's a keeper," she whispered, nodding at Gabe. "He's the kind of man you deserve, cara."

Ellie didn't know about *deserved*, but she knew about wanted and loved. Every time she was with Gabe, her emotions went zooming joyously into the stratosphere. *Oh, Lord, please!* was her constant prayer. *Please let this work out. Please don't let me get hurt. Please let him love me. Please help me be worthy of his love.*

If the kiss he gave her when he dropped her at the house before taking Nick to school for what remained of the day was any indication, the Lord was coming through big time.

All the next day Ellie felt like singing, and the terrible thing was, she gave in to the urge. *Just think of it as a joyful noise, Lord.*

There was no other way to think of the cackling sound that issued from her mouth as she joined the praise music on her play list. As she cleaned the Montessoris' house, their dog, an ugly/cute and bowlegged English bull, refused to stay in the same room with her once she started singing. Every time she moved to a new room to work, Archibald moved to the room farthest from her. If he could have put a pillow over his head to drown out the caterwauling, he probably would have. When she was ready to leave, Archibald gave her a hearty going away slurp.

"I know they're kisses of relief, Archie," she said as she petted him. "But I'll take kisses for any reason."

Archie's affection made finding that Mrs. Montessori hadn't left Ellie's check a little less irritating, but only a little. It was the second time in the past four weeks the Montessoris had pulled this stunt. They took the time to write her long missives of orders, but they couldn't take the time to pay her?

She grabbed a pen from her purse and scrawled in big letters across the to-do list No Check, No Cleaning!!

But the missing payment was only a tiny blip in her happiness. Nothing could get her down for long today. She floated out of the house and floated home. She floated into the house.

The cathartic effect of confession—to Gabe—and confrontation—with Joey—was amazing. Then there was the energizing effect of falling in love.

It was six-thirty when she and the boys sat down to dinner, a ham steak, twice baked potatoes, the frozen kind, and broccoli with butter and lots of Kraft parmesan shaken on top.

"I got some great footage of Nick at practice today," Kenny said as he cut up his ham.

"You should only cut up two or three pieces at a time," Ellie told him. "Not the whole thing."

Kenny frowned. "Why? It seems smarter to get all the cutting over with at once."

"I don't know why but take my word. It's good manners."

"Huh," was Kenny's profound reaction. He put his knife down.

"So you got all my missed catches and bad passes?" Nick speared another forkful of broccoli.

"Yep, but I'll edit them out of your recruitment films."

"Not before I watch them to see what I was doing wrong."

"Maybe it wasn't you," Kenny said. "Maybe it was the guy who threw you the pass or the guy who should have been blocking for you."

"If the play is executed accurately and a pattern is run correctly, the ball should be where expected. Whether it's me or him, I need to know."

"Coach'll tell you."

"Yeah, but I need to see for myself."

Kenny looked at Ellie. "The difference between a good player and a great one."

A horn sounded out front.

"Andy's here." Nick grabbed his plate from the table and took the one step necessary to put it on the counter.

"Where are you going?" Ellie asked.

"Youth group."

"I thought that was Thursday."

"It is, but this week that's Thanksgiving, so we're meeting tonight, and Andy's going with us. His first time. Come on, Kenny."

Kenny stood with his plate and glass. "It was a delicious meal, Ms. L." He grinned. "I mean Mom. I'm excited Andy's coming. Look at what going has done for me."

"What has it done?" Ellie asked, curious to see what his answer would be.

"It helped me find Jesus."

Ellie smiled, blinking back tears. "I know all about what that can do for you."

"New life," Kenny headed after Nick.

"New life." Hand over her happy heart, she followed them into the living room. "What time will you guys be home?"

"We'll be back by eleven." Nick rushed out the door.

"Closer to ten," she called after him. "It's a game night."

Kenny paused at the door and said happily, "Curfew, that mom thing. I'll tell him and Andy."

The boy was unnatural, Ellie thought as she watched him run across the lawn after Nick. Kids were supposed to stretch their wings, to push against authority. Unless, perhaps, they had never had any authority or structure previously, and somehow it now gave them comfort.

As she cleaned up the dinner dishes, the house seemed to sigh as silence settled through the rooms. She was alone for the evening. Gabe would be over later, but he had a township meeting he had to attend first, so he wasn't certain when.

"We need to talk, El," he said when he called to tell her about his meeting.

"What about?"

"Later," and he was gone.

She was pretty certain that her imagination was going to drive her crazy before he got there.

She wandered through the house feeling slightly uneasy as she thought of Joey out there somewhere. She tried to convince herself that everything was fine where he was concerned. She'd confronted him, looked him in the eye, seen he didn't have horns and a pitch fork in hand. He was just a man. Granted, a not very nice one, but still just a man. And she wasn't that cowed woman she'd been years ago.

Of course it wasn't that simple. She heard him again as he hissed at her as she left the deli with Nick and Gabe. *"I'll get you for this, Angel Eyes. You can count on it."* Just the memory of his voice—*Angel Eyes*—set off all her own automatic responses. Accelerated breathing. Damp palms. Queasy stomach.

But he was there. She was here. And Gabe was coming.

She went to her bedroom and what she liked to call her studio which was really the corner next to the window. She'd occupy herself until Gabe got here. She knew what she wanted to paint next, so she started the preliminary drawings of a little girl sitting in a tree, the wind blowing her wild hair as leaves rained around her.

When she became aware of the knocking on the back door off the kitchen, she had to blink herself back to the present. She glanced at the clock. Two hours had passed, and she hadn't even noticed. She stood and sheets of paper crackled underfoot. She glanced down at all her aborted tries before she got the balance she wanted. She glanced at the sheet still on the table. Sometimes it was so frustrating trying to make her hands with their limited skill reproduce the image in her mind.

She walked cautiously through the darkened house to the back door. What if it was Joey, though if it was him, she wouldn't expect him to knock so politely. The cats watched her from the living room with that feline combination of curiosity and caution, ready to dash for cover should they need to.

She flicked on the porch light and blinked at the sight of Avery wearing her camo outfit, the desired effect ruined slightly by her pink winter coat and pink knit hat with the pink and white pompom.

Ellie threw the door open. "Avery! What are you doing here? Were you up in the tree again?"

"Turn out the light!" Avery almost fell inside in her hurry. "He's coming back."

"What?" Ellie's heart started to race.

Avery reached up and hit the switches that threw both the porch and the kitchen into darkness. She ran to the living room and peered at the road. "See? Here he comes."

"Who?" But Ellie knew as she stood beside the girl and stared out too. The cats joined them, sitting on the sill.

"He keeps driving by your house. It's creepy."

"What do you mean he keeps driving by?"

"At least six times. Once would be just a guy going someplace. Twice or even three times could be a guy who got lost going some place. Six times is a weirdo watching your house, especially since he slows way down when he passes. I could walk by faster than he drives. It gives me the shudders."

"I'll get you for this, Angel Eyes. Don't think I won't."

They watched a car roll slowly by, the driver invisible in the dark night.

Ellie stepped away from the window, pressing against the wall even though she knew he couldn't see her in the dark house any more than she could see him. She grabbed her cell phone and dialed Gabe. Her heart sank as she was kicked immediately into voice mail. He had his phone turned off for the meeting.

"Gabe, there's a car cruising by the house repeatedly. It's probably just some girl who wants to see Nick, but it makes me nervous."

"It's a man," Avery said. "I saw him through my binoculars."

For the first time Ellie noticed the binoculars hanging around Avery's neck.

Avery put them to her eyes. "Well, they're really my father's and he doesn't like me to use them because I change the setting." She took a moment to look earnestly at Ellie. "I plan to wipe my prints and put the setting back like I found it. He'll never know."

Ellie heard more hope than certainty in that pronouncement. "It's a man," she repeated to Gabe. "Avery saw him. It's probably not Joey, but still…."

"Uh-oh," Avery said. "He just pulled to the side of the road and parked a couple of houses down. He's getting out." She turned her intelligent gaze on Ellie. "If it was summer and there were leaves on the trees, we'd never even know he was there. I've been mad because the leaves are gone and you can see me, but now I'm glad. If there was still leaves, he could sneak right up on us."

"If it weren't for you, kiddo, he'd be sneaking up on me, leaves or no leaves. I owe you big time."

Avery grinned as she pulled her hat off by the pompom. "I'll collect."

Of that Ellie had no doubt. She stared down the road and watched as the man turned toward the house, and though his face wasn't clearly visible, the way he held his body screamed Joey.

"It's Joey!" she told Gabe's phone. She swallowed hard. "It's Joey."

Fight or flight. Flight! Her car was mere steps away out in the drive, but she doubted she could get to it and away before

Joey reached the house. She looked around for some place to hide.

None of the usual places would work. The few closets were so small and shallow the hangers had to be put sideways on pegs rather than hung on a rod. She and Avery'd never fit. Under the beds was out because the space was full of cardboard storage units used to help make up for the lack of closets. She grimaced. The attic crawl space was the only possible option.

As she dialed 911, Ellie pulled Avery into her bedroom and to the door that led to the small attic. When she'd first seen it when they moved in, she'd been happy there wasn't a pull-down stairs. They always felt so wobbly. Then she'd gone up, thinking there would be good storage up here. Not so. The treads were so narrow and the walls pressed so close, it was almost impossible for an adult to ascend, let alone carry something up. She pulled the door open, looked up, and shuddered. It was claustrophobic even in the daytime. She hated the thought of going up there into darkness, but she had no choice.

Buddy and Midnight watched with interest from their new positions on the bed, but they made no move to go with her. At the first sign of trouble, they'd doubtless slink under the beds between the storage boxes and be perfectly safe.

"There's a man outside, and he's going to try and break in and hurt us," Ellie told the 911 woman. "We need help immediately!"

"Has he come in your house?"

"Not yet, but he will. He's threatened me before, struck me before." She gave her name and address.

"We'll send someone immediately," she said.

"Please let Gabe Hyland know." Ellie's breath came in nervous gasps. "He's at the township meeting and his phone's off."

She hung up and took a deep breath. "Come on, Avery. Up we go."

The girl hesitated as she looked up. "I can't see."

"And we can't turn on the light. He'd see. There are windows at each end for ventilation. Here, take my hand." Ellie held it out, and Avery grabbed on tight. "Close the door behind you."

Avery did, and what had been moonless midnight in the bedroom became pitch black in the stairwell. Avery gave a little hiccup of distress.

Ellie tapped her cell phone, and the weak light it gave seemed a million candle power in the stygian darkness. At least they could see as step by step they climbed, hand against the wall to balance themselves,

"What was that noise?" Avery asked in a trembly voice as they neared the top.

"That scurrying? Just a little mouse running away from us." *Please, Lord, just a mouse. Not anything worse.*

"I don't like it up here." Avery sounded like Ellie felt.

"That just shows what an intelligent girl you are."

"But God'll take care of us. Right?"

"Right." *Oh, Lord, please!*

Ellie squeezed Avery's hand as they climbed deeper and deeper into the darkness. The fear pressed in on her, making even the act of drawing a breath an effort.

Downstairs a window shattered.

———

Gabe stretched as he walked out of the meeting room for the short break in the discussion of the police force. Should Lyndale keep its own department, or should they become part of the county force? Several smaller towns and townships already shared a force for financial reasons. So far Lyndale had kept its own department, but some of the new members of the Board of Supervisors were questioning the wisdom of continuing to do so.

Absently Gabe checked his phone. He'd felt it vibrate against his hip earlier, but it hadn't been at a time in the discussion he could check it. He had been too busy fighting for Hollis and Dottie and the rest of his staff.

"Gabe!"

His blood chilled when he heard the tension and fear in Ellie's voice as she told him about the man driving by her house. Then he heard the little piping voice of Avery, the wonder kid.

"It's Joey!" Ellie screamed and the phone went dead.

"I gotta go!" Gabe yelled to the Board secretary who was leaning over the drinking fountain. "Emergency—which is why we need to keep the local force!"

He hit the road with his Kojak light flashing.

Hang on, Ellie! I'm coming! Right behind that thought came a desperate prayer. *Oh, Lord, keep her safe! I can't take losing a second woman I love.*

He called Dottie. "Get Hollis to Ellie's right away!" He gave the address.

"He's on his way. She called 911," Dottie said.

Gabe grunted and hung up. Red, he suddenly thought. If Robyn had been golden yellow, all openness and sunshine, Ellie was red. Strong. Vibrant. A fighter and an overcomer. An achiever and a survivor.

His marriage to Rob had been a lot like sinking into a warm tub of water, all nerveless relaxation and pampered ease. He had thoroughly enjoyed her gentle spirit and loving heart, and he knew he would have been happy with her all his life if she had lived.

Life with Ellie, on the other hand, would be all challenge and discovery, energy and exhilaration, confrontation and reconciliation. And, he realized with astonishing certainty, the man he had become since Robyn's death wanted that life. Badly. He pushed his foot harder on the accelerator.

———

"We'll just hide out up here until he goes," Ellie whispered to Avery as the sound of the broken glass faded.

"What if he looks for us up here?" Avery's voice shook. "He's going to see the door and check what's behind it."

"Ellie! I know you're here!" The thud of heavy footfalls sounded below them as Joey walked methodically from room to room. She heard doors open and shut.

"He's looking in closets," Avery whispered.

"Shh!" Ellie hit 911 again. "He's in the house," she whispered with desperation. "I can hear him moving upstairs."

"Help's on the way," came the response. "Just hold on."

Ellie was so tense her neck and back had the flexibility of an iron rod. She and Avery were sitting in the middle of an empty space. All Joey had to do was open the door. The light would pour up the stairwell and there they'd be.

Think, Ellie! She flashed her phone again as she looked wildly around the attic.

She looked at the support beam at the back of the room. It wasn't very wide, but it was all there was, and anyone coming up the stairs would be facing away from it.

The idea of ducking behind it evoked visions of vicious spiders spinning huge webs waiting to entangle her so she would be cocooned like Frodo in the scene with the giant spider in *Lord of the Rings: Return of the King*, the scene she could never bring herself to watch, much to Nick's amusement. But what choice was there? It might give them a few more minutes of safety so Gabe could get here.

Ellie crossed to the pillar, pulling Avery with her. She hesitated a minute before committing to the hiding place, but she had no other choice. She made herself move forward, and a cobweb caught her across the cheek. She felt sweat pop out all over her body. It was all she could do not to scream. Arachnophobia. The only fear stronger was of Joey.

She brushed the cobweb off her face with a shaking hand and crouched with her arms around Avery, her back against the support. Downstairs she could hear Joey on a rampage. He swore viciously as he knocked things over, and he yelled all that he would do when he got his hands on her.

"Why's he so mad at you?" Avery whispered. "You're nice."

Ellie sighed. What to say? She went with the current reason. "Nick came home with me instead of staying with him."

"That's Nick's dad? The one he went with last night?" Avery sounded scandalized.

Ellie made a little humming sound of assent.

"Huh." Avery jumped at a particularly loud crash that sounded directly below them. "Maybe my dad's not so bad after all."

The attic door crashed open and light from downstairs flooded up. Ellie leaned into the support beam. Avery huddled against her. The attic light blazed on, and Ellie felt more vulnerable than she ever remembered feeling. Wild as he used to get, Joey'd never been this purposefully destructive and bent on revenge. All the insecurities and fears flooded back.

As Joey ascended the stairs, Ellie's whole body began to shake.

"I know you're up here, Angel Eyes."

The superiority and contempt in his voice hung heavy in the air, a great weight pressing on her chest, forcing her back in time. She felt herself becoming that girl huddled at Joey's feet, waiting for the next blow.

No! Oh, Lord, don't let that happen!

"You think you can get away from me?" Joey gave a sharp laugh at such an absurd idea.

With a dry mouth and pounding heart, she peered around the beam and watched the back of his head appear as he climbed.

She retreated, a turtle withdrawing into the safety of her shell, and stayed as still as she could with her heart running a marathon in her chest.

"I can smell your fear you know." He spoke with satisfaction as he paused half-way up the stairs and looked around.

Ellie closed her eyes and tried to make herself and Avery as small as possible.

Joey came the rest of the way up, turned in a circle, and looked at her support beam. She could feel the moment of discovery.

"Well, hello, Angel Eyes." He grinned as he came to stand mere inches from her. "I always did like you cowering at my feet."

Her legs were shaking so much she wasn't sure they'd hold her, but Ellie forced herself to stand. She might be so terrified she was afraid she'd throw up, but she was never cowering at his feet again. She pushed Avery behind her.

Joey grabbed Ellie's wrist, and her skin contracted under his touch. He tried to yank her toward him. She resisted. "No! No, no, no!"

"It's me or that fugitive warrant and jail, Angel Eyes." He grinned. "Take your pick."

"What fugitive warrant?" She felt her feet slipping on the plywood flooring as he continued to haul her in. "And I'll take jail!"

A flashing light appeared in the window at the other end of the attic. At the same time the cobweb brushed across her face again, only this time the spider that went with it crawled across it, looking the size of a baseball with great hairy legs.

She wasn't certain who screamed loudest, Joey, Avery or herself. They all jumped and raced to the center of the attic. She brushed frantically at her face and hair.

"It's not on you." Avery pulled on her arm. "It's on him." She pointed and Ellie watched the spider, probably every bit as frightened of them as they were of it, climb over the edge of Joey's black leather jacket collar and disappear inside as Joey disappeared down the stairs, muttering and brushing at his neck. She heard the back door fly open at the same time the front door slammed against the wall.

"Help!" she screamed. "Up here!"

Avery raced down the stairs. "Spider! Spider! And a man!"

———

"Ellie!" Gabe had heard the screams as he ran across the yard. "Ellie!" He threw his shoulder into the door and fell into the house as the lock gave way. When he heard her yell, "Up here," he went weak with relief.

He ran toward her voice and met Avery racing out of Ellie's bedroom yelling about spiders and a man. Spiders? The screaming was about a spider?

"It's a huge spider!" Avery began to cry now that help was here. "Huge!" She spread her hands as far apart as she could.

Gabe rushed to the stairs, Avery at his heels, only to be forced to go slowly up as his shoulders barely fit.

Ellie stood in the center of the attic, hand pressed to her mouth, looking slightly hysterical with what seemed like laughter in spite of what she'd just been through.

"Spi-spider! Crawling on him. Big." She held her hands almost as far apart as Avery.

Clearly he'd missed the Goliath of spiders. And she was both laughing and crying.

"Oh, Gabe, I was so scared! And then the spider—" She pointed at her neck. "Down his collar." She slapped her hand over her mouth again as a half laugh-half sob escaped. "Out the back door."

Gabe wrapped his arms around her. "It's okay, El. It's over. You're safe." She shook as she clung to him. "He's not going very far. Hollis is waiting for him at his car."

"We were so scared." Ellie reached for Avery. "But this kid was one brave little girl."

Avery snuggled against Ellie. Gabe rested one hand on the girl's head as he rubbed his other hand up and down, up and down Ellie's spine. He could feel the shaking slowly lessen. "I'm proud of you both."

Ellie rested her forehead on his chest. "Thanks. Knowing you were coming helped a lot."

"You're red, you know," he said. "And red's my new favorite color."

She frowned up at him. "What does that mean?"

He stroked her hair. "It means you're strong and invincible and very, very special."

She blinked. Avery said, "Wow."

More footfalls sounded downstairs. "Hey, Mom, where are you? Why's the light flashing on top of Coach's car? And why's the cop car down the street?"

Avery charged down the steps. "Nick, Nick! You'll never guess what just happened!"

Gabe took advantage of the momentary solitude to kiss Ellie, really kiss her. "I meant what I said."

"I'm glad." She cuddled into him. "You make me feel wondrously, blessedly safe."

Safe? Not the most romantic of sentiments, but given her history and the night she'd had, safe was good. It meant she trusted him and depended on him. It was early to talk of love. They needed time to be sure, but as he wrapped his arms around her, he smiled. He'd found the woman for him.

Avery's voice floated up to them. "You should have seen it. A gigantic spider! It landed on the bad guy and scared him away!"

Ellie pulled back and her smile faded. "Quick, before the kids come up here. Joey said there's a fugitive warrant out for me. What's that mean? He said I'd go to jail."

"There is such a warrant. I went into the law enforcement data bases today and found it. It was issued when you first left Philadelphia when Joey reported your taking Nick as a kidnapping. It's issued for Gabriella Francella."

"But I didn't kidnap Nick. I saved him."

Gabe nodded. "I agree, and I don't think you'll have a problem showing that, especially after tonight. Cases of one parent running with a child or children and the other parent pressing charges are touchy, but they're usually resolved without jail time. It's a matter of both of you sitting down with your attorneys in the judge's chambers and talking things through to a reasonable compromise."

"There was no room for compromise then and there isn't now, not after tonight."

"Which is what your lawyer will tell the judge. Nonna's testimony will help, and the destruction downstairs will make your case."

"No jail?"

"No jail, at least not for you. Joey has a bit to answer for though."

She started down the stairs. "It's pretty bad down there?" She looked apprehensively through the open door into her bedroom.

Nick appeared, his face a mix of anger, disbelief, and vulnerability. "Mom! Everything's a mess! He ruined our stuff!"

Gabe trailed as she walked through her house looking at all her possessions, including the wonderful picture over the sofa, broken, torn, and defaced. Tears filled her eyes, and he was afraid she was blaming herself.

Hollis came in through the front door, looked around and whistled. "What a mess!"

Gabe left Ellie to talk with his officer. "You have always been one of my most observant officers."

"Well, it is," Hollis said defensively.

Gabe rubbed his forehead. "Sorry for the sarcasm. Rough night. Where's Terafino?"

"Don't know. He never came near his car. He must have seen me and kept going. Dottie sent over Patsy Finnegan, and she's watching the vehicle now."

"Pictures." Gabe waved his hand to indicate the devastation. "Lots of pictures. Camera's in my car."

Hollis disappeared for a few seconds, then reappeared and began recording the damages.

Gabe found Ellie in Nick's bedroom. Nick and Kenny were collecting all the broken things and piling them on the bed. Several of Nick's trophies had been snapped in half.

"I'm so sorry, Nick." Ellie's eyes brimmed with tears. "If I—"

"Don't!" Gabe set his finger across her lips. "It isn't your fault, El."

"It isn't, Mom." Nick laid one of the damaged trophies on the bed. "And they can be repaired."

Ellie bent and picked up an Eagles team poster ripped into pieces. She stared at it as two tears rolled down.

Gabe leaned close. "Ellie, do not accept responsibility that isn't yours."

"But if I hadn't—"

"El, couples break up every day. Ninety-nine point nine percent of men would merely be sad or relieved, depending on who did the breaking up. They would not go into their former girl's home and destroy it. No one has the right to behave like this toward another. It's wrong and the sign of a sick man, especially with the passage of eight years."

And he couldn't forget that the man was still out there, free to weave his web and inject his venom whenever he chose.

But not for long if Gabe could help it.

CHAPTER 28

Finally things calmed down and everyone who didn't live here left. They cleaned up the mess without saying much, then went to bed. Nick lay in the dark and felt as if his brain might explode. His father—his father!—had broken into their home and wrecked it. How could he do such a thing?

He punched his pillow into a mound and closed his eyes. They popped open as thoughts ricocheted wildly and images did replays on his mental TV. Broken trophies were the least of it. He could always get them fixed. But Mom's big painting and her paint supplies and the dishes and the pitcher that had been Grandmom Francella's, one of Mom's few things from her mom.

It struck him how mean vandals and vandalism were. Mean. There was no other word for it. People destroyed things that meant nothing to them but which meant a lot to the people they belonged to. Like that pitcher. Grandmom Francella was dead. Mom couldn't get another pitcher from her. Something precious had been taken by someone mean.

His father.

Vindictive had been a vocabulary word last week in English, and he'd now seen that word in action. It was like taking vandalism one step further. It wasn't just destruction for the fun of destroying. It was a personal attack. When Coach said most guys who broke up with their girls or wives just moved on, he was right. Dad's need to dominate, to always be the one who was right, who was in control, led to thinking that said you were right even when it was obvious you were wrong. It made you think you had every right to get even.

How much of what had happened tonight was his fault for not staying with Dad?

In his mind he heard Coach tell Mom it wasn't her fault. Nick agreed. And it wasn't his fault either. Not really. He took a deep breath as he embraced that thought.

He stared at the crack in the ceiling, its outline a black fissure in the flat gray of the darkened room. His father's anger made him feel sick. It also made him realize what he'd been thinking for years without even realizing it. He'd been hoping against hope that all would be well. After all, except for that one night, his memories of Dad toward him were full of approval and love.

He snorted in self-disgust, then held his breath as Kenny snuffled in his sleep. The last thing he wanted was Kenny to wake up and try to make him feel better. He turned on his side and his thoughts followed.

He was as bad as some little kid who thought his absentee father was a prince among men, a rich guy with a big house and a fancy car, someone who loved him unconditionally and would fix all the problems in his life. How pathetic was that.

He was smart. He should have accepted that the violence hadn't been just that one night toward him. He'd heard the insults, the slaps, the cries for years, and he should have known better. Maybe Dad learned to be violent from his father who maybe learned it from his father. Who knew how far back it went? It was like the Old Testament said, the sins of the fathers were visited on the children to the third and fourth generation.

His breath caught. Did that mean he had to be violent too? Was he born that way and he couldn't avoid it even though he hated it? Was the tendency to violence like a disease you had from birth, like spina bifida or cystic fibrosis, and you couldn't get rid of it no matter how hard you tried?

Another thought gripped him. Was that why he liked football so much? Because it could be brutal? He thought of the hard tackle that had taken him down, the one that rattled his bones. He knew that player had purposely hit him to hurt him. He knew some played the game that way—kill the other guy. Some pro teams paid their players bonuses to hurt the quarterback.

Did he play that way without realizing it? Was he too aggressive, maybe even cruel on the field, and he was too dumb to see it?

Oh, God, I don't want to be that way! I don't!

"Therefore, if anyone is in Christ, he is a new creation; the old is gone, the new has come."

The verse, memorized long ago in Sunday school, struck him with such force that he actually sat up. He could feel his mouth hanging open.

"What's wrong?" Kenny asked from his sleeping bag on the floor.

The old was gone! Nick grinned. Kenny thought he was smiling at him and grinned back. "So you're okay?"

The generational chain was broken! His father might be an abuser. His grandfather might have been an abuser. Maybe even his great-grandfathers for generations back, but he didn't have to be that way. He was a new creation! He was a Jesus man, a man of the day, not the night, a man of the Light.

What a relief! The fog in his brain cleared, and he could see clearly. He could feel whole in spite of half of his genetics.

"Good night, Kenny." He lay back down and in minutes was sound asleep.

CHAPTER 29

Thanksgiving Day and the possibility of an undefeated season arrived cold and overcast with snow predicted by late afternoon. Ellie took her seat in the stadium at ten in the morning wrapped in her warmest coat. She lost no time tucking a fleece blanket around her legs. She pulled her red beret down over her ears, tugged her red and black wool blend scarf up over her mouth, and stuffed her gloved hands in her pockets.

Avery sat beside her bundled in pink. The girl stared at her pink mittens in disgust. "When I grow up, I'm never wearing pink again," she muttered. "I tell them and tell them, but do they listen?" She glared at Ellie.

Ellie extended her red blanket to cover Avery's knees. "You look cute in pink."

The glare intensified. "Cute? Me? Please." She pointed at the red blanket. "I like red. I want a red jacket. I want red frames for my glasses. I want a red hat like yours. Well, not exactly like yours. They'd laugh me out of school in that, but the color."

Grinning, Ellie tried to short circuit the mood of the day. "I hear Santa likes red, and Christmas is coming."

"Yeah, and they'll probably go away and leave me behind then too."

Ellie flinched inside, but she didn't let her sympathy show. Avery needed no encouragement in her sour mood. "It's wonderful to see you in such a good humor this morning."

"It's 'cause I love holidays so much."

Ellie heard the hurt below the pique. "What are you and Mrs. Cotton doing for Thanksgiving dinner?"

"She's taking me to her sister's house." She made it sound as painful as a pre-Novocain day in the dentist's chair.

"Does she have a big family?"

"Two sisters. They'll both be there." She shrugged. "They're okay, I guess, if you don't mind lots of wheezing and teeth-sucking. They let me watch all the TV I want."

Avery was spending Thanksgiving with three old ladies? No wonder she was cranky. Not for the first time, Ellie wondered what was wrong with the girl's parents.

"Would you like to spend Thanksgiving with us?" she asked. "All day, I mean. Not just this morning for the game."

Avery's eyes went wide. "You mean it? I could have Thanksgiving dinner with you and Nick and Kenny?"

"And Coach and his mom and dad and family. And you can meet my nonna. What do you say? Shall I speak to Mrs. Cotton?"

Avery jumped to her feet and hugged Ellie. "Mrs. Cotton won't care. She'll be glad to get rid of me. Oh, thank you, thank you!"

As Ellie hugged the girl back, she hoped Maris wouldn't care either.

Gabe and the team ran onto the field, and a great roar went up. The bottom dropped out of Ellie's stomach as she jumped to her feet, clapping her gloved hands together and joining the crowd in its cheers. She had no trouble spotting Gabe, running with his team, his fair hair standing out among the sea of helmets. Her blood fizzed at the sight of him.

Oh, Lord, this game means so much to him. Help him do well. And if You want to let us win, that'd be nice, too. But mostly Ellie prayed God would help him coach wisely so he could look back on the game without regrets, whatever the final score.

And Nick. She searched the jerseys until she found his number. It seemed like yesterday he was Avery's size, all active little boy, and somehow, while she blinked, he had become this tall, strong young man. *Keep him from injury, Lord. Help him play well.*

The cheerleaders, wearing black leggings under their little skirts, anoraks in the school colors, and fuzzy earmuffs, released scores of balloons. The band played the school song and the National Anthem. An unbeaten season was on the line, and Avery jumped up and down at the excitement of her first live game. "This is so cool! This is so cool!"

Ellie wondered how long it would take her to become bored.

"Oh, I'm so nervous I can hardly stand it," Andy Rode's mother said from her seat behind Ellie. "I think I'm going to be sick."

"Spare us," her husband said. "Please."

But Ellie knew exactly what Andy's mom meant. She tried to swallow her nerves and wished she hadn't eaten that granola bar for breakfast.

"Think we can squeeze in three more?"

Ellie looked up at a smiling Maris with Dr. Hyland and Matt right behind her.

Ellie and Avery slid over to make room. "Sit here at your peril. It tends to get a bit loud."

"Just the right place for us," Dr. Hyland said. "Maris cheers very enthusiastically."

Maris grinned. "I do, and I'm proud of it. You can never cheer too loudly for your babies."

"We're cheering for Nick," Avery announced.

"Tell you what," Maris said to the girl. "I'll cheer for Nick too if you cheer for Gabe."

"You mean Coach?"

Maris nodded. "He's my boy."

Avery looked like she couldn't believe Coach had a mother, but she nodded. "Deal."

"Does he know you're here?" Ellie asked.

"He knows I'm here." Matt Hyland climbed around his parents and Avery and sat down on Ellie's other side.

Ellie grinned up at Gabe's little brother. "You're hard to miss."

"So they tell me."

A drum roll sounded and a great cheer went up as the opposing team kicked off to Lyndale. The team moved the ball to the opposition's forty-five yard line before they had to punt. The opposition made it back to Lyndale's forty. Back and forth the ball went as both teams worked off their big game nerves. Lyndale finally scored after Nick caught a pass on the eight yard line to set them up, but the other team scored on their next possession. Ellie's nerves were more than ready for half time.

"It's a good thing it's so cold and I need to wear gloves, or I would have all my nails chewed off by now," Ellie muttered.

Maris laughed. "When Gabe played, the pressure was due to the fact that they lost every game, poor kids. Things improved a lot when he played at Wexford, but this is by far the biggest game he's ever been involved in. I don't even want to think what my blood pressure is."

Avery tugged on Ellie's sleeve. "Can I have a hot dog?"

"Sure." Ellie stood. "And a Coke?"

"I'll take her," Matt said. "I think the rest of us could use some hot chocolate."

"Hot chocolate?" Avery looked like she'd swoon. "With marshmallows?" She danced after Matt as they left to find the concession stand.

"Ellie," Maris said, her voice serious. She put her hand over Ellie's.

Ellie tensed. Somehow Maris knew how she felt about Gabe and didn't approve. Maybe she even knew about the fugitive warrant.

If Ellie'd thought she was nervous before, it had been like a Pennsylvania winter compared to the Antarctic winter now deep freezing her. She wasn't certain she wanted to know how Maris and Dr. Hyland felt about her as a potential successor to the wonderful Robyn. She was too afraid of the answer. She and Robyn couldn't be more different, the perfect Christian and the woman with the tainted history. One of the most obvious proofs of the wide gulf fixed was the young man out on the football field. But much as she regretted Joey, she could never regret Nick.

"I asked Avery to come to dinner with us," Ellie blurted. Change the topic. Delay the keep-away-from-my-boy lecture. "I hope that's okay?" And how awkward would dinner be after the lecture?

Maris waved a hand. "She's little. She won't take up much space."

"Her parents went to the Caribbean for the week and left her with their elderly housekeeper."

Maris shook her head in disgust. "Some people. And of course she can come. We'd be delighted to have her."

"Thanks." Ellie grinned wryly. "I seem to be collecting wounded souls and sharing them with you. Avery. Kenny. And there's Nick and me."

Maris patted Ellie's knee. "Your compassion is one of the many things I like about you. Which brings me to what I want to say while we're alone."

"I'm here," Dr. Hyland pointed out as he leaned into his wife. "And the stadium is rather full."

"Yes, but they're all busy." Maris flicked a hand to brush the several hundred people away. "And you, my dear, are discreetly not listening. Or pretending you're not listening."

He gave her a sardonic grin and turned his attention to the band on the field.

Ellie's stomach fluttered as she waited for whatever it was Maris wanted to say. *Help me handle this well, Lord!*

"I—we want to thank you for the change you've made in Gabe," Maris said.

Ellie blinked. "Change? Gabe? Me?"

"Oh, yes. When Robyn and their baby were killed, something shut down in him. He drew into himself. Oh, he did all that was expected of him and more as far as work and church, but he'd been so badly hurt that he kept himself in emotional neutral. At first we weren't worried. He needed time to heal, and we ached with him. But in recent years we've been concerned about him, all of us. He's needed to love again, to care again, to invest himself in someone special again." Maris beamed. "And here you are."

Relief made Ellie dizzy. Maris and Dr. Hyland approved! "But I can't be what you had hoped for Gabe. I come with so much baggage and such a terrible history." And potential present troubles too, though she'd been advised by her new lawyer, obtained only yesterday, not to talk about the fugitive warrant with anyone.

"What I've prayed for Gabe since he was born was a woman who loved him and who loved the Lord. Robyn was all that, but she didn't stay with us long. As time's passed since her death, I've prayed that very same prayer for him." She smiled. "I've put no other restrictions on my hopes."

"Still you didn't expect someone like me. I know that."

"You're right; I didn't expect you. I expected a good little Christian like Robyn, a woman who had followed the Lord all her life. But God had other plans, and here you are. And it's clear that Gabe cares for you very much."

Ellie flushed with pleasure. She didn't know what to say. "Thank you. I never imagined I'd meet a man like him."

Maris took Ellie's hands in hers. "I can't imagine how hard it's been, Ellie. Your experience is outside mine, but while you were struggling, all unknowing I've been praying God's protection on you. And though I didn't even know he existed, on Nick. I've also been asking the Lord what was keeping you so long, but He was growing you for our son." She smiled. "I began to wonder if Gabe would ever find the right woman, but I think he has."

Ellie's eyes swam with tears. "But my past."

"Is the past. That's what Christ's forgiveness is all about. You've proven yourself since you became a believer. You've become a woman of character." She gave a quick grin.

Dr. Hyland leaned over his wife. "Ellie, let me say that I agree with Maris. We thank God for you." He glanced at his wife, put his arm around her and squeezed. "Of course, I wasn't listening and I'm merely assuming here."

Ellie watched the last of the band show without seeing a thing. *Thank You, Lord! Thank You, thank You!*

Avery came dancing back to her seat, and Ellie felt like dancing with her.

"I got a hot dog and chips and hot chocolate." Avery held out her booty, stored in a little cardboard holder, for Ellie to see.

Maris helped drape the blanket back over the little girl's knees as Avery frowned at her food. She couldn't balance things on her knees because they sloped down too much.

"Let me hold that for you," Ellie offered, and took Avery's beverage as visions of hot chocolate running down the back of the man sitting in front of them flashed through her mind.

"I'll eat fast," Avery promised as she took a bite of her hot dog.

"Take your time," Ellie said. "We've got the whole second half."

Matt doled out the hot chocolates he was carrying, leaving Ellie with a cup in each hand, and they settled in for the second half.

When Nick scored at the end of the third quarter, Avery jumped up and down and screamed her delight. "He is so cool!" she shouted. "He is so cool!"

That touchdown proved to be the winning one, and the game ended with Lyndale enjoying their first ever undefeated season. The crowd went crazy. From somewhere, some of the guys on the team had gotten a tub of Gatorade that they dumped all over Gabe who sputtered and shuddered at the drenching, grinning the whole time.

"Just like on TV!" Avery shouted, delighted.

"Hope he doesn't catch his death," Maris said through a broad grin. "What a day!"

Ellie knew that no one else was as deeply happy over the outcome as she was. Her boy did well and her boyfriend—stupid word, but what else could she call him?—did too. The two men in her life.

At that moment Gabe turned to the stands and began to scan the crowd. He quickly found her and his parents thanks to Matt's height. Gabe's joy radiated from him. Dr. Hyland clasped his hands over his head in a classic victory symbol, and Gabe waved. Then he zeroed in on Ellie and blew a kiss.

"Ellie!" Mrs. Rode shrieked. "Did I really see what I saw?"

Ellie nodded as she smiled back at Gabe with all the love in her heart. Then he turned and trotted out onto the field to shake the hand of the opposing coach.

Her chest swelling with joy, she scanned the happy faces in the stadium, sharing the special moment with all of them—and froze. A frisson of fear danced up her spine. Was that Joey up there?

Matt clapped her on the back, rocking her in place. She grinned automatically at him, then turned and looked for Joey again. How like him to think himself beyond consequences for what he did the other night. Show up like nothing's wrong. But if it had been him, he'd disappeared.

She looked around for a cop to report him but caught herself. She wasn't even sure she'd seen him. Besides, if it was him, he wouldn't harm Nick and couldn't harm her. She had friends to protect her today. He'd never dare come near her.

Loving the wonderful luxury of feeling safe, she pushed Joey from her mind and joined the stream of happy fans making their way to the stadium exits, Avery's hand firmly clasped in her hers.

"We'll see you at five," Maris kissed Ellie on the cheek. "You too, young lady," she added to Avery who bounced in delight.

When Ellie and Avery reached the ground, Kenny, wearing a team jersey over his coat, played a salmon swimming upstream as he made his way to them through the crowd. Nick and the rest of the team had already disappeared into the locker room as had Gabe.

Kenny was vibrating with happiness. "Wasn't that the greatest?"

"I saw you taking movies." Avery stared at him through her pink specs, clearly impressed.

"I'm the team videographer," Kenny said, pride in his job evident.

"Wow!" Avery said, and Ellie thought Nick was in danger of being supplanted as the girl's hero. Football games faded from memory, but movies went on forever.

"Ms. L, can you do me a big favor?" Kenny looked apologetic.

"Sure, if I can."

"I think I ought to go wish my mom Happy Thanksgiving. She never asked me to come over or anything, but...." He shrugged. "I only want to stay about ten minutes."

"I think that's a very good idea. And you'd like me to take you?"

He nodded.

"Not a problem. Let's go."

"I've got to put the camera stuff away, and then I'll be with you. Five minutes tops."

Ten minutes later, Kenny appeared. "The locker room's chaos! Everyone's underage, so no champagne. Instead they're squirting soda all over the place. I had to escape or have my clothes ruined!" He brushed a hand down the jacket she'd gotten him at Clothes 2 Go. She knew that underneath he wore his blue sweater.

They drove to the old house on Main Street.

"Whoops, what's going on here?" Ellie asked. Sawhorses blocked the curb with a Men at Work sign beside them.

"Maybe they're actually going to fix the curb and sidewalk." Kenny seemed impressed at the possibility. "I think I'll have to revise my opinion of the landlord."

"On Thanksgiving?" Ellie continued down the street and parked at the first available spot.

"Don't look a gift horse in the mouth and all that," Kenny said.

"What's a gift horse?" After releasing her seat belt, Avery leaned over the front seat.

Ellie and Kenny looked at each other blankly.

"That's a very good question, Avery," Ellie said. "I haven't the vaguest idea. You, Kenny?"

He shook his head. "A horse that's a gift?"

"Don't worry about it," Avery said graciously. "We'll google it when we get home."

Kenny climbed out of the car. "I won't be long."

Ellie climbed out too. "Come on, Avery. We're going to wait for Kenny inside. It's too cold to sit in the car."

The three walked down the sidewalk and into the house. Ellie sighed with pleasure as she felt the heat of the little lobby. "Go, Kenny. We'll wait here." She shooed him up the stairs. As he climbed, the door of #1 opened. A skinny boy and very pale girl peered out.

"We heard voices. She gone crazy again?" The boy pointed up the stairs.

"Who?" Ellie looked up. Only two apartments. Kenny's mom and Mr. Achmed.

"Mitzi. She's nuts."

Ellie frowned. Had Kenny heard?

"Hi, Mr. Achmed. Happy Thanksgiving." Kenny waved toward a door Ellie could just see was open about five inches. She relaxed. Kenny hadn't heard. He was talking to the famous Crazy Achmed. She was disappointed that from here in the lobby she couldn't see his eye peering out.

When Ellie didn't say anything and it became obvious that nothing interesting was going to happen, the couple disappeared into their apartment looking disappointed.

"Is Mitzi Kenny's mother?" Avery looked concerned.

Ellie nodded.

"They weren't very nice." She scowled at the closed door to #1.

"But Kenny didn't hear, and we won't say anything."

Avery nodded. "We won't say anything."

Ellie lowered herself to the third step, and Avery sat beside her. She looked around the unkempt entrance hall. "This house is very old. Does Kenny really live here?"

For a little girl who had known only top of the line, this crumbling Victorian was a revelation.

"Yes, Kenny really lived here. His mother still does." She pointed to Mitzi's door. "Right there. #3. And #4 is Mr. Achmed's apartment." She swallowed a smile as she noted the door was still open a crack.

"Who lives there?" Avery pointed to a closed door to their left with #2 on its peeling black panel.

"I don't know. I've never met them."

As she said that, two men in hoodies carrying fat duffels came walking down the hall from the back of the house. They seemed surprised to see her and Avery there, but they nodded as they rang the doorbell beside apartment #2. A young man opened the door, looked equally surprised to see Ellie and Avery, and let the men in, all without saying a word.

Ellie grinned at Avery. "Now you know who lives in #2."

Still running in overdrive from the excitement of the game, Avery couldn't remain sitting. She began to climb the steps. Up two, down two. Up three, down three. Up four, down four. As she ascended and descended, she counted. Ellie leaned into the railing to get out of her way.

"Your jeans with the pretty flowers and sparkly stones look very nice, Avery."

Avery paused on step number ten and looked at her legs. "Pink flowers," she said sadly. She unzipped her coat. "Pink top."

Ellie refrained from mentioning the pink sneakers. "The flowers on your top match the ones on your jeans, don't they?"

Avery nodded. "I wanted to look nice for Nick today. I wanted him to be proud of me at the game." She started down the steps again.

When she reached the bottom, Ellie took the girl's hands and pulled her close. "You are a very kind girl, Avery, wearing something you dislike because you think it will make another happy." Ellie hugged her and kissed her on the cheek. "Thank you."

Avery wrapped her arms around Ellie's neck and buried her face in Ellie's coat. She held on for a long time, then pulled away. She gave a sniff and wiped a hand across her damp cheek. "What number am I on?"

"Eleven," Ellie said quietly, her heart breaking for this brave, lonely child.

"One, two," and Avery began her climb. When she came down, she turned on her pink sneaker and immediately started up again. "Twelve, thirteen. Fourteen," she called as she reached the top step. She didn't start down as Ellie expected but walked right up to #3 and knocked.

Kenny must have opened the door, though Ellie couldn't see from where she sat. She heard Avery ask, "Can I come in and see where you live?"

"Sure, kid, right this way. Hey, Mom, we've got company."

The sound of the door closing was followed by the sound of another opening. Footsteps advanced from the rear of the house toward the lobby. Ellie looked over her shoulder and felt her heart seize.

Joey!

CHAPTER 30

Joey smirked at her look of panic as she sat huddled against the banister. She stared at him and said nothing, too frightened by his appearance to even speak. There was something profoundly satisfying in the knowledge that he had such immense power over her.

"Hello, Angel Eyes," he said cheerfully. "Imagine bumping into you here."

She climbed to her feet, and it looked like she had to lean against the wall to remain upright. He hoped she was terrified. If she wasn't, she would be before he was finished with her.

It had infuriated him to watch her during the football game. She'd sat surrounded by a group who considered her one of them. They talked with her, laughed with her. A tall guy even went with some kid to get food for her at half time. Another boyfriend? His kid? Her kid?

He thought many of the people around her were the parents of other players because they congratulated specific people if a certain kid made a good play. They cheered with Ellie a lot because Nick did so well, patting her on the back as if she had somehow helped Nick.

Those congratulations infuriated him the most. *He* should have been in that cluster of people. He, not she. He should have been receiving praise for his son's prowess. He should have been talking with the other fathers about the previous games, the outstanding plays, the heartbreaking mistakes. As he shivered among strangers, he shook with suppressed rage at Ellie for denying him the chance to watch Nick develop over the years. Just think how much better the kid'd be if he'd had his old man to coach him. Not that blond interfering guy who came to Terafino's with Ellie but him!

Keeping his hate hidden as he approached her in the hallway of this dingy apartment, he smiled. "My boy did well today, don't you think? Won the game for them."

Ellie watched him as if he were a tiger preparing to spring and devour her. "He did."

"He tells me he's being recruited."

She nodded. "His coach is helping us sort things out."

"The coach is the guy you had dinner with, the guy who came to the deli with you."

She nodded again.

"The one who blew you a kiss."

She didn't respond though she blanched.

"*I'll* help Nick with his recruitment choices." Spite seeped through even with his best efforts to contain it. "Me! Not some stupid coach."

"Only if Nick asks," she said.

The quietly delivered insult broke his restraint, and he sprang.

————

Ellie didn't even have time to scream before he was on her. Her mistake had been assuming he wouldn't dare touch her in a public place. Sure, no one was in the lobby at the moment, but this wasn't a remote solitary location. Kenny was just upstairs. So was Crazy Achmed. And there were at least three people behind door #2 and the couple in #1.

But Joey didn't care. All he wanted was to give her pain as payback for his perceived hurts. He saw himself as justified in whatever actions he took and immune from consequences, and that fact scared her more than anything.

When he grabbed her, he bent one of her arms painfully behind her, and pain stabbed her.

"Joey! Don't!"

He dropped her arm and pulled her against him, her back to his chest. One arm ringed her waist, the other pressed against her windpipe.

"Please, Joey." Her voice was thready. She struggled to get air. "I can't breathe."

He laughed and yanked her up and off her feet so that her own weight intensified the pressure on her throat.

She clawed at his arm, trying to remove the constriction, trying to get a breath. Had she ever felt so scared?

"You think you can get away with making a fool of me?" he hissed in her ear. "You think you can turn my son against me?"

"I didn't—" she gasped. "I wouldn—"

He jerked her head back. "And you called the cops on me the other night!"

Of course she did. It's what any woman did when someone broke into her house. She'd point that out to him if she could speak, but the force he was exerting on her throat was too great. Not that he'd hear even if she could speak. He was well past the point where any logic but his own distorted reasoning could make any impression.

"I had to walk for miles because the police were watching my car and I couldn't get it," he hissed in her ear. "I had to call Antony to come get me. And I've still got a great sore on my back from a spider bite. You can just be glad it didn't kill me. You could be tried for murder by spider, Ellie." His hot breath raked across her face. "I mean attempted murder, and You've. Got. To. Pay."

She heard the slow, deliberate threat as her vision grayed at the edges. She clutched his arm, trying to pull it away. If she didn't get air, she was going to pass out. In desperation she kicked back, her boot striking his shin.

He grunted but the pressure didn't lessen. "You will so regret that." He released her waist and reached into his coat pocket and pulled out a gun. He pressed the barrel hard against her temple.

"All those years without my son." His voice was hoarse with hatred. "I will never forgive you for that, Ellie. Never! And I believe in payback." He said the last slowly, emphasizing every icy word.

Her insides turned to water. "Don't," she tried to say. "Think of Nick." But nothing came out. Her vision was going black and her legs could no longer hold her.

As she slid toward unconsciousness, she heard him snarl, "I could shoot you right here and right now if I wanted to. Who's to stop me?"

Who indeed?

Just when she was certain she was going to pass out, Joey eased his hold and her feet touched the ground. She staggered and gasped for air, then gave a little scream as he grabbed her arm again and twisted it higher.

"You're going to break it!" Her voice was raspy, her throat aflame.

"Like I care." But to her surprise he released her with a shove.

She stumbled and grabbed the bannister with her good arm. She faced him so he couldn't grab her without her seeing it coming. She slowly lowered the arm he'd bent, her shoulder screaming protest at the abuse it had received. She cradled the arm and began rubbing her shoulder to ease the pain.

Joey back handed her, catching her full in the face. She was so startled at his unexpected move she made no sound. The force of the blow knocked her off her feet. She fell hard against the stair treads, gasping as the wind was knocked from her.

All his hatred and resentment, nine years worth, poured over her, a Niagara Falls of rage intent on destroying. He aimed the gun at her face at the same time he pulled his foot back to kick her. Her head spun from the punch and her ribs ached from the fall. She braced for the agony of the kick.

"Stop! You cannot do this in America!"

———

Achmed Azziz had been hovering at his partly opened door ever since he heard Kenny come upstairs. He heard the lady and the girl talking. He heard the girl counting the steps and asking to go into Kenny's apartment. Common sounds. Safe sounds.

When he heard a man's voice, he frowned. The words were spoken in such an ugly manner. Who had come in to bother the lady? He hadn't heard the front door open. The back door. That had to be it. The young couple downstairs, the ones who called the police all the time on Mitzi, they left the back door open when it was supposed to be locked. It was also the way the strange, silent men came and went.

Achmed's few friends always used the front door. You used the front door when you had nothing to hide.

He heard a scuffling noise and the lady give a little gasp of pain. He opened his door and peeked over the railing just in time to see a big man with dark hair hit the lady so hard she fell. Then the man pointed a gun at her and brought his foot back to kick her.

"Stop!" Achmed yelled. "You cannot do that in America."

———

Ellie'd forgotten how much a punch in the face hurt. She wanted to curl in a ball and protect herself while she cried, but the gun held her mesmerized.

Through the ringing in her ears she heard Crazy Achmed challenging Joey.

No, Achmed, no! Go back into your apartment and watch. Then you can tell the police what happened when they find my body.

Joey paused mid-kick and looked up to see who was yelling at him. He wasn't used to people interfering with anything he wanted to do, and some of his fury was now diverted to the dark-haired man on the upper landing.

Achmed looked frightened and uncertain, but he stood his ground. "Do not hurt her!"

"This is not your business," Joey roared as he leveled his gun at Achmed who ducked but didn't go away.

She couldn't let anything happen to this innocent man who had spoken in her defense. Her face throbbed, and it hurt to swallow from the near strangling, but she pulled herself to her feet. She was not going to lie there waiting for Joey to shoot Achmed or kick her. She was not falling back into the destructive patterns of the past. She was not cowering before a bully intent on exerting his power over anyone who disagreed with him. Not anymore. Not ever again. Not even if he shot her.

She was taking her stand. She was fighting back.

She looked wildly around the lobby. Where was a statue of the Virgin when you needed one? A scream would have to do.

She opened her mouth and let loose.

———

Gabe grinned at Nick as they climbed into the car. Nick settled himself in the passenger seat, the game ball held firmly in his arms. Gabe suspected both of them could have flown home on waves of euphoria except for that little thing called gravity.

"Undefeated, Nick. I still can't believe it."

"Undefeated," Nick repeated, grinning and running his hands lovingly over the ball. It was covered with the signatures of the entire team.

"Back when I was in school," Gabe began.

"Is that when you had to walk ten miles to get there and it was up hill both ways?"

"Smart mouth," Gabe said without heat. "It was only five miles."

They grinned at each other. In fact Gabe couldn't stop grinning. "Back then we lost every game."

"A perfect season!"

"Perfectly awful. I like this kind of perfect better."

They were headed toward Nick's when Gabe's cell phone vibrated on his hip. He glanced down at the readout. It was Dottie.

———

Ellie got all the reaction she wanted with her blood curdling scream, everything happening at once.

Joey jumped and spun to her, his face going white with shock and fury.

Achmed's eyes went wide, and he looked more frightened than ever.

The young man in #2 ran into the hall, followed by the men with duffels though they weren't holding them at the moment. The couple in #1 threw their door open, phones in hand.

Kenny exploded from his mother's apartment, Avery and Mitzi on his heels. "What's wrong, Ms. L?" he yelled., peering down at her. Then he spotted Joey. "Call 911, Mom! Quick!"

"I already dialed," the skinny girl from #1 said, but her words were lost in the general confusion.

Mitzi ignored Kenny and smiled down the stairs. "Joey, what are you doing here?"

"I got a phone." Avery pulled a pink one from her coat pocket and shoved it at Kenny.

"What's going on?" The guy from #2 looked up at Mitzi.

"It's not me this time!" Mitzi pointed at Ellie. "It's her."

"I'm calling 911," Kenny yelled.

"I already did," the skinny girl repeated.

"He is hit her," Achmed indicated Joey. "Is not allowed in America."

"Really, Joey?" Mitzi scowled. "I thought you had more class."

"Shut up, Mitzi! Shut up, all of you!" Joey's eyes were wide and wild. He waved his gun. "Get away, all of you."

Immediately the two visitors to #2 produced their own weapons, both trained on Joey. "Drop it!" they ordered.

At that moment the front door burst open and people wearing navy jackets with lettering on the back rushed in, guns drawn.

"This is a raid!" yelled a man that Ellie recognized as the not-drunk man who told her she'd ruin everything. "DEA! Drop your weapons!"

In the confusion of the door slamming open and the men yelling, Joey pocketed the gun he had no intention of dropping. No one, no matter the agency they worked for, was taking away what was his. He stared at the agents from the Drug Enforcement Agency, at their guns and somber expressions, and tried to look innocent. He held his hands out and away from his body. His heart was hammering so loudly he could hardly hear. How had the cops gotten here already? Ellie's scream was still vibrating in the air.

But they weren't the local law. They were DEA. This was a planned raid. He cursed silently. They would pick today to break a local drug ring and time it for when he was here.

"Who screamed?" one of the agents demanded.

Ellie raised her hand. "Me." Joey saw her lips move, but no sound came. The scream must have fried her already sore vocal cords. She looked frail, staring down at them from halfway up the stairs.

"You all right, lady?"

She nodded.

The agent turned to the man from #2. "Melvin Vining?"

The man nodded.

"She with you?" The agent indicated Ellie.

Mel Vining hesitated. *Claim her!* Joey loved the idea of her getting in trouble. But the guy blinked and shook his head. "I never saw her before in my life."

The agent nodded and slapped a piece of paper in the man's hand. "Melvin Vining, we have a warrant to search your apartment."

Vining took a step back, shaking his head. "You have no right." But it was hollow bluster. If they had a warrant, they had the right.

Joey noted with amusement that the couple in #1 had disappeared into their apartment, and the two men who came out of Vining's apartment were trying to slowly slip down the hall, attempting to distance themselves from disaster. Their weapons had disappeared from view too.

Joey pointed to them. "They're with Vining," he said as loudly as he could. Misdirection. He and his gun needed to get out of here before Ellie said anything. He'd fade away to live and fight another day.

"Thanks, we know," said a woman agent standing near him. "Just hang close, will you? We'll need to talk to you." She looked at Ellie and at Mitzi who watched open-mouthed from the second floor with her kid and the foreign guy. "You folks too."

As she spoke, three agents appeared from the back of the house, preventing the escape of the two trying to slink away. An agent pulled out the familiar laminated card and began to read as the others snapped on wrist restraints. Both slinkers were relieved of their weapons.

Vining looked furious as two agents led him away. The remaining agents disappeared into Vining's apartment, no doubt to begin tearing it apart for drugs and/or drug money.

Joey looked at Ellie, the bright red mark on her cheek clearly visible. She had a hand holding her throat. He lifted his hand, formed a finger gun, and shot her. Bang, he mouthed and loved it when she flinched.

He backed slowly toward the door. No one appeared interested in him, intent as they were on their DEA responsibilities. They'd asked him to wait, and they assumed he'd obey like a good little boy. He sniffed. He was the one who gave the orders, not the one who obeyed. He pushed the door open and slid through. Moving slowly, innocently, just a guy leaving for a walk, he crossed the porch and started down the creaky front stairs.

———

"First, congratulations, Chief," Dottie said, "You and your boys did good."

"Thanks, Dottie. What's up?"

She cleared her throat. "Not to bring you down, but I thought you'd like to know. Hollis just called in. Something's going down over at Uplanders' house."

"Another domestic?"

"No. Not something we're involved in. But trouble, big trouble."

And Ellie was there! He grabbed his Kojak light, slammed it on the roof, and hit the accelerator. His stomach felt hollow. Who cared about an undefeated season if something happened to Ellie? *Oh, Lord, please!*

He slowed, looked, then blew through a red light. He turned onto Main and could see congestion ahead. Cars at all angles, men rushing, even a TV van from one of the Philadelphia stations.

"When the news beats the local law to a situation, things are pretty bad," Gabe muttered.

"They were at the ball game," Nick said, sounding thrilled to be speeding through town with the light flashing. "They interviewed me about having an undefeated season."

Gabe pulled his Rav4 as close to Uplanders as he could, threw the car in park, grabbed his gun, and sprinted for the house. Where was Hollis? Where was Ellie? And Kenny and Avery?

"Stay in the car," he yelled back to Nick. "Anything happens to you, your mom will kill me."

Anything happens to her, it'll kill me.

Gabe had spent all day yesterday trying to find out who the man was that Ellie spoke with, the one pretending to be a drunk, and he'd hit nothing but stone walls. The very inability to find answers told him something big was up, but he had no idea what. He certainly hadn't expected anything to happen on Thanksgiving.

As he raced toward the house, he wondered if these guys were Homeland Security after Achmed. Maybe the kid in #1 had been right. Maybe he'd had a terrorist living in his jurisdiction and he hadn't known. There was a depressing and distressing thought.

Then he saw DEA in large letters across the agents' jackets. Who were they after? Mitzi? For Kenny's sake he hoped not. The kid had enough to contend with without his mother being jailed for possession or sales. But what if the source of her new condo and improved looks wasn't Morelli after all?

He'd almost reached the house when the front door opened and a familiar figure slipped out, then hurried down the steps. Gabe's nape prickled. What was Joey doing here?

There was no reason except Ellie.

———

When the agents burst through the front door, Ellie's sense of relief was so great she had to lean into the wall to remain upright. Joey wasn't going to shoot her or Achmed or anyone else, and the duffel men weren't going to shoot Joey.

She climbed part way up the stairs to get out of the way. From this vantage point she watched the couple in #1 fade away and the duffle guys try to slip out the back.

She saw Joey point at the duffel guys and yell, "They're with Vining!" She watched the duffel guys get arrested, Mel Vining be led away, and the not-drunk undercover agent lead a large contingent of his force into #2 to conduct a search. The congestion in the hall suddenly lessened considerably. She flinched when Joey finger-shot her, then slid quietly out the door.

Should she say anything to the agents about him? But they weren't interested in her domestic problems. They had bigger issues to deal with. But on the other hand Joey shouldn't be allowed to just walk away. The police were looking for him.

"I called 911," Kenny called down to her. "Coach'll be here soon."

She nodded and tried to say thanks. All that came out was a squeak, her bruised throat not cooperating. She looked at Achmed. "Thank you," she mouthed. He flushed and looked embarrassed.

She hurried toward the door, glancing in #2 as she passed.

She skidded to a halt in astonishment. Lying on the coffee table in the living room were bricks of white powder and plastic bags filled with a colorful pharmacopeia. A photographer was busy shooting it all. An agent was holding up one of the duffel bags, showing the money stuffed inside. Mel Vining had been quite the entrepreneur.

But he wasn't her problem. Joey was. She grabbed the front door and rushed outside. Joey was walking down the street, about to disappear in the crowd that was gathering.

"Stop that man!" But she made next to no sound. She ran down the steps, pointing at him, mouthing *stop him, stop him!*

Joey must have felt her because he glanced back over his shoulder. When he saw her, he stopped and again held up his hand to finger-shoot her.

Only it wasn't his finger he pointed at her.

———

Nick watched Coach race toward Kenny's house, gun in hand. When the man had reached over Nick and pulled the gun from the glove compartment, Nick had swallowed hard. Sure, cops carried guns. Sure, Coach was a cop. But seeing him with it in his hand as he ran toward a situation others ran from was unnerving. Real. Too real.

Nick's stomach flip-flopped. This was nothing like watching stuff on TV. This scene went way past scary straight into terrifying. And Mom was in there!

Then he saw his father walking away from the house. He was trying to be casual, innocent, like he hoped no one noticed him. But his dad wasn't innocent; he was all about slyness and deceit. Nick threw open the car door and got out. Had his father somehow hurt his mother like he'd threatened? Was that why all the cars were here?

The front door to Kenny's opened and Mom rushed out. At the sight of her in one piece, Nick's knees went weak with relief.

She pointed at Dad and yelled something Nick couldn't hear. Then she started to run after him.

No one but Coach seemed to notice her or hear her. "Stay back, Ellie," he called as he raced after Dad. Then a couple of the DEA agents seemed to realize something serious was going on, something they hadn't expected, and they drew their guns.

Dad was going to get shot! Or maybe Coach. They wouldn't realize he was a cop.

Nick was surprised at how much he didn't want his father shot. He didn't like his dad. He was angry at him and wanted nothing to do with him anymore, but he didn't want him killed.

And the thought of Coach getting killed made his chest ache. He imagined Butch Cassidy and Sundance getting riddled with bullets in slow motion. That couldn't happen to Dad and Coach!

Nick began running toward his father, going faster than he'd ever run on the gridiron. But the stakes were higher than a mere undefeated season or a great scholarship.

Dad must have realized Mom and Coach were after him because he stopped, turned, and to Nick's horrified disbelief, pointed a gun at Mom. She froze, a look of disbelief on her face.

"No, Dad," he screamed. "No!"

"Ellie!" Coach yelled. "Get down! Get inside!" Coach flicked his arm toward the house though he never took his eyes off Dad.

Dad shifted his aim from Mom to Coach. "You stay away from her, Hyland! She's mine!"

Nick blocked all the yelling and all the guns and focused, grasping his perfect weapon. He drew his arm back and launched the game ball he'd continued to hold when he climbed from the car. He threw a perfect spiral straight at his father.

CHAPTER 31

When Joey turned the gun on Gabe, Ellie's heart began to hammer like a mad thing trying to escape a locked room. "No! No!"

Then Nick yelled, and her breath stopped. He was out there, exposed to all the guns and the possibility of injury or even death. "Go back, Nick! Go back!"

But only a raspy frog noise came out. Even if she had screamed and he'd heard her, she knew he wouldn't listen. Pride and fear made her insides a battlefield. *Oh, God! Only You!*

What she didn't expect was the football bullet Nick threw. It took the unsuspecting Joey right in the head and knocked him off his feet. His gun went flying.

Behind her Kenny, Mitzi, and Achmed crowded out the door just in time to see Joey hit the ground.

"Way to go, Nick!" Kenny jumped in the air and popped a victory fist.

"Joey!" Mitzi gave a distressed squeal.

Achmed said nothing, his face impassive, but he followed them all to where Joey lay. He quietly walked to the gun, lying in the grass. He picked it up and offered it, butt first, to Gabe who had his gun trained on Joey. "For you, Mr. Policeman."

Joey pushed himself to a sitting position, groaning and holding the top of his skull where he took the hit. Hollis appeared from somewhere and rushed to Gabe's side. Not that Gabe needed him. He had wrist restraints on Joey in seconds and dragged him to his feet.

Ellie rushed to Nick who was walking slowly toward his father.

"Are you all right, Nick?" she managed to whisper when she reached him.

He looked at her with sad eyes. "I'm fine." He studied the mark of Joey's slap and the red ring where the gun had been pressed to her temple. He looked from the bruises beginning to form on her neck to his father and back to her. "Are you all right?"

"I'm okay." She put a hand to her cheek. "Bruises disappear." But the pain of a father who was warped didn't go away as easily. She slid her arm around Nick's waist and gave him a quick squeeze. "Thanks for your quick thinking. You may well have saved me or Gabe or both of us."

"He's a hero!" Kenny said. "Hey, TV guys! Over here!"

Nick shook his head and tried to look invisible.

"Ellie." Gabe turned his attention to her. "Look at me."

She turned and he studied her face. His jaw went rigid at the proof of Joey's violence. She could see the anger burning in his eyes, but he held it in check.

"I'm fine, Gabe," she whispered. "Really, I am."

He looked unconvinced. "I have to take Joey in and book him."

"Book me? What'd I do?" Joey demanded. "I was just walking down the street."

Ellie couldn't believe his audacity. Here she stood, voice raspy from the near throttling, face red from the slap, ribs maybe cracked from her fall, and he thought he'd done nothing wrong? And then there was waving a gun and threatening both her and Gabe.

"We'll start with assault and battery and public endangerment and go on from there," Gabe said.

Joey took surly to a new low. "I want a lawyer."

"You're going to need one." Gabe led him toward Hollis's cruiser.

As they passed Nick, Joey pulled to a stop and glared at the son he claimed to love. "You threw that ball at me!"

Ellie watched anxiously. Joey was unstable, and he'd hurt Nick enough already.

Nick looked his father in the eye. "I did," he said quietly, "and if you ever again threaten people I love in any way, I'll defend them then too."

Joey went white with rage. "I want an apology! I deserve one. I am your father!"

Nick shook his head and said nothing.

"Then you're no son of mine! I disown you! I never want to see you again!" The last floated on the air as Gabe shoved Joey into the back seat of Hollis's squad car.

Gabe slapped the roof and Hollis drove off with Joey raging still.

Ellie's chest was tight with pain for her son. "Don't listen to him, Nick. He won't even remember he said those things tomorrow." The problem was that Nick would remember his whole life.

Nick slung an arm around her shoulder. "Don't worry, Mom. I consider the source." But his sad smile was heartrending. His beautiful victory just an hour ago was tainted. How could he ever think of it without thinking of the aftermath?

Gabe returned to them and studied Nick. "I'm sorry your day had to be ruined by all this. You deserved to be able to celebrate to your heart's content."

Nick shrugged. "I bet you need to impound the game ball as evidence or something, don't you?"

"More likely your arm," Gabe said lightly. "But I promise we'll give it back after the trial."

———

When Ellie, Gabe, Avery, and the boys arrived at Nonna's, she had a pot of her pasta e fagioli waiting for them.

"To warm you after that cold game," she said. "Louie went to the store for me." She smiled at Mr. Salerno who held a chair for her.

"You sit, Sophia. Ellie and I will serve."

Soon fragrant bowls of bean soup were before all of them. Nonna offered a prayer and they all echoed her with amens.

"So tell me," Nonna said to Nick. "I want to know all about your game."

And he told her or tried to since everyone kept interrupting with their take on things.

"It was my first game," Avery said in an infrequent silence. She gave a little bounce. "And Kenny took movies!"

Ellie grinned at Nick. Kenny was definitely replacing him as Avery's number one.

It was clear after an hour that Nonna was tiring. Everyone pitched in to wash the dishes and put them away. They crowded the front hall as they slipped on their coats and hats.

"It's snowing!" Avery hopped up and down as she looked outside. "It's so pretty!"

When Ellie hugged her grandmother goodbye, Nonna whispered, "He's even better than I thought!"

Ellie eyed Gabe and whispered, "I think I'm in love."

Nonna blinked. "You only think?"

"Nonna," Gabe said, his jacket on but not zipped. "May I see you for a moment in private?"

Nonna nodded solemnly. "In the living room." She glanced at Ellie and winked.

"What's that about?" Nick asked as the two disappeared.

Ellie just grinned, and Kenny said, "He's asking for your mom's hand. That's the way it's done, right, Mom?"

"Why do you say that?" Ellie waited for his answer.

Kenny laughed. "I got eyes."

"Why's he want your hand?" Avery asked. "That's silly."

"Nonna's my closest relative, sweetheart, so Mr. Hyland is asking for her permission to marry me."

"Really? Shouldn't he ask you?"

"He will, but it's polite to ask the parents—or in my case, grandparent—for permission. It's good manners."

"Huh," Avery said, "What if she says no?"

Ellie grinned. "She won't." And neither would she. She left with joy spiraling through her because at last she had given Nonna something to be thankful about.

———

Thanksgiving dinner at the Hylands had been wonderful and a bit overwhelming. There had been thirteen crowded around the table including Dr. and Mrs. Hyland, Matt, Gabe's two sisters, Dinah and Gracie, and one brother-in-law Connor, Grandma Hyland, as well as Avery, Nick, Kenny and last-minute addition Achmed.

Earlier in the day after Joey had been taken away, Ellie had turned to Achmed. "How can I thank you?" she croaked. "You put yourself at risk for me."

Achmed glowed. "I am glad to help."

"We all thank you." Gabe shook Achmed's hand as did a solemn Nick and Kenny.

"Today is Thanksgiving, Mr. Achmed," Ellie said. "I am very thankful for you."

"Azziz," Achmed said. "My name is Achmed Azziz."

GAYLE ROPER

"Mr. Azziz," Gabe said, "will you join us for Thanksgiving dinner?"

His eyes lit. "I look up the story on my laptop. Is nice story. Pilgrims and Indians. I don't understand Pilgrims, but I know Indians."

Ellie smiled at the shy man, wondering if he knew Native Americans or India Indians, not that it mattered. "Come and celebrate a genuine American tradition with us. We'll come for you at ten minutes before five."

They had all eaten themselves into a stupor, and when Gabe and Matt weren't recounting the glories of today's football game, they were watching more football on TV with the boys, trying to explain the finer points to Achmed. In spite of Joey, it turned out to be a good day.

After taking Achmed home, everyone slid out of their coats back at the little gray house. There was barely room to move without inadvertently punching someone.

Mrs. Cotton never came back that night, so Avery was bedded down in Ellie's bed.

"So where will you sleep?" Gabe asked as the two of them sat at the table in the kitchen, the only unoccupied room. In the living room the boys lounged in front of the TV and another football game.

Ellie shrugged. "Probably the sofa."

Gabe reached across the table and took her hand. "I spoke with your nonna."

Ellie nodded, her blood fizzing with anticipation.

He ran his thumb back and forth over her knuckles. "I was wondering—"

"Hey, Mom." Nick and Kenny crowded into the kitchen. "Have we got anything to eat?" The two of them stormed the cabinets and the refrigerator, forcing Gabe to stand so they could get out a pair of sodas.

308

Ellie looked at Gabe with a what-can-you-do smile.

Gabe held out a hand. "Come on, Ellie. I want to take a walk."

"It's snowing," Nick said.

"It's cold," Kenny added.

"It's private." Gabe bundled Ellie into her coat, red beret, and boots.

She glanced back over her shoulder as Gabe led her outside. Nick was watching her, a smile on his face. He gave her a thumbs up. She smiled back and followed Gabe into the cold, her heart warm.

EPILOGUE

One year later

Another Thanksgiving and another football season concluded. Ellie cuddled into her coat and waited for Gabe to emerge from the school. She hoped he hurried. They were hosting the family Thanksgiving dinner this evening, and there were still a multitude of chores to be done.

Nick and Kenny came out with Andy Rode. The three were flying high with the delight of another undefeated season.

"We're going to drop Andy off at his house, then go see Kenny's mom for a couple of minutes," Nick called. He loved the novelty of being the kid with the car.

Ellie nodded. "Don't stay too long. There's—"

"I know. There's lots still to do."

She wrinkled her nose at him. "Sorry. I'm obsessing." But she wanted everything to be just right for Gabe's family.

He came back and gave her a quick hug. "They love you, Mom. Relax. They're not going to stop loving you if the house is dusty or the veggies are scorched."

Ellie blinked. "How'd you get so perceptive?" she muttered at his back as he walked to the used car that Gabe had helped him pick out over the summer. A trio of girls waited near the car.

"Hey, Nick," said one with a come-hither smile. It was a lost cause for her, poor girl. Nick still had eyes only for Stephanie.

"Hi, Andy," said another, practically panting over the boy.

Kenny looked back over his shoulder at Ellie and rolled his eyes. Then he froze as a sweet young thing said, "Hi, Kenny." Eyes wide with either disbelief or fright, he turned to the cute little redhead. Ellie hoped that for the girl's sake he managed to smile.

The locker room door opened, and Gabe walked out, eyes dancing with delight.

She stood and went to him. She wrapped her arms around him and said in as sultry a voice as she could manage, "Hey, Coach, want a reward for the great game?"

He grinned down at her. "What have you got in mind?"

She reached up and kissed him. He responded enthusiastically.

"Make sure you don't tell my wife about this." He held her close. "She doesn't think much of sports groupies."

Ellie tsk-tsked. "She is so narrow minded."

They walked to Gabe's car arm in arm. This year there would be no Joey to mar the day. He was serving five to ten with court ordered counseling to help him control his anger issues. Ellie pitied whatever woman he charmed next.

Antony had taken over the running of Antonio's, and it failed within six months. Terafino's at the Italian Market was still doing well, and Antony seemed satisfied with that business. At least that's what Mitzi told Kenny. Antony still kept her in her new condo in Lyndale, but for some reason was unwilling to move her to South Philly or make an honest woman out of her. Ellie suspected the reason was named Angelina or Carmela or Delores.

"Are we supposed to pick up Avery on our way home?" Gabe asked.

Ellie nodded. "She told me she's wearing her new red sweater that she ordered online with her birthday money. 'If they won't buy me anything but pink, I'll have to buy it myself!' she said."

"Someday some man is going to have an interesting life with that girl."

"I'm praying for just the right one," Ellie said. "Just like I pray for the right women for Nick and Kenny." She squeezed Gabe's hand. "I know how wonderful the right person is."

Gabe grinned. "Remind me to give you a thank you kiss when I'm not driving."

They passed the old gray house and turned into the cul de sac where Avery lived.

"Do you realize what a strange family we have?" Gabe asked as they watched Avery run out, her overnight duffel in hand. "Starting with a little girl who has adopted us."

"Then there's the wonderful old lady whose health is starting to decline again," Ellie said with sorrow.

"But she had a good year with us," Gabe said. "Never forget that."

"That's because you made her delirious with joy when you married me."

Gabe nodded. "I did it just for her."

"I know. It was very magnanimous of you." Ellie laid her head briefly on his shoulder as Avery yanked open the rear door and climbed in. "Then there's Nick, of course."

"I love Nick," Avery announced.

"The most normal of all," Gabe said. "Thank goodness he's signed his letter of intent and all that recruitment nonsense is over!"

"Then we've got the musical comedy star/movie mogul who literally sings for his supper now that he's comfortable enough around us to be natural. By the way, a cute little redhead was waiting for him when the guys left. I think she scared him to death."

"Is my bedroom ready for me?" Avery strained forward against her seatbelt.

"It's always ready for you," Ellie said. "It's yours."

"Yeah. It's mine." She relaxed against the seat.

When they reached home, Avery was out of the car and in the house before Ellie was even unbuckled.

"Hey, Nonna, I'm here," she yelled as she disappeared from sight.

Taking advantage of the open door, Mister Thomas slipped out, wiggling with delight that they were home. He jumped about them as Gabe and Ellie walked hand in hand into the house. They could hear Avery and Nonna talking in the living room, Mr. Salerno's raspy bass a fine counterpoint.

Gabe took Ellie's coat as she slid out of it. "You sure you don't want to say anything today?" He rested his hand on her still flat abdomen.

"Too soon," Ellie said. "Let's just enjoy our secret for a little while. We can tell everyone at Christmas."

Gabe pulled her into a hug, and they were standing with her head resting on his shoulder when Nick and Kenny exploded into the room from one direction, Avery, Nonna and Mr. Salerno at a more restrained pace from the other. Gabe and Ellie opened their arms and invited their family into the hug. Avery snuggled into the center, Nonna wrapped a frail arm around Ellie, and Nick and Kenny slipped arms around shoulders.

After years of hiding, of seeking she didn't know what, she had found the Lord, and He had given her more than she could ever have imagined. She blinked back tears of joy.

"Okay, everyone" she said. "Let me give you your assignments. We're going to make this the best Thanksgiving ever."

CPSIA information can be obtained
at www.ICGtesting.com
Printed in the USA
LVHW081826090220
646320LV00008B/429

"A joy to read. You'll remember [it]
long after you've turned the last page."
—ROMANTIC TIMES

★ "It's romantic without being gooey and tear-jerking
without being campy—what more could a reader want?"
—BCCB, starred review

★ "This is a passionate, vulnerable, wonderfully
complete and irresistible book."
—VOYA, starred review

"[Nelson] writes with abandon . . . it's a headlong kind
of book, preferably devoured at a single setting."
—LOS ANGELES TIMES

"Brimming with humor and life, full of music
and the poems Lennie drops all over town,
The Sky Is Everywhere explores betrayal and
forgiveness through a vibrant cast of characters."
—SLJ

"A finely-drawn portrait of grief and first love."
—THE DAILY BEAST

"A story of love, loss, and healing that will resonate
with readers long after they've finished reading."
—BOOKLIST

"A story about love and loss . . . both heartfelt and literary."
—KIRKUS REVIEWS

"Jandy Nelson (remember that name) has written a YA novel with the best voice I have read since Laurie Halse Anderson's *Speak*."
—Jane Yolen

"Jandy Nelson has cast the intensity of first love together with the intensity of grief to produce a novel that is unusually rich with both insight and breathless romance. She writes with abandon, setting her characters free to live their excesses. . . . It's a headlong sort of book, preferably devoured at a single sitting." —*Los Angeles Times*

"Those who think young-adult books can't be as literary, rich, and mature as their adult counterparts will be disabused of that notion after reading *The Sky Is Everywhere*. . . . First-time author and literary agent Jandy Nelson has created a finely-drawn portrait of grief and first love, with vivid characters and melodic prose."
—*The Daily Beast*

★ "Nelson documents Lennie's stumbling negotiation of her emotional maelstrom with delicacy and shimmering clarity, writing with sorrowful, consoling tenderness of the journey through various stages of bereavement. . . . The characterization is clear-eyed and evocative. . . . It's romantic without being gooey and tear-jerking without being campy—what more could a reader want?"
—*BCCB*, starred review

"Buoyantly written and brimming with humor and life as it plumbs the depths and ambiguities of grief, full of music and the poems Lennie drops all over town, *The Sky Is Everywhere* explores betrayal and forgiveness through a vibrant cast of characters."
—*School Library Journal*

"From the opening paragraph, the author brilliantly navigates Lennie's course between despair and hope, sorrow and humor. . . . Debut novelist Jandy Nelson possesses a rare gift for language and a finely tuned ear . . . a suspenseful and gripping love triangle."
—*Shelf Awareness*

"In this amazing tale of love and loss, Nelson introduces a cast of characters who make the reader laugh and cry and want to know these people in real life. It's a wonderful book."
—NPR's *The Roundtable*

★ "Extremely difficult to put down. Teenagers of any age should fall in love with the book's charm, intensity, humor and poignancy."
—*VOYA*, starred review

★ "This honest, complex debut is distinguished by a dreamy California setting and poetic images that will draw readers into Lennie's world. . . ."   —*Publishers Weekly*, starred review

"Nearly everyone who's staggered through life in the wake of a loved one's death will recognize themselves in this brilliant, piercing story. It's a warm, deeply honest story that resonates with truth."
—*The Denver Post*

"How grief and love run side by side is sensitively and intensely explored in this energetic, poetic and warm-blooded novel."
—*The Guardian*, UK

"By turns both heart-wrenching and very funny . . . hard to put down."
—*Athens Banner-Herald*

What kind of girl?

I roll onto my back and before long I'm holding my pillow in my arms and kissing the air with an embarrassing amount of passion. Not again, I think. What's wrong with me? What kind of girl wants to kiss every boy at a funeral, wants to maul a guy in a tree after making out with her [dead] sister's boyfriend the previous night? *Speaking of which, what kind of girl makes out with her sister's boyfriend, period?*

OTHER BOOKS YOU MAY ENJOY

Hold Still	Nina LaCour
If I Stay	Gayle Forman
I'll Give You the Sun	Jandy Nelson
Impossible	Nancy Werlin
Looking for Alaska	John Green
My Life Next Door	Huntley Fitzpatrick
The Secret Year	Jennifer Hubbard
When It Happens	Susane Colasanti
Willow	Julia Hoban
Wintergirls	Laurie Halse Anderson

THE
SKY
IS
EVERY
WHERE

JANDY NELSON

speak

SPEAK
An imprint of Penguin Random House LLC
375 Hudson Street
New York, New York 10014

First published in the United States of America by Dial Books,
an imprint of Penguin Group (USA) Inc., 2010
Published by Speak, an imprint of Penguin Group (USA) Inc., 2011

THE LIBRARY OF CONGRESS HAS CATALOGED THE DIAL BOOKS EDITION AS FOLLOWS:
Nelson, Jandy.
The sky is everywhere / by Jandy Nelson.
p. cm.
Summary: In the months after her sister dies, seventeen-year-old Lennie falls into a love triangle
and discovers the strength to follow her dream of becoming a musician.
ISBN: 978-0-8037-3495-1 (hc)
[1. Grief—Fiction. 2. Death—Fiction. 3. Sisters—Fiction. 4. Musicians—Fiction.] I. Title.
PZ7.N433835Sk 2010
[Fic]—dc22 2009022809

Speak ISBN 978-0-14-241780-5

Designed by Jennifer Kelly

Printed in the United States of America

21

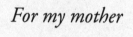

For my mother

part
one

chapter 1

GRAM IS WORRIED about me. It's not just because my sister Bailey died four weeks ago, or because my mother hasn't contacted me in sixteen years, or even because suddenly all I think about is sex. She is worried about me because one of her houseplants has spots.

Gram has believed for most of my seventeen years that this particular houseplant, which is of the nondescript variety, reflects my emotional, spiritual, and physical well-being. I've grown to believe it too.

Across the room from where I sit, Gram—all six feet and floral frock of her, looms over the black-spotted leaves.

"What do you mean it might not get better this time?" She's asking this of Uncle Big: arborist, resident pothead, and mad scientist to boot. He knows something about everything, but he knows everything about plants.

To anyone else it might seem strange, even off the wall, that Gram, as she asks this, is staring at me, but it doesn't to Uncle Big, because he's staring at me as well.

"This time it has a very serious condition." Big's voice trumpets as if from stage or pulpit; his words carry weight, even *pass the salt* comes out of his mouth in a thou-shalt-Ten-Commandments kind of way.

Gram raises her hands to her face in distress, and I go back to scribbling a poem in the margin of *Wuthering Heights*. I'm huddled into a corner of the couch. I've no use for talking, would just as soon store paper clips in my mouth.

"But the plant's always recovered before, Big, like when Lennie broke her arm, for instance."

"That time the leaves had white spots."

"Or just last fall when she auditioned for lead clarinet but had to be second chair again."

"Brown spots."

"Or when—"

"This time it's different."

I glance up. They're still peering at me, a tall duet of sorrow and concern.

Gram is Clover's Garden Guru. She has the most extraordinary flower garden in Northern California. Her roses burst with more color than a year of sunsets, and their fragrance is so intoxicating that town lore claims breathing in their scent can cause you to fall in love on the spot. But despite her nurturing and renowned green thumb, this plant seems to follow the trajectory of my life, independent of her efforts or its own vegetal sensibility.

I put my book and pen down on the table. Gram leans in close to the plant, whispers to it about the importance of *joie de vivre,* then lumbers over to the couch, sitting down next to me.

Then Big joins us, plopping his enormous frame down beside Gram. We three, each with the same unruly hair that sits on our heads like a bustle of shiny black crows, stay like this, staring at nothing, for the rest of the afternoon.

This is us since my sister Bailey collapsed one month ago from a fatal arrhythmia while in rehearsal for a local production of *Romeo & Juliet*. It's as if someone vacuumed up the horizon while we were looking the other way.

chapter 2

The morning of the day Bailey died,
she woke me up
by putting her finger in my ear.
I hated when she did this.
She then started trying on shirts, asking me:
Which do you like better, the green or the blue?
The blue.
You didn't even look up, Lennie.
Okay, the green. Really, I don't care what shirt you wear . . .
Then I rolled over in bed and fell back asleep.
I found out later
she wore the blue
and those were the last words I ever spoke to her.

(Found written on a lollipop wrapper on the trail to the Rain River)

MY FIRST DAY back to school is just as I expect, the hall does a Red Sea part when I come in, conversations hush, eyes swim with nervous sympathy, and everyone stares as if I'm holding Bailey's dead body in my arms, which I guess I am. Her death is all over me, I can feel it and everyone can see it, plain as a big black coat wrapped around me on a beautiful spring day. But what I don't expect is the unprecedented hubbub over some new boy, Joe Fontaine, who arrived in my month-long absence. Everywhere I go it's the same:

"Have you seen him yet?"

"He looks like a Gypsy."

"Like a rock star."

"A pirate."

"I hear he's in a band called Dive."

"That he's a musical genius."

"Someone told me he used to live in Paris."

"That he played music on the streets."

"Have you seen him yet?"

I have seen him, because when I return to my band seat, the one I've occupied for the last year, he's in it. Even in the stun of grief, my eyes roam from the black boots, up the miles of legs covered in denim, over the endless torso, and finally settle on a face so animated I wonder if I've interrupted a conversation between him and my music stand.

"Hi," he says, and jumps up. He's treetop tall. "You must be Lennon." He points to my name on the chair. "I heard about— I'm sorry." I notice the way he holds his clarinet, not precious with it, tight fist around the neck, like a sword.

"Thank you," I say, and every available inch of his face busts

5

into a smile—whoa. Has he blown into our school on a gust of wind from another world? The guy looks unabashedly jack-o'-lantern happy, which couldn't be more foreign to the sullen demeanor most of us strove to perfect. He has scores of messy brown curls that flop every which way and eyelashes so spider-leg long and thick that when he blinks he looks like he's batting his bright green eyes right at you. His face is more open than an open book, like a wall of graffiti really. I realize I'm writing *wow* on my thigh with my finger, decide I better open my mouth and snap us out of this impromptu staring contest.

"Everyone calls me Lennie," I say. Not very original, but better than *guh,* which was the alternative, and it does the trick. He looks down at his feet for a second and I take a breath and regroup for Round Two.

"Been wondering about that actually, Lennon after John?" he asks, again holding my gaze—it's entirely possible I'm going to faint. Or burst into flames.

I nod. "Mom was a hippie." This is *northern* Northern California after all—the final frontier of freakerdom. Just in the eleventh grade we have a girl named Electricity, a guy named Magic Bus, and countless flowers: Tulip, Begonia, and Poppy— all parent-given-on-the-birth-certificate names. Tulip is a two-ton bruiser of a guy who would be the star of our football team if we were the kind of school that had a football team. We're not. We're the kind of school that has optional morning medi-tation in the gym.

"Yeah," Joe says. "My mom too, and Dad, as well as aunts, uncles, brothers, cousins . . . welcome to Commune Fontaine."

I laugh out loud. "Got the picture."

But whoa again—should I be laughing so easily like this? And should it feel this good? Like slipping into cool river water.

I turn around, wondering if anyone is watching us, and see that Sarah has just walked—rather, exploded—into the music room. I've hardly seen her since the funeral, feel a pang of guilt.

"Lennieeeee!" She careens toward us in prime goth-gone-cowgirl form: vintage slinky black dress, shit-kicker cowboy boots, blond hair dyed so black it looks blue, all topped off with a honking Stetson. I note the breakneck pace of her approach, wonder for an instant if she's going to actually jump into my arms right before she tries to, sending us both skidding into Joe, who somehow retains his balance, and ours, so we all don't fly through the window.

This is Sarah, subdued.

"Nice," I whisper in her ear as she hugs me like a bear even though she's built like a bird. "Way to bowl down the gorgeous new boy." She cracks up, and it feels both amazing and disconcerting to have someone in my arms shaking from laughter rather than heartbreak.

Sarah is the most enthusiastic cynical person on the planet. She'd be the perfect cheerleader if she weren't so disgusted by the notion of school spirit. She's a literature fanatic like me, but reads darker, read Sartre in tenth grade—*Nausea*—which is when she started wearing black (even at the beach), smoking cigarettes (even though she looks like the healthiest girl you've ever seen), and obsessing about her existential crisis (even as she partied to all hours of the night).

"Lennie, welcome back, dear," another voice says. Mr. James—also known in my mind as Yoda for both outward

7

appearance and inward musical mojo—has stood up at the piano and is looking over at me with the same expression of bottomless sadness I've gotten so used to seeing from adults. "We're all so very sorry."

"Thank you," I say, for the hundredth time that day. Sarah and Joe are both looking at me too, Sarah with concern and Joe with a grin the size of the continental United States. Does he look at everyone like this, I wonder. Is he a wingnut? Well, whatever he is, or has, it's catching. Before I know it, I've matched his continental U.S. and raised him Puerto Rico and Hawaii. I must look like The Merry Mourner. Sheesh. And that's not all, because now I'm thinking what it might be like to kiss him, to *really* kiss him—uh-oh. This is a problem, an entirely new un-Lennie-like problem that began (*WTF-edly?!*) at the funeral: I was drowning in darkness and suddenly all these boys in the room were glowing. Guy friends of Bailey's from work or college, most of whom I didn't know, kept coming up to me saying how sorry they were, and I don't know if it's because they thought I looked like Bailey, or because they felt bad for me, but later on, I'd catch some of them staring at me in this charged, urgent way, and I'd find myself staring back at them, like I was someone else, thinking things I hardly ever had before, things I'm mortified to have been thinking in a church, let alone at my sister's funeral.

This boy beaming before me, however, seems to glow in a class all his own. He must be from a very friendly part of the Milky Way, I'm thinking as I try to tone down this nutso smile on my face, but instead almost blurt out to Sarah, "He looks like Heathcliff," because I just realized he does, well, except for the happy smiling part—but then all of a sudden the breath is kicked out of me and I'm shoved onto the cold hard concrete floor of my life now, because I remember I can't run home after school and tell Bails about a new boy in band.

My sister dies over and over again, all day long.

"Len?" Sarah touches my shoulder. "You okay?"

I nod, willing away the runaway train of grief barreling straight for me.

Someone behind us starts playing "Approaching Shark," aka the *Jaws* theme song. I turn to see Rachel Brazile gliding toward us, hear her mutter, "Very funny," to Luke Jacobus, the saxophonist responsible for the accompaniment. He's just one of many band-kill Rachel's left in her wake, guys duped by the fact that all that haughty horror is stuffed into a spectacular body, and then further deceived by big brown fawn eyes and Rapunzel hair. Sarah and I are convinced God was in an ironic mood when he made her.

"See you've met The Maestro," she says to me, casually touching Joe's back as she slips into her chair—first chair clarinet—where I should be sitting.

She opens her case, starts putting together her instrument. "Joe studied at a conservatory in *Fronce*. Did he tell you?" Of course she doesn't say *France* so it rhymes with *dance* like a normal English-speaking human being. I can feel Sarah bristling beside me. She has zero tolerance for Rachel ever since she got first chair over me, but Sarah doesn't know what really happened—no one does.

Rachel's tightening the ligature on her mouthpiece like she's trying to asphyxiate her clarinet. "Joe was a *fabulous* second in your absence," she says, drawing out the word *fabulous* from here to the Eiffel Tower.

I don't fire-breathe at her: "Glad everything worked out for you, Rachel." I don't say a word, just wish I could curl into a ball and roll away. Sarah, on the other hand, looks like she wishes there were a battle-ax handy.

The room has become a clamor of random notes and scales. "Finish up tuning, I want to start at the bell today," Mr. James calls from the piano. "And take out your pencils, I've made some changes to the arrangement."

"I better go beat on something," Sarah says, throwing Rachel a disgusted look, then huffs off to beat on her timpani.

Rachel shrugs, smiles at Joe—no not smiles: twinkles—oh brother. "Well, it's true," she says to him. "You were—I mean, are—*fabulous*."

"Not so." He bends down to pack up his clarinet. "I'm a hack, was just keeping the seat warm. Now I can go back to where I belong." He points his clarinet at the horn section.

"You're just being modest," Rachel says, tossing fairy-tale locks over the back of her chair. "You have *so* many colors on your tonal palette."

I look at Joe expecting to see some evidence of an inward groan at these imbecilic words, but see evidence of something else instead. He smiles at Rachel on a geographical scale too. I feel my neck go hot.

"You know I'll miss you," she says, pouting.

"We'll meet again," Joe replies, adding an eye-bat to his repertoire. "Like next period, in history."

I've disappeared, which is good really, because suddenly I

don't have a clue what to do with my face or body or smashed-up heart. I take my seat, noting that this grinning, eye-batting fool from Fronce looks nothing like Heathcliff. I was mistaken.

I open my clarinet case, put my reed in my mouth to moisten it and instead bite it in two.

At 4:48 p.m. on a Friday in April,
my sister was rehearsing the role of Juliet
and less than one minute later
she was dead.
To my astonishment, time didn't stop
with her heart.
People went to school, to work, to restaurants;
they crushed crackers into their clam chowder,
fretted over exams,
sang in their cars with the windows up.
For days and days, the rain beat its fists
on the roof of our house—
evidence of the terrible mistake
God had made.
Each morning, when I woke
I listened for the tireless pounding,
looked at the drear through the window
and was relieved
that at least the sun had the decency
to stay the hell away from us.

(Found on a piece of staff paper, spiked on a low branch, Flying Man's Gulch)

chapter 3

THE REST OF the day blurs by and before the final bell, I sneak out and duck into the woods. I don't want to take the roads home, don't want to risk seeing anyone from school, especially Sarah, who informed me that while I've been in hiding, she's been reading up on loss and according to all the experts, it's time for me to talk about what I'm going through—but she, and the experts, and Gram, for that matter, don't get it. I can't. I'd need a new alphabet, one made of falling, of tectonic plates shifting, of the deep devouring dark.

As I walk through the redwood trees, my sneakers sopping up days of rain, I wonder why bereaved people even bother with mourning clothes when grief itself provides such an unmistakable wardrobe. The only one who didn't seem to spot it on me today—besides Rachel, who doesn't count—was the new boy. He will only ever know this new sisterless me.

I see a scrap of paper on the ground dry enough to write on, so I sit on a rock, take out the pen that I always keep in my back pocket now, and scribble a conversation I remember having with Bailey on it, then fold it up and bury it in the moist earth.

When I break out of the forest onto the road to our house, I'm flooded with relief. I want to be at home, where Bailey is most alive, where I can still see her leaning out the window, her wild black hair blowing around her face as she says, "C'mon, Len, let's get to the river pronto."

"Hey you." Toby's voice startles me. Bailey's boyfriend of two years, he's part cowboy, part skate rat, all love slave to my sister, and totally MIA lately despite Gram's many invitations. "We really need to reach out to him now," she keeps saying.

He's lying on his back in her garden with the neighbor's two red dogs, Lucy and Ethel, sprawled out asleep beside him. This is a common sight in the springtime. When the angel's trumpets and lilacs bloom, her garden is positively soporific. A few moments among the blossoms and even the most energetic find themselves on their backs counting clouds.

"I was, uh, doing some weeding for Gram," he says, obviously embarrassed about his kick-back position.

"Yeah, it happens to the best of us." With his surfer flop of hair and wide face sun-spattered in freckles, Toby is the closest a human can come to lion without jumping species. When Bailey first saw him, she and I were out road-reading (we all road-read; the few people who live on our street know this about our family and inch their way home in their cars just in case one of us is out strolling and particularly rapt). I was reading *Wuthering Heights*, as usual, and she was reading *Like Water for Chocolate*, her favorite, when a magnificent chestnut brown horse trotted past us on the way to the trailhead. *Nice horse*, I thought, and went back to Cathy and Heathcliff, only looking up a few seconds later when I heard the thump of Bailey's book as it hit the ground.

She was no longer by my side but had stopped a few paces back.

"What's wrong with you?" I asked, taking in my suddenly lobotomized sister.

"Did you see that guy, Len?"

"What guy?"

"God, what's wrong with *you*, that gorgeous guy on that horse, it's like he popped out of my novel or something. I can't believe you didn't see him, Lennie." Her exasperation at my disinterest in boys was as perpetual as my exasperation at her preoccupation with them. "He turned around when he passed us and smiled right at me—he was *so* good-looking . . . just like the Revolutionary in this book." She reached down to pick it up, brushing the dirt off the cover. "You know, the one who whisks Gertrudis onto his horse and steals her away in a fit of passion—"

"Whatever, Bailey." I turned back around, resumed reading, and made my way to the front porch, where I sunk into a chair and promptly got lost in the stampeding passion of the two on the English moors. I liked love safe between the covers of my novel, not in my sister's heart, where it made her ignore me for months on end. Every so often though, I'd look up at her, posing on a rock by the trailhead across the road, so obviously feigning reading her book that I couldn't believe she was an actress. She stayed out there for hours waiting for her Revolutionary to come back, which he finally did, but from the other direction, having traded in his horse somewhere for a skateboard. Turns out he didn't pop out of her novel after all, but out of Clover High like the rest of us, only he hung out with the ranch kids and skaters, and because she was exclusively a drama diva, their paths never crossed until that day. But by that point it didn't matter where he came from or what he rode in on because that image of him galloping by had burned into Bailey's psyche and stolen from her the capacity for rational thought.

I've never really been a member of the Toby Shaw fan club. Neither his cowboy bit nor the fact that he could do a 180 Ollie into a Fakie Feeble Grind on his skateboard made up for the fact that he had turned Bailey into a permanent love zombie.

That, and he's always seemed to find me as noteworthy as a baked potato.

"You okay, Len?" he asks from his prone position, bringing me back to the moment.

For some reason, I tell the truth. I shake my head, back and forth, back and forth, from disbelief to despair, and back again.

He sits up. "I know," he says, and I see in his marooned expression that it's true. I want to thank him for not making me say a word, and getting it all the same, but I just remain silent as the sun pours heat and light, as if from a pitcher, all over our bewildered heads.

He pats the grass with his hand for me to join him. I sort of want to but feel hesitant. We've never really hung out before without Bailey.

15

I motion toward the house. "I need to go upstairs."

This is true. I want to be back in The Sanctum, full name: The Inner Pumpkin Sanctum, newly christened by me, when Bailey, a few months ago, persuaded me the walls of our bedroom just had to be orange, a blaringly unapologetic orange that had since made our room sunglasses optional. Before I'd left for school this morning, I'd shut the door, purposefully, wishing I could barricade it from Gram and her cardboard boxes. I want The Sanctum the way it is, which means exactly the way it was. Gram seems to think this means: *I'm out of my tree and running loose through the park,* Gramese for *mental.*

"Sweet pea." She's come out onto the porch in a bright purple frock covered in daisies. In her hand is a paintbrush, the first time I've seen her with one since Bailey died. "How was your first day back?"

I walk over to her, breathe in her familiar scent: patchouli, paint, garden dirt.

"It was fine," I say.

She examines my face closely like she does when she's preparing to sketch it. Silence tick-tocks between us, as it does lately. I can feel her frustration, how she wishes she could shake me like she might a book, hoping all the words will just fall out.

"There's a new boy in honor band," I offer.

"Oh yeah? What's he play?"

"Everything, it seems." Before I escaped into the woods at lunch, I saw him walking across the quad with Rachel, a guitar swinging from his hand.

"Lennie, I've been thinking . . . it might be good for you now, a real comfort . . ." Uh-oh. I know where this is going. "I mean, when you were studying with Marguerite, I couldn't rip that instrument out of your hands—"

"Things change," I say, interrupting her. I can't have this conversation. Not again. I try to step around her to go inside. I just want to be in Bailey's closet, pressed into her dresses, into the lingering scents of riverside bonfires, coconut suntan lotion, rose perfume—her.

"Listen," she says quietly, reaching her free hand out to straighten my collar. "I invited Toby for dinner. He's quite out of his tree. Go keep him company, help him weed or something."

It occurs to me she probably said something similar to him about me to get him to finally come over. Ugh.

And then without further ado, she dabs my nose with her paintbrush.

"Gram!" I cry out, but to her back as she heads into the house. I try to wipe off the green with my hand. Bails and I spent much of our lives like this, ambushed by Gram's swashbuckling green-tipped paintbrush. Only green, mind you. Gram's paintings line the walls of the house, floor to ceiling, stack behind couches, chairs, under tables, in closets, and each and every one of them is a testament to her undying devotion to the color green. She has every hue from lime to forest and uses them to paint primarily one thing: willowy women who look half mermaid, half Martian. "They're my ladies," she'd tell Bails and me. "Halfway between here and there."

Per her orders, I drop my clarinet case and bag, then plant myself in the warm grass beside a supine Toby and the sleeping dogs to help him "weed."

"Tribal marking," I say, pointing to my nose.

He nods disinterestedly in his flower coma. I'm a green-nosed baked potato. Great.

I turtle up, tucking my knees to my chest and resting my head in the crevice between them. My eyes move from the wisteria cascading down the trellis to the several parties of daffodils gossiping in the breeze to the indisputable fact that springtime has shoved off its raincoat today and is just prancing around—it makes me queasy, like the world has already forgotten what's happened to us.

"I'm not going to pack up her things in cardboard boxes," I say without thinking. "Ever."

Toby rolls on his side, shields his face with his hand trying to block the sun so he can see me, and to my surprise says, "Of course not."

I nod and he nods back, then I flop down on the grass, cross my arms over my head so he can't see that I'm secretly smiling a little into them.

The next thing I know the sun has moved behind a mountain and that mountain is Uncle Big towering over us. Toby and I must have both crashed out.

"I feel like Glinda the Good Witch," Big says, "looking down on Dorothy, Scarecrow, and two Totos in the poppy field outside of Oz." A few narcotic springtime blooms are no match for Big's bugle of a voice. "I guess if you don't wake up, I'm going to have to make it snow on you." I grin groggily up at him with his enormous handlebar mustache poised over his lip like a grand Declaration of Weird. He's carrying a red cooler as if it were a briefcase.

"How's the distribution effort going?" I ask, tapping the

cooler with my foot. We are in a ham predicament. After the funeral, there seemed to be a prime directive in Clover that everyone had to stop by our house with a ham. Hams were everywhere; they filled the fridge, the freezer, lined the counters, the stove, sat in the sink, the cold oven. Uncle Big attended to the door as people stopped by to pay their respects. Gram and I could hear his booming voice again and again, "Oh a ham, how thoughtful, thank you, come in." As the days went on Big's reaction to the hams got more dramatic for our benefit. Each time he exclaimed "A ham!" Gram and I found each other's eyes and had to suppress a rush of inappropriate giggles. Now Big is on a mission to make sure everyone in a twenty-mile radius has a ham sandwich a day.

He rests the cooler on the ground and reaches his hand down to help me up. "It's possible we'll be a hamless house in just a few days."

Once I'm standing, Big kisses my head, then reaches down for Toby. When he's on his feet, Big pulls him into his arms, and I watch Toby, who is a big guy himself, disappear in the mountainous embrace. "How you holding up, cowboy?"

"Not too good," he admits.

Big releases him, keeping one hand on his shoulder, and puts the other one on mine. He looks from Toby to me. "No way out of this but through . . . for any of us." He says it like Moses, so we both nod as if we've been bestowed with a great wisdom. "And let's get you some turpentine." He winks at me. Big's an ace winker—five marriages to his name to prove it. After his beloved fifth wife left him, Gram insisted he move in with us, saying, "Your poor uncle will starve himself if he stays in this lovelorn condition much longer. A sorrowing heart poisons recipes."

This has proven to be true, but for Gram. Everything she cooks now tastes like ashes.

Toby and I follow Big into the house, where he stops before the painting of his sister, my missing mother: Paige Walker. Before she left sixteen years ago, Gram had been painting a portrait of her, which she never got to finish but put up anyway. It hovers over the mantel in the living room, half a mother, with long green hair pooling like water around an incomplete face.

Gram had always told us that our mother would return. "She'll be back," she'd say like Mom had gone to the store for some eggs, or a swim at the river. Gram said it so often and with such certainty that for a long while, before we learned more, we didn't question it, just spent a whole lot of time waiting for the phone to ring, the doorbell to sound, the mail to arrive.

I tap my hand softly against Big, who's staring up at The Half Mom like he's lost in a silent mournful conversation. He sighs, puts an arm around me and one around Toby, and we all plod into the kitchen like a three-headed, six-legged, ten-ton sack of sad.

Dinner, unsurprisingly, is a ham and ash casserole that we hardly touch.

After, Toby and I camp out on the living room floor, listening to Bailey's music, poring over countless photo albums, basically blowing our hearts to smithereens.

I keep sneaking looks at him from across the room. I can almost see Bails flouncing around him, coming up from behind and dropping her arms around his neck the way she always did.

She'd say sickeningly embarrassing things in his ear, and he'd tease her back, both of them acting like I wasn't there.

"I feel Bailey," I say finally, the sense of her overwhelming me. "In this room, with us."

He looks up from the album on his lap, surprised. "Me too. I've been thinking it this whole time."

"It's *so* nice," I say, relief spilling out of me with the words.

He smiles and it makes his eyes squint like the sun is in his face. "It is, Len." I remember Bailey telling me once that Toby doesn't talk all that much to humans but is able to gentle startled horses at the ranch with just a few words. Like St. Francis, I'd said to her, and I believe it—the low slow lull of his voice is soothing, like waves lapping the shore at night.

I return to the photos of Bailey as Wendy in the Clover Elementary production of *Peter Pan*. Neither of us mentions it again, but the comfort of feeling Bailey so close stays with me for the rest of the evening.

Later, Toby and I stand by the garden, saying good-bye. The dizzy, drunk fragrance of the roses engulfs us.

"It was great hanging out with you, Lennie, made me feel better."

"Me too," I say, plucking a lavender petal. "Much better, really." I say this quietly and to the rosebush, not sure I even want him to hear, but when I peek back up at his face, it's kind, his leonine features less lion, more cub.

"Yeah," he says, looking at me, his dark eyes both shiny and sad. He lifts his arm, and for a second I think he's going to touch my face with his hand, but he just runs his fingers through the tumble of sunshine that is his hair.

We walk the few remaining steps to the road in slow motion. Once there, Lucy and Ethel emerge out of nowhere and start climbing all over Toby, who has dropped to his knees to say good-bye to them. He holds his skateboard in one hand, ruffling and petting the dogs with the other as he whispers unintelligible words into their fur.

"You really are St. Francis, huh?" I have a thing for the saints—the miracles, not the mortifications.

"It's been said." A soft smile meanders across the broad planes of his face, landing in his eyes. "Mostly by your sister." For a split second, I want to tell him it was me who thought that, not Bailey.

He finishes his farewell, stands back up, then drops his skateboard to the ground, steadying it with his foot. He doesn't get on. A few years pass.

"I should go," he says, not going.

"Yeah," I say. A few more.

Before he finally hops on his board, he hugs me good-bye and we hold on to each other so tightly under the sad, starless sky that for a moment I feel as if our heartbreak were one instead of two.

But then all of a sudden, I feel a hardness against my hip, him, *that. Holy fucking shit!* I pull back quickly, say good-bye, and run back into the house.

I don't know if he knows that I felt him.

I don't know anything.

Someone from Bailey's drama class
yelled *bravo* at the end of the service
and everyone jumped to their feet
and started clapping
I remember thinking the roof would blow
from the thunder in our hands
that grief was a room filled
with hungry desperate light
We clapped for nineteen years
of a world with Bailey in it
did not stop clapping
when the sun set, moon rose
when all the people streamed into our house
with food and frantic sorrow
did not stop clapping
until dawn
when we closed the door
on Toby
who had to make his sad way home
I know we must have moved from that spot
must have washed and slept and ate
but in my mind, Gram, Uncle Big and I
stayed like that for weeks
just staring at the closed door
with nothing between our hands
but air

(Found on a piece of notebook paper blowing down Main Street)

chapter 4

THIS IS WHAT happens when Joe Fontaine has his debut trumpet solo in band practice: I'm the first to go, swooning into Rachel, who topples into Cassidy Rosenthal, who tumbles onto Zachary Quittner, who collapses onto Sarah, who reels into Luke Jacobus—until every kid in band is on the floor in a bedazzled heap. Then the roof flies off, the walls collapse, and when I look outside I see that the nearby stand of redwoods has uprooted and is making its way up the quad to our classroom, a gang of giant wooden men clapping their branches together. Lastly, the Rain River overflows its banks and detours left and right until it finds its way to the Clover High music room, where it sweeps us all away—he is *that* good.

When the rest of us lesser musical mortals have recovered enough to finish the piece, we do, but as we put our instruments away at the end of practice, the room is as quiet and still as an empty church.

Finally, Mr. James, who's been staring at Joe like he's an ostrich, regains the power of speech and says, "Well, well. As you all say, that sure sucked." Everyone laughs. I turn around to see what Sarah thought. I can just about make out an eye under a giant Rasta hat. She mouths *unfreakingbelievable*. I look over at Joe. He's wiping his trumpet, blushing from the response or flushed from playing, I'm not sure which. He looks up, catches my eye, then raises his eyebrows expectantly at me, almost like the storm that has just come out of his horn has been for me. But why would that be? And why is it I keep catching him watching me play? It's not interest, I mean, *that* kind of interest, I can tell. He watches me clinically, intently, the way Marguerite used to during a lesson when she was trying to figure out what in the world I was doing wrong.

"Don't even think about it," Rachel says as I turn back around. "That trumpet player's accounted for. Anyway, he's like so out of your league, Lennie. I mean, when's the last time you had a boyfriend? Oh yeah, never."

I think about lighting her hair on fire.

I think about medieval torture devices: The Rack, in particular.

I think about telling her what really happened at chair auditions last fall.

Instead I ignore her like I have all year, swab my clarinet, and wish I were indeed preoccupied by Joe Fontaine rather than by what happened with Toby—each time I recall the sensation of him pressing into me, shivers race all through my body— definitely not the appropriate reaction to your sister's boyfriend's hard-on! And what's worse is that in the privacy of my mind, I don't pull away like I actually did but stay wrapped in his arms under the still sky, and that makes me flush with shame.

I shut my clarinet case wishing I could do the same on these thoughts of Toby. I scan the room—the other horn players have gathered around Joe, as if the magic were contagious. Not a word between him and me since my first day back. Hardly a word between me and anyone at school really. Even Sarah.

Mr. James claps to get the attention of the class. In his excited, crackly voice, he begins talking about summer band practice because school's out in less than a week. "For those who are around, we will be practicing, starting in July. Who shows up will determine what we play. I'm thinking jazz"— he snaps his fingers like a flamenco dancer—"maybe some hot Spanish jazz, but I'm open to suggestions."

He raises his arms like a priest before a congregation. "Find the beat and keep it, my friends." The way he ends every class. But then after a moment he claps again. "Almost forgot, let me see a show of hands of those who plan on auditioning for All-State next year." Oh no. I drop my pencil and bend over to avoid any possible eye collision with Mr. James. When I emerge from my careful inspection of the floor, my phone vibrates in my pocket. I turn to Sarah, whose visible eye is popping out of her head. I sneak out my phone and read her text.

Y didn't u raise ur hand???
Solo made me think of u—that day!
Come over 2nite???

I turn around, mouth: *Can't.*

She picks up one of her sticks and dramatically feigns stabbing it into her stomach with both hands. I know behind the hari-kari is a hurt that's growing, but I don't know what to do about it. For the first time in our lives, I'm somewhere she can't find, and I don't have the map to give her that leads to me.

I gather my things quickly to avoid her, which is going to be easy because Luke Jacobus has cornered her, and as I do, the day she mentioned comes racing back. It was the beginning of freshman year and we had both made honor band. Mr. James, particularly frustrated with everyone, had jumped on a chair and shouted, "What's wrong with you people? You think you're musicians? You have to stick your asses in the wind!" Then he said, "C'mon, follow me. Those of you who can, bring your instruments."

We filed out of the room, down the path into the forest where the river rushed and roared. We all stood on the banks, while he climbed up onto a rock to address us.

"Now, listen, learn, and then play, just *play*. Make *noise*. Make *something*. Make *muuuuuuuuusic*." Then he began conducting the river, the wind, the birds in the trees like a total loon. After we got over our hysterics and piped down, one by one, those of us who had our instruments started to play. Unbelievably, I was one of the first to go, and after a while, the river and wind and birds and clarinets and flutes and oboes mixed all together in a glorious cacophonous mess and Mr. James turned his attention from the forest back to us, his body swaying, his arms flailing left and right, saying, "That's it, that's it. *That's it!*"

And it was.

When we got back to the classroom, Mr. James came over to me and handed me Marguerite St. Denis's card. "Call her," he said. "Right away."

I think about Joe's virtuoso performance today, can feel it in my fingers. I ball them into fists. Whatever it was, whatever that thing is Mr. James took us in the woods that day to find, whether it's abandon, or passion, whether it's innovation, or simply courage, Joe has it.

His ass is in the wind. Mine is in second chair.

chapter 5

Lennie?

Yeah?

You awake?

Yeah.

We did it.

Did what?

Toby and I did it, had sex last night.

I thought you already had, like 10,000 times.

Nope.

Well . . .

It was incredible.

Congratulations then.

Sheesh, why can't you ever be happy for me about Toby?

I don't know.

What is it, are you jealous?

I don't know . . . sorry.

It's okay. Forget it, go to sleep.

Talk about it if you want to.

I don't want to anymore.

Fine.

Fine.

(Found on a to-go
cup along the banks
of the Rain River)

I KNOW IT'S him, and wish I didn't. I wish my first thought was of anyone in the world but Toby when I hear the ping of a pebble on the window. I'm sitting in Bailey's closet, writing a poem on the wall, trying to curb the panic that hurls around inside my body like a trapped comet.

I take off the shirt of Bailey's I'd put on over mine, grab the doorknob, and hoist myself back into The Sanctum. Crossing to the window, my bare feet press into the three flattened blue rugs that scatter the room, pieces of bright sky that Bailey and I pounded down with years of cut-throat dance competitions to out-goofball the other without cracking up. I always lost because Bailey had in her arsenal The Ferret Face, which when combined with her masterful Monkey Moves, was certifiably deadly; if she pulled the combo (which took more unself-consciousness than I could ever muster), I was a goner, reduced to a helpless heap of hysterics, every time.

I lean over the sill, see Toby, as I knew I would, under a near full moon. I've had no luck squelching the mutiny inside me. I take a deep breath, then go downstairs and open the door.

"Hey, what's up?" I say. "Everyone's sleeping." My voice sounds creaky, unused, like bats might fly out of my mouth. I take a good look at him under the porch light. His face is wild with sorrow. It's like looking in a mirror.

"I thought maybe we could hang out," he says. This is what I hear in my mind: *boner, boner, erection, hard-on, woody, boner, boner, boner*—"I have something to tell you, Len, don't know who else to tell." The need in his voice sends a shudder right through me. Over his head, the red warning light could not be flashing brighter, but still I can't seem to say no, don't want to. "C'mon in, sir."

He touches my arm in a friendly, brotherly way as he passes, which sets me at ease, maybe guys get hard-ons all the time, for no reason—I have zero knowledge of boner basics. I've only ever kissed three guys, so I'm totally inexperienced with real-life boys, though quite an expert at the kind in books, especially Heathcliff, who doesn't get erections—wait, now that I'm thinking about it, he must get them *all the time* with Cathy on the moors. Heathcliff must be a total freaking boner boy.

I close the door behind him and motion for him to be quiet as he follows me up the steps to The Sanctum, which is sound-proofed so as to protect the rest of the house against years of barky bleating clarinet notes. Gram would have a coronary that he's here visiting me at almost two a.m. on a school night. *On any night, Lennie.* This is most definitely not what she had in mind by reaching out to him.

Once the door of The Sanctum is closed, I put on some of the indie-kill-yourself music I've been listening to lately, and sit down next to Toby on the floor, our backs to the wall, legs outstretched. We sit in silence like two stone slabs. Several centuries pass.

When I can't handle it anymore, I joke, "It's possible you've taken this whole strong silent type thing to an extreme."

"Oh, sorry." He shakes his head, embarrassed. "Don't even realize I'm doing it."

"Doing it?"

"Not talking . . ."

"Really? What is it you think you're doing?"

He tilts his head, smiling squintily, adorably. "I was going for the oak tree in the yard."

I laugh. "Very good then, you do a perfect oak impersonation."

"Thank you . . . think it drove Bails mad, my silent streak."

"Nah, she liked it, she told me, less chance of disagreements . . . plus more stage time for her."

"True." He's quiet for a minute, then in a voice ragged with emotion, says, "We were so different."

"Yeah," I say softly. Quintessential opposites, Toby always serene and still (when not on horse or board) while Bailey did everything: walk, talk, think, laugh, party, at the speed of light, and with its gleam.

"*You* remind me of her . . ." he says.

I want to blurt out: *What!? You've always acted like I was a baked potato!* but instead I say, "No way, don't have the wattage."

"You have plenty . . . it's me that has the serious shortage," he says, sounding surprisingly like a spud.

"Not to her," I say. His eyes warm at that—it kills me. What are we going to do with all this love?

He shakes his head in disbelief. "I got lucky. That chocolate book . . ."

The image assaults me: Bailey leaping off the rock the day they met when Toby returned on his board. "I knew you'd come back," she'd exclaimed, throwing the book in the air. "Just like in this story. I knew it!"

I have a feeling the same day is playing out in Toby's mind, because our polite levity has screeched to a halt—all the past tense in our words suddenly stacking up as if to crush us.

31

I can see the despair inching across his face as it must be across mine.

I look around our bedroom, at the singing orange paint we'd slathered over the dozy blue we'd had for years. Bailey had said, "If this doesn't change our lives, I don't know what will—this, Lennie, is *the color of extraordinary*." I remember thinking I didn't want our lives to change and didn't understand why she did. I remember thinking I'd always liked the blue.

I sigh. "I'm really glad you showed up, Toby. I'd been hiding in Bailey's closet freaking out for hours."

"Good. That you're glad, I mean, didn't know if I should bug you, but couldn't sleep either . . . did some stupid-ass skating that could've killed me, then ended up here, sat under the plum tree for an hour trying to decide . . ."

The rich timbre of Toby's voice suddenly makes me aware of the other voice in the room, the singer blaring from the speakers who sounds like he's being strangled at best. I get up to put on something more melodic, then when I sit back down, I confide, "No one gets it at school, not really, not even Sarah."

He tips his head back against the wall. "Don't know if it's possible to get it until you're in it like we are. I had no idea . . ."

"Me neither," I say, and suddenly, I want to hug Toby because I'm just so relieved to not have to be in it by myself anymore tonight.

He's looking down at his hands, his brow furrowed, like he's struggling with how to say something. I wait.

And wait.

Still waiting here. How did Bailey brave the radio silence?

When he looks up, his face is all compassion, all cub. The words spill out of him, one on top of the next. "I've never known sisters so close. I feel so bad for you, Lennie, I'm just so sorry. I keep thinking about you without her."

"Thanks," I whisper, meaning it, and all of a sudden wanting to touch him, to run my hand over his, which rests on his thigh just inches from mine.

I glance at him sitting there so close to me that I can smell his shampoo, and I am stuck with a startling, horrifying thought: He is really good-looking, alarmingly so. How is it I never noticed before?

I'll answer that: He's Bailey's boyfriend, Lennie. What's wrong with you?

Dear Mind, I write on my jeans with my finger, *Behave*.

I'm sorry, I whisper to Bailey inside my head, I don't mean to think about Toby this way. I assure her it won't happen again.

It's just that he's the only one who understands, I add. *Oh brother*.

After a wordless while, he pulls a pint of tequila out of his jacket pocket, uncaps it.

"Want some?" he asks. Great, that'll help.

"Sure." I hardly ever drink, but maybe it will help, maybe it'll knock this madness out of me. I reach for the pint and our fingers graze a moment too long as I take it—I decide I imagined it, put the bottle to my lips, take a healthy sip, and then very daintily spit it out all over us. "Yuck, that's disgusting." I wipe my mouth with my sleeve. "Whoa."

He laughs, holds out his arms to show what a mess I've made of him. "It takes time to get used to it."

"Sorry," I say. "Had no idea it was so nasty."

He cheers the bottle to the air in response and takes a swig. I'm determined to try again and not projectile spew. I reach for the bottle, bring it to my lips, and let the liquid burn down my throat, then take another sip, bigger.

"Easy," Toby says, taking the pint from me. "I need to tell you something, Len."

"Okay." I'm enjoying the warmth that has settled over me.

"I asked Bailey to marry me . . ." He says it so quickly it doesn't register at first. He's looking at me, trying to gauge my reaction. It's stark, raving WTF!

"Marry you? Are you kidding?" Not the response he wants, I'm sure, but I'm totally blindsided; he could have just as easily told me she'd been secretly planning a career in fire-eating. Both of them were just nineteen, and Bailey a marriage-o-phobe to boot.

"What'd she say?" I'm afraid to hear the answer.

"She said yes." He says it with as much hope as hopelessness, the promise of it still alive in him. *She said yes.* I take the tequila, swig, don't even taste it or feel the burn. I'm stunned that Bailey wanted this, hurt that she wanted it, really hurt that she never told me. I have to know what she'd been thinking. I can't believe I can't ask her. Ever. I look at Toby, see the earnestness in his eyes; it's like a soft, small animal.

"I'm sorry, Toby," I say, trying to bottle my incredulity and hurt feelings, but then I can't help myself. "I don't know why she didn't tell me."

"We were going to tell you guys that very next week. I'd just asked . . ." His use of *we* jars me; the big *we* has always been

Bailey and me, not Bailey and Toby. I suddenly feel left out of a future that isn't even going to happen.

"But what about her acting?" I say instead of: *What about me?*

"She was acting . . ."

"Yeah, but . . ." I look at him. "You know what I mean." And then I see by his expression that he doesn't know what I mean at all. Sure some girls dream of weddings, but Bailey dreamt of Juilliard: the Juilliard School in New York City. I once looked up their mission statement on the Web: *To provide the highest caliber of artistic education for gifted musicians, dancers, and actors from around the world, so that they may achieve their fullest potential as artists, leaders, and global citizens.* It's true after the rejection she enrolled last fall at Clover State, the only other college she applied to, but I'd been certain she'd reapply. I mean, how could she not? It was her dream.

We don't talk about it anymore. The wind's picked up and has begun rattling its way into the house. I feel a chill run through me, grab a throw blanket off the rocker, pull it over my legs. The tequila makes me feel like I'm melting into nothing, I want to, want to disappear. I have an impulse to write all over the orange walls—I need an alphabet of endings ripped out of books, of hands pulled off of clocks, of cold stones, of shoes filled with nothing but wind. I drop my head on Toby's shoulder. "We're the saddest people in the world."

"Yup," he says, squeezing my knee for a moment. I ignore the shivers his touch sends through me. *They were getting married.*

"How will we do this?" I say under my breath. "Day after day after day without her . . ."

35

"Oh, Len." He turns to me, smoothes the hair around my face with his hand.

I keep waiting for him to move his hand away, to turn back around, but he doesn't. He doesn't take his hand or gaze off of me. Time slows. Something shifts in the room, between us. I look into his sorrowful eyes and he into mine, and I think, *He misses her as much as I do*, and that's when he kisses me—his mouth: soft, hot, so alive, it makes me moan. I wish I could say I pull away, but I don't. I kiss him back and don't want to stop because in that moment I feel like Toby and I together have, somehow, in some way, reached across time, and pulled Bailey back.

He breaks away, springs to his feet. "I don't understand this." He's in an instant-just-add-water panic, pacing the room.

"God, I should go, I *really* should go."

But he doesn't go. He sits down on Bailey's bed, looks over at me and then sighs as if giving in to some invisible force. He says my name and his voice is so hoarse and hypnotic it pulls me up onto my feet, pulls me across miles of shame and guilt. I don't want to go to him, but I do want to too. I have no idea what to do, but still I walk across the room, wavering a bit from the tequila, to his side. He takes my hand and tugs on it gently.

"I just want to be near you," he whispers. "It's the only time I don't die missing her."

"Me too." I run my finger along the sprinkle of freckles on his cheek. He starts to well up, then I do too. I sit down next to him and then we lie down on Bailey's bed, spooning. My last thought before falling asleep in his strong, safe arms is that I hope we are not replacing our scents with the last remnants of Bailey's own that still infuse the bedding.

When I wake again, I'm facing him, our bodies pressed together, breath intermingling. He's looking at me.

"You're beautiful, Len."

"No," I say. Then choke out one word. "Bailey."

"I know," he says. But he kisses me anyway. "I can't help it." He whispers it right into my mouth.

I can't help it either.

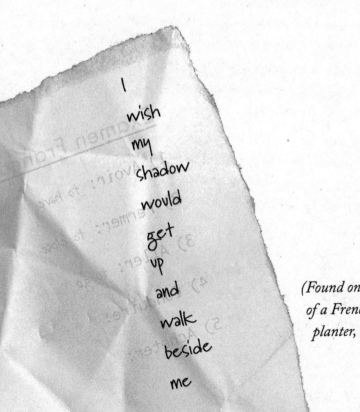

I
wish
my
shadow
would
get
up
and
walk
beside
me

(Found on the back
of a French quiz in a
planter, Clover High)

chapter 6

There were once two sisters who shared the same room,
the same clothes,
the same thoughts at the same moment.
These two sisters did not have a mother
but they had each other.
The older sister walked ahead of the younger
so the younger one always knew where to go.
The older one took the younger to the river
where they floated on their backs
like dead men.
The older girl would say:
Dunk your head under a few inches,
then open your eyes and look up at the sun
The younger girl:
I'll get water up my nose
The older:
C'mon, do it
and so the younger girl did it
and her whole world filled with light.

(Found on a piece of notebook paper caught in a fence up on the ridge)

JUDAS, BRUTUS, BENEDICT Arnold, and me.

And the worst part is every time I close my eyes I see Toby's lion face again, his lips a breath away from mine, and it makes me shudder head to toe, not with guilt, like it should, but with desire—and then, just as soon as I allow myself the image of us kissing, I see Bailey's face twisting in shock and betrayal as she watches us from above: her boyfriend, her *fiancé* kissing her traitorous little sister *on her own bed*. Ugh. Shame watches me like a dog.

I'm in self-imposed exile, cradled between split branches, in my favorite tree in the woods behind school. I've been coming here every day at lunch, hiding out until the bell rings, whittling words into the branches with my pen, allowing my heart to break in private. I can't hide a thing—everyone in school sees clear to my bones.

I'm reaching into the brown bag Gram packed for me, when I hear twigs crack underneath me. Uh-oh. I look down and see Joe Fontaine. I freeze. I don't want him to see me: Lennie Walker: Mental Patient Eating Lunch in a Tree (it being decidedly out of your tree to hide out in one!). He walks in confused circles under me like he's looking for someone. I'm hardly breathing but he isn't moving on, has settled just to the right of my tree. Then I inadvertently crinkle the bag and he looks up, sees me.

"Hi," I say, like it's the most normal place to be eating lunch.

"Hey, there you are—" He stops, tries to cover. "I was wondering what was back here . . ." He looks around. "Perfect spot for a gingerbread house or maybe an opium den."

"You already gave yourself away," I say, surprised at my own boldness.

"Okay, guilty as charged. I followed you." He smiles at me—that same smile—wow, no wonder I'd thought—

He continues, "And I'm guessing you want to be alone. Probably don't come all the way out here and then climb a tree because you're starving for conversation." He gives me a hopeful look. He's charming me, even in my pitiful emotional state, my Toby turmoil, even though he's accounted for by Cruella de Vil.

"Want to come up?" I present him a branch and he bounds up the tree in about three seconds, finds a suitable seat right next to me, then bats his eyelashes at me. I'd forgotten about the eyelash endowment. Wow squared.

"What's to eat?" He points to the brown bag.

"You kidding? First you crash my solitude, now you want to scavenge. Where were you raised?"

"Paris," he says. "So I'm a scavenger *raffiné*."

Oh so glad *j'étudie le français*. And jeez, no wonder the school's abuzz about him, no wonder I'd wanted to kiss him. I even momentarily forgive Rachel the idiotic baguette she had sticking out of her backpack today. He goes on, "But I was born in California, lived in San Francisco until I was nine. We moved back there about a year ago and now we're here. Still want to know what's in the bag though."

"You'll never guess," I tell him. "I won't either, actually. My grandmother thinks it's really funny to put all sorts of things in our—my lunch. I never know what'll be inside: e. e. cummings, flower petals, a handful of buttons. She seems to have lost sight of the original purpose of the brown bag."

"Or maybe she thinks other forms of nourishment are more important."

"That's exactly what she thinks," I say, surprised. "Okay, you want to do the honors?" I hold up the bag.

"I'm suddenly afraid, is there ever anything alive in it?" Bat. Bat. Bat. Okay, it might take me a little time to build immunity to the eyelash bat.

"Never know . . ." I say, trying not to sound as swoony as I feel. And I'm going to just pretend that sitting-in-a-tree k-i-s-s-i-n-g rhyme did not just pop into my head.

He takes the bag, then reaches in with a grand gesture, and pulls out—an apple.

"An apple? How anti-climactic!" He throws it at me. "Everyone gets apples."

I urge him to continue. He reaches in, pulls out a copy of *Wuthering Heights*.

"That's my favorite book," I say. "It's like a pacifier. I've read it twenty-three times. She's always putting it in."

"*Wuthering Heights*—twenty-three times! Saddest book ever, how do you even function?"

"Do I have to remind you? I'm sitting in a tree at lunch."

"True." He reaches in again, pulls out a stemless purple peony. Its rich scent overtakes us immediately. "Wow," he says, breathing it in. "Makes me feel like I might levitate." He holds it under my nose. I close my eyes, imagine the fragrance lifting me off my feet too. I can't. But something occurs to me.

"My favorite saint of all time is a Joe," I tell him. "Joseph of Cupertino, he levitated. Whenever he thought of God, he would float into the air in a fit of ecstasy."

He tilts his head, looks at me skeptically, eyebrows raised. "Don't buy it."

I nod. "Tons of witnesses. Happened all the time. Right during Mass."

"Okay, I'm totally jealous. Guess I'm just a wannabe levitator."

"Too bad," I say. "I'd like to see you drifting over Clover playing your horn."

"Hell yeah," he exclaims. "You could come with, grab my foot or something."

We exchange a quick searching glance, both of us wondering about the other, surprised at the easy rapport—it's just a moment, barely perceptible, like a lady bug landing on your arm.

He rests the flower on my leg and I feel the brush of his fingers through my jeans. The brown bag is empty now. He hands it to me, and then we're quiet, just listening to the wind rustle around us and watching the sun filter through the redwoods in impossibly thick foggy rays just like in children's drawings.

Who is this guy? I've talked more to him in this tree than I have to anyone at school since I've been back. But how could he have read *Wuthering Heights* and still fall for Rachel Bitchzilla? Maybe it's because she's been to Fronce. Or because she pretends to like music that no one else has heard of, like the wildly popular Throat Singers of Tuva.

"I saw you the other day," he says, picking up the apple. He tosses it with one hand, catches it with the other. "By The Great Meadow. I was playing my guitar in the field. You were across the way. It looked like you were writing a note or something against a car, but then you just dropped the piece of paper—"

"Are you stalking me?" I ask, trying to keep my sudden delight at that notion out of my voice.

"Maybe a little." He stops tossing the apple. "And maybe I'm curious about something."

"Curious?" I ask. "About what?"

He doesn't answer, starts picking at moss on a branch. I notice his hands, his long fingers full of calluses from guitar strings.

"What?" I say again, dying to know what made him curious enough to follow me up a tree.

"It's the way you play the clarinet . . ."

The delight drains out of me. "Yeah?"

"Or the way you don't play it, actually."

"What do you mean?" I ask, knowing exactly what he means.

"I mean you've got loads of technique. Your fingering's quick, your tonguing fast, your range of tones, man . . . but it's like it all stops there. I don't get it." He laughs, seemingly unaware of the bomb he just detonated. "It's like you're sleep-playing or something."

Blood rushes to my cheeks. Sleep-playing! I feel caught, a fish in a net. I wish I'd quit band altogether like I'd wanted to. I look off at the redwoods, each one rising to the sky surrounded only by its loneliness. He's staring at me, I can feel it, waiting for a response, but one is not forthcoming—this is a no trespassing zone.

"Look," he says cautiously, finally getting a clue that his charms have worn off. "I followed you out here because I wanted to see if we could play together."

"Why?" My voice is louder and more upset than I want it to be. A slow familiar panic is taking over my body.

"I want to hear John Lennon play for real, I mean, who wouldn't, right?"

His joke crashes and burns between us.

"I don't think so," I say as the bell rings.

"Look—" he starts, but I don't let him finish.

"I don't want to play with you, okay?"

"Fine." He hurls the apple into the air. Before it hits the ground and before he jumps out of the tree, he says, "It wasn't my idea anyway."

chapter 7

I WAKE TO Ennui, Sarah's Jeep, honking down the road—it's an ambush. I roll over, look out the window, see her jump out in her favorite black vintage gown and platform combat boots, back-to-blond hair tweaked into a nest, cigarette hanging from bloodred lips in a pancake of ghoulish white. I look at the clock: 7:05 a.m. She looks up at me in the window, waves like a windmill in a hurricane.

I pull the covers over my head, wait for the inevitable.

"I've come to suck your blood," she says a few moments later.

I peek out of the covers. "You really do make a stunning vampire."

"I know." She leans into the mirror over my dresser, wiping some lipstick off her teeth with her black-nail-polished finger. "It's a good look for me . . . Heidi goes goth." Without the accoutrements, Sarah could play Goldilocks. She's a sun-kissed beach girl who goes gothgrungepunkhippierockeremocoremetalfreakfashionistabraingeekboycrazyhiphoprastagirl to keep it under wraps. She crosses the room, stands over me, then pulls a corner of the covers down and hops into bed with me, boots and all.

"I miss you, Len." Her enormous blue eyes are shining down on me, so sincere and incongruous with her getup. "Let's go to breakfast before school. Last day of junior year and all. It's tradition."

"Okay," I say, then add, "I'm sorry I've been so awful."

"Don't say that, I just don't know what to do for you. I can't imagine . . ." She doesn't finish, looks around The Sanctum. I see the dread overtake her. "It's so unbearable . . ." She stares at Bailey's bed. "Everything is just as she left it. God, Len."

"Yeah." My life catches in my throat. "I'll get dressed."

She bites her bottom lip, trying not to cry. "I'll wait downstairs. I promised Gram I'd talk with her." She gets out of bed and walks to the door, the leap in her from moments before now a shuffle. I pull the covers back over my head. I know the bedroom is a mausoleum. I know it upsets everyone (except Toby, who didn't even seem to notice), but I want it like this. It makes me feel like Bailey's still here or like she might come back.

On the way to town, Sarah tells me about her latest scheme to bag a babe who can talk to her about her favorite existentialist, Jean-Paul Sartre. The problem is her insane attraction to lumphead surfers who (not to be prejudicial) are not customarily the most well-versed in French literature and philosophy, and therefore must constantly be exempted from Sarah's Must-Know-Who-Sartre-Is-or-at-Least-Have-Read-Some-of-D.H.-Lawrence-or-at-the-minimum-One-of-the-Brontës-Preferably-Emily criteria of going out with her.

"There's an afternoon symposium this summer at State in French Feminism," she tells me. "I'm going to go. Want to come?"

I laugh. "That sounds like the perfect place to meet guys."

"You'll see," she says. "The coolest guys aren't afraid to be feminists, Lennie."

I look over at her. She's trying to blow smoke rings, but blowing smoke blobs instead.

I'm dreading telling her about Toby, but I have to, don't I? Except I'm too chicken, so I go with less damning news.

"I hung out with Joe Fontaine the other day at lunch."

"You didn't!"

"I did."

"No way."

"Yes way."

"Nah-uh."

"Uh-huh."

"Not possible.

"So possible."

We have an incredibly high tolerance for yes-no.

"You duck! You flying yellow duck! And you took this long to tell me?!" When Sarah gets excited, random animals pop into her speech like she has an Old MacDonald Had a Farm kind of Tourette syndrome. "Well, what's he like?"

"He's okay," I say distractedly, looking out the window. I can't figure out whose idea it could've been that we play together. Mr. James, maybe? But why? And argh, how freaking mortifying.

"Earth to Lennie. Did you just say Joe Fontaine is *okay*? The

47

guy's holy horses *unfreakingbelievable*! And I heard he has two older brothers: holy horses to the third power, don't you think?"

"Holy horses, Batgirl," I say, which makes Sarah giggle, a sound that doesn't seem quite right coming out of her Batgoth face. She takes a last drag off her cigarette and drops it into a can of soda. I add, "He likes Rachel. What does that say about him?"

"That he has one of those Y chromosomes," Sarah says, shoving a piece of gum into her orally fixated mouth. "But really, I don't see it. I heard all he cares about is music and she plays like a screeching cat. Maybe it's those stupid Throat Singers she's always going on about and he thinks she's in the musical know or something." Great minds . . . Then suddenly Sarah's jumping in her seat like she's on a pogo stick. "Oh Lennie, do it! Challenge her for first chair. Today! C'mon. It'll be so exciting—probably never happened in the history of honor band, a chair challenged on the last day of school!"

I shake my head. "Not going to happen."

"But why?"

I don't answer her, don't know how to.

An afternoon from last summer pops into my head. I'd just quit my lessons with Marguerite and was hanging out with Bailey and Toby at Flying Man's. He was telling us that Thoroughbred racing horses have these companion ponies that always stay by their sides, and I remember thinking, *That's me*. I'm a companion pony, and companion ponies don't solo. They don't play first chair or audition for All-State or compete nationally or seriously consider a certain performing arts conservatory in New York City like Marguerite had begun insisting.

They just don't.

Sarah sighs as she swerves into a parking spot. "Oh well, guess I'll have to entertain myself another way on the last day of school."

"Guess so."

We jump out of Ennui, head into Cecilia's, and order up an obscene amount of pastries that Cecilia gives us for free with that same sorrowful look that follows me everywhere I go now. I think she would give me every last pastry in the store if I asked.

We land on our bench of choice by Maria's Italian Deli, where I've been chief lasagna maker every summer since I was fourteen. I start up again tomorrow. The sun has burst into millions of pieces, which have landed all over Main Street. It's a gorgeous day. Everything shines except my guilty heart.

"Sarah, I have to tell you something."

A worried look comes over her. "Sure."

"Something happened with Toby the other night." Her worry has turned into something else, which is what I was afraid of. Sarah has an ironclad girlfriend code of conduct regarding guys. The policy is sisterhood before all else.

"Something like something? Or something like *something*?" Her eyebrow has landed on Mars.

My stomach churns. "Like *something* . . . we kissed." Her eyes go wide and her face twists in disbelief, or perhaps it's horror. This is the face of my shame, I think, looking at her. *How could I have kissed Toby?* I ask myself for the thousandth time.

"Wow," she says, the word falling like a rock to the ground. She's making no attempt to hold back her disdain. I bury my head in my hands, assume the crash position—I shouldn't have told her.

"It felt right in the moment, we both miss Bails so much, he just gets it, gets me, he's like the only one who does. . . and I was drunk." I say all this to my jeans.

"Drunk?" She can't contain her surprise. I hardly ever even have a beer at the parties she drags me to. Then in a softer voice, I hear, "Toby's the only one who gets you?"

Uh-oh.

"I didn't mean that," I say, lifting my head to meet her eyes, but it's not true, I did mean it, and I can tell from her expression she knows it. "Sarah."

She swallows, looks away from me, then quickly changes the topic back to my disgrace. "I guess it does happen. Grief sex is kind of a thing. It was in one of those books I read." I still hear the judgment in her voice, and something more now too.

"We didn't have sex," I say. "I'm still the last virgin standing."

She sighs, then puts her arm around me, awkwardly, as if she has to. I feel like I'm in a headlock. Neither of us has a clue how to deal with what's not being said, or what is.

"It's okay, Len. Bailey would understand." She sounds totally unconvincing. "And it's not like it's ever going to happen again, right?"

"Of course not," I say, and hope I'm not lying.

And hope I am.

Everyone has always said I look like Bailey,
but I don't.
I have gray eyes to her green,
an oval face to her heart-shaped one,
I'm shorter, scrawnier, paler,
flatter, plainer, tamer.
All we shared is a madhouse of curls
that I imprison in a ponytail
while she let hers rave
like madness
around her head.
I don't sing in my sleep
or eat the petals off flowers
or run into the rain instead of out of it.
I'm the unplugged-in one,
the side-kick sister,
tucked into a corner of her shadow.
Boys followed her everywhere;
they filled the booths at the restaurant
where she waitressed,
herded around her at the river.
One day, I saw a boy come up behind her
and pull a strand of her long hair.
I understood this—
I felt the same way.
In photographs of us together,
she is always looking at the camera,
and I am always looking at her.

*(Found on a folded-up piece of paper half buried in pine
needles on the trail to the Rain River)*

chapter 8

I AM SITTING at Bailey's desk with St. Anthony: Patron of Lost Things.

He doesn't belong here. He belongs on the mantel in front of The Half Mom where I've always kept him, but Bailey must've moved him, and I don't know why. I found him tucked behind the computer in front of an old drawing of hers that's tacked to the wall—the one she made the day Gram told us our mother was an explorer (of the Christopher Columbus variety).

I've drawn the curtains, and though I want to, I won't let myself peek out the window to see if Toby is under the plum tree. I won't let myself imagine his lips lost and half wild on mine either. No. I let myself imagine igloos, nice frigid arctic igloos. I've promised Bailey nothing like what happened that night will ever happen again.

It's the first day of summer vacation and everyone from school is at the river. I just got a drunken call from Sarah informing me that not one, not two, but three unfreakingbelievable Fontaines are supposed to be arriving momentarily at Flying Man's, that they are going to play outside, that she just found out the two older Fontaines are in a seriously awesome band in L.A., where they go to college, and I better get my butt down there to witness the glory. I told her I was staying in and to revel in their Fontainely glory for me, which resurrected the bristle from yesterday: "You're not with Toby, are you, Lennie?"

Ugh.

I look over at my clarinet abandoned in its case on my playing chair. It's in a coffin, I think, then immediately try to unthink it. I walk over to it, unlatch the lid. There never was a question what instrument I'd play. When all the other girls ran to the flutes in fifth-grade music class, I beelined for a clarinet. It reminded me of me.

I reach in the pocket where I keep my cloth and reeds and feel around for the folded piece of paper. I don't know why I've kept it (for over a year!), why I fished it out of the garbage later that afternoon, after Bailey had tossed it with a cavalier "Oh well, guess you guys are stuck with me," before throwing herself into Toby's arms like it meant nothing to her. But I knew it did. How could it not? It was Juilliard.

Without reading it a final time, I crumple Bailey's rejection letter into a ball, toss it into the garbage can, and sit back down at her desk.

I'm in the exact spot where I was that night when the phone blasted through the house, through the whole unsuspecting world. I'd been doing chemistry, hating every minute of it like I always do. The thick oregano scent of Gram's chicken fricassee was wafting into our room and all I wanted was Bailey to hurry home already so we could eat because I was starving and hated isotopes. How can that be? How could I have been thinking about fricassee and carbon molecules when across town my sister had just taken her very last breath? What kind of world is this? And what do you do about it? What do you do when the worst thing that can happen actually happens? When you get *that* phone call? When you miss your sister's roller coaster of a voice so much that you want to take apart the whole house with your fingernails?

This is what I do: I take out my phone and punch in her number. In a blind fog of a moment the other day I called to see when she'd be home and discovered her account hadn't yet been canceled.

Hey, this is Bailey, Juliet for the month, so dudes, what say'st thou? Hast thou not a word of joy? Some comfort . . .

I hang up at the tone, then call back, again and again, and again, and again, wanting to just pull her out of the phone. Then one time I don't hang up.

"Why didn't you tell me you were getting married?" I whisper, before snapping the phone shut and laying it on her desk. Because I don't understand. Didn't we tell each other everything? *If this doesn't change our lives, Len, I don't know what will,* she'd said when we painted the walls. Is that the change she'd wanted then? I pick up the cheesy plastic St. Anthony. And what about him? Why bring him up here? I look more closely at the drawing he was leaning against. It's been up so long that the paper has yellowed and the edges have curled, so long that I haven't taken notice of it for years. Bailey drew it when she was around eleven, the time she started questioning Gram about Mom with an unrelenting ferocity.

She'd been at it for weeks.

"How do you know she'll be back?" Bailey asked for the millionth time. We were in Gram's art room, Bailey and I lay sprawled out on the floor drawing with pastels while Gram painted one of her ladies at a canvas in the corner, her back to us. She'd been skirting Bailey's questions all day, artfully changing the subject, but it wasn't working this time. I watched Gram's arm drop to her side, the brush sending droplets of a hopeful green onto the bespattered floor. She sighed, a big lonely sigh, then turned around to face us.

"I guess you're old enough, girls," she said. We perked up, immediately put down our pastels, and gave her our undivided attention. "Your mother is . . . well . . . I guess the best way to describe it . . . hmmm . . . let me think . . ." Bailey looked at me in shock—we'd never known Gram to be at a loss for words.

"What, Gram?" Bailey asked. "What is she?"

"Hmmm . . ." Gram bit her lip, then finally, hesitantly, she said, "I guess the best way to say it is . . . you know how some people have natural tendencies, how I paint and garden, how Big's an arborist, how you, Bailey, want to grow up and be an actress—"

"I'm going to go to Juilliard," she told us.

Gram smiled. "Yes, we know, Miss Hollywood. Or Miss Broadway, I should say."

"Our mom?" I reminded them before we ended up talking some more about that dumb school. All I'd hoped was that it was in walking distance if Bailey was going there. Or at least close enough so I could ride my bike to see her every day. I'd been too scared to ask.

Gram pursed her lips for a moment. "Okay, well, your mother, she's a little different, she's more like a . . . well, like an explorer."

"Like Columbus, you mean?" Bailey asked.

"Yes, like that, except without the *Niña, Pinta,* and *Santa Maria*. Just a woman, a map, and the world. A solo artist." Then she left the room, her favorite and most effective way of ending a conversation.

Bailey and I stared at each other. In all our persistent musings on where Mom was and why she left, we never ever imagined anything remotely this good. I followed after Gram to try and find out more, but Bailey stayed on the floor and drew this picture.

In it, there's a woman at the top of a mountain looking off into the distance, her back to us. Gram, Big, and I—with our names beneath our feet—are waving up at the lone figure from the base of the mountain. Under the whole drawing, it says in green *Explorer*. For some reason, Bailey did not put herself in the picture.

I bring St. Anthony to my chest, hold him tight. I need him now, but why did Bailey? What had she lost?

What was it she needed to find?

I put on her clothes.
I button one of her frilly shirts
over my own T-shirt.
Or I wrap one, sometimes two,
sometimes all of her diva scarves around my neck.
Or I strip and slip one of her slinkier dresses over my head,
letting the fabric
fall over my skin like water.
I always feel better then,
like she's holding me.
Then I touch all the things
that haven't moved since she died:
crumpled-up dollars
dredged from a sweaty pocket,
the three bottles of perfume
always with the same amount of liquid in them now,
the Sam Shepherd play
Fool For Love
where her bookmark will never move forward.
I've read it for her twice now,
always putting the bookmark back
where it was when I finish—
it kills me
she will never find out
what happens
in the end.

(Found on the inside cover of
Wuthering Heights, Clover High library)

chapter 9

Gram spends the night
in front of The Half Mom.
I hear her weeping—
sad
endless
rain.
I sit at the top of the stairs,
know she's touching

Mom's cold flat cheek
as she says: I'm sorry
I'm so sorry.
I think a terrible thing.
I think: You should be.
I think: How could you have   let this happen?
How could you have let both   of them leave me?

(Found written on the wall of the bathroom at Cecilia's Bakery)

SCHOOL'S BEEN OUT for two weeks. Gram, Big, and I are certifiably out of our trees and running loose through the park—all in opposite directions.

Exhibit A: Gram's following me around the house with a teapot. The pot is full. I can see the steam coming out the spout. She has two mugs in her other hand. Tea is what Gram and I used to do together, before. We'd sit around the kitchen table in the late afternoons and drink tea and talk before the others came home. But I don't want to have tea with Gram anymore because I don't feel like talking, which she knows but still hasn't accepted. So she's followed me up the stairs and is now standing in the doorway of The Sanctum, pot in hand.

I flop onto the bed, pick up my book, pretend to read.

"I don't want any tea, Gram," I say, looking up from *Wuthering Heights,* which I note is upside down and hope she doesn't.

Her face falls. Epically.

"Fine." She puts a mug on the ground, fills the other one in her hand for herself, takes a sip. I can tell it's burned her tongue, but she pretends it hasn't. "Fine, fine, fine," she chants, taking another sip.

She's been following me around like this since school got out. Normally, summer is her busiest time as Garden Guru, but she's told all her clients she is on hiatus until the fall. So instead of guruing, she happens into Maria's while I'm at the deli, or into the library when I'm on my break, or she tails me to Flying Man's and paces on the path while I float on my back and let my tears spill into the water.

But teatime is the worst.

"Sweet pea, it's not healthy . . ." Her voice has melted into a familiar river of worry. I think she's talking about my remoteness, but when I glance over at her I realize it's the other thing. She's staring at Bailey's dresser, the gum wrappers strewn about, the hairbrush with a web of her black hair woven through the teeth. I watch her gaze drifting around the room to Bailey's dresses thrown over the back of her desk chair, the towel flung over her bedpost, Bailey's laundry basket still piled over with her dirty clothes . . . "Let's just pack up a few things."

"I told you, I'll do it," I whisper so I don't scream at the top of my lungs. "I'll do it, Gram, if you stop stalking me and leave me alone."

"Okay, Lennie," she says. I don't have to look up to know I've hurt her.

When I do look up, she's gone. Instantly, I want to run after her, take the teapot from her, pour myself a mug and join her, just spill every thought and feeling I'm having.

But I don't.

I hear the shower turn on. Gram spends an inordinate amount of time in the shower now and I know this is because she thinks she can cry under the spray without Big and me hearing. We hear.

Exhibit B: I roll onto my back and before long I'm holding my pillow in my arms and kissing the air with an embarrassing amount of passion. Not again, I think. What's wrong with me? What kind of girl wants to kiss every boy at a funeral, wants to maul a guy in a tree after making out with her sister's boyfriend the previous night? *Speaking of which, what kind of girl makes out with her sister's boyfriend, period?*

Let me just unsubscribe to my own mind already, because

I don't get any of it. I hardly ever thought about sex before, much less did anything about it. Three boys at three parties in four years: Casey Miller, who tasted like hot dogs; Dance Rosencrantz, who dug around in my shirt like he was reaching into a box of popcorn at the movies. And Jasper Stolz in eighth grade because Sarah dragged me into a game of spin the bottle. Total blobfish feeling inside each time. Nothing like Heathcliff and Cathy, like Lady Chatterley and Oliver Mellors, like Mr. Darcy and Elizabeth Bennet! Sure, I've always been into the Big Bang theory of passion, but as something theoretical, something that happens in books that you can close and put back on a shelf, something that I might secretly want bad but can't imagine ever happening to me. Something that happens to the heroines like Bailey, to the commotion girls in the leading roles. But now I've gone mental, kissing everything I can get my lips on: my pillow, arm chairs, doorframes, mirrors, always imagining the one person I should not be imagining, the person I promised my sister I will never ever kiss again. The one person who makes me feel just a little less afraid.

The front door slams shut, jarring me out of Toby's forbidden arms.

It's Big. Exhibit C: I hear him stomp straight into the dining room, where only two days ago, he unveiled his pyramids. This is always a bad sign. He built them years ago, based on some hidden mathematics in the geometry of the Egyptian pyramids. (Who knows? The guy also talks to trees.) According to Big, his pyramids, like the ones in the Middle East, have extraordinary properties. He's always believed his replicas would be able to prolong the life of cut flowers and fruit, even revive bugs, all of which he would place under them for ongoing study. During his pyramid spells, Big, Bails, and I would spend hours searching the house for dead spiders or flies, and then each morning we'd run to the pyramids hoping to witness a resurrection. We never did. But whenever Big's really upset, the necromancer in him comes out, and with it, the pyramids. This time, he's at it with a fervor, sure it will work, certain that he only failed before because he forgot a key element: an electrically charged coil, which he's now placed under each pyramid.

A little while later, a stoned Big drifts past my open door. He's been smoking so much weed that when he's home he seems to hover above Gram and me like an enormous balloon—every time I come upon him, I want to tie him to a chair.

He backtracks, lingers in my doorway for a moment.

"I'm going to add a few dead moths tomorrow," he says, as if picking up on a conversation we'd been having.

I nod. "Good idea."

He nods back, then floats off to his room, and most likely, right out the window.

This is us. Two months and counting. Booby Hatch Central.

THE NEXT MORNING, a showered and betoweled Gram is fixing breakfast ashes, Big is sweeping the rafters for dead moths to put under the pyramids, and I am trying not to make out with my spoon, when there's a knock at the door. We freeze, all of us suddenly panicked that someone might witness the silent sideshow of our grief. I walk to the front door on tiptoe, so as not to let on that we are indeed home, and peek through the peep-hole. It's Joe Fontaine, looking as animated as ever, like the front door is telling him jokes. He has a guitar in his hand.

"Everybody hide," I whisper. I prefer all boys safe in the recesses of my sex-crazed mind, not standing outside the front door of our capsizing house. Especially this minstrel. I haven't even taken my clarinet out of its case since school ended. I have no intention of going to summer band practice.

"Nonsense," Gram says, making her way to the front of the house in her bright purple towel muumuu and pink towel turban ensemble. "Who is it?" she asks me in a whisper hundreds of decibels louder than her normal speaking voice.

"It's that new kid from band, Gram, I can't deal." I swing my arms back and forth trying to shoo her into the kitchen.

I've forgotten how to do anything with my lips but kiss furniture. I have no conversation in me. I haven't seen anyone from school, don't want to, haven't called back Sarah, who's taken to writing me long e-mails (essays) about how she's not judging me at all about what happened with Toby, which just lets me know how much she's judging me about what happened with Toby. I duck into the kitchen, back into a corner, pray for invisibility.

"Well, well, a troubadour," Gram says, opening the door. She has obviously noticed the mesmery that is Joe's face and has already begun flirting. "Here I thought we were in the twenty-first century . . ." She is starting to purr. I have to save him.

I reluctantly come out of hiding and join swami seductress Gram. I get a good look at him. I've forgotten quite how luminous he is, like another species of human that doesn't have blood but light running through their veins. He's spinning his guitar case like a top while he talks to Gram. He doesn't look like he needs saving, he looks amused.

"Hi, John Lennon." He's beaming at me like our tree-spat never happened.

What are you doing here? I think so loudly my head might explode.

"Haven't seen you around," he says. Shyness overtakes his face for a quick moment—it makes my stomach flutter. Uh, I think I need to get a restraining order for all boys until I can get a handle on this newfound body buzz.

"Do come in," Gram says, as if talking to a knight. "I was just preparing breakfast." He looks at me, asking if it's okay with his eyes. Gram's still talking as she walks back into the kitchen. "You can play us a song, cheer us up a bit." I smile at him, it's impossible not to, and motion a welcome with my arm. As we enter the kitchen, I hear Gram whisper to Big, still in knight parlance, "I daresay, the young gentleman batted his extraordinarily long eyelashes at me."

We haven't had a real visitor since the weeks following the funeral and so don't know how to behave. Uncle Big has seemingly floated to the floor and is leaning on the broom he had been using to sweep up the dead. Gram stands, spatula in hand, in the middle of the kitchen with an enormous smile on her face. I'm certain she's forgotten what she's wearing. And I sit upright in my chair at the table. No one says anything and all of us stare at Joe like he's a television we're hoping will just turn itself on.

It does.

"That garden is wild, never seen flowers like that, thought some of those roses might chop off *my* head and put me in a vase." He shakes his head in amazement and his hair falls too adorably into his eyes. "It's like Eden or something."

"Better be careful in Eden, all that temptation." The thunder of Big's God voice surprises me—he's been my partner in muteness lately, much to Gram's displeasure. "Smelling Gram's flowers has been known to cause all sorts of maladies of the heart."

"Really?" Joe says. "Like what?"

"Many things. For instance, the scent of her roses causes a mad love to flourish." At that, Joe's gaze ever so subtly shifts to me—whoa, or did I imagine it? Because now his eyes are back on Big, who's still talking. "I believe this to be the case from personal experience and five marriages." He grins at Joe. "Name's Big, by the way, I'm Lennie's uncle. Guess you're new around here or you'd already know all this."

What he would know is that Big is the town lothario. Rumors have it that at lunchtime women from all over pack a picnic and set out to find which tree that arborist is in, hoping for an invitation to lunch with him in his barrel high in the canopy. The stories go that shortly after they dine, their clothes flutter down like leaves.

I watch Joe taking in my uncle's gigantism, his wacked-out mustache. He must like what he sees, because his smile immediately brightens the room a few shades.

"Yup, we moved here just a couple months ago from the city, before that we were in Paris—" Hmm. He must not have read the warning on the door about saying the word *Paris* within a mile radius of Gram. It's too late. She's already off on a Franco-philiac rhapsody, but Joe seems to share her fanaticism.

He laments, "Man, *if only* we still lived—"

"Now, now," she interrupts, wagging her finger like she's scolding him. Oh no. Her hands have found her hips. Here it comes: She singsongs, "*If only* I had wheels on my ass, I'd be a trolley cart." A Gram standard to forestall wallowing. I'm appalled, but Joe cracks up.

Gram's in love. I don't blame her. She's taken him by the hand and is now escorting him on a docent walk through the house, showing off her willowy women, with whom he seems duly and truly impressed, from the exclamations he's making, in French, I might add. This leaves Big to resume his scavenging for bugs and me to replace fantasies of my spoon with Joe Fontaine's mouth. I can hear them in the living room, know they are standing in front of The Half Mom because everyone who comes in the house has the same reaction to it.

"It's so haunting," Joe says.

"Hmm, yes . . . that's my daughter, Paige. Lennie and Bailey's mom, she's been away for a long, long time . . ." I'm shocked. Gram hardly ever talks about Mom voluntarily. "One day I'll finish this painting, it's not done . . ." Gram has always said she'll finish it when Mom comes back and can pose for her.

"Come now, let's eat." I can hear the heartache in Gram's voice through three walls. Mom's absence has grown way more pronounced for her since Bailey's death. I keep catching her and Big staring at The Half Mom with a fresh, almost desperate kind of longing. It's become more pronounced for me too.

Mom was what Bails and I did together before bed when we'd imagine where she was and what she was doing. I don't know how to think about Mom without her.

I'm jotting down a poem on the sole of my shoe when they come back in.

"Run out of paper?" Joe asks.

I put my foot down. Ugh. What's your major, Lennie? Oh yeah: Dorkology.

Joe sits down at the table, all limbs and graceful motion, an octopus.

We are staring at him again, still not certain what to make of the stranger in our midst. The stranger, however, appears quite comfortable with us.

"What's up with the plant?" He points to the despairing Lennie houseplant in the middle of the table. It looks like it has leprosy. We all go silent, because what do we say about my doppelganger houseplant?

"It's Lennie, it's dying, and frankly, we don't know what to do about it," Big booms with finality. It's as if the room itself takes a long awkward breath, and then at the same moment Gram, Big, and I lose it—Big slapping the table and barking laughter like a drunk seal, Gram leaning back against the counter wheezing and gasping for breath, and me doubled over trying to breathe in between my own uncontrolled gasping and snorting, all of us lost in a fit of hysterics the likes of which we haven't had in months.

"Aunt Gooch! Aunt Gooch!" Gram is shrieking in between peals of laugher. Aunt Gooch is the name Bailey and I gave to Gram's laugh because it would arrive without notice like a crazy relative who shows up at the door with pink hair, a suitcase full of balloons, and no intention of leaving.

Gram gasps, "Oh my, oh my, I thought she was gone for good."

Joe seems to be taking the outburst quite well. He's leaned back in his chair, is balancing on its two back legs; he looks entertained, like he's watching, well, like he's watching three heartbroken people lose their marbles. I finally settle enough to explain to Joe, amidst tears and residual giggles, the story of the plant. If he hadn't already thought he'd gained entry to the local loony bin, he was sure to now. To my amazement, he doesn't make an excuse and fly out the door, but takes the predicament quite seriously, like he actually cares about the fate of the plain, sickly plant that will not revive.

After breakfast, Joe and I go onto the porch, which is still eerily cloaked in morning fog. The moment the screen door closes behind us, he says, "One song," as if no time has elapsed since we were in the tree.

I walk over to the railing, lean against it, and cross my arms in front of my chest. "You play. I'll listen."

"I don't get it," he says. "What's the deal?"

"The deal is I don't want to."

"But why? Your pick, I don't care what."

"I told you, I don't—"

He starts to laugh. "God, I feel like I'm pressuring you to have sex or something." Every ounce of blood in a ten-mile radius rushes to my cheeks. "C'mon. I know you want to . . ." he jokes, raising his eyebrows like a total dork. What I want is to hide under the porch, but his giant loopy grin makes me laugh. "Bet you like Mozart," he says, squatting to open his case. "All clarinetists do. Or maybe you're a Bach's Sacred Music devotee?" He squints up at me. "Nah, don't seem like one of those." He takes the guitar out, then sits on the edge of the coffee table, swinging it over his knee. "I've got it. No clarinet player with blood in her veins can resist Gypsy jazz." He plays a few sizzling chords. "Am I right? Or I know!" He starts beating a rhythm on his guitar with his hand, his foot pounding the floor. "Dixieland!"

The guy's life-drunk, I think, makes Candide look like a sourpuss. Does he even know that death exists?

"So, whose idea was it?" I ask him.

He stops finger-drumming. "What idea?"

"That we play together. You said—"

"Oh, that. Marguerite St. Denis is an old friend of the family—the one I blame actually for my exile up here. She might've mentioned something about how Lennie Walker *joue de la clarinette comme un reve*." He twirls his hand in the air like Marguerite. *"Elle joue a ravir, de merveille."*

I feel a rush of something, everything, panic, pride, guilt, nausea—it's so strong I have to hold on to the railing. I wonder what else she told him.

"Quel catastrophe," he continues. "You see, I thought *I* was her only student who played like a dream." I must look confused, because he explains, "In France. She taught at the conservatory, most summers."

As I take in the fact that my Marguerite is also Joe's Marguerite, I see Big barreling past the window, back at it, broom overhead, looking for creatures to resurrect. Joe doesn't seem to notice, probably a good thing. He adds, "I'm joking, about me, clarinet's never been my thing."

"Not what I heard," I say. "Heard you were *fabulous*."

"Rachel doesn't have much of an ear," he replies matter-of-factly, without insult. Her name falls too easily from his lips, like he says it all the time, probably right before he kisses her. I feel my face flush again. I look down, start examining my shoes. What's with me? I mean really. He just wants to play music together like normal musicians do.

Then I hear, "I thought about you . . ."

I don't dare look up for fear I imagined the words, the sweet tentative tone. But if I did, I'm imagining more of them. "I thought about how crazy sad you are, and . . ."

He's stopped talking. *And what?* I lift my head to see that he's examining my shoes too. "Okay," he says, meeting my gaze. "I had this image of us holding hands, like up at The Great Meadow or somewhere, and then taking off into the air."

Whoa—I wasn't expecting that, but I like it. "A la St. Joseph?"

He nods. "Got into the idea."

"What kind of launch?" I ask. "Like rockets?"

"No way, an effortless takeoff, Superman-style." He raises one arm up and crosses his guitar with the other to demonstrate. "You know."

I do know. I know I'm smiling just to look at him. I know that what he just said is making something unfurl inside. I know that all around the porch, a thick curtain of fog hides us from the world.

I want to tell him.

"It's not that I don't want to play with you," I say quickly so I don't lose my nerve. "It's that, I don't know, it's different, playing is." I force out the rest. "I didn't want to be first chair, didn't want to do the solos, didn't want to do any of it. I blew it, the chair audition . . . on purpose." It's the first time I've said it aloud, to anyone, and the relief is the size of a planet. I go on. "I hate soloing, not that you'd understand that. It's just so . . ." I'm waving my arm around, unable to find the words. But then I point my hand in the direction of Flying Man's. "So like jumping from rock to rock in the river, but in this kind of thick fog, and you're all alone, and every single step is . . ."

"Is what?"

I suddenly realize how ridiculous I must sound. I have no clue what I'm talking about, no clue. "It doesn't matter," I say.

He shrugs. "Tons of musicians are afraid to face-plant."

I can hear the steady whoosh of the river as if the fog's parted to let the sound through.

It's not just performance anxiety though. That's what Marguerite thought too. It's why she thought I quit—*You must work on the nerves, Lennie, the nerves*—but it's more than that, way more. When I play, it's like I'm all shoved and crammed and scared inside myself, like a jack-in-the-box, except one without a spring. And it's been like that for over a year now.

Joe bends down and starts flipping through the sheet music in his case; lots of it is handwritten. He says, "Let's just try. Guitar and clarinet's a cool duet, untapped."

He's certainly not taking my big admission too seriously. It's like finally going to confession only to find out the priest has earplugs in.

I tell him, "Maybe sometime," so he'll drop it.

"Wow." He grins. "Encouraging."

And then it's as if I've vanished. He's bent over the strings, tuning his guitar with such passionate attention I almost feel like I should look away, but I can't. In fact, I'm full-on gawking, wondering what it would be like to be cool and casual and fearless and passionate and so freaking alive, just like he is—and for a split second, I want to play with him. I want to disturb the birds.

Later, as he plays and plays, as all the fog burns away, I think, he's right. That's exactly it—I am crazy sad, and somewhere deep inside, all I want is to fly.

chapter 10

Grief is a house
where the chairs
have forgotten how to hold us
the mirrors how to reflect us
the walls how to contain us
Grief is a house that disappears
each time someone knocks at the door
or rings the bell
a house that blows into the air
at the slightest gust
that buries itself deep in the ground
while everyone is sleeping
Grief is a house where no one can protect you
where the younger sister
will grow older than the older one
where the doors
no longer let you in
or out

(Found under a stone in Gram's garden)

As usual I can't sleep and am sitting at Bailey's desk, holding St. Anthony, in a state of dread about packing up her things. Today, when I got home from lasagna detail at the deli, there were cardboard boxes open by her desk. I've yet to crack a drawer. I can't. Each time I touch the wooden knobs, I think about her never thumbing through her desk for a notebook, an address, a pen, and all the breath races out of my body with one thought: *Bailey's in that airless box—*

No. I shove the image into a closet in my mind, kick the door shut. I close my eyes, take one, two, three breaths, and when I open them, I find myself staring again at the picture of Explorer Mom. I touch the brittle paper, feel the wax of the crayon as I glide my finger across the fading figure. Does her human counterpart have any idea one of her daughters has died at nineteen years old? Did she feel a cold wind or a hot flash or was she just eating breakfast or tying her shoe like it was any other ordinary moment in her extraordinary itinerant life?

Gram told us our mom was an explorer because she didn't know how else to explain to us that Mom had what generations of Walkers call the "restless gene." According to Gram, this restlessness has always plagued our family, mostly the women. Those afflicted keep moving, they go from town to town, continent to continent, love to love—this is why Gram explained Mom had no idea who either of our fathers were, and so neither did we—until they wear themselves out and return home. Gram told us her aunt Sylvie and a distant cousin Virginia also had the affliction, and after many years adventuring across the globe, they, like all the others before them, found their way back. It's their destiny to leave, she told us, and their destiny to return, as well.

"Don't boys get it?" I asked Gram when I was ten years old and "the condition" was becoming more understandable to me. We were walking to the river for a swim.

"Of course they do, sweet pea." But then she stopped in her tracks, took my hands in hers, and spoke in a rare solemn tone. "I don't know if at your mature age you can understand this, Len, but this is the way it is: When men have it, no one seems to notice, they become astronauts or pilots or cartographers or criminals or poets. They don't stay around long enough to know if they've fathered children or not. When women get it, well, it's complicated, it's just different."

"How?" I asked. "How is it different?"

"Well, for instance, it's not customary for a mother to not see her own girls for this many years, is it?"

She had a point there.

"Your mom was born like this, practically flew out of my womb and into the world. From day one, she was running, running, running."

"Running away?"

"Nope, sweet pea, never *away*, know that." She squeezed my hand. "She was always running toward."

Toward what? I think, getting up from Bailey's desk. What was my mother running toward then? What is she running toward now? What was Bailey? What am I?

I walk over to the window, open the curtain a crack and see Toby, sitting under the plum tree, under the bright stars, on the green grass, in the world. Lucy and Ethel are draped over his legs—it's amazing how those dogs only come around when he does.

I know I should turn off the light, get into bed, and moon about Joe Fontaine, but that is not what I do.

I meet Toby under the tree and we duck into the woods to the river, wordlessly, as if we've had a plan to do this for days. Lucy and Ethel follow on our heels a few paces, then turn back around and go home after Toby has an indecipherable talk with them.

I'm leading a double life: Lennie Walker by day, Hester Prynne by night.

I tell myself, I will not kiss him, no matter what.

It's a warm, windless night and the forest is still and lonely. We walk side by side in the quiet, listening to the fluted song of the thrush. Even in the moonlit stillness, Toby looks sun-drenched and windswept, like he's on a sailboat.

"I know I shouldn't have come, Len."

"Probably not."

"Was worried about you," he says quietly.

"Thanks," I say, and the cloak of being fine that I wear with everyone else slips right off my shoulders.

Sadness pulses out of us as we walk. I almost expect the trees to lower their branches when we pass, the stars to hand down some light. I breathe in the horsy scent of eucalyptus, the thick sugary pine, aware of each breath I take, how each one keeps me in the world a few seconds longer. I taste the sweetness of the summer air on my tongue and want to just gulp and gulp and gulp it into my body—this living, breathing, heart-beating body of mine.

"Toby?"

"Hmm?"

"Do you feel more alive since . . ." I'm afraid to ask this, like I'm revealing something shameful, but I want to know if he feels it too.

He doesn't hesitate. "I feel more *everything* since."

Yeah, I think, more everything. Like someone flipped on the switch of the world and everything is just on now, including me, and everything in me, bad and good, all cranking up to the max.

He grabs a twig off a branch, snaps it between his fingers. "I keep doing this stupid stuff at night on my board," he says, "gnarly-ass tricks only show-off dip-shits do, and I've been doing it alone . . . and a couple times totally wasted."

Toby is one of a handful of skaters in town who regularly and spectacularly defy gravity. If he thinks he's putting himself in danger he's going full-on kamikaze.

"She wouldn't want that, Toby." I can't keep the pleading out of my voice.

He sighs, frustrated. "I know that, I know." He picks up his pace as if to leave behind what he just told me.

"She'd kill me." He says it so definitively and passionately that I wonder if he's really talking about skating or what happened between us.

"I won't do it anymore," he insists.

"Good," I say, still not totally sure what he's referring to, but if it's us, he doesn't have to worry, right? I've kept the curtains drawn. I've promised Bailey nothing will ever happen again.

Though even as I think this, I find my eyes drinking him in, his broad chest and strong arms, his freckles. I remember his mouth hungrily on mine, his big hands in my hair, the heat coursing through me, how it made me feel—

"It's just so reckless . . ." he says.

"Yeah." It comes out a little too breathy.

"Len?"

I need smelling salts.

He looks at me funny, but then I think he reads in my eyes what has been going on in my head, because his eyes kind of widen and spark, before he quickly looks away.

GET A GRIP, LENNIE.

We walk in silence then through the woods and it snaps me back into my senses. The stars and moon are mostly hidden over the thick tree cover, and I feel like I'm swimming through darkness, my body breaking the air as if it were water. I can hear the rush of the river getting louder with every step I take, and it reminds me of Bailey, day after day, year after year, the two of us on this path, lost in talk, the plunge into the pool, and then the endless splaying on the rocks in the sun—

I whisper, "I'm left behind."

"Me too . . ." His voice catches. He doesn't say anything else, doesn't look at me; he just takes my hand and holds it and doesn't let it go as the cover above us gets thicker and we push together farther into the deepening dark.

I say softly, "I feel so guilty," almost hoping the night will suck my words away before Toby hears.

"I do too," he whispers back.

"But about something else too, Toby . . ."

"What?"

With all the darkness around me, with my hand in Toby's, I feel like I can say it. "I feel guilty that I'm still here . . ."

"Don't. Please, Len."

"But she was always so much . . . more—"

"No." He doesn't let me finish. "She'd hate for you to feel that way."

"I know."

And then I blurt out what I've forbidden myself to think, let alone say: "She's in a coffin, Toby." I say it so loud, practically shriek it—the words make me dizzy, claustrophobic, like I need to leap out of my body.

I hear him suck in air. When he speaks, his voice is so weak I barely hear it over our footsteps. "No, she isn't."

I know this too. I know both things at once.

Toby tightens his grip around my hand.

Once at Flying Man's, the sky floods through the opening in the canopy. We sit on a flat rock and the full moon shines so brightly on the river, the water looks like pure rushing light.

"How can the world continue to shimmer like this?" I say as I lie down under a sky drunk with stars.

Toby doesn't answer, just shakes his head and lies down next to me, close enough for him to put his arm around me, close enough for me to put my head on his chest if he did so. But he doesn't, and I don't.

He starts talking then, his soft words dissipating into the night like smoke. He talks about how Bailey wanted to have the wedding ceremony here at Flying Man's so they could jump into the pool after saying their vows. I lean up on my elbows and can see it as clearly in the moonlight as if I were watching a movie, can see Bailey in a drenched bright orange wedding dress laughing and leading the party down the path back to the house, her careless beauty so huge it had to walk a few paces ahead of her, announcing itself. I see in the movie of Toby's words how happy she would have been, and suddenly, I just don't know where all that happiness, her happiness, and ours, will go now, and I start to cry, and then Toby's face is above mine and his tears are falling onto my cheeks until I don't know whose are whose, just know that all that happiness is gone, and that we are kissing again.

When I'm with him,
there is someone with me
in my house of grief,
someone who knows
its architecture as I do,
who can walk with me,
from room to sorrowful room,
making the whole rambling structure
of wind and emptiness
not quite as warm as lonely
as it was before.

(Found on a branch of a tree outside Clover High)

chapter 11

JOE FONTAINE'S KNOCKING. I'm lying awake in bed, thinking about moving to Antarctica to get away from this mess with Toby. I prop myself up on an elbow to look out the window at the early, bony light.

Joe's our rooster. Each morning since his first visit, a week and a half ago, he arrives at dawn with his guitar, a bag of chocolate croissants from the bakery, and a few dead bugs for Big. If we aren't up, he lets himself in, makes a pot of coffee thick as tar, and sits at the kitchen table strumming melancholy chords on his guitar. Every so often he asks me if I feel like playing, to which I reply *no,* to which he replies *fine.* A polite standoff. He hasn't mentioned Rachel again, which is okay by me.

The strangest part about all this is that it's not strange at all, for any of us. Even Big, who is not a morning person, pads down the stairs in his slippers, greets Joe with a boisterous back slap, and after checking the pyramids (which Joe has already checked), he jumps right back into their conversation from the previous morning about his obsession du jour: exploding cakes.

Big heard that a woman in Idaho was making a birthday cake for her husband when the flour ignited. They were having a dry spell, so there was lots of static electricity in the air. A cloud of flour dust surrounded her and due to a spark from a static charge in her hand, it exploded: an inadvertent flour bomb. Now Big is trying to enlist Joe to reenact the event with him for the sake of science. Gram and I have been adamantly opposed to this for obvious reasons. "We've had enough catastrophe, Big," Gram said yesterday, putting her foot down. I think the amount of pot Big's been smoking has made the idea of the exploding cake much funnier and more fascinating than it really is, but somehow Joe is equally enthralled with the concept.

It's Sunday and I have to be at the deli in a few hours. The kitchen's bustling when I stumble in.

"Morning, John Lennon," Joe says, looking up from his guitar strings and throwing me a jaw-dropping grin—what am I doing making out with Toby, *Bailey's* Toby, I think as I smile back at the holy horses unfreakingbelievable Joe Fontaine, who has seemingly moved into our kitchen. Things are so mixed up—the boy who should kiss me acts like a brother and the boy who should act like a brother keeps kissing me. Sheesh.

"Hey, John Lennon," Gram echoes.

Unbelievable. This can't be catching on. "Only Joe's allowed to call me that," I grumble at her.

"John Lennon!" Big whisks into the kitchen and me into his arms, dancing me around the room. "How's my girl today?"

"Why's everyone in such a good mood?" I feel like Scrooge.

"I'm not in a good mood," Gram says, beaming ear to ear, looking akin to Joe. I notice her hair is dry too. No grief-shower this morning. A first. "I just got an idea last night. It's a surprise." Joe and Big glance at me and shrug. Gram's ideas often rival Big's on the bizarre scale, but I doubt this one involves explosions or necromancy.

"We don't know what it is either, honey," Big bellows in a baritone unfit for eight a.m. "In other breaking news, Joe had an epiphany this morning: He put the Lennie houseplant under one of the pyramids—I can't believe I never thought of that." Big can't contain his excitement, he's smiling down on Joe like a proud father. I wonder how Joe slipped in like this, wonder if it's somehow because he never knew her, doesn't have one single memory of her, he's like the world without our heartbreak—

My cell phone goes off. I glance at the screen. It's Toby. I let it go to voicemail, feeling like the worst person in the world because just seeing his name recalls last night, and my stomach flies into a sequence of contortions. How could I have let this happen?

I look up, all eyes are on me, wondering why I didn't pick up the phone. I have to get out of the kitchen.

"Want to play, Joe?" I say, heading upstairs for my clarinet.

"Holy shit," I hear, then apologies to Gram and Big.

Back on the porch, I say, "You start, I'll follow."

He nods and starts playing some sweet soft chords in G minor. But I feel too unnerved for sweet, too unnerved for soft. I can't shake off Toby's call, his kisses. I can't shake off cardboard boxes, perfume that never gets used, bookmarks that don't move, St. Anthony statues that do. I can't shake off the fact that Bailey at eleven years old did not put herself in the drawing of our family, and suddenly, I am so upset I forget I'm playing music, forget Joe's even there beside me.

I start to think about all the things I haven't said since Bailey died, all the words stowed deep in my heart, in our orange bedroom, all the words in the whole world that aren't said after someone dies because they are too sad, too enraged, too devastated, too guilty, to come out—all of them begin to course inside me like a lunatic river. I suck in all the air I can, until there's probably no air left in Clover for anyone else, and then I blast it all out my clarinet in one mad bleating typhoon of a note. I don't know if a clarinet has ever made such a terrible sound, but I can't stop, all the years come tumbling out now—Bailey and me in the river, the ocean, tucked so snug into our room, the backseat of cars, bathtubs, running through the trees, through days and nights and months and years without Mom—I am breaking windows, busting through walls, burning up the past, pushing Toby off me, taking the dumb-ass Lennie houseplant and hurling it into the sea—

I open my eyes. Joe's staring at me, astonished. The dogs next door are barking.

"Wow, I think I'll follow next time," he says.

I'd been making decisions for days.
I picked out the dress Bailey would wear forever—
a black slinky one—inappropriate—that she loved.
I chose a sweater to go over it, earrings, bracelet, necklace,
her most beloved strappy sandals.
I collected her makeup to give to the funeral director with a recent photo—
I thought it would be that would dress her;
I didn't think a strange man should see her naked
touch her body
shave her legs
apply her lipstick
but that's what happened all the same.
I helped Gram pick out the casket,
the plot at the cemetery.
I changed a few lines
in the obituary that Big composed.
I wrote on a piece of paper what I thought
should go on the headstone.
I did all this without uttering a word.
Not one word, for days,
until I saw Bailey before the funeral
and lost my mind.
I hadn't realized that when people say so-and-so
snapped
that's what actually happens—
I started shaking her—
I thought I could wake her up
and get her the hell out of that box.
When she didn't wake,
I screamed: *Talk to me.*
Big swooped me up into his arms,
carried me out of the room, the church,
into the slamming rain,
and down to the creek
where we sobbed together
under the black coat he held over our heads
to protect us from the weather.

(Found on a piece of staff paper crumpled up by the trailhead)

chapter 12

I WISH I had my clarinet, I think as I walk home from the deli. If I did, I'd head straight into the woods where no one could hear me and face-plant like I did on the porch this morning. *Play the music, not the instrument,* Marguerite always said. And Mr. James: *Let the instrument play you.* I never got either instruction until today. I always imagined music trapped inside my clarinet, not trapped inside of me. But what if music is what escapes when a heart breaks?

I turn onto our street and see Uncle Big road-reading, tripping over his massive feet, greeting his favorite trees as he passes them. Nothing too unusual, but for the flying fruit. There are a few weeks every year when if circumstances permit, like the winds are just so and the plums particularly heavy, the plum trees around our house become hostile to humans and begin using us for target practice.

Big waves his arm east to west in enthusiastic greeting, narrowly escaping a plum to the head.

I salute him, then when he's close enough, I give a hello

twirl to his mustache, which is waxed and styled to the hilt, the fanciest (i.e., freakiest) I've seen it in some time.

"Your friend is over," he says, winking at me. Then he puts his nose back into his book and resumes his promenade. I know he means Joe, but I think of Sarah and my stomach twists a little. She sent me a text today: *Sending out a search party for our friendship.* I haven't responded. I don't know where it is either.

A moment later, I hear Big say, "Oh, Len, Toby called for you, wants you to ring him right away."

He called me on my cell again too while I was at work. I didn't listen to the voicemail. I reiterate the oath I've been swearing all day that I will never see Toby Shaw again, then I beg my sister for a sign of forgiveness—*no need for subtlety either, Bails, an earthquake will do.*

As I get closer, I see that the house is inside out—in the front yard are stacks of books, furniture, masks, pots and pans, boxes, antiques, paintings, dishes, knickknacks—then I see Joe and someone who looks just like him but broader and even taller coming out of the house with our sofa.

"Where do you want this, Gram?" Joe says, like it's the most natural thing in the world to be moving the couch outside. This must be Gram's surprise. We're moving into the yard. Great.

"Anywhere's fine, boys," Gram says, then sees me. "Lennie." She glides over. "I'm going to figure out what's causing the terrible luck," she says. "This is what came to me in the middle of the night. We'll move anything suspicious out of the house, do a ritual, burn sage, then make sure not to put anything unlucky back inside. Joe was nice enough to go get his brother to help."

"Hmmm," I say, not knowing what else to say, wishing I could've seen Joe's face as Gram very sanely explained this INSANE idea to him. When I break away from her, Joe practically gallops over. He's such a downer.

"Just another day at the psych ward, huh?" I say.

"What's quite perplexing . . ." he says, pointing a finger professorially at his brow, "is just how Gram is making the lucky or unlucky determination. I've yet to crack the code." I'm impressed at how quickly he's caught on that there is nothing to do but grab a wing when Gram's aflight with fancy.

His brother comes up then, rests his hand carelessly on Joe's shoulder, and it instantly transforms Joe into a little brother—the slice into my heart is sharp and sudden—*I'm no longer a little sister*. No longer a sister, period.

Joe can barely mask his adulation and it topples me. I was just the same—when I introduced Bailey I felt like I was presenting the world's most badass work of art.

"Marcus is here for the summer, goes to UCLA. He and my oldest brother are in a band down there." Brothers and brothers and brothers.

"Hi," I say to another beaming guy. Definitely no need for lightbulbs Chez Fontaine.

"I heard you play a mean clarinet," Marcus says. This makes me blush, which makes Joe blush, which makes Marcus laugh and punch his brother's arm. I hear him whisper, "Oh Joe, you've got it so bad." Then Joe blushes even more, if that's possible, and heads into the house for a lamp.

I wonder why though if Joe's got it so bad he doesn't make a move, even a suggestion of one. I know, I know, I'm a feminist, I could make a move, but a) I've never made a move on anyone in my life and therefore have no moves to make, b) I've been a wee bit preoccupied with the bat in my belfry who doesn't belong there, and c) Rachel—I mean, I know he spends mornings at our house, but how do I know he doesn't spend evenings at hers.

Gram's taken a shine to the Fontaine boys. She's flitting around the yard, telling them over and over again how handsome they are, asking if their parents ever thought about selling them. "Bet they'd make a bundle on you boys. Shame to give boys eyelashes like yours. Don't you think so, Lennie? Wouldn't you kill for eyelashes like that?" God, I'm embarrassed, though she's right about the eyelashes. Marcus doesn't blink either, they both bat.

She sends Joe and Marcus home to get their third brother, convinced that all Fontaine brothers have to be here for the ritual. It's clear both Marcus and Joe have fallen under her spell. She probably could get them to rob a bank for her.

"Bring your instruments," she yells after them. "You too, Lennie."

I do as I'm told and get my clarinet from the tree it's resting in with an assortment of my worldly possessions. Then Gram and I take some of the pots and pans she has redeemed lucky back into the kitchen to cook dinner. She prepares the chickens while I quarter the potatoes and spice them with garlic and rosemary. When everything is roasting in the oven, we go outside to gather some strewn plums to make a tart. She is rolling out the dough for the crust while I slice tomatoes and avocados for the salad. Every time she passes me, she pats my head or squeezes my arm.

"This is nice, cooking together again, isn't it, sweet pea?"

I smile at her. "It is, Gram." Well, it was, because now she's looking at me in her talk-to-me-Lennie way. The Gramouncements are about to begin.

"Lennie, I'm worried about you." Here goes.

"I'm all right."

"It's really time. At the least, tidy up, do her laundry, or allow me to. I can do it while you're at work."

"I'll do it," I say, like always. And I will, I just don't know when.

She slumps her shoulders dramatically. "I was thinking you and I could go to the city for the day next week, go to lunch—"

"That's okay."

I drop my eyes back to my task. I don't want to see her disappointment.

She sighs in her big loud lonely way and goes back to the crust. Telepathically, I tell her I'm sorry. I tell her I just can't confide in her right now, tell her the three feet between us feels like three light-years to me and I don't know how to bridge it.

Telepathically, she tells me back that I'm breaking her broken heart.

When the boys come back they introduce the oldest Fontaine, who is also in town for the summer from L.A.

"This is Doug," Marcus says just as Joe says, "This is Fred."

90

"Parents couldn't make up their mind," the newest Fontaine offers. This one looks positively deranged with glee. Gram's right, we should sell them.

"He's lying," Marcus pipes in. "In high school, Fred wanted to be sophisticated so he could hook up with lots of French girls. He thought Fred was way too uncivilized and Flintstone-ish so decided to use his middle name, Doug. But Joe and I couldn't get used to it."

"So now everyone calls him DougFred on two continents." Joe hand-butts his brother's chest, which provokes a counter-attack of several jabs to the ribs. The Fontaine boys are like a litter of enormous puppies, rushing and swiping at each other, stumbling all around, a whirl of perpetual motion and violent affection.

I know it's ungenerous, but watching them, their camaraderie, makes me feel lonely as the moon. I think about Toby and me holding hands in the dark last night, kissing by the river, how with him, I'd felt like my sadness had a place to be.

We eat sprawled out on what is now our lawn furniture. The wind has died down a bit, so we can sit without being pelted by fruit. The chicken tastes like chicken, the plum tart like plum tart. It's too soon for there not to be one bite of ash.

Dusk splatters pink and orange across the sky, beginning its languorous summer stroll. I hear the river through the trees sounding like possibility—

She will never know the Fontaines.

She will never hear about this dinner on a walk to the river.

She will not come back in the morning or Tuesday or in three months.

She will not come back ever.

She's gone and the world is ambling on without her—

I can't breathe or think or sit for another minute.

I try to say "I'll be right back," but nothing comes out, so I just turn my back on the yard full of concerned faces and hurry toward the tree line. When I get to the path, I take off, trying to outrun the heartache that is chasing me down.

I'm certain Gram or Big will follow me, but they don't, Joe does. I'm out of breath and writing on a piece of paper I found on the path when he comes up to me. I ditch the note behind a rock, try to brush away my tears.

This is the first time I've seen him without a smile hidden somewhere on his face.

"You okay?" he asks.

"You didn't even know her." It's out of my mouth, sharp and accusatory, before I can stop it. I see the surprise cross his face.

"No."

He doesn't say anything more, but I can't seem to shut my insane self up. "And you have all these brothers." As if it were a crime, I say this.

"I do."

"I just don't know why you're hanging out with us all the time." I feel my face get hot as embarrassment snakes its way through my body—the real question is why I am persisting like a full-fledged maniac.

"You don't?" His eyes rove my face, then the corners of his mouth begin to curl upward. "I like you, Lennie, duh." He looks at me incredulously. "I think you're amazing . . ." Why would he think this? Bailey is amazing and Gram and Big, and of course Mom, but not me, I am the two-dimensional one in a 3-D family.

He's grinning now. "Also I think you're really pretty and I'm incredibly shallow."

I have a horrible thought: *He only thinks I'm pretty, only thinks I'm amazing, because he never met Bailey,* followed by a really terrible, horrible thought: *I'm glad he never met her.* I shake my head, try to erase my mind, like an Etch A Sketch.

"What?" He reaches his hand to my face, brushes his thumb slowly across my cheek. His touch is so tender, it startles me. No one has ever touched me like this before, looked at me the way he's looking at me right now, deep into me. I want to hide from him and kiss him all at the same time.

And then: Bat. Bat. Bat.

I'm sunk.

I think his acting-like-a-brother stint is over.

"Can I?" he says, reaching for the rubber band on my ponytail.

I nod. Very slowly, he slides it off, the whole time holding my eyes in his. I'm hypnotized. It's like he's unbuttoning my shirt. When he's done, I shake my head a little and my hair springs into its habitual frenzy.

"Wow," he says softly. "I've wanted to do that . . ."

I can hear our breathing. I think they can hear it in New York.

"What about Rachel?" I say.

"What about her?"

"You and her?"

"You," he answers. Me!

I say, "I'm sorry I said all that, before . . ."

He shakes his head like it doesn't matter, and then to my surprise he doesn't kiss me but wraps his arms around me instead. For a moment, in his arms, with my mind so close to his heart, I listen to the wind pick up and think it just might lift us off our feet and take us with it.

chapter 13

THE DRY TRUNKS of the old growth redwoods creak and squeak eerily over our heads.

"Whoa. What is *that*?" Joe asks, all of a sudden pulling away as he glances up, then over his shoulder.

"What?" I ask, embarrassed how much I still want his arms around me. I try to joke it off. "Sheesh, how to ruin a moment. Don't you remember? I'm having a crisis?"

"I think you've had enough freak-outs for one day," he says, smiling now, and twirling his finger by his ear to signify what a wack-job I am. This makes me laugh out loud. He's looking all around again in a mild panic. "Seriously, what was that?"

"Are you scared of the deep, dark forest, city boy?"

"Of course I am, like most sane people, remember lions and tigers and bears, oh my?" He curls his finger around my belt loop, starts veering me back to the house, then stops suddenly. "That, right then. That creepy horror movie noise that happens right before the ax murderer jumps out and gets us."

"It's the old growths creaking. When it's really windy, it

sounds like hundreds of doors squeaking open and shut back here, all at the same time, it's beyond spooky. Don't think you could handle it."

He puts his arm around me. "A dare? Next windy day then." He points to himself—"Hansel"—then at me—"Gretel."

Right before we break from the trees, I say, "Thanks, for following me, and . . ." I want to thank him for spending all day moving furniture for Gram, for coming every morning with dead bugs for Big, for somehow being there for them when I can't be. Instead, I say, "I really love the way you play." Also true.

"Likewise."

"C'mon," I say. "That wasn't playing. It was honking. Total face-plant."

He laughs. "No way. Worth the wait. Testament to why if given the choice I'd rather lose the ability to talk than play. By far the superior communication."

This I agree with, face-plant or not. Playing today was like finding an alphabet—it was like being sprung. He pulls me even closer to him and something starts to swell inside, something that feels quite a bit like joy.

I try to ignore the insistent voice inside: *How dare you, Lennie? How dare you feel joy this soon?*

When we emerge from the woods, I see Toby's truck parked in front of the house and it has an immediate bone-liquefying effect on my body. I slow my pace, disengage from Joe, who looks quizzically over at me. Gram must have invited Toby to be part of her ritual. I consider staging another freak-out and running back into the woods so I don't have to be in a room with Toby and Joe, but I am not the actress and know I couldn't

96

pull it off. My stomach churns as we walk up the steps, past Lucy and Ethel, who are, of course, sprawled out on the porch awaiting Toby's exit, and who, of course, don't move a muscle as we pass. We push through the door and then cross the hall into the living room. The room is aglow with candles, the air thick with the sweet scent of sage.

DougFred and Marcus sit on two of the remaining chairs in the center of the room playing flamenco guitar. The Half Mom hovers above them as if she's listening to the coarse, fiery chords that are overtaking the house. Uncle Big towers over the mantel clapping his hand on his thigh to the feverish beat. And Toby stands on the other side of the room, apart from everyone, looking as lonely as I felt earlier—my heart immediately lurches toward him. He leans against the window, his golden hair and skin gleaming in the flickery light. He watches us enter the room with an inappropriate hawkish intensity that is not lost on Joe and sends shivers through me. I can feel Joe's bewilderment without even looking to my side.

Meanwhile, I am now imagining roots growing out of my feet so I don't fly across the room into Toby's arms, because I have a big problem: Even in this house, on this night, with all these people, with Joe Fabulous Fontaine, who is no longer acting like my brother, right beside me, I still feel this invisible rope pulling me across the room toward Toby and there doesn't seem to be anything I can do about it.

I turn to Joe, who looks like I've never seen him: unhappy, his body stiff with confusion, his gaze shifting from Toby to me and back again. It's as if all the moments between Toby and me that never should have happened are spilling out of us in front of Joe.

"Who's that guy?" Joe asks, with none of his usual equanimity.

"Toby." It comes out oddly robotic.

Joe looks at me like: *Well, who's Toby, retard?*

"I'll introduce you," I say, because I have no choice and cannot just keep standing here like I've had a stroke.

There's no other way to put it: THIS BLOWS.

And on top of everything, the flamenco has begun to crescendo all around us, whipping fire and sex and passion every which way. Perfect. Couldn't they have chosen some sleepy sonata? Waltzes are lovely too, boys. With me on his heels, Joe crosses the room toward Toby: the sun on a collision course with the moon.

The dusky sky pours through the window, framing Toby. Joe and I stop a few paces in front of him, all of us now caught in the uncertainty between day and night. The music continues its fiery revolution all around us and there is a girl inside of me that wants to give in to the fanatical beat—she wants to dance wild and free all around the thumping room, but unfortunately, that girl's in me, not me. Me would like an invisibility cloak to get the hell out of this mess.

I look over at Joe and am relieved to see that the fevered chords have momentarily hijacked his attention. His one hand plays his thigh, his foot drums the ground, and his head bobs around, which flops his hair into his eyes. He can't stop smiling at his brothers, who are pounding their guitars into notes so ferocious they probably could overthrow the government. I realize I'm smiling like a Fontaine as I watch the music riot through Joe. I can feel how intensely he wants his guitar, just as, all of a sudden, I can feel how intensely Toby wants me. I steal a glance at him, and as I suspected, he's watching me watch Joe, his eyes clamped on me. How did we get ourselves into this? It doesn't feel like solace in this moment at all, but something else. I look down, write *help* on my jeans with my finger, and when I look back up I see that Toby's and Joe's eyes have locked. Something passes silently between them that has everything to do with me, because as if on cue they look from each other to me, both saying with their eyes: *What's going on, Lennie?*

Every organ in my body switches places.

Joe puts his hand gently on my arm as if it will remind me to open my mouth and form words. At the contact, Toby's eyes flare. What's going on with him tonight? He's acting like my boyfriend, not my sister's, not someone I made out with twice under very extenuating circumstances. And what about me and this inexplicable and seemingly inescapable pull to him despite everything?

I say, "Joe just moved to town." Toby nods civilly and I sound human, a good start. I'm about to say "Toby was Bailey's boyfriend," which I loathe saying for the *was* and for how it will make me feel like the traitorous person that I am.

But then Toby looks right at me and says, "Your hair, it's down." Hello? This is not the right thing to say. The right thing to say is "Oh, where'd you move from, dude?" or "Clover's pretty cool." Or "Do you skate?" Or basically anything but "Your hair, it's down."

Joe seems unperturbed by the comment. He's smiling at me like he's proud that he was the one that let my hair out of its bondage.

Just then, I notice Gram in the doorway, looking at us. She blows over, holding her burning stick of sage like a magic wand. She gives me a quick once-over, seems to decide I've recovered, then points her wand at Toby and says, "Let me introduce you boys. Joe Fontaine, this is Toby Shaw, Bailey's boyfriend."

Whoosh—I see it: a waterfall of relief pours over Joe. I see the case close in his mind, as he probably thinks there couldn't be anything going on—because what kind of sister would ever cross that kind of line?

"Hey, I'm so sorry," he tells Toby.

"Thanks." Toby tries to smile, but it comes out all wrong and homicidal. Joe, however, so unburdened by Gram's revelation, doesn't even notice, just turns around buoyant as ever, and goes to join his brothers, followed by Gram.

"I'm going to go, Lennie." Toby's voice is barely audible over the music. I turn around, see that Joe is now bent over his guitar, oblivious to everything but the sound his fingers are making.

"I'll walk you out," I say.

Toby says good-bye to Gram, Big, and the Fontaines, all of whom are surprised he's leaving so soon, especially Gram, who I can tell is adding some things up.

I follow him to his truck—Lucy, Ethel, and I, all yapping at his feet. He opens the door, doesn't get in, leans against the cab. We are facing each other and there's not a trace of the calm or gentleness I've become so accustomed to seeing in his expression, but something fierce and unhinged in its place. He's in total tough-skater-dude mode, and though I don't want to, I'm finding it arresting. I feel a current coursing between us, feel it begin to rip out of control inside of me. *What is it?* I think as he looks into my eyes, then at my mouth, then sweeps his gaze slowly, proprietarily over my body. *Why can't we stop this?* I feel so reckless—like I'm reeling with him into the air on his board with no regard for safety or consequence, with no regard for anything but speed and daring and being hungrily, greedily alive—but I tell him, "No. Not now."

"When?"

"Tomorrow. After work," I say, against my better judgment, against any judgment.

What do you girls want for dinner?
What do you girls think about my new painting?
What do the girls want to do this weekend?
Did the girls leave for school yet?
I haven't seen the girls yet today.
I told those girls to hurry up!
Where are those girls?
Girls, don't forget your lunches.
Girls, be home by 11 p.m.
Girls, don't even think of swimming—it's freezing out.
Are the Walker Girls coming to the party?
The Walker Girls were at the river last night.
Let's see if the Walker Girls are home.

(Found written on the wall of Bailey's closet)

chapter 14

I FIND GRAM, who is twirling around the living room with her sage wand like an overgrown fairy. I tell her that I'm sorry, but I don't feel well and need to go upstairs.

She stops mid-whirl. I know she senses trouble, but she says, "Okay, sweet pea." I apologize to everyone and say good night as nonchalantly as possible.

Joe follows me out of the room, and I decide it might be time to join a convent, just cloister up with the Sisters for a while.

He touches my shoulder and I turn around to face him. "I hope what I said in the woods didn't freak you out or something . . . hope that's not why you're crashing . . ."

"No, no." His eyes are wide with worry. I add, "It made me pretty happy, actually." Which of course is true except for the slight problem that immediately after hearing his declaration, I made a date with my dead sister's boyfriend to do *God knows what!*

"Good." He brushes his thumb on my cheek, and again his tenderness startles me. "Because I'm going crazy, Lennie." Bat.

Bat. Bat. And just like that, I'm going crazy too because I'm thinking Joe Fontaine is about to kiss me. Finally.

Forget the convent.

Let's get this out of the way: My previously nonexistent floozy-factor is blowing right off the charts.

"I didn't know you knew my name," I say.

"So much you don't know about me, *Lennie*." He smiles and takes his index finger and presses it to my lips, leaves it there until my heart lands on Jupiter: three seconds, then removes it, turns around, and heads back into the living room. Whoa—well, that was either the dorkiest or sexiest moment of my life, and I'm voting for sexy on account of my standing here dumb-struck and giddy, wondering if he did kiss me after all.

I am totally out of control.

I do not think this is how normal people mourn.

When I can move my legs one in front of the other, I make my way up to The Sanctum. Thankfully, it has been deemed fairly lucky by Gram so is mostly untouched, especially Bailey's things, which she mercifully didn't touch at all. I go straight over to her desk and start talking to the explorer picture like we sometimes talk to The Half Mom.

Tonight, the woman on the mountaintop will have to be Bailey.

I sit down and tell her how sorry I am, that I don't know what's wrong with me and that I'll call Toby and cancel the date first thing in the morning. I also tell her I didn't mean to think what I thought in the woods and I would do anything for her to be able to meet Joe Fontaine. Anything. And then I ask her again to please give me a sign that she forgives me before the list of unpardonable things I think and do gets too long and I become a lost cause.

I look over at the boxes. I know I'm going to have to start eventually. I take a deep breath, banish all morbid thoughts from my mind, and put my hands on the wooden knobs of the top desk drawer. Only to immediately think about Bailey and my anti-snooping pact. I never broke it, not once, despite a natural propensity for nosing around. At people's houses, I open medicine cabinets, peek behind shower curtains, open drawers and closet doors whenever possible. But with Bailey, I adhered to the pact—

Pacts. So many between us, breaking now. And what about the unspoken ones, those entered into without words, without pinky swears, without even realizing it? A squall of emotion lands in my chest. Forget talking to the picture, I take out my phone, punch in Bailey's number, listen impatiently to her as Juliet, heat filling my head, then over the tone, I hear myself say, "What happens to a stupid companion pony when the racehorse dies?" There's both anger and despair in my voice and immediately and illogically I wish I could erase the message so she won't hear it.

I slowly open the desk drawer, afraid of what I might find, afraid of what else she might not have told me, afraid of this rollicking bananas pact-breaking me. But there are just things, inconsequential things of hers, some pens, a few playbills from shows at Clover Repertory, concert tickets, an address book, an old cell phone, a couple of business cards, one from our dentist reminding her of her next appointment, and one from Paul Booth, Private Investigator with a San Francisco address.

WTF?

I pick it up. On the back in Bailey's writing it says *4/25 4 p.m., Suite 2B*. The only reason I can think of that she would go see a private investigator would be to find Mom. But why would she do that? We both knew that Big already tried, just a few years ago in fact, and that the PI had said it would be impossible to find her.

The day Big told us about the detective, Bailey had been furious, torpedoing around the kitchen while Gram and I snapped peas from the garden for dinner.

Bailey said, "I know you know where she is, Gram."

"How could I know, Bails?" Gram replied.

"Yeah, how could she know, Bails?" I repeated. I hated when Gram and Bailey fought, and sensed things were about to blow.

Bailey said, "I could go after her. I could find her. I could bring her back." She grabbed a pod, putting the whole thing, shell and all, into her mouth.

"You couldn't find her, and you couldn't bring her back either." Big stood in the doorway, his words filled the room like gospel. I had no idea how long he'd been listening.

Bailey went to him. "How do you know that?"

"Because I've tried, Bailey."

Gram and I stopped snapping and looked up at Big. He hulked over to the table and sat in a kitchen chair, looking like a giant in a kindergarten classroom. "I hired a detective a few years back, a good one, figured I would tell you all if he came up with something, but he didn't. He said it's the easiest thing to be lost if you don't want to be found. He thinks Paige changed her name and probably changes her social security number if she moves . . ." Big strummed his fingers on the table—it sounded like little claps of thunder.

"How do we even know she's alive?" Big said under his breath, but we all heard it as if he hollered it from the mountaintop. Strangely, this had never occurred to me and I don't think it had ever occurred to Bailey either. We were always told she would be back and we believed it, deeply.

"She's alive, she's most certainly alive," Gram said to Big. "And she will be back."

I saw suspicion dawn again on Bailey's face.

"How do you know, Gram? You must know something if you're so sure."

"A mother knows, okay? She just does." With that, Gram left the room.

I put the card back in the desk drawer, take St. Anthony with me, and get into bed. I put him on the nightstand. Why was she keeping so many secrets from me? And how in the world can I possibly be mad at her about it now? About anything. Even for a moment.

Bailey and I didn't talk too much
about Gram's spells,
what she called her Private Times,
days spent in the art room
without break.
It was just a part of things,
like green summer leaves,
burning up in fall.
I'd peek through the crack in the door,
see her surrounded by easels
of green women, half formed—
the paint still wet and hungry.
She'd work on them all at once,
and soon, she'd begin
to look like one of them too,
all that green spattered on her clothes,
her hands, her face.
Bails and I would pack
our own brown bags those days,
would pull out our sandwiches at noon,
hating the disappointment of a world
where polka-dotted scarves,
sheets of music, blue feathers,
didn't surprise us at lunch.

After school, we'd bring her tea
or a sliced apple with cheese,
but it'd just sit on the table, untouched.
Big would tell us to ride it out—
that everyone needs a break
from the routine now and then.
So we did—
it was like Gram would go
on vacation with her ladies
and like them
would get caught somewhere
between here and there.

(Found on a brown paper bag in Lennie's clarinet case)

Len, you awake?

Yeah.

Let's do Mom.

Okay, I'll start. She's in Rome—

She's always in Rome lately—

Well, now she's a famous Roman pizza chef and it's late at night, the restaurant just closed and she's drinking a glass of wine with—

With Luigi, the drop-dead gorgeous waiter, they just grabbed the bottle of wine and are walking through the moonlit streets, it's hot, and when they come to a fountain she takes off her shoes and jumps in . . .

Luigi doesn't even take off his shoes, just jumps in and splashes her, they're laughing. . .

But standing in the fountain under the big, bright moon makes her think of Flying Man's, how she used to swim at night with Big . . .

You really think so, Bails? You really think she's in a fountain in Rome on a hot summer night with gorgeous Luigi and thinking about us? About Big?

Sure.

No way.

We're thinking about her.

That's different.

Why?

Because we're not in a fountain in Rome on a hot summer night with gorgeous Luigi.

True.

Night, Bails.

(Found on a piece of notebook paper balled up in a shoe in Lennie's closet)

chapter 15

THE DAY EVERYTHING happens begins like all others lately with Joe's soft knock. I roll over, peek out the window, and see only the lawn through the morning fog. Everything must have been moved back into the house after I'd gone to sleep.

I go downstairs, find Gram sitting at her seat at the kitchen table, her hair wrapped in a towel. She has her hands around a mug of coffee and is staring at Bailey's chair. I sit down next to her. "I'm really sorry about last night," I say. "I know how much you wanted to do a ritual for Bailey, for us."

"It's okay, Len, we'll do one. We have plenty of time." She takes my hand with one of hers, rubs it absentmindedly with the other. "And anyway, I think I figured out what was causing the bad luck."

"Yeah?" I say. "What?"

"You know that mask Big brought back from South America when he was studying those trees. I think that it might have a curse on it."

I've always hated that mask. It has fake hair all over it, eyebrows that arch in astonishment, and a mouth baring shiny, wolfish teeth. "It always gave me the creeps," I tell her. "Bailey too."

Gram nods but she seems distracted. I don't think she's really listening to me, which couldn't be more unlike her lately.

"Lennie," she says tentatively. "Is everything okay between you and Toby?"

My stomach clenches. "Of course," I say, swallowing hard, trying to make my voice sound casual. "Why?" She owl-eyes me.

"Don't know, you both seemed funny last night around each other." Ugh. Ugh. Ugh.

"And I keep wondering why Sarah isn't coming around. Did you get in a fight?" she says to further send me into a guilt spiral.

Just then, Big and Joe come in, saving me. Big says, "We thought we saw life in spider number six today."

Joe says, "I swear I saw a flutter."

"Almost had a heart attack, Joe here, practically launched through the roof, but it must have been a breeze, little guy's still dead as a doornail. The Lennie plant's still languishing too. I might have to rethink things, maybe add a UV light."

"Hey," Joe says, coming behind me, dropping a hand to my shoulder. I look up at the warmth in his face and smile at him. I think he could make me smile even while I was hanging at the gallows, which I'm quite certain I'm headed for. I put my hand over his for a second, see Gram notice this as she gets up to make us breakfast.

I feel somehow responsible for the scrambled ashes that we are all shoveling into our mouths, as if I've somehow derailed the path to healing that our household was on yesterday morning. Joe and Big banter on about resurrecting bugs and exploding cakes—the conversation that would not die—while I actively avoid Gram's suspicious gaze.

"I need to get to work early today, we're catering the Dwyers' party tonight." I say this to my plate but can see Gram nodding in my periphery. She knows because she's been asked to help with the flower arrangements. She's asked all the time to oversee flower arrangements for parties and weddings but rarely says yes because she hates cut flowers. We all knew not to prune her bushes or cut her blooms under penalty of death. She probably said yes this time just to get out of the house for an afternoon. Sometimes I imagine the poor gardeners all over town this summer without Gram, standing in their yards, scratching their heads at their listless wisteria, their forlorn fuchsias.

Joe says, "I'll walk you to work. I need to go to the music store anyway." All the Fontaine boys are supposedly working for their parents this summer, who've converted a barn into a workshop where his dad makes specialty guitars, but I get the impression they spend all day working on new songs for their band Dive.

We embark on the seven-block walk to town, which looks like it's going to take two hours because Joe comes to a standstill every time he has something to say, which is every three seconds.

"You can't walk and talk at the same time, can you?" I ask.

He stops in his tracks, says "Nope." Then continues on for a minute in silence until he can't take it anymore and stops, turns to me, takes my arm, forcing me to stop, while he tells me how I have to go to Paris, how we'll play music in the metro, make tons of money, eat only chocolate croissants, drink red wine, and stay up all night every night because no one ever sleeps in Paris. I can hear his heart beating the whole time and I'm thinking, *Why not?* I could step out of this sad life like it's an old sorry dress, and go to Paris with Joe—we could get on a plane and fly over the ocean and land in *France*. We could do it today even. I have money saved. I have a beret. A hot black bra. I know how to say *Je t'aime*. I love coffee and chocolate and Baudelaire. And I've watched Bailey enough to know how to wrap a scarf. We could really do it, and the possibility makes me feel so giddy I think I might catapult into the air. I tell him so. He takes my hand and puts his other arm up Superman-style.

"You see, I was right," he says with a smile that could power the state of California.

"God, you're gorgeous," I blurt out and want to die because I can't believe I said it aloud and neither can he—his smile, so huge now, he can't even get any words past it.

He stops again. I think he's going to go on about Paris some more—but he doesn't. I look up at him. His face is serious like it was last night in the woods.

"Lennie," he whispers.

I look into his sorrowless eyes and a door in my heart blows open.

And when we kiss, I see that on the other side of that door is sky.

chapter 16

I can't shove the dark out of my way

*(Found written
on the bench outside of Maria's Italian Deli)*

I MAKE A million lasagnas in the window at the deli, listening to Maria gossip with customer after customer, then come home to find Toby lying on my bed. The house is still as stone with Gram at the Dwyers' and Big at work. I punched Toby's number into my phone ten times today, but stopped each time before pressing send. I was going to tell him I couldn't see him. Not after promising Bailey. Not after kissing Joe. Not after

Gram's inquisition. Not after reaching into myself and finding some semblance of conscience. I was going to tell him that we had to stop this, had to think how it would make Bailey feel, how bad it makes us feel. I was going to tell him all these things, but didn't because each time I was about to complete the call, I got transported back to the moment by his truck last night and that same inexplicable recklessness and hunger would overtake me until the phone was closed and lying silent on the counter before me.

"Hi, you." His voice is deep and dark and unglues me instantly.

I'm moving toward him, unable not to, the pull, unavoidable, tidal. He gets up quickly, meets me halfway across the room. For one split second we face each other; it's like diving into a mirror. And then I feel his mouth crushing into mine, teeth and tongue and lips and all his raging sorrow crashing right into mine, all our raging sorrow together now crashing into the world that did this to us. I'm frantic as my fingers unbutton his shirt, slip it off his shoulders, then my hands are on his chest, his back, his neck, and I think he must have eight hands because one is taking off my shirt, another two are holding my face while he kisses me, one is running through my hair, another two are on my breasts, a few are pulling my hips to his and then the last undoes the button on my jeans, unzips the fly and we are on the bed, his hand edging its way between my legs, and that is when I hear the front door slam shut—

We freeze and our eyes meet—a midair collision of shame: All the wreckage explodes inside me. I can't bear it. I cover my face with my hands, hear myself groan. What am I doing? What did we almost do? I want to press the rewind button. Press it and press it and press it. But I can't think about that now, can only think about not getting caught in this bed with Toby.

"Hurry," I say, and it unfreezes and de-panics both of us.

He springs to his feet and I scramble across the floor like a crazed crab, put on my shirt, throw Toby his. We're both dressing at warp speed—

"No more," I say, fumbling with the buttons on my shirt, feeling criminal and wrong, full of ick and shame. "Please."

He's straightening the bedding, frenetically puffing pillows, his face flushed and wild, blond hair flying in every direction. "I'm sorry, Len—"

"It doesn't make me miss her less, not anymore." I sound half resolute, half frantic. "It makes it worse."

He stops what he's doing, nods, his face a wrestling match of competing emotions, but it looks like hurt is winning out. God, I don't want to hurt him, but I don't want to do this anymore either. I can't. And what is *this* anyway? Being with him just now didn't feel like the safe harbor it did before—it was different, desperate, like two people struggling for breath.

"John Lennon," I hear from downstairs. "You home?"

This can't be happening, it can't. Nothing used to happen to me, nothing at all for seventeen years and now everything at once. Joe is practically singing my name, he sounds so elated, probably still riding high from that kiss, that sublime kiss that could make stars fall into your open hands, a kiss like Cathy and Heathcliff must have had on the moors with the sun beat-

115

ing on their backs and the world streaming with wind and possibility. A kiss so unlike the fearsome tornado that moments before ripped through Toby and me.

Toby is dressed and sitting on my bed, his shirt hanging over his lap. I wonder why he doesn't tuck it in, then realize he's trying to cover a freaking hard-on—oh God, who am I? How could I have let this get so out of hand? And why doesn't my family do anything normal like carry house keys and lock front doors?

I make sure I'm buttoned and zipped. I smooth my hair and wipe my lips before I swing open the bedroom door and stick my head out just as Joe is barreling down the hallway. He smiles wildly, looks like love itself stuffed into a pair of jeans, black T-shirt, and backward baseball cap.

"Come over tonight. They're all going to the city for some jazz show." He's out of breath—I bet he ran all the way here. "Couldn't wait . . ." He reaches for my hand, takes it in his, then sees Toby sitting on the bed behind me. First he drops my hand, and then the impossible happens: Joe Fontaine's face shuts like a door.

"Hey," he says to Toby, but his voice is pinched and wary.

"Toby and I were just going through some of Bailey's things," I blurt out. I can't believe I'm using Bailey to lie to Joe to cover up fooling around with her boyfriend. A new low even for the immoral girl I've become. I'm a Gila monster of a girl. Loch Ness Lennie. No convent would even take me.

Joe nods, mollified by that, but he's still looking at me and Toby and back again with suspicion. It's as if someone hit the dimmer switch and turned down his whole being.

Toby stands up. "I need to get home." He crosses the room, his carriage slumped, his gait awkward, uncertain. "Good seeing you again," he mumbles at Joe. "I'll see you soon, Len." He slips past us, sad as rain, and I feel terrible. My heart follows after him a few paces, but then it ricochets back to Joe, who stands before me without a trace of death anywhere on him.

"Lennie, is there—"

I have a pretty good idea what Joe is about to ask and so I do the only thing I can think of to stop the question from coming out of his mouth: I kiss him. I mean *really* kiss him, like I've wanted to do since that very first day in band. No sweet soft peck about it. With the same lips that just kissed someone else, I kiss away his question, his suspicion, and after a while, I kiss away the someone else too, the something else that almost just happened, until it is only the two of us, Joe and me, in the room, in the world, in my crazy swelling heart.

Holy horses.

I put aside for a moment the fact that I've turned into a total strumpet-harlot-trollop-wench-jezebel-tart-harridan-chippy-nymphet because I've just realized something incredible. *This is it*—what all the hoopla is about, what *Wuthering Heights* is about—it all boils down to this feeling rushing through me in this moment with Joe as our mouths refuse to part. Who knew all this time I was one kiss away from being Cathy and Juliet and Elizabeth Bennet and Lady Chatterley!?

Years ago, I was crashed in Gram's garden and Big asked me what I was doing. I told him I was looking up at the sky. He said, "That's a misconception, Lennie, the sky is everywhere, it begins at your feet."

Kissing Joe, I believe this, for the first time in my life.

I feel delirious, Joelirious, I think as I pull away for a moment, and open my eyes to see that the Joe Fontaine dimmer switch has been cranked back up again and that he is Joelirious too.

"That was—" I can hardly form words.

"Incredible," he interrupts. "Fucking *incroyable*."

We're staring at each other, stunned.

"Sure," I say, suddenly remembering he invited me over tonight.

"Sure what?" He looks at me like I'm speaking Swahili, then smiles and puts his arms around me, says, "Ready?" He lifts me off my feet and spins me around and I am suddenly in the dorkiest movie ever, laughing and feeling a happiness so huge I am ashamed to be feeling it in a world without my sister.

"Sure, I'll come over tonight," I say as everything stops spinning and I land back on my own two feet.

chapter 17

What's wrong, Lennie?

Nothing.

Tell me.

No.

C'mon, spill it.

Okay. It's just that you're different now.

How?

Like Zombieville.

I'm in love, Len—I've never felt like this before.

Like what?

Like forever.

Forever?

Yeah, this is it. He's it.

How do you know?

My toes told me. The toes knows.

(Found on a napkin stuffed in a mug, Cecilia's Bakery)

"I'M GOING OVER to Joe's," I say to Gram and Big, who are both home now, camped out in the kitchen, listening to a baseball game on the radio, circa 1930.

"That sounds like a plan," Gram says. She's taken the still despairing Lennie houseplant out from under the pyramid and is sitting beside it at the table, singing to it softly, something about greener pastures. "I'll just freshen up and get my bag, sweet pea."

She can't be serious.

"I'll go too," says Big, who is hunched over a crossword puzzle. He's the fastest puzzler in all Christendom. I look over and note, however, that this time he's putting numbers in the boxes instead of letters. "As soon as I finish this, we can all head up to the Fontaines'."

"Uh, I don't think so," I say.

They both look up at me, incredulous.

Big says, "What do you mean, Len, he's here every single morning, it's only fair that—"

And then he can't keep it up anymore and bursts out laughing, as does Gram. I'm relieved. I had actually started to imagine trucking up the hill with Gram and Big in tow: the Munsters follow Marilyn on a date.

"Why, Big, she's all dressed up. And her hair's down. Look at her." This is a problem. I was going for the short flowery dress and heels and lipstick and wild hair look that no one would notice is any different from the jeans, ponytail, and no makeup look I've mastered every other day of my life. I know I'm blushing, also know I better get out of the house before I run back upstairs and challenge Bailey's Guinness-Book-of-

Changing-Clothes-Before-a-Date record of thirty-seven outfits. This was only my eighteenth, but clothes-changing is an exponential activity, the frenzy only builds, it's a law of nature. Even St. Anthony peering at me from the nightstand, reminding me of what I'd found in the drawer last night, couldn't snap me out of it. I'd remembered something about him though. He was like Bailey, charismatic as all get out. He had to give his sermons in marketplaces because he overflowed even the largest of churches. When he died all the church bells in Padua rang of their own accord. Everyone thought angels had come to earth.

"Good-bye, you guys," I say to Gram and Big, and head for the door.

"Have fun, Len . . . and not too late, okay?"

I nod, and am off on the first real date of my life. The other nights I've had with boys don't count, not the ones with Toby I'm actively trying not to think about, and definitely not the parties, after which I'd spent the next day, week, month, year thinking of ways to get my kisses back. Nothing has been like this, nothing has made me feel like I do right now walking up the hill to Joe's, like I have a window in my chest where sunlight is pouring in.

chapter 18

When
Joe
plays
his
horn
I
fall

out
of
my
chair
and
onto
my

knees
When
he
plays
all
the
flowers

swap
colors
and
years
and
decades
and

centuries
of
rain
pour
back
into
the
sky

(Found on the bathroom wall, music room, Clover High)

THE FEELING I had earlier today with Joe in The Sanctum overwhelms me the moment I see him sitting on the stoop of the big white house playing his guitar. He's bent over it, singing softly, and the wind is carrying his words through the air like fluttering leaves.

"Hey, John Lennon," he says, putting aside his guitar, standing up and jumping off the front step. "Uh-oh. You look *vachement* amazing. Too good to be alone with me all night long." He's practically leaping over. His delight quotient mesmerizes me. At the human factory, someone must have messed up and just slipped him more than the rest of us. "I've been thinking about a duet we could do. I just need to rearrange—"

I'm not listening anymore. I hope he just keeps talking up a storm, because I can't utter a word. I know the expression *love bloomed* is metaphorical, but in my heart in this moment, there is one badass flower, captured in time-lapse photography, going from bud to wild radiant blossom in ten seconds flat.

"You okay?" he asks. His hands are on either side of my arms and he's peering into my face.

"Yes." I'm wondering how people breathe in these situations. "I'm fine."

"You are *fine*," he says, looking me over like a major dork, which immediately snaps me out of my love spell.

"Ugh, *quel dork*," I say, pushing him away.

He laughs and slips his arm around my shoulders. "C'mon, you enter Maison Fontaine at your own risk."

The first thing I notice about Maison Fontaine is that the phone is ringing and Joe doesn't seem to notice. I hear a girl's voice on an answering machine far away in another room and think for a minute it sounds like Rachel before deciding it doesn't. The second thing I notice is how opposite this house is to Maison Walker. Our house looks like Hobbits live there. The ceilings are low, the wood is dark and gnarly, colorful rag rugs line the floors, paintings, the walls, whereas Joe's house floats high in the sky with the clouds. There are windows everywhere that reveal sunburned fields swimming in the wind, dark green woods that cloister the river, and the river itself as it wends from town to town in the distance. There are no tables piled with weeks of mail, shoes kicked around under furniture, books open on every surface. Joe lives in a museum. Hanging all over the walls are gorgeous guitars of every color, shape, and size. They look so animate, like they could make music all by themselves.

"Pretty cool, huh? My dad makes amazing instruments. Not just guitars either. Mandolins, lutes, dulcimers," he says as I ogle one and then the next.

And now for something completely different: Joe's room. The physical manifestation of chaos theory. It's overflowing with instruments I've never seen before and can't even imagine what kind of sound they'd make, CDs, music magazines, library books in French and English, concert posters of French bands I've never heard of, comic books, notebooks with tiny boxlike weirdo boy writing in them, sheets of music, stereo equipment unplugged and plugged, broken-open amps and other sound equipment I don't recognize, odd rubber animals, bowls of blue marbles, decks of cards, piles of clothes as high as my knee, not to mention the dishes, bottles, glasses . . . and over his desk a small poster of John Lennon.

"Hmm," I say, pointing to the poster. I look around, taking it all in. "I think your room is giving me new insight into Joe Fontaine aka freaking madman."

"Yeah, thought it best to wait to show you the bombroom until . . ."

"Until what?"

"I don't know, until you realized . . ."

"Realized what?"

"I don't know, Lennie." I can see he's embarrassed. Somehow things have turned uncomfortable.

"Tell me," I say. "Wait until I realized what?"

"Nothing, it's stupid." He looks down at his feet, then back up at me. Bat. Bat. Bat.

"I want to know," I say.

"Okay, I'll say it: Wait until you realized that maybe you liked me too."

The flower is blooming again in my chest, this time three seconds from bud to showstopper.

"I do," I say, and then without thinking, add, "A lot." What's gotten into me? Now I really can't breathe. A situation made worse by the lips that are suddenly pressing into mine.

Our tongues have fallen madly in love and gotten married and moved to Paris.

After I'm sure I've made up for all my former years of kisslessness, I say, "I think if we don't stop kissing, the world is going to explode."

"Seems like it," he whispers. He's staring dreamily into my eyes. Heathcliff and Cathy have nothing on us. "We can do something else for a while," he says. "If you want . . ." He smiles. And then: Bat. Bat. Bat. I wonder if I am going to survive the night.

"Want to play?" he asks.

"I do," I tell him, "but I didn't bring my instrument."

"I'll get one." He leaves the room, which gives me a chance to recover, and unfortunately, to think about what happened with Toby earlier. How scary and out of control it was today, like we were trying to break each other apart. But why? To find Bailey? To wrench her from the other's heart? The other's body? Or was it something worse? Were we trying to forget her, to wipe out her memory for one passionate moment? But no, it's not that, it can't be, can it? When we're together, Bailey's all around us like air we can breathe; that's been the comfort until today, until it got so out of hand. I don't know. The only thing I do know is that it's all about her, because even now if I imagine Toby alone with his heartache while I am here with Joe obliterating my own, I feel guilty, like I've abandoned him, and with him, my grief, and with my grief, my sister.

The phone rings again and it mercifully ejects me from these thoughts, and crash-lands me back into the bombroom—this room where Joe sleeps in this unmade bed and reads these books strewn everywhere and drinks out of these five hundred half-full glasses seemingly at once. I feel giddy with the intimacy of being where he thinks and dreams, where he changes his clothes and flings them absolutely all over the place, where he's naked. *Joe, naked.* The thought of it, him, all of him—*guh.* I've never even seen a real live guy totally naked, ever. Only some Internet porn Sarah and I devoured for a while. That's it. I've always been scared of seeing all, seeing *it.* The first time Sarah saw one hard, she said more animal names came flying out of her mouth in that one moment than all other moments in her life combined. Not animals you'd think either. No pythons and eels. According to her it was a full-on menagerie: hippos, elephants, orangutans, tapirs, gazelles, etc.

All of a sudden I'm walloped with missing her. How could I be in Joe Fontaine's freaking bedroom without her knowing? How could I have blown her off like this? I take out my phone, text: *Call back the search party. Please. Forgive.*

I look around again, curbing all impulses to go through drawers, peek under the bed, read the notebook lying open at my feet. Okay, I curb two out of three of those impulses. It's been a bad day for morality. And it's not really reading someone's journal if it's open and you can glance down and make out your name, well, your name to him, in a sentence that says . . .

I bend my knees, and without touching the notebook in any way, read just the bit around the initials JL.

I'VE NEVER MET ANYONE AS HEARTBROKEN AS JL, I WANT TO MAKE HER FEEL BETTER, WANT TO BE AROUND HER ALL THE TIME, IT'S CRAZY, IT'S LIKE SHE'S ON FULL BLAST, AND EVERYONE ELSE IS JUST ON MUTE, AND SHE'S HONEST, SO HONEST, NOTHING LIKE GENEVIEVE, NOTHING AT ALL LIKE GENEVIEVE . . .

I hear his steps in the hall, stand up. The phone is ringing yet again.

He comes back with two clarinets, a B flat and a bass, holds them up. I go for the soprano like I'm used to.

"What's the deal with the phone?" I say, instead of saying *Who's Genevieve?* Instead of falling to my knees and confessing that I'm anything but honest, that I'm probably just exactly like Genevieve, whoever she is, but without the exotic French part.

He shrugs. "We get a lot of calls," he says, then begins his tuning ritual that makes everything in the world but him and a handful of chords disappear.

The untapped duet of guitar and clarinet is awkward at first. We stumble around in sound, fall over each other, look up embarrassed, try again. But after a while, we begin to click and when we don't know where the other is going, we lock eyes and listen so intently that for fleeting moments it's like our souls are talking. One time after I improvise alone for a while, he exclaims, "Your tone is awesome, so so lonely, like, I don't know, a day without birds or something," but I don't feel lonely at all. I feel like Bailey is listening.

"WELL, YOU'RE NO different late at night, exactly the same John Lennon." We're sitting on the grass, drinking some wine Joe swiped from his father. The front door is open and a French chanteuse is blasting out of it into the warm night. We're swigging out of the bottle and eating cheese and a baguette. I'm finally in France with Joe, I think, and it makes me smile.

"What?" he asks.

"I don't know. This is nice. I've never drunk wine before."

"I have my whole life. My dad mixed it with water for us when we were little."

"Really? Drunken little Fontaine boys running into walls?"

He laughs. "Yup, exactly. That's my theory of why French children are so well behaved. They're drunk off their *petits mignons* asses most of the time." He tips the bottle and takes a sip, passes it to me.

"Are both your parents French?"

"Dad is, born and raised in Paris. My mom's from around here originally. But Dad makes up for it, he's Central Casting French." There's a bitterness in his voice, but I don't pursue it. I've only just recovered from the consequences of my snooping, have almost forgotten about Genevieve and the importance of honesty to Joe, when he says, "Ever been in love?" He's lying on his back, looking up at a sky reeling with stars.

I don't holler, *Yes, right now, with you, stupid,* like I suddenly want to, but say, "No. I've never been anything."

He gets up on one elbow, looks over at me. "What do you mean?"

I sit, hugging my knees, looking out at the spattering of lights down in the valley.

"It's like I was sleeping or something, happy, but sleeping, for seventeen years, and then Bailey died . . ." The wine has made it easier to talk but I don't know if I'm making any sense. I look over at Joe. He's listening to me so carefully, like he wants to catch my words in his hands as they fall from my lips.

"And now?"

"Well, now I don't know. I feel so different." I pick up a pebble and toss it into the darkness. I think how things used to be: predictable, sensible. How I used to be the same. I think how there is no inevitability, how there never was, I just didn't know it then. "I'm awake, I guess, and maybe that's good, but it's more complicated than that because now I'm someone who knows the worst thing can happen at any time."

Joe's nodding like I'm making sense, which is good, because I have no idea what I just said. I know what I meant though. I meant that I know now how close death is. How it lurks. And who wants to know that? Who wants to know we are just one carefree breath away from the end? Who wants to know that the person you love and need the most can just vanish forever?

He says, "But if you're someone who knows the worst thing can happen at any time, aren't you also someone who knows the best thing can happen at any time too?"

I think about this and instantly feel elated. "Yeah, that's right," I say. "Like right now with you, actually . . ." It's out of my mouth before I can stop it, and I see the delight wash across his face.

"Are we drunk?" I ask.

He takes another swig. "Quite possibly."

"Anyway, have you ever . . ."

"I've never experienced anything like what you're going through."

"No, I mean, have you ever been in love?" My stomach clenches. I want him to say no so badly, but I know he won't, and he doesn't.

"Yeah, I was. I guess." He shakes his head. "I think so anyway."

"What happened?"

A siren sounds in the distance. Joe sits up. "During the summers, I boarded at school. I walked in on her and my roommate, killed me. I mean really killed me. I never talked to her again, or him, threw myself into music in kind of an insane way, swore off girls, well, until now, I guess . . ." He smiles, but not like usual. There's a vulnerability in it, a hesitancy; it's all over his face, swimming around in his beautiful green eyes too. I shut my eyes to not have to see it, because all I can think about is how he almost walked in on Toby and me today.

Joe grabs the bottle of wine and drinks. "Moral of the story: Violinists are insane. I think it's that crazy-ass bow." Genevieve, the gorgeous French violinist. Ugh.

"Yeah? What about clarinetists?"

He smiles. "The most soulful." He trails his finger across my face, forehead to cheek to chin, then down my neck. "And so beautiful." Oh my, I totally get why King Edward VIII of

England abdicated his throne for love. If I had a throne, I'd abdicate it just to relive the last three seconds.

"And horn players?" I ask, intertwining my fingers with his.

He shakes his head. "Crazy hellions, steer clear. All-or-nothing types, no middle ground for the blowhards." Uh-oh. "Never want to cross a horn player," he adds flippantly, but I don't hear it flippantly. I can't believe I lied to him today. I have to stay away from Toby. Far away.

A pair of coyotes howl in the distance, sending a shiver up my spine. Nice timing, dogs.

"Didn't know you horn guys were so scary," I say, letting go of his hand and taking a swig off the bottle. "And guitarists?"

"You tell me."

"Hmm, let me think . . ." I trail my finger over his face this time. "Homely and boring, and of course, talentless—" He cracks up. "I'm not done. But they make up for all that because they are so, so passionate—"

"Oh, God," he whispers, reaching his hand behind my neck and bringing my lips to his. "Let's let the whole fucking world explode this time."

And we do.

chapter 19

I'M LYING IN bed, hearing voices.

"What do you think is wrong with her?"

"Not sure. Could be the orange walls getting to her." A pause, then I hear: "Let's think about it logically. Symptoms: still in bed at noon on a sunny Saturday, goofy grin on her face, stains on her lips likely from red wine, a beverage she's not allowed to drink, which we will address later, and the giveaway, still in her clothes, a dress I might add, with flowers on it."

"Well, my expert opinion, which I draw from vast experience and five glorious, albeit flawed marriages, is that Lennie Walker aka John Lennon is out of her mind in love."

Big and Gram are smiling down at me. I feel like Dorothy waking in her bed, surrounded by her Kansans after having been over the rainbow.

"Do you think you're ever going to get up again?" Gram is sitting on the bed now, patting my hand, which is in hers.

"I don't know." I roll over to face her. "I just want to lie here forever and think about him." I haven't decided which is better: experiencing last night, or the blissed-out replay in my mind where I can hit pause and turn ecstatic seconds into whole hours, where I can loop certain moments until the sweet grassy taste of Joe is again in my mouth, the clove scent of his skin is in the air, until I can feel his hands running through my hair, all over my dress, just one thin, thin layer between us, until the moment when he slipped his hands under the fabric and I felt his fingers on my skin like music—all of it sending me again and again right off the cliff that is my heart.

This morning, for the first time, Bailey wasn't my first thought on waking and it had made me feel guilty. But the guilt didn't have much of a chance against the dawning realization that I was falling in love. I had stared out the window at the early-morning fog, wondering for a moment if she had sent Joe to me so I would know that in the same world where she could die, this could happen.

Big says, "Would you look at her. We've got to cut down those damn rosebushes." His hair is particularly coiled and springy today, and his mustache is unwaxed, so it looks like a squirrel is running across his face. In any fairy tale, Big plays the king.

Gram chides him, "Hush now, you don't even believe in that." She doesn't like anyone to perpetuate the rumor about the aphrodisiacal nature of her roses, because there was a time when desperate lovers would come and steal them to try to change the hearts of their beloveds. It made her crazy. There is not much Gram takes more seriously than proper pruning.

Big won't let it go though. "I follow the proof-is-in-the-pudding scientific method: Please examine the empirical evidence in this bed. She's worse than me."

"No one is worse than you, you're the town swain." Gram rolls her eyes.

"You say swain, but imply swine," Big retorts, twisting his squirrel for effect.

I sit up in bed, lean my back against the sill to better enjoy their verbal tennis match. I can feel the summery day through the window, deliciously warming my back. But when I look over at Bailey's bed, I'm leveled. How can something this momentous be happening to me without her? And what about all the momentous things to come? How will I go through each and every one of them without her? I don't care that she was keeping things from me—I want to tell her absolutely everything about last night, about everything that will ever happen to me! I'm crying before I even realize it, but I don't want us all to tailspin, so I swallow and swallow it all down, and try to focus on last night, on falling in love. I spot my clarinet across the room, half covered with the paisley scarf of Bailey's I recently started wearing.

"Joe didn't come by this morning?" I ask, wanting to play again, wanting to blow all this everything I'm feeling out my clarinet.

Big replies, "No, bet a million dollars he's exactly where you are, though he probably has his guitar with him. Have you asked him if he sleeps with it yet?"

"He's a musical genius," I say, feeling my earlier giddiness returning. Without a doubt, I've gone bipolar.

"Oh, jeez. C'mon Gram, she's a lost cause." Big winks at me, then heads for the door.

Gram stays seated next to me, ruffling my hair like I'm a

little kid. She's looking at me closely and a little too long. Oh no. I've been in such a trance, I forget that I haven't really been talking to Gram lately, that we've hardly been alone like this in weeks.

"Len." This is definitely her Gramouncement tone, but I don't think it's going to be about Bailey. About expressing my feelings. About packing up Bailey's things. About going to the city for lunch. About resuming my lessons. About all the things I haven't wanted to do.

"Yeah?"

"We talked about birth control, diseases and all that . . ." Phew. This one's harmless.

"Yeah, like a million times."

"Okay, just as long as you haven't suddenly forgotten it all."

"Nope."

"Good." She's patting my hand again.

"Gram, there's no need yet, okay?" I feel the requisite blush from revealing this, but better to not have her freaking out about it and constantly questioning me.

"Even better, even better," she says, the relief evident in her voice, and it makes me think. Things with Joe last night were intense, but they were paced to savor. Not so with Toby. I worry what might've happened if we weren't interrupted. Would I have had the sense to stop us? Would he have? All I know is that everything was happening really quickly, I was totally out of control, and condoms were the furthest thing from my mind. God. How did that happen? How did Toby Shaw's hands ever end up on my breasts? *Toby's!* And only hours before Joe's. I want to dive under the bed, make it my perma-

135

nent residence. How did I go from bookworm and band geek to two-guys-in-the-same-day hussy?

Gram smiles, oblivious of the sudden bile rising in my throat, the twisting in my guts. She ruffles my hair again. "In the middle of all this tragedy, you're growing up, sweet pea, and that is such a wonderful thing."

Groan.

chapter 20

"LENNIE! LENNIE! LENNNNNNNNNNIE! God, I've missed you!" I pull the cell phone away from my ear. Sarah hadn't texted me back, so I assumed she was really pissed. I cut in to say so, and she responds, "I *am* furious! And I'm *not* speaking to you!" then she launches into all the summer gossip I've missed. I soak it up but can tell there was some true vitriol in her words. I'm lying on my bed, wiped after practicing Cavallini's Adagio and Tarantella for two straight hours—it was incredible, like turning the air into colors. It made me think of the Charlie Parker quote Mr. James liked to repeat: *If you don't live it, it can't come out of your horn.* It also made me think I might go to summer band practice after all.

Sarah and I make a plan to meet at Flying Man's. I'm dying to tell her about Joe. Not about Toby. I'm thinking if I don't talk about it, I can just pretend it didn't happen.

She's lying on a rock in the sun reading Simone de Beauvoir's *The Second Sex*—in preparation, I'm sure, for her very promising guy-poaching expedition to State's Women's Studies Department feminism symposium. She springs to her feet when she sees me, and hugs me like crazy despite the fact that she's completely naked. We have our own secret pool and mini-falls behind Flying Man's that we've been coming to for years. We've declared it clothing optional and we opt not. "God, it's been forever," she says.

"I'm so sorry, Sarah," I say, hugging her back.

"It's okay, really," she says. "I know I need to give you a free pass right now. So that's . . ." She pulls away for a second, studies my face. "Wait a minute? What's wrong with you? You look weird. I mean *really* weird."

I can't stop smiling. I must look like a Fontaine.

"What, Lennie? What happened?"

"I think I'm falling in love." The moment the words are out of my mouth, I feel my face go hot with shame. I'm supposed to be grieving, not falling in love. Not to mention everything else I've been doing.

"Whaaaaaaaaaaaaaaaaaaaaaaaat! That is so unfreakingfreaking-freakingfreakingbelieveable! Cows on the moon, Len! Cows. On. The. Moon!" Well, so much for my shame. Sarah is in full-on cheerleader mode, arms flailing, hopping up and down. Then she stops abruptly. "Wait, with whom? NOT Toby, I hope."

"No, no, of course not," I say as a speeding eighteen-wheeler of guilt flattens me.

"Whew," Sarah, says, sweeping her hand off her brow dramatically. "Who then? Who could you be in love with? You haven't gone anywhere, at least that I know of, and this town is beyond Loserville, so where'd you find him?"

"Sarah, it's Joe."

"It's not."

"Yeah, it is."

"No!"

"Yup."

"Not true."

"Is true."

"Nah-uh, nah-uh, nah-uh."

"Uh-huh, uh-huh, uh-huh."

Etc.

Her previous display of enthusiasm was nothing compared to the one that is going on now. She's doing circles around me, saying, "Oh my God. I am soooooooooooooo jealous. Every girl in Clover is after one Fontaine or another. No wonder you've been a shut-in. I would be too, if I could shut in with one of them. God, let me live vicariously through you. Tell me every freaking detail. That beautiful, beautiful boy, those eyes, those *eyelashes*, that unfreakingbelievable smile, that trumpet playing, wow, Lennnnnnnnnie." She's pacing now, has lit another cigarette, is chain smoking in glee—a naked smokestack maniac. I'm so happy to be hanging out with the marvel that is my best friend Sarah. And I'm so happy to be happy about it.

I tell her every detail. How he came over every morning with croissants, how we played music together, how he made Gram and Big so happy just by being in the house, how we drank wine last night and kissed until I was sure I had walked right into the sky. I told her how I think I can hear his heart beating even when he's not there, how I feel like flowers—Gramgantuan ones—are blooming in my chest, how I'm sure I feel just the way Heathcliff did for Cathy before—

"Okay, stop for a second." She's still smiling but she looks a bit worried and surprised too. "Lennie, you're not in love, you're demented. I've never heard anyone talk about a guy like this."

I shrug. "Then I'm demented."

"Wow, I want to be demented too." She sits down next to me on the rock. "It's like you've hardly kissed three guys in your whole life and now this. Guess you were saving it up or something . . ."

I tell her my Rip Van Lennie theory of having slept my whole life until recently.

"I don't know, Len. You always seemed awake to me."

"Yeah, I don't know either. It was a wine-induced theory."

Sarah picks up a stone, tosses it into the water with a little too much force. "What?" I ask.

She doesn't answer right away, picks up another stone and hurls it too. "I am mad at you, but I'm not allowed to be, you know?"

It's exactly how I feel toward Bailey sometimes lately.

"You've just been keeping so much from me, Lennie. I thought . . . I don't know."

It's as if she were speaking my lines in a play.

"I'm sorry," I say again feebly. I want to say more, give her an explanation, but the truth is I don't know why I've felt so closed off to her since Bailey died.

"It's okay," she says again quietly.

"It'll be different now," I say, hoping it's true. "Promise."

I look out at the sun courting the river's surface, the green leaves, the wet rocks behind the falls. "Want to go swimming?"

"Not yet," she says. "I have news too. Not breaking news, but still." It's a clear dig and I deserve it. I didn't even ask how she was.

She's smirking at me, quite dementedly, actually. "I hooked up with Luke Jacobus last night."

"Luke?" I'm surprised. Besides for his recent lapse in judgment, which resulted in his band-kill status, he's been devotedly, unrequitedly in love with Sarah since second grade. King of the Nerdiverse, she used to call him. "Didn't you make out with him in seventh grade and then drop him when that idiot surfer glistened at you?"

"Yeah, it's probably dumb," she says. "I agreed to do lyrics for this incredible music he wrote, and we were hanging out, and it just happened."

"What about the Jean-Paul Sartre rule?"

"Sense of humor trumps literacy, I've decided—and jumping giraffes, Len, growth geyser, the guy's like the Hulk these days."

"He is funny," I agree. "And green."

She laughs, just as my phone signals a text. I rifle through my bag and take it out hoping for a message from Joe.

Sarah's singing, "Lennie got a love note from a Fontaine," as she tries to read over my shoulder. "C'mon let me see it." She grabs the phone from me. I pull it out of her hands, but it's too late. It says: *I need to talk to you. T.*

"As in Toby?" she asks. "But I thought . . . I mean, you just said . . . Lennie, what're you doing?"

"Nothing," I tell her, shoving the phone back in my bag, already breaking my promise. "Really. Nothing."

"Why don't I believe you?" she says, shaking her head. "I have a bad feeling about this."

"Don't," I say, swallowing my own atrocious feeling. "Really. I'm demented, remember?" I touch her arm. "Let's go swimming."

We float on our backs in the pool for over an hour. I make her tell me everything about her night with Luke so I don't have to think about Toby's text, what might be so urgent. Then we climb up to the falls and get under them, screaming FUCK over and over into the roar like we've done since we were little.

I scream bloody murder.

chapter 21

There were once two sisters
who were not afraid of the dark
because the dark was full of the other's voice
across the room,
because even when the night was thick
and starless
they walked home together from the river
seeing who could last the longest
without turning on her flashlight,
not afraid
because sometimes in the pitch of night
they'd lie on their backs
in the middle of the path
and look up until the stars came back
and when they did,
they'd reach their arms up to touch them
and did.

*(Found on an envelope stuck
under the tire of a car on Main Street)*

By THE TIME I walk home from the river through the woods, I've decided Toby, like me, feels terrible about what happened, hence the urgency of the text. He probably just wants to make sure it will never happen again. Well, agreed. No argument from demented ol' moi.

Clouds have gathered and the air feels thick with the possibility of a rare summer rain. I see a to-go cup on the ground, so I sit down, write a few lines on it, and then bury it under a mound of pine needles. Then I lie down on my back on the spongy forest floor. I love doing this—giving it all up to the enormity of the sky, or to the ceiling if the need arises while I'm indoors. As I reach my hands out and press my fingers into the loamy soil, I start wondering what I'd be doing right now, what I'd be feeling right this minute if Bailey were still alive. I realize something that scares me: I'd be happy, but in a mild kind of way, nothing demented about it. I'd be turtling along, like I always turtled, huddled in my shell, safe and sound.

But what if I'm a shell-less turtle now, demented and devastated in equal measure, an unfreakingbelievable mess of a girl, who wants to turn the air into colors with her clarinet, and what if somewhere inside I prefer this? What if as much as I fear having death as a shadow, I'm beginning to like how it quickens the pulse, not only mine, but the pulse of the whole world. I doubt Joe would even have noticed me if I'd still been in that hard shell of mild happiness. He wrote in his journal that he thinks I'm on full blast, *me,* and maybe I am now, but I never was before. How can the cost of this change in me be so great? It doesn't seem right that anything good should come out of Bailey's death. It doesn't seem right to even have these thoughts.

But then I think about my sister and what a shell-less turtle she was and how she wanted me to be one too. *C'mon, Lennie*, she used to say to me at least ten times a day. *C'mon, Len*. And that makes me feel better, like it's her life rather than her death that is now teaching me how to be, who to be.

I know Toby's there even before I go inside, because Lucy and Ethel are camped out on the porch. When I walk into the kitchen, I see him and Gram sitting at the table talking in hushed voices.

"Hi," I say, dumbfounded. Doesn't he realize he can't be here?

"Lucky me," Gram says. "I was walking home with armfuls of groceries and Toby came whizzing by on his skateboard." Gram hasn't driven since the 1900s. She walks everywhere in Clover, which is how she became Garden Guru. She couldn't help herself, started carrying her shears on her trips to town and people would come home and find her pruning their bushes to perfection: ironic yes, because of her hands-off policy with her own garden.

"Lucky," I say to Gram as I take in Toby. Fresh scrapes cover his arms, probably from wiping out on his board. He looks wild-eyed and disheveled, totally unmoored. I know two things in this moment: I was wrong about the text and I don't want to be unmoored with him anymore.

What I really want is to go up to The Sanctum and play my clarinet.

Gram looks at me, smiles. "You swam. Your hair looks like a cyclone. I'd like to paint it." She reaches her hand up and touches my cyclone. "Toby's going to have dinner with us."

I can't believe this. "I'm not hungry," I say. "I'm going upstairs."

Gram gasps at my rudeness, but I don't care. Under no circumstances am I sitting through dinner with Toby, *who touched my breasts,* and Gram and Big. What is he thinking?

I go up to The Sanctum, unpack and assemble my clarinet, then take out the Edith Piaf sheet music that I borrowed from a certain garçon, turn to "La Vie en Rose," and start playing. It's the song we listened to last night while the world exploded. I'm hoping I can just stay lost in a state of Joeliriousness, and I won't hear a knock at my door after they eat, but of course, I do.

Toby, *who touched my breasts and let's not forget put his hand down my pants too,* opens the door, walks tentatively across the room, and sits on Bailey's bed. I stop playing, rest my clarinet on my stand. Go away, I think heartlessly, just go away. Let's pretend it didn't happen, none of it.

Neither of us says a word. He's rubbing his thighs so intently, I bet the friction is generating heat. His gaze is drifting all around the room. It finally locks on a photograph of Bailey and him on her dresser. He takes a breath, looks over at me. His gaze lingers.

"Her shirt . . ."

I look down. I forgot I had it on. "Yeah." I've been wearing Bailey's clothes more and more outside The Sanctum as well as in it. I find myself going through my own drawers and thinking, Who was the girl who wore these things? I'm sure a shrink would love this, all of it, I think, looking over at Toby. She'd probably tell me I was trying to take Bailey's place. Or worse, competing with her in a way I never could when she was alive. But is that it? It doesn't feel like it. When I wear her clothes, I just feel safer, like she's whispering in my ear.

I'm lost in thought, so it startles me when Toby says in an uncharacteristic shaky voice, "Len, I'm sorry. About every-thing." I glance at him. He looks so vulnerable, frightened. "I got way out of control, feel so bad." Is this what he needed to tell me? Relief tumbles out of my chest.

"Me too," I say, thawing immediately. We're in this together.

"Me more, trust me," he says, rubbing his thighs again. He's so distraught. Does he think it's all his fault or something?

"We both did it, Toby," I say. "Each time. We're both hor-rible."

He looks at me, his dark eyes warm. "You're not horrible, Lennie." His voice is gentle, intimate. I can tell he wants to reach out to me. I'm glad he's across the room. I wish he were across the equator. Do our bodies now think whenever they're together they get to touch? I tell mine that is most definitely not the case, no matter that I feel it again. No matter.

And then a renegade asteroid breaks through the earth's atmosphere and hurtles into The Sanctum: "It's just that I can't stop thinking about you," he says. "I can't. I just . . ." He's ball-ing up Bailey's bedspread in his fists. "I want—"

"Please don't say more." I cross the room to my dresser, open the middle drawer, reach in and pull out a shirt, my shirt. I have to take Bailey's off. Because I'm suddenly thinking that imaginary shrink is spot on.

147

"It's not me," I say quietly as I open the closet door and slip inside. "I'm not her."

I stay in the dark quiet getting my breathing under control, my life under control, getting my own shirt on my own body. It's like there's a river under my feet tumbling me toward him, still, even with everything that's happened with Joe, a roaring, passionate, despairing river, but I don't want to go this time. I want to stay on the shore. We can't keep wrapping our arms around a ghost.

When I come out of the closet, he's gone.

"I'm so sorry," I say aloud to the empty orange room.

As if in response, thousands of hands begin tapping on the roof. I walk over to my bed, climb up to the window ledge and stick my hands out. Because we only get one or two storms a summer, rain is an event. I lean far over the ledge, palms to the sky, letting it all slip through my fingers, remembering what Big told Toby and me that afternoon. *No way out of this but through.* Who knew what through would be?

I see someone rushing down the road in the downpour. When the figure gets near the lit-up garden I realize it's Joe and am instantly uplifted. My life raft.

"Hey," I yell out and wave like a maniac.

He looks up at the window, smiles, and I can't get down the stairs, out the front door, into the rain and by his side fast enough.

"I missed you," I say, reaching up and touching his cheek with my fingers. Raindrops drip from his eyelashes, stream in rivulets all down his face.

"God, me too." Then his hands are on my cheeks and we

are kissing and the rain is pouring all over our crazy heads and once again my whole being is aflame with joy.

I didn't know love felt like this, like turning into brightness.

"What are you doing?" I say, when I can finally bring myself to pull away for a moment.

"I saw it was raining—I snuck out, wanted to see you, just like this."

"Why'd you have to sneak out?" The rain's drenching us, my shirt clings to me, and Joe's hands to it, rubbing up and down my sides.

"I'm in prison," he says. "Got busted big-time, that wine we drank was like a four-hundred-dollar bottle. I had no idea. I wanted to impress you so took it from downstairs. My dad went ape-shit when he saw the empty bottle—he's making me sort wood all day and night in the workshop while he talks to his girlfriend on the phone the whole time. I think he forgets I speak French."

I'm not sure whether to address the four-hundred-dollar bottle of wine we drank or the girlfriend, decide on the latter. "His girlfriend?"

"Never mind. I had to see you, but now I have to go back, and I wanted to give you this." He pulls a piece of paper out of his pocket, stuffs it quickly into mine before it can get soaked.

He kisses me again. "Okay, I'm leaving." He doesn't move. "I don't want to leave you."

"I don't want you to," I say. His hair's black and snaky all around his glistening face. It's like being in the shower with him. Wow—to be in the shower with him.

He turns to go for real then and I notice his eyes narrow as he peers over my shoulder. "Why's he always here?"

I turn around. Toby's in the doorframe, *watching us*—he looks like he's been hit by a wrecking ball. God. He must not have left, must have been in the art room with Gram or something. He pushes open the door, grabs his skateboard, and rushes past without a word, huddled against the downpour.

"What's going on?" Joe asks, X-raying me with his stare. His whole body has stiffened.

"Nothing. Really," I answer, just as I did with Sarah. "He's upset about Bailey." What else can I tell him? If I tell him what's going on, what went on even after he kissed me, I'll lose him.

So when he says, "I'm being stupid and paranoid?" I just say, "Yeah." And hear in my head: *Never cross a horn player.*

He smiles wide and open as a meadow. "Okay." Then he kisses me hard one last time and we are again drinking the rain off each other's lips. "Bye, John Lennon."

And he's off.

I hurry inside, worrying about what Toby said to me and what I didn't say to Joe, as the rain washes all those beautiful kisses off of me.

chapter 22

I'M LYING DOWN on my bed, holding in my hands the antidote to worrying about anything. It's a sheet of music, still damp from the rain. At the top, it says in Joe's boxlike weirdo boy handwriting: *For a soulful, beautiful clarinetist, from a homely, boring, talentless though passionate guitarist. Part 1, Part 2 to come.*

I try to hear it in my head, but my facility to hear without playing is terrible. I get up, find my clarinet, and moments later the melody spills into the room. I remember as I play what he said about my tone being so lonely, like a day without birds, but it's as if the melody he wrote is nothing but birds and they are flying out of the end of my clarinet and filling the air of a still summer day, filling the trees and sky—it's exquisite. I play it over and over again, until I know it by heart.

It's two a.m. and if I play the song one more time, my fingers will fall off, but I'm too Joelirious to sleep. I go downstairs to get something to eat, and when I come back into The Sanctum, I'm blindsided by a want so urgent I have to cover my mouth to stifle a shriek. I want Bails to be sprawled out on her bed reading. I want to talk to her about Joe, want to play her this song.

I want my sister.

I want to hurl a building at God.

I take a breath and exhale with enough force to blow the orange paint right off the walls.

It's no longer raining—the scrubbed newness of the night rolls in through the open window. I don't know what to do, so I walk over to Bailey's desk and sit down like usual. I look at the detective's business card again. I thought about calling him but haven't yet, haven't packed up a thing either. I pull over a carton, decide to do one or two drawers. I hate looking at the empty boxes almost more than I hate the idea of packing up her things.

The bottom drawer's full of school notebooks, years of work, now useless. I take one out, glide my fingers over the cover, hold it to my chest, and then put it in the carton. All her knowledge is gone now. Everything she ever learned, or heard, or saw. Her particular way of looking at Hamlet or daisies or thinking about love, all her private intricate thoughts, her inconsequential secret musings—they're gone too. I heard this expression once: Each time someone dies, a library burns. I'm watching it burn right to the ground.

I stack the rest of the notebooks on top of the first, close the drawer, and do the same with the one above it. I close the carton and start a new one. There are more school notebooks in this drawer, some journals, which I will not read. I flip through the stack, putting them, one by one, into the box. At the very bottom of the drawer, there is an open one. It has Bailey's chicken scrawl handwriting all over it; columns of words cover the whole page, with lines crossing out most of them. I take it out, feel a pang of guilt, but then my guilt turns to surprise, then fear, when I see what the words are.

They're all combinations of our mother's name combined with other names and things. There is a whole section of the name Paige combined with people and things related to John Lennon, my namesake, and we assume her favorite musician because of it. We know practically nothing about Mom. It's like when she left, she took all traces of her life with her, leaving only a story behind. Gram rarely talks about anything but her amazing wanderlust, and Big isn't much better.

"At five years old," Gram would tell us over and over again, holding up her fingers for emphasis, "your mother snuck out of her bed one night and I found her halfway to town, with her little blue backpack and a walking stick. She said she was on an adventure—at five years old, girls!"

So that was all we had, except for a box of belongings we kept in The Sanctum. It's full of books we foraged over the years from the shelves downstairs, ones that had her name in them: *Oliver Twist*, *On the Road*, *Siddhartha*, *The Collected Poems of William Blake*, and some Harlequins, which threw us for a loop, book snobs that we are. None of them are dog-eared or annotated. We have some yearbooks, but there are no scribbles from friends in them. There's a copy of *The Joy of Cooking* with food spattered all over it. (Gram did once tell us that Mom was magical in the kitchen and that she suspects she makes her living on the road by cooking.)

But mostly, what we have are maps, lots and lots of them: road maps, topographic maps, maps of Clover, of California, of the forty-nine other states, of country after country, continent after continent. There are also several atlases, each of which looks as read and reread as my copy of *Wuthering Heights*. The maps and atlases reveal the most about her: a girl for whom the world beckoned. When we were younger, Bailey and I would spend countless hours poring over the atlases imagining routes and adventures for her.

I start leafing through the notebook. There are pages and pages of these combinations: Paige/Lennon/Walker, Paige/Lennon/Yoko, Paige/Lennon/Imagine, Paige/Dakota/Ono, and on and on. Sometimes there are notes under a name combination. For instance, scribbled under the words *Paige/Dakota* is an address in North Hampton, MA. But then that's crossed out and the words *too young* are scrawled in.

I'm shocked. We'd both put our mother's name into search engines many times to no avail, and we would sometimes try to think of pseudonyms she might have chosen and search them to no avail as well, but never like this, never methodically, never with this kind of thoroughness and persistence. The notebook is practically full. Bailey must have been doing this in every free moment, every moment I wasn't around, because I so rarely saw her at the computer. But now that I'm thinking about it, I did see her in front of The Half Mom an awful lot before she died, studying it intently, almost like she was waiting for it to speak to her.

I turn to the first page of the notebook. It's dated February 27, less than two months before she died. How could she have done all this in that amount of time? No wonder she needed St. Anthony's help. I wish she'd asked for mine.

I put the notebook back in the drawer, walk back over to my bed, take my clarinet out of the case again, and play Joe's song.

I want to be in that summer day again, I want to be there with
my sister.

At night,
when we were little,
we tented Bailey's covers,
crawled underneath with our flashlights
and played cards: Hearts,
Whist, Crazy Eights,
and our favorite: Bloody Knuckles.
The competition was vicious.
All day, every day,
we were the Walker Girls—
two peas in a pod
thick as thieves—
but when Gram closed the door
for the night,
we bared our teeth.
We played for chores,
for slave duty,
for truths and dares and money.
We played to be better, brighter,
to be more beautiful,
more,
just more.
But it was all a ruse—
we played
so we could fall asleep
in the same bed
without having to ask,
so we could wrap together
like a braid,
so while we slept
our dreams could switch bodies.

chapter 23

I used to talk to The Half Mom a lot,
but I'd wait until no one else was home
and then I'd say:
I imagine you
up there
not like a cloud or a bird or a star
but like a mother,
except one who lives in the sky
who doesn't make a fuss
about gravity
who just goes about her business
drifting around with the wind.

*(Found on a piece
of newspaper
under the Walkers'
porch)*

WHEN I COME down to the kitchen the next morning, Gram
is at the stove cooking sausages, her shoulders hunched into a
broad frown. Big slouches over his coffee at the table. Behind
them the morning fog shrouds the window, like the house is
hovering inside a cloud. Standing in the doorway I'm filled
with the same scared, hollow feeling I get when I see abandoned
houses, ones with weeds growing through the front steps, paint
cracked and dirty, windows broken and boarded up.

"Where's Joe?" Big asks. I realize then why the despair is so naked this morning: Joe's not here.

"In prison," I say.

Big looks up, smirks. "What'd he do?" Instantly, the mood is lifted. Wow. I guess he's not only my life raft.

"Took a four-hundred-dollar bottle of wine from his father and drank it one night with a girl named John Lennon."

At the same time, Gram and Big gasp, then exclaim, "Four hundred dollars?!"

"He had no idea."

"Lennie, I don't like you drinking." Gram waves her spatula at me. The sausages sizzle and sputter in the pan behind her.

"I don't drink, well hardly. Don't worry."

"Damn, Len. Was it good?" Big's face is a study of wonder.

"I don't know. I've never had red wine before, guess so." I'm pouring a cup of coffee that is thin as tea. I've gotten used to the mud Joe makes.

"Damn," Big repeats, taking a sip of his coffee and making a disgusted face. I guess he now prefers Joe's sludge too. "Don't suppose you will drink it again either, with the bar set that high."

I'm wondering if Joe will be at the first band practice today— I've decided to go—when suddenly he walks through the door with croissants, dead bugs for Big, and a smile as big as God for me.

"Hey!" I say.

"They let you out," says Big. "That's terrific. Is it a conjugal visit or is your sentence over?"

"Big!" Gram chastises. "Please."

Joe laughs. "It's over. My father is a very romantic man, it's his best and worst trait, when I explained to him how I was feeling—" Joe looks at me, proceeds to turn red, which of course makes me go full-on tomato. It surely must be against the rules to feel like this when your sister is dead!

Gram shakes her head. "Who would have thought Lennie such a romantic?"

"Are you kidding?" Joe exclaims. "Her reading *Wuthering Heights* twenty-three times didn't give it away?" I look down. I'm embarrassed at how moved I am by this. *He knows me.* Somehow better than they do.

"Touché, Mr. Fontaine," Gram says, hiding her grin as she goes back to the stove.

Joe comes up behind me, wraps his arms around my waist. I close my eyes, think about his body, naked under his clothes, pressing into me, naked under mine. I turn my head to look up at him. "The melody you wrote is so beautiful. I want to play it for you." Before the last word is out of my mouth, he kisses me. I twist around in his arms so that we are facing each other, then throw my arms around his neck while his find the small of my back, and sweep me into him. Oh God, I don't care if this is wrong of me, if I'm breaking every rule in the Western World, I don't care about freaking anything, because our mouths, which momentarily separated, have met again and anything but that ecstatic fact ceases to matter.

How do people function when they're feeling like this?

How do they tie their shoes?

Or drive cars?

Or operate heavy machinery?

How does civilization continue when this is going on?

A voice, ten decibels quieter than its normal register, stutters out of Uncle Big. "Uh, kids. Might want to, I don't know, mmmm . . ." Everything screeches to a halt in my mind. Is *Big* stammering? Uh, Lennie? Probably not cool to make out like this in the middle of the kitchen in front of your grandmother and uncle. I pull away from Joe; it's like breaking suction. I look at Gram and Big, who are standing there fiddly and sheepish while the sausages burn. Is it possible that we've succeeded in embarrassing the Emperor and Empress of Weird?

I glance back at Joe. He looks totally cartoon-dopey, like he's been bonked on the head with a club. The whole scene strikes me as hysterical, and I collapse into a chair laughing.

Joe smiles an embarrassed half smile at Gram and Big, leans against the counter, his trumpet case now strategically held over his crotch. Thank God I don't have one of those. Who'd want a lust-o-meter sticking out the middle of their body?

"You're going to rehearsal, right?" he asks.

Bat. Bat. Bat.

Yes, if we make it.

WE DO MAKE it, though in my case, in body only. I'm surprised my fingers can find the keys as I glide through the pieces Mr. James has chosen for us to play at the upcoming River Festival. Even with Rachel sending me death-darts about Joe and repeatedly turning the stand so I can't see it, I'm lost in the music, feel like I'm playing with Joe alone, improvising, reveling in not knowing what is going to happen note to note . . . but mid-practice, mid-song, mid-note, a feeling of dread sweeps over me as I start thinking about Toby, how he looked when he left last night. What he said in The Sanctum. He has to know we need to stay away from each other now. He has to. I tuck the panic away but spend the rest of rehearsal painfully alert, following the arrangement without the slightest deviation.

After practice, Joe and I have the whole afternoon together because he's out of prison and I'm off work. We're walking back to my house, the wind whipping us around like leaves.

"I know what we should do," I say.

"Didn't you want to play me the song?"

"I do, but I want to play it for you somewhere else. Remember I dared you in the woods that night to brave the forest with me on a really windy day? Today is it."

We veer off the road and hike in, bushwhacking through thickets of brush until we find the trail I'm looking for. The sun filters sporadically through the trees, casting a dim and shadowy light over the forest floor. Because of the wind, the trees are creaking symphonically—it's a veritable philharmonic of squeaking doors. Perfect.

After a while, he says, "I think I'm holding up remarkably well, considering, don't you?"

"Considering what?"

"Considering we're hiking to the soundtrack of the creepiest horror movie ever made and all the world's tree trolls have gathered above us to open and close their front doors."

"It's broad daylight, you can't be scared."

"I can be, actually, but I'm trying not to be a wuss. I have a very low eerie threshold."

"You're going to love where I'm taking you, I promise."

"I'm going to love it if you take off all your clothes there, I

160

promise, or at least some of them, maybe even just a sock." He comes over to me, drops his horn, and swings me around so we are facing each other.

I say, "You're very repressed, you know? It's maddening."

"Can't help it. I'm half French, *joie de vivre* and all. In all seriousness though, I haven't yet seen you in any state of undress, and it's been three whole days since our first kiss, *quel catastrophe*, you know?" He tries to get my wind-blown hair out of my face, then kisses me until my heart busts out of my chest like a wild horse. "Though I do have a very good imagination . . ."

"Quel dork," I say, pulling him forward.

"You know, I only act like a dork so you'll say *quel dork*," he replies.

The trail climbs to where the old growth redwoods rocket into the sky and turn the forest into their private cathedral. The wind has died down and the woods have grown unearthly still and peaceful. Leaves flicker all around us like tiny pieces of light.

"So, what about your mom?" Joe asks all of a sudden.

"What?" My head couldn't have been further away from thoughts of my mother.

"The first day I came over, Gram said she'd finish the portrait when your mother comes back. Where is she?"

"I don't know." Usually I leave it at that and don't fill in the spare details, but he hasn't run away yet from all our other family oddities. "I've never met my mother," I say. "Well, I met her, but she left when I was one. She has a restless nature, guess it runs in the family."

He stops walking. "That's it? That's the explanation? For her leaving? And *never coming back*?" Yes, it's nutso, but this Walker nutso has always made sense to me.

"Gram says she'll come back," I say, my stomach knotting up, thinking of her coming back right now. Thinking of Bailey trying so hard to find her. Thinking of slamming the door in her face if she did come back, of screaming, *You're too late*. Thinking of her never coming back. Thinking I'm not sure how to believe all this anymore without Bailey believing it with me. "Gram's aunt Sylvie had it too," I add, feeling imbecilic. "She came back after twenty years away."

"Wow," Joe says. I've never seen his brow so furrowed.

"Look, I don't know my mother, so I don't miss her or anything . . ." I say, but I feel like I'm trying to convince myself more than Joe. "She's this intrepid, free-spirited woman who took off to traipse all around the globe alone. She's mysterious. It's cool." It's *cool*? God, I'm a ninny. But when did everything change? Because it did used to be cool, super-cool, in fact—she was our Magellan, our Marco Polo, one of the wayward Walker women whose restless boundless spirit propels her from place to place, love to love, moment to unpredictable moment.

Joe smiles, looks at me so warmly, I forget everything else. "You're cool," he says. "Forgiving. Unlike dickhead me." Forgiving? I take his hand, wondering from his reaction, and my own, if I'm cool and forgiving or totally delusional. And what about this dickhead him? Who is it? Is it the Joe that never talked to that violinist again? If so, I don't want to meet that guy, ever. We continue in silence, both of us soaring around in the sky of our minds for another mile or so and then we are

162

there, and all thoughts of dickhead him and my mysterious missing mother are gone.

"Okay, close your eyes," I say. "I'll lead you." I reach up from behind him and cover my hands over his eyes and steer him down the path.

"Okay, open them."

There is a bedroom. A whole bedroom in the middle of the forest.

"Wow, where's Sleeping Beauty?" Joe asks.

"That would be me," I say, and take a running leap onto the fluffy bed. It's like jumping into a cloud. He follows me.

"You're too awake to be her, we've already covered this." He stands at the edge of the bed, looking around. "This is unbelievable, how is this here?"

"There's an inn about a mile away on the river. It was a commune in the sixties, and the owner Sam's an old hippie. He set up this forest bedroom for his guests to happen upon if they hike up here, for surprise romance, I guess, but I've never seen a soul pass through and I've been coming forever. Actually, I did see someone here once: Sam, changing the sheets. He throws this tarp over when it rains. I write at that desk, read in that rocker, lie here on this bed and daydream. I've never brought a guy here before though."

He smiles, sits on the bed next to where I'm lying on my back and starts trailing his fingers over my belly.

"What do you daydream about?" he asks.

"This," I say as his hand spreads across my midriff under my shirt. My breathing's getting faster—I want his hands everywhere.

163

"John Lennon, can I ask you something?"

"Uh-oh, whenever people say that, something scary comes next."

"Are you a virgin?"

"You see—scary question came next," I mumble, mortified—what a mood-killer. I squirm out from under his hand. "Is it that obvious?"

"Sort of." Ugh. I want to crawl under the covers. He tries to backtrack. "No, I mean, I think it's cool that you are."

"It's decidedly uncool."

"For you maybe, but not for me, if . . ."

"If what?" My stomach is suddenly churning. Roiling.

Now he looks embarrassed—good. "Well, if sometime, not now, but sometime, you might not want to be one anymore, and I could be your first, that's where the cool part comes in, you know, for me." His expression is shy and sweet, but what he's saying makes me feel scared and excited and overwhelmed and like I'm going to burst into tears, which I do, and for once, I don't even know why.

"Oh, Lennie, I'm sorry, was that bad to say? Don't cry, there's no pressure at all, kissing you, being with you in any way is amazing—"

"No," I say, now laughing and crying at the same time. "I'm crying because . . . well, I don't know why I'm crying, but I'm happy, not sad . . ."

I reach for his arm, and he lies down on his side next to me, his elbow resting by my head, our bodies touching length to length. He's peering into my eyes in a way that's making me tremble.

"Just looking into your eyes . . ." he whispers. "I've never felt anything like this."

I think about Genevieve. He'd said he was in love with her, does that mean . . .

"Me neither," I say, not able to stop the tears from spilling over again.

"Don't cry." His voice is weightless, mist. He kisses my eyes, gently grazes my lips.

He looks at me then so nakedly, it makes me lightheaded, like I need to lie down even though I'm lying down. "I know it hasn't been that long, Len, but I think . . . I don't know . . . I might be . . ."

He doesn't have to say it, I feel it too; it's not subtle—like every bell for miles and miles is ringing at once, loud, clanging, hungry ones, and tiny, happy, chiming ones, all of them sounding off in this moment. I put my hands around his neck, pull him to me, and then he's kissing me hard and so deep, and I am flying, sailing, soaring . . .

He murmurs into my hair, "Forget what I said earlier, let's stick with this, I might not survive anything more." I laugh. Then he jumps up, finds my wrists, and pins them over my head. "Yeah, right. Totally joking, I want to do *everything* with you, whenever you're ready, I'm the one, promise?" He's above me, batting and grinning like a total hooplehead.

"I promise," I say.

"Good. Glad that's decided." He raises an eyebrow. "I'm going to deflower you, John Lennon."

"Oh my God, so, so embarrassing, *quel, quel major dork.*" I try to cover my face with my hands, but he won't let me. And then we are wrestling and laughing and it's many, many minutes before I remember that my sister has died.

165

chapter 24

The.
World.
Is.
Not.
A.
Safe.
Place.

*(Found on a candy
wrapper in the woods
behind Clover High)*

I SEE TOBY'S truck out front and a bolt of anger shoots through me. Why can't he just stay away from me for one freaking day even? I just want to hang on to this happiness. *Please.*

I find Gram in the art room, cleaning her brushes. Toby is nowhere in sight.

"Why is he always here?" I hiss at Gram.

She looks at me, surprised. "What's wrong with you, Lennie? I called him to help me fix the trellising around my garden and he said he would stop by after he was done at the ranch."

"Can't you call someone else?" My voice is seething with anger and exasperation, and I'm sure I sound completely bonkers to Gram. I am bonkers—I just want to be in love. I want to feel this joy. I don't want to deal with Toby, with sorrow and grief and guilt and DEATH. I'm so sick of DEATH.

Gram does not look pleased. "God, Len, have a heart, the guy's destroyed. It makes him feel better to be around us. We're the only ones who understand. He said as much last night." She is drying her brushes over the sink, snapping her wrist dramatically with each shake. "I asked you once if everything was all right between you two and you said yes. I believed you."

I take a deep breath and let it out slowly, trying to coerce Mr. Hyde back into my body. "It's okay, it's fine, I'm sorry. I don't know what's wrong with me." Then I pull a Gram and walk right out of the room.

I go up to The Sanctum and put on the most obnoxious head-banging punk music I have, a San Francisco band called Filth. I know Toby hates any kind of punk because it was always a point of contention with Bailey, who loved it. He finally won her over to the alt-country he likes, and to Willie Nelson, Hank Williams, and Johnny Cash, his holy trinity, but he never came around to punk.

The music is not helping. I'm jumping up and down on the blue dance rug, banging around to the incessant beat, but I'm too angry to even bang around BECAUSE I DON'T WANT TO DANCE IN THE INNER PUMPKIN SANCTUM ALONE. In one instant, all the rage that I felt moments before for Toby has transferred to Bailey. I don't understand how she could have done this to me, left me here all alone. Especially because she promised me her whole life that she would never EVER disappear like Mom did, that we would always have each other, always, ALWAYS, ALWAYS. "It's the only pact that mattered, Bailey!" I cry out, taking the pillow and pounding it again and again into the bed, until finally, many songs later, I feel a little bit calmer.

I drop on my back on the bed, panting and sweating. How will I survive this missing? How do others do it? People die all the time. Every day. Every hour. There are families all over the world staring at beds that are no longer slept in, shoes that are no longer worn. Families that no longer have to buy a particular cereal, a kind of shampoo. There are people everywhere standing in line at the movies, buying curtains, walking dogs, while inside, their hearts are ripping to shreds. For years. For their whole lives. I don't believe time heals. I don't want it to. If I heal, doesn't that mean I've accepted the world without her?

I remember the notebook then. I get up, turn off Filth, put on a Chopin Nocturne to see if that'll settle me down, and go over to the desk. I take out the notebook, turn to the last page, where there are a few combinations that haven't yet been crossed out. The whole page is combinations of Mom's name with Dickens characters. Paige/Twist, Paige/Fagan, Walker/Havisham, Walker/Oliver/Paige, Pip/Paige.

I turn on the computer, plug in *Paige Twist* and then search through pages of docs, finding nothing that could relate to our mom, then I put in *Paige Dickens* and find some possibilities, but the documents are mostly from high school athletic teams and college alumni magazines, none that could have anything to do with her. I go through more Dickens combinations but don't find even the remotest possibility.

An hour's passed and I've just done a handful of searches. I look back over the pages and pages that Bailey did, and wonder again when she did it all, and where she did it, maybe at the computer lab at the State, because how could I not have noticed her bleary-eyed at this computer for hours on end? It strikes me again how badly she wanted to find Mom, because why else would she have devoted all this time to it? What could have happened in February to take her down this road? I wonder if that was when Toby asked her to marry him. Maybe she wanted Mom to come to the wedding. But Toby said he had asked her right before she died. I need to talk to him.

I go downstairs, apologize to Gram, tell her I've been emotional all day, which is true every freaking day lately. She looks at me, strokes my hair, says, "It's okay, sweet pea, maybe we could go on a walk together tomorrow, talk some—" When will she *get* it? I don't want to talk to her about Bailey, about anything.

When I come out of the house, Toby's standing on a ladder, working on the trellis in the front of the garden. Streamers of gold and pink peel across the sky. The whole yard is glowing with the setting sun, the roses look lit from within, like lanterns.

He looks over at me, exhales dramatically, then climbs slowly down the ladder, leaning against it with arms crossed in front of his chest. "Wanted to say sorry . . . again." He sighs. "I'm half out of my mind lately." His eyes search mine. "You okay?"

"Yeah, except for the half out of my mind part," I say.

He smiles at that, his whole face alighting with kindness and understanding. I relax a little, feel bad for wanting to behead him an hour before.

"I found this notebook in Bailey's desk," I tell him, eager to find out if he knows anything and very eager not to talk or think about yesterday. "It's like she was looking for Mom, but feverishly, Toby, page after page of possible pseudonyms that she must have been putting in search engines. She'd tried every-thing, must have done it around the clock. I don't know where she did it, don't know why she did it . . ."

"Don't know either," he says, his voice trembling slightly. He looks down. Is he hiding something from me?

"The notebook is dated. She started doing this at the end of February—did anything happen then that you know of?"

Toby's bones unhinge and he slides down the trellis, and drops his head into his hands and starts to cry.

What's going on?

I lower to him, kneel in front of him, put my hands on his arms. "Toby," I say gently. "It's okay." I'm stroking his hair with my hand. Fear prickles my neck and arms.

He shakes his head. "It's not okay." He can barely get the words out. "I wasn't ever going to tell you."

"What? What weren't you going to tell me?" My voice comes out shrill, crazy.

"It makes it worse, Len, and I didn't want it to be any harder for you."

"What?" Every hair on my body is on end. I'm really fright-ened now. What could possibly make Bailey's death any worse?

He reaches for my hand, holds it tight in his. "We were going to have a baby." I hear myself gasp. "She was pregnant when she died." No, I think, this can't be. "Maybe she was looking for your mom because of that. The end of February would have been around the time when we found out."

The idea begins to avalanche inside me, gaining speed and mass. My other hand has landed on his shoulder and although I'm looking at his face, I'm watching my sister hold their baby up in the air, making ferret faces at it, watching as she and Toby each take a hand of their child and walk him to the river. Or her. God. I can see in Toby's eyes all that he has been carrying alone, and for the first time since Bailey's death I feel more sorry for someone else than I do for myself. I close my arms around him and rock him. And then, when our eyes meet and we are again there in that helpless house of grief, a place where Bailey can never be and Joe Fontaine does not exist, a place where it's only Toby and me left behind, I kiss him. I kiss him to comfort him, to tell him how sorry I am, to show him I'm here and that I'm alive and so is he. I kiss him because I'm in way over my head and have been for months. I kiss him and keep kissing and holding and caressing him, because for whatever fucked-up reason, that is what I do.

The moment Toby's body stiffens in my arms, I know.

I know, but I don't know who it is.

At first, I think it's Gram, it must be. But it's not.

It's not Big either.

I turn around and there he is, a few yards away, motionless, a statue.

Our eyes hold, and then, he stumbles backward. I jump out of Toby's grasp, find my legs, and rush toward Joe, but he turns away, starts to run.

"Wait, please," I yell out. "Please."

He freezes, his back to me—a silhouette against a sky now burning up, a wildfire racing out of control toward the horizon. I feel like I'm falling down stairs, hurtling and tumbling with no ability to stop. Still, I force myself forward and go to him. I take his hand to try to turn him around, but he rips it away as if my touch disgusts him. Then he's turning, slowly, like he's moving underwater. I wait, scared out of my mind to look at him, to see what I've done. When he finally faces me, his eyes are lifeless, his face like stone. It's as if his marvelous spirit has evacuated his flesh.

Words fly out of my mouth. "It's not like us, I don't feel— it's something else, my sister . . ." *My sister was pregnant*, I'm about to say in explanation, but how would that explain anything? I'm desperate for him to get it, but I don't get it.

"It's not what you think," I say predictably, pathetically.

I watch the rage and hurt erupt simultaneously in his face. "Yes, it *is*. It's *exactly* what I think, it's exactly what I *thought*." He spits his words at me. "How could you . . . I thought you—"

"I do, I do." I'm crying hard now, tears streaming down my face. "You don't understand."

His face is a riot of disappointment. "You're right, I *don't*. Here."

He pulls a piece of paper out of his pocket. "This is what I came to give you." He crumples it up and throws it at me, then turns around and runs as fast as he can away into the falling night.

I bend over and grab the crumpled piece of paper, smooth it out. At the top it says *Part 2: Duet for aforementioned clarinetist and guitarist*. I fold it carefully, put it in my pocket, then sit down on the grass, a heap of bones. I realize I'm in the same exact spot Joe and I kissed last night in the rain. The sky's lost its fury, just some straggling gold wisps steadily being consumed by darkness. I try to hear the melody he wrote for me in my head, but can't. All I hear is him saying: *How could you?*

How could I?

172

Someone might as well roll up the whole sky, pack it away for good.

Soon, there's a hand on my shoulder. Toby. I reach up and rest my hand on his. He squats down on one knee next to me.

"I'm sorry," he says quietly, and a moment later, "I'm going to go, Len." Then just the coldness on my shoulder where his hand had been. I hear his truck start and listen to the engine hum as it follows Joe down the road.

Just me. Or so I think until I look up at the house to see Gram silhouetted in the doorway like Toby was last night. I don't know how long she's been there, don't know what she's seen and what she hasn't. She swings open the door, walks to the end of the porch, leans on the railing with both hands.

"Come in, sweet pea."

I don't tell her what happened with Joe, just as I never told her what has been going on with Toby. Yet I can see in her mournful eyes as she looks into mine that she most likely already knows it all.

"One day, you'll talk to me again." She takes my hands. "I miss you, you know. So does Big."

"She was pregnant," I whisper.

Gram nods.

"She told you?"

"The autopsy."

"They were engaged," I say. This, I can tell from her face, she didn't know.

She encloses me in her arms and I stay in her safe and sound embrace and let the tears rise and rise and fall and fall until her dress is soaked with them and night has filled the house.

chapter 25

I DO NOT go to the altar of the desk to talk to Bailey on the mountaintop. I do not even turn on the light. I go straight into bed with all my clothes on and pray for sleep. It doesn't come.

What comes is shame, weeks of it, waves of it, rushing through me in quick hot flashes like nausea, making me groan into my pillow. The lies and half-truths and abbreviations I told and didn't tell Joe tackle and hold me down until I can hardly breathe. How could I have hurt him like this, done to him just what Genevieve did? All the love I have for him clobbers around in my body. My chest aches. All of me aches. He looked like a completely different person. He is a different person. Not the one who loved me.

I see Joe's face, then Bailey's, the two of them looming above me with only three words on their lips: *How could you?*

I have no answer.

I'm sorry, I write with my finger on the sheets over and over until I can't stand it anymore and flip on the light.

But the light brings actual nausea and with it all the moments with my sister that will now remain unlived: holding her baby in my arms. Teaching her child to play the clarinet. Just getting older together day by day. All the future we will not have rips and retches out of me into the garbage pail I am crouched over until there's nothing left inside, nothing but me in this ghastly orange room.

And that's when it hits.

Without the harbor and mayhem of Toby's arms, the sublime distraction of Joe's, there's only me.

Me, like a small seashell with the loneliness of the whole ocean roaring invisibly within.

Me.

Without.

Bailey.

Always.

I throw my head into my pillow and scream into it as if my soul itself is being ripped in half, because it is.

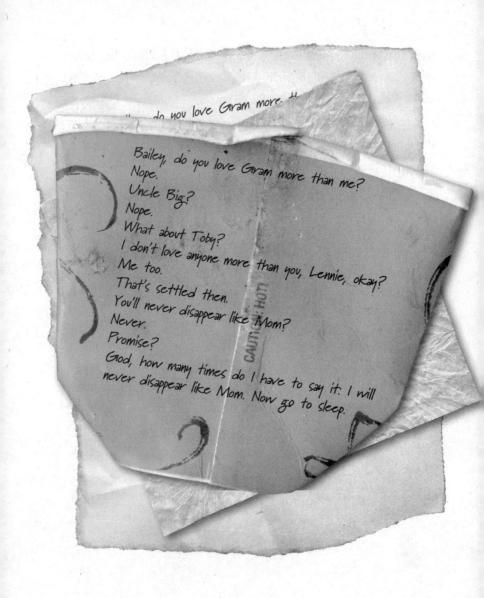

do you love Gram more. H

Bailey, do you love Gram more than me?
Nope.
Uncle Big?
Nope.
What about Toby?
I don't love anyone more than you, Lennie, okay?
Me too.
That's settled then.
You'll never disappear like Mom?
Never.
Promise?
God, how many times do I have to say it. I will
never disappear like Mom. Now go to sleep.

(Found on a to-go cup, Rain River)
(Found on a lollipop wrapper in the parking lot, Clover High)
(Found on a piece of paper in a trash can, Clover Public Library)

part
two

Len, where is she tonight?

I was sleeping.

C'mon, Len.

Okay, India climbing in the Himalayas.

We did that one last week.

You start then.

All right. She's in Spain. Barcelona. A scarf covering her head, sitting by the water, drinking sangria, with a man named Pablo.

Are they in love?

Yes.

But she will leave him come morning.

Yes.

She'll wake before dawn, sneak her suitcase out from under the bed, put on a red wig, a green scarf, a yellow dress, white pumps. She'll catch the first train out.

Will she leave a note?

No.

She never does.

No.

She'll sit on the train and stare out the window at the sea. A woman will sit next to her and they'll strike up a conversation. The woman will ask her if she has any children, and she'll say, "No."

Wrong, Len. She'll say, "I'm on the way to see my girls right now."

(Found on a piece of paper stuck between two rocks at Flying Man's)

chapter 26

I WAKE UP later with my face mashed into the pillow. I lean up on my elbows and look out the window. The stars have bewitched the sky of darkness. It's a shimmery night. I open the window, and the sound of the river rides the rose-scented breeze right into our room. I'm shocked to realize that I feel a little better, like I've slept my way to a place with a little more air. I push away thoughts of Joe and Toby, take one more deep breath of the flowers, the river, the world, then I get up, take the garbage pail into the bathroom, clean it and myself, and when I return head straight over to Bailey's desk.

I turn on the computer, pull out the notebook from the top desk drawer where I keep it now, and decide to continue from where I left off the other day. I need to do something for my sister and all I can think to do is to find our mother for her.

I start plugging in the remaining combinations in Bailey's notebook. I can understand why becoming a mother herself would have compelled Bailey to search for Mom like this. It makes sense to me somehow. But there is something else I suspect. In a far cramped corner of my mind, there is a dresser, and in that dresser there is a thought crammed into the back of the bottom-most drawer. I know it's there because I put it there where I wouldn't have to look at it. But tonight I open that creaky drawer and face what I've always believed, and that is this: Bailey had it too. Restlessness stampeded through my sister her whole life, informing everything she did from running cross-country to changing personas on stage. I've always thought that was the reason behind why she wanted to find our mother. And I know it was the reason I never wanted her to. I bet this is why she didn't tell me she was looking for Mom like this. She knew I'd try to stop her. I didn't want our mother to reveal to Bailey a way out of our lives.

One explorer is enough for any family.

But I can make up for that now by finding Mom. I put combination after combination into a mix of search engines. After an hour, however, I'm ready to toss the computer out the window. It's futile. I've gotten all the way to the end of Bailey's notebook and have started one of my own using words and symbols from Blake poems. I can see in the notebook that Bailey was working her way through Mom's box for clues to the pseudonym. She'd used references from *Oliver Twist, Siddhartha, On the Road,* but hadn't gotten to William Blake yet. I have his book of poems open and I'm combining words like *Tiger* or *Poison Tree* or *Devil* with *Paige* or *Walker* and the words *chef, cook, restaurant,* thinking as Gram did that that's how she might make money while traveling, but it's useless. After yet another hour of no possible matches, I tell the mountaintop Bailey in the explorer picture, I'm not giving up, I just need a break, and head downstairs to see if anyone is still awake.

Big's on the porch, sitting in the middle of the love seat like it's a throne. I squeeze in beside him.

"Unbelievable," he murmurs, goosing my knee. "Can't remember the last time you joined me for a nighttime chat. I was just thinking that I might play hooky tomorrow, see if a new lady-friend of mine wants to have lunch with me in a restaurant. I'm sick of dining in trees." He twirls his mustache a little too dreamily.

Uh-oh.

"Remember," I warn. "You're not allowed to ask anyone to marry you until you've been with her a whole year. Those were your rules after your last divorce." I reach over and tug on his mustache, add for effect, "Your fifth divorce."

"I know, I know," he says. "But boy do I miss proposing, nothing so romantic. Make sure you try it, at least once, Len—it's skydiving with your feet on the ground." He laughs in a tinkley way that might be called a giggle if he weren't thirty feet tall. He's told Bailey and me this our whole lives. In fact, until Sarah went into a diatribe about the inequities of marriage in sixth grade, I had no idea proposing wasn't always considered an equal-opportunity endeavor.

I look out over the small yard where hours before Joe left me, probably forever. I think for a minute about telling Big that Joe probably won't be around anymore, but I can't face breaking it to him. He's almost as attached to him as I am. And anyway, I want to talk to him about something else.

"Big?"

"Hmmm?"

"Do you really believe in this restless gene stuff?"

He looks at me, surprised, then says, "Sounds like a fine load of crap, doesn't it?"

I think about Joe's incredulous response today in the woods, about my own doubts, about everybody's, always. Even in this town where free-spiritedness is a fundamental family value, the few times I've ever told anyone my mother took off when I was one year old to live a life of freedom and itinerancy, they looked like they wanted to commit me to a nice rubber room somewhere. Even so, to me, this Walker family gospel never seemed all that unlikely. Anyone who's read a novel or walked down the street or stepped through the front door of my house knows that people are all kinds of weird, especially my people, I think, glancing at Big, who does God knows what in trees, marries perennially, tries to resurrect dead bugs, smokes more pot than the whole eleventh grade, and looks like he should reign over some fairy tale kingdom. So why wouldn't his sister be an adventurer, a blithe spirit? Why shouldn't my mother be like the hero in so many stories, the brave one who left? Like Luke Skywalker, Gulliver, Captain Kirk, Don Quixote, Odysseus. Not quite real to me, okay, but mythical and magical, not unlike my favorite saints or the characters in novels I hang on to perhaps a little too tightly.

"I don't know," I answer honestly. "Is it all crap?"

Big doesn't say anything for a long time, just twirls away at his mustache, thinking. "Nah, it's all about classification, know what I mean?" I don't, but won't interrupt. "Lots of things run through families, right? And this tendency, whatever it is, for whatever reason, runs through ours. Could be worse, we could have depression or alcoholism or bitterness. Our afflicted kin just hit the road—"

"I think Bailey had it, Big," I say, the words tumbling out of me before I can catch them, revealing just how much I might actually believe in it after all. "I've always thought so."

"Bailey?" His brow creases. "Nah, don't see it. In fact, I've never seen a girl so relieved as when she got rejected from that school in New York City."

"Relieved?" Now *this* is a fine load of crap! "Are you kidding? She *always* wanted to go to Juilliard. She worked sooooooooooo hard. It was her dream!"

Big studies my burning face, then says gently, "Whose dream, Len?" He positions his hands like he's playing an invisible clarinet. "Because the only one I used to see working sooooooooooo hard around here was you."

God.

Marguerite's trilling voice fills my head: *Your playing is ravishing. You work on the nerves, Lennie, you go to Juilliard.*

Instead, I quit.

Instead, I shoved and crammed myself into a jack-in-the-box of my own making.

"C'mere." Big opens his arm like a giant wing and closes it over me as I snuggle in beside him and try not to think about how terrified I'd felt each time Marguerite mentioned Juilliard, each time I'd imagine myself—

"Dreams change," Big says. "I think hers did."

Dreams change, yes, that makes sense, but I didn't know dreams could hide inside a person.

He wraps his other arm around me too and I sink into the bear of him, breathing in the thick scent of pot that infuses his clothes. He squeezes me tight, strokes my hair with his enormous hand. I'd forgotten how comforting Big is, a human furnace. I peek up at his face. A tear runs down his cheek.

After a few minutes, he says, "Bails might have had some ants in the pants, like most people do, but I think she was more like me, and you lately, for that matter—*a slave to love*." He smiles at me like he's inducting me into a secret society. "Maybe it's those damn roses, and for the record, those I believe in: hook, line, and sinker. They're deadly on the heart—I swear, we're like lab rats breathing in that aroma all season long . . ." He twirls his mustache, seems to have forgotten what he was saying. I wait, remembering that he's stoned. The rose scent ribbons through the air between us. I breathe it in, thinking of Joe, knowing full well that it's not the roses that have spurred this love in my heart, but the boy, such an amazing boy. *How could I?*

Far away, an owl calls—a hollow, lonesome sound that makes me feel the same.

Big continues talking as if no time has passed. "Nah, it wasn't Bails who had it—"

"What do you mean?" I ask, straightening up.

He stops twirling. His face has grown serious. "Gram was different when we were growing up," he says. "If anyone else had it, she did."

"Gram hardly leaves the neighborhood," I say, not following.

He chuckles. "I know. Guess that's how much I don't believe in the gene though. I always thought my mother had it. I thought she just bottled it up somehow, trapped herself in that art room for weeks on end, and threw it onto those canvases."

"Well, if that's the case, why didn't *my mother* just bottle it up, then?" I try to keep my voice down but I feel suddenly infuriated. "Why'd she have to leave if Gram just had to make some paintings?"

"I don't know, honey, maybe Paige had it worse."

"Had *what* worse?"

"I don't know!" And I can tell he doesn't know, that he's as frustrated and bewildered as I am. "Whatever makes a woman leave two little kids, her brother, and her mother, and not come back for sixteen years. That's what! I mean, we call it wanderlust, other families might not be so kind."

"What would other families call it?" I ask. He's never intimated anything like this before about Mom. Is it all a cover story for crazy? Was she really and truly out of her tree?

"Doesn't matter what anyone else would call it, Len," he says. "This is *our* story to tell."

This is our story to tell. He says it in his Ten Commandments way and it hits me that way: profoundly. You'd think for all the reading I do, I would have thought about this before, but I haven't. I've never once thought about the interpretative, the storytelling aspect of life, of my life. I always felt like I was in a story, yes, but not like I was the author of it, or like I had any say in its telling whatsoever.

You can tell your story any way you damn well please.

It's your solo.

chapter 27

This is the secret I kept from you, Bails,
from myself too:
I think I liked that Mom was gone,
that she could be anybody,
anywhere,
doing anything.
I liked that she was our invention,
a woman living
on the last page of the story
with only what we imagined
spread out before her.
I liked that she was ours, alone.

(Found on a page ripped out of Wuthering Heights, *spiked
on a branch, in the woods)*

JOELESSNESS SETTLES OVER the morning like a pall. Gram and I are slumped spineless over the kitchen table, staring off in opposite directions.

When I got back to The Sanctum last night, I put Bailey's notebook into the carton with the others and closed up the box. Then I returned St. Anthony to the mantel in front of The Half Mom. I'm not sure how I'm going to find our mother, but I know it isn't going to be on the Internet. All night, I thought about what Big said. It's possible no one in this family is quite who I believed, especially me. I'm pretty sure he hit the jackpot with me.

And maybe with Bailey too. Maybe he's right and she didn't have it—whatever *it* is. Maybe what my sister wanted was to stay here and get married and have a family.

Maybe that was her color of extraordinary.

"Bailey had all these secrets," I say to Gram.

"Seems to run in the family," she replies with a tired sigh.

I want to ask her what she means, remembering what Big said about her too last night, but can't because he's just stomped in, dressed for work after all, a dead ringer for Paul Bunyan. He takes one look at us and says, "Who died?" Then stops mid-step, shakes his head. "I *cannot* believe I just said that." He knocks on his head nobody-home-style. Then he looks around. "Hey, where's Joe this morning?"

Gram and I both look down.

"What?" he asks.

"I don't think he'll be around anymore," I say.

"Really?" Big shrinks from Gulliver to Lilliputian before my eyes. "Why, honey?"

I feel tears brimming. "I don't know."

Thankfully, he lets it drop and leaves the kitchen to check on the bugs.

The whole way to the deli I think of the crazy French violinist Genevieve with whom Joe was in love and how he never spoke to her again. I think of his assessment of horn players as all-or-nothing types. I think how I had all of him and now I'm going to have none of him unless I can somehow make him understand what happened last night and all the other nights with Toby. But how? I already left two messages on his cell this morning and even called the Fontaine house once. It went like this:

Lennie (shaking in her flip-flops): Is Joe home?

Marcus: Wow, Lennie, shocker . . . brave girl.

Lennie (looks down to see scarlet letter emblazoned on her T-shirt): Is he around?

Marcus: Nope, left early.

Marcus and Lennie: Awkward Silence

Marcus: He's taking it pretty hard. I've never seen him so upset about a girl before, about anything, actually . . .

Lennie (close to tears): Will you tell him I called?

Marcus: Will do.

Marcus and Lennie: Awkward Silence

Marcus (tentative): Lennie, if you like him, well, don't give up.

Dial tone.

And that's the problem, I madly like him. I make an SOS call to Sarah to come down to the deli during my shift.

NORMALLY, I AM The Zen Lasagna Maker. After three and a half summers, four shifts a week, eight lasagnas a shift: 896 lasagnas to date—done the math—I have it down. It's my meditation. I separate noodle after noodle from the glutinous lump that comes out of the refrigerator with the patience and precision of a surgeon. I plunge my hands into the ricotta and spices and fold the mixture until fluffy as a cloud. I slice the cheese into cuts as thin as paper. I spice the sauce until it sings. And then I layer it all together into a mountain of perfection. My lasagnas are sublime. Today, however, my lasagnas are not singing. After nearly chopping off a finger on the slicer, dropping the glutinous lump of noodles onto the floor, overcooking the new batch of pasta, dumping a truck-load of salt into the tomato sauce, Maria has me on moron-detail stuffing cannolis with a blunt object while she makes the lasagnas by my side. I'm cornered. It's too early for customers, so it's just us trapped inside the *National Enquirer*—Maria's the town crier, chatters nonstop about the lewd and lascivious goings-on in Clover, including, of course, the arboreal escapades of the town Romeo: my uncle Big.

"How's he doing?"

"You know."

"Everyone's been asking about him. He used to stop at The Saloon every night after he returned to earth from the tree-tops." Maria's stirring a vat of sauce beside me, a witch at her cauldron, as I try to cover the fact that I've broken yet another pastry shell. I'm a lovesick mess with a dead sister. "The place isn't the same without him. He holding up?" Maria turns to me, brushes a dark curl of hair from her perspiring brow, notes with irritation the growing pile of broken cannoli shells.

"He's just okay, like the rest of us," I say. "He's been coming home after work." I don't add, *And smoking three bowls of weed to numb the pain.* I keep looking up at the door, imagining Joe sailing through it.

"I did hear he had a treetop visitor the other day," Maria singsongs, back to everyone else's business.

"No way," I say, knowing full well that this is most likely the case.

"Yup. Dorothy Rodriguez, you know her, right? She teaches second grade. Last night at the bar, I heard that she rode up with him in the barrel high into the canopy, and *you know* . . ." She winks at me. "They picnicked."

I groan. "Maria, it's my uncle, please."

She laughs, then blathers on about a dozen more Clover trysts until at last Sarah floats in dressed like a fabric shop specializing in paisley. She stands in the doorway, puts her arms up, and makes peace signs with both hands.

"Sarah! If you don't look like the spitting image of me twenty years—sheesh, almost thirty years ago," Maria says, heading into the walk-in cooler. I hear the door thump behind her.

"Why the SOS?" Sarah says to me. The summer day has followed her in. Her hair is still wet from swimming. When I called earlier she and Luke were at Flying Man's "working" on some song. I can smell the river on her as she hugs me over the counter.

"Are you wearing toe rings?" I ask to postpone my confession a little longer.

"Of course." She lifts her kaleidoscopic pantalooned leg into the air to show me.

"Impressive."

She hops on the stool across the counter from where I'm working, throws her book on the counter. It's by a Hélène Cixous. "Lennie, these French feminists are so much cooler than those stupid existentialists. I'm so into this concept of *jouissance*, it means transcendent rapture, which I'm sure you and Joe know all about—" She plays the air with invisible sticks.

"Knew." I take a deep breath. Prepare for the *I told you so* of the century.

Her face is stuck somewhere between disbelief and shock. "What do you mean, *knew*?"

"I mean, *knew*."

"But yesterday . . ." She's shaking her head, trying to catch up to the news. "You guys frolicked off from practice making the rest of us sick on account of the indisputable, irrefutable, unmistakable true love that was seeping out of every pore of your attached-at-the-hip bodies. Rachel nearly exploded. It was so beautiful." And then it dawns on her. "You didn't."

"Please don't have a cow or a horse or an aardvark or any other animal about it. No morality police, okay?"

"Okay, promise. Now tell me you didn't. I told you I had a bad feeling."

"I did." I cover my face with my hands. "Joe saw us kissing last night."

"You've got to be kidding?"

I shake my head.

As if on cue, a gang of miniature Toby skate rats whiz by on their boards, tearing apart the sidewalk, quiet as a 747.

"But why, Len? Why would you do that?" Her voice is surprisingly without judgment. She really wants to know. "You don't love Toby."

"No."

"And you're dementoid over Joe."

"Totally."

"Then why?" This is the million-dollar question.

I stuff two cannolis, deciding how to phrase it. "I think it has to do with how much we both love Bailey, as crazy as that sounds."

Sarah stares at me. "You're right, that does sound crazy. Bailey would *kill* you."

My heart races wild in my chest. "I know. But Bailey is *dead,* Sarah. And Toby and I don't know how to deal with it. And that's what happened. Okay?" I've never yelled at Sarah in my life and that was definitely approaching a yell. But I'm furious at her for saying what I know is true. Bailey *would* kill me, and it just makes me want to yell at Sarah more, which I do. "What should I do? Penance? Should I mortify the flesh, soak my hands in lye, rub pepper into my face like St. Rose? Wear a hair shirt?"

Her eyes bug out. "Yes, that's exactly what I think you should do!" she cries, but then her mouth twitches a little. "That's right, wear a hair shirt! A hair hat! A whole hair ensemble!" Her face is scrunching up. She bleats out, "St. Lennie," and then folds in half in hysterics. Followed by me, all our anger morphing into uncontrollable spectacular laughter—we're both bent over trying to breathe and it feels so great even though I might die from lack of oxygen.

"I'm sorry," I say between gasps.

She manages out, "No, me. I promised I wouldn't get like that. Felt good though to let you have it."

"Likewise," I squeal.

Maria sweeps back in, apron loaded with tomatoes, peppers, and onions, takes one look at us, and says, "You and your crazy cohort get out of here. Take a break."

Sarah and I drop onto our bench in front of the deli. The street's coming to life with sunburned couples from San Francisco stumbling out of B and Bs, swaddled in black, looking for pancakes or inner tubes or weed.

Sarah shakes her head as she lights up. I've confounded her. A hard thing to do. I know she'd still like to holler: *What in flying foxes were you thinking, Lennie?* but she doesn't.

"Okay, the matter at hand is getting that Fontaine boy back," she says calmly.

"Exactly."

"Clearly making him jealous is out of the question."

"Clearly." I sink my chin into my palms, look up at the thousand-year-old redwood across the street—it's peering down at me in consternation. It wants to kick my sorry newbie-to-the-earth ass.

"I know!" Sarah exclaims. "You'll seduce him." She lowers her eyelids, puckers her lips into a pout around her cigarette, inhales deeply, and then exhales a perfect smoke blob. "Seduction always works. I can't even think of one movie where it doesn't work, can you?"

"You can't be serious. He's so hurt and pissed. He's not even speaking to me, I called three times today . . . and it's me, not you, remember? I don't know how to seduce anyone." I'm miserable—I keep seeing Joe's face, stony and lifeless, like it was last night. If ever there was a face impervious to seduction, it's that one.

Sarah twirls her scarf with one hand, smokes with the other. "You don't have to *do* anything, Len, just show up to band practice tomorrow looking F-I-N-E, looking *irresistible*." She says *irresistible* like it has ten syllables. "His raging hormones and wild passion for you will do the rest."

"Isn't that incredibly superficial, Ms. French Feminist?"

"*Au contraire, ma petite.* These feminists are all about celebrating the body, its *langage*." She whips the scarf in the air. "Like I said, they're all after *jouissance*. As a means, of course, of subverting the dominant patriarchal paradigm and the white male literary canon, but we can get into that another time." She flicks her cigarette into the street. "Anyway, it can't hurt, Len. And it'll be fun. For me, that is . . ." A cloud of sadness crosses her face.

We exchange a glance that holds weeks of unsaid words.

"I just didn't think you could understand me anymore," I blurt out. I'd felt like a different person and Sarah had felt like the same old one, and I bet Bailey had felt similarly about me, and she was right to. Sometimes you just have to soldier through in your own private messy way.

"I couldn't understand," Sarah exclaims. "Not really. Felt—*feel* so useless, Lennie. And man, those grief books suck, so formulaic, total hundred percent dreck."

"Thanks," I say. "For reading them."

She looks down at her feet. "I miss her too." Until this

moment, it hadn't occurred to me she might've read those books for herself also. But of course. She revered Bailey. I've left her to grieve all on her own. I don't know what to say, so I reach across the bench and hug her. Hard.

A car honks with a bunch of hooting doofuses from Clover High in it. Way to ruin the moment. We disengage, Sarah waving her feminist book at them like a religious zealot—it makes me laugh.

When they pass, she takes another cigarette out of her pack, then gently touches my knee with it. "This Toby thing, I just don't get it." She lights the smoke, keeps shaking the match after it's out, like a metronome. "Were you competitive with Bailey? You guys never seemed like those King Lear type of sisters. I never thought so anyway."

"No we weren't. No . . . but . . . I don't know, I ask myself the same thing—"

I've crashed head-on into that something Big said last night, that awfully huge something.

"Remember that time we watched the Kentucky Derby?" I ask Sarah, not sure if this will make sense to anyone but me.

She looks at me like I'm crazy. "Yeah, uh, why?"

"Did you notice the racehorses had these companion ponies that didn't leave their sides?"

"I guess."

"Well, I think that was us, me and Bails."

She pauses a minute, exhales a long plume of smoke, before she says, "You were both racehorses, Len." I can tell she doesn't believe it though, that she's just trying to be nice.

I shake my head. "C'mon, be real, I wasn't. God, no way. I'm not." And it's been no one's doing but my own. Bailey went as crazy as Gram when I quit my lessons.

"Do you want to be?" Sarah asks.

"Maybe," I say, unable to quite manage a yes.

She smiles, then in silence, we both watch car after car creep along, most of them filled with ridiculously bright rubber river gear: giraffe boats, elephant canoes, and the like. Finally she says, "Being a companion pony must suck. Not metaphorically, I mean, you know, if you're a horse. Think about it. Self-sacrifice twenty-four/seven, no glory, no glamour . . . they should start a union, have their own Companion Pony Derby."

"A good new cause for you."

"No. My new cause is turning St. Lennon into a femme fatale." She smirks. "C'mon, Len, say yes."

Her *C'mon, Len* reminds me of Bails, and the next thing I know, I hear myself saying, "Okay, fine."

"It'll be subtle, I promise."

"Your strong suit."

She laughs. "Yeah, you're so screwed."

It's a hopeless idea, but I have no other. I have to do something, and Sarah's right, looking sexy, assuming I *can* look sexy, can't hurt, can it? I mean it is true that seduction hardly ever fails in movies, especially French ones. So I defer to Sarah's expertise, experience, to the concept of *jouissance,* and Operation Seduction is officially under way.

I HAVE CLEAVAGE. Melons. Bazumbas. Bodacious tatas. Handfuls of bosom pouring out of a minuscule black dress that I'm going to wear in broad daylight to band practice. I can't stop looking down. I'm stacked, a buxom babe. My scrawny self is positively zaftig. How can a bra possibly do this? Note to the physicists: Matter can indeed be created. Not to mention that I'm in platforms, so I look nine feet tall, and my lips are red as pomegranates.

Sarah and I have ducked into a classroom next to the music room.

"Are you sure, Sarah?" I don't know how I got myself into this ridiculous *I Love Lucy* episode.

"Never been more sure of anything. No guy will be able to resist you. I'm a little worried Mr. James won't survive it though."

"All right. Let's go," I say.

The way I get down the hallway is to pretend I'm someone else. Someone in a movie, a black-and-white French movie where everyone smokes and is mysterious and alluring. I'm a woman, not a girl, and I'm going to seduce a man. Who am I kidding? I freak out and run back to the classroom. Sarah follows, my bridesmaid.

"Lennie, c'mon." She's exasperated.

There it is again, *Lennie, c'mon*. I try again. This time I think of Bailey, the way she sashayed, making the ground work for her, and I glide effortlessly through the door of the music room.

I notice right away that Joe isn't there, but there's still time until rehearsal starts, like fifteen seconds, and he's always early, but maybe something held him up.

Fourteen seconds: Sarah was right, all the boys are staring at me like I've popped out of a centerfold. Rachel almost drops her clarinet.

Thirteen, twelve, eleven: Mr. James throws his arms up in celebration. "Lennie, you look ravishing!" I make it to my seat.

Ten, nine: I put my clarinet together but don't want to get lipstick all over my mouthpiece. I do anyway.

Eight, seven: Tuning.

Six, five: Tuning still.

Four, three: I turn around. Sarah shakes her head, mouths *unfreakingbelievable*.

Two, one: The announcement I now am expecting. "Let's begin class. Sorry to say we've lost our only trumpet player for the festival. Joe's going to perform with his brothers instead. Take out your pencils, I have changes."

I drop my glamorous head into my hands, hear Rachel say, "I told you he was out of your league, Lennie."

chapter 28

(Found on the back of a flyer on the sidewalk, Main Street)

There once was a girl who found herself dead.
She peered over the ledge of heaven
and saw that back on earth
her sister missed her too much,
was way too sad,
so she crossed some paths
that would not have crossed,
took some moments in her hand
shook them up
and spilled them like dice
over the living world.
It worked.
The boy with the guitar collided
with her sister.
"There you go, Len," she whispered. "The rest is up to you."

"MAY THE FORCE be with you," Sarah says, and sends me on my way, which is up the hill to the Fontaines' in aforementioned black cocktail dress, platforms, and bodacious tatas. The whole way up I repeat a mantra: *I am the author of my story and I can tell it any way I want. I am a solo artist. I am a racehorse.* Yes, this puts me into the major freaker category of human, but it does the trick and gets me up the hill, because fifteen minutes later I am looking up at Maison Fontaine, the dry summer grass crackling all around me, humming with hidden insects, which reminds me: How in the world does Rachel know what happened with Joe?

When I get to the driveway, I see a man dressed all in black with a shock of white hair, waving his arms around like a dervish, shouting in French at a stylish woman in a black dress (hers fits her) who looks equally peeved. She is hissing back at him in English. I definitely do not want to walk past those two panthers, so I sneak around the far side of the property and then duck under the enormous willow tree that reigns like a queen over the yard, the thick drapes of leaves falling like a shimmering green ball gown around the ancient trunk and branches, creating the perfect skulk den.

I need a moment to bolster my nerve, so I pace around in my new glimmery green apartment trying to figure out what I'm going to actually say to Joe, a point both Sarah and I forgot to consider.

That's when I hear it: clarinet music drifting out from the house, the melody Joe wrote for me. My heart does a hopeful flip. I walk over to the side of Maison Fontaine that abuts the tree and, still concealed by a drape of leaves, I stand up on tiptoe and see through the open window a sliver of Joe playing a bass clarinet in the living room.

And thus begins my life as a spy.

I tell myself, after this song, I will ring the doorbell and literally face the music. But then, he plays the melody again and again and the next thing I know I'm lying on my back listening to the amazing music, reaching into Sarah's purse for a pen, which I find as well as a scrap of paper. I jot down a poem, spike it with a stick into the ground. The music is making me rapturous; I slip back into that kiss, again drinking the sweet rain off his lips—

To be rudely interrupted by DougFred's exasperated voice. "Dude, you're driving me berserk—this same song over and over again, for two days now, I can't deal. We're all going to jump off the bridge right after you. Why don't you just talk to her?" I jump up and scurry over to the window: Harriet the Spy in drag. *Please say you'll talk to her*, I mind-beam to Joe.

"No way," he says.

"Joe, it's pathetic . . . c'mon."

Joe's voice is pinched, tight. "I *am so* pathetic. She was lying to me the whole time . . . just like Genevieve, just like Dad to Mom for that matter . . ."

Ugh. Ugh. Ugh. Boy, did I blow it.

"Whatever, already, with all of that—shit's complicated sometimes, man." *Hallelujah, DougFred.*

"Not for me."

"Just get your horn, we need to practice."

Still concealed under the tree, I listen to Joe, Marcus, and DougFred practicing: It goes like this, three notes, then a cell phone rings: Marcus: *Hey Ami*, then five minutes later, another ring: Marcus: *Salut Sophie*, then DougFred: *Hey Chloe*, then fifteen minutes later: *Hi Nicole*. These guys are Clover catnip. I remember how the phone rang pretty much continually the evening I spent here. Finally, Joe says: *Turn off the cell phones or we won't even get through a song*—but just as he finishes the sentence, his own cell goes off and his brothers laugh. I hear him say, *Hey Rachel*. And that's the end of me. *Hey Rachel* in a voice that sounds happy to hear from her, like he was expecting the call, waiting for it even.

I think of St. Wilgefortis, who went to sleep beautiful and woke up with a full beard and mustache, and wish that fate on Rachel. Tonight.

Then I hear: *You were totally right. The Throat Singers of Tuva are awesome.*

Call 911.

Okay, calm down, Lennie. Stop pacing. Don't think about him batting his eyelashes at Rachel Brazile! Grinning at her, kissing her, making her feel like she's part sky . . . *What have I done?* I lie down on my back in the grass under the umbrella of trembling sun-lit leaves. I'm leveled by a phone call. How must it have been for him to actually see me kiss Toby?

I suck, there's no other way to put it.

There's also no other way to put this: I'm so freaking in love—it's just blaring every which way inside me, like some psycho opera.

But back to BITCHZILLA!?

Be rational, I tell myself, systematic, think of all the many innocuous unromantic reasons she could be calling him. I can't think of one, though I'm so consumed with trying I don't even hear the truck pull up, just a door slamming. I get up, peek out through the thick curtain of leaves, and almost pass out to see Toby walking toward the front door. WTF-asaurus? He hesitates before ringing the bell, takes a deep breath, then presses the button, waits, then presses it again. He steps back, looks toward the living room, where the music is now blasting, then knocks hard. The music stops and I hear the pounding of feet, then watch the door open and hear Toby say: "Is Joe here?"

Gulp.

Next, I hear Joe still in the living room: "What's his problem? I didn't want to talk to him yesterday and I don't want to talk to him today."

Marcus is back in the living room. "Just talk to the guy."

"No."

But Joe must have gone to the door, because I hear muffled words and see Toby's mouth moving, although he's quieted down too much for me to make out the words.

I don't plan what happens next. It just happens. I just happen to have that stupid it's-my-story-I'm-a-racehorse mantra back on repeat in my head and so I somehow decide that whatever is going to happen, good or bad, I don't want to be hiding in a tree when it does. I muster all my courage and part the curtain of leaves.

The first thing I notice is the sky, so full of blue and the kind of brilliant white clouds that make you ecstatic to have eyes. Nothing can go wrong under this sky, I think as I make my way across the lawn, trying not to wobble in my platforms. The Fontaine panther-parents are nowhere in sight; probably they took their hissing match into the barn. Toby must hear my footsteps; he turns around.

"Lennie?"

The door swings open and three Fontaines pile out like they've been stuffed in a car.

Marcus speaks first: "Va va va voom."

Joe's mouth drops open.

Toby's too, for that matter.

"Holy shit" comes out of DougFred's perpetually deranged-with-glee face. The four of them are like a row of dumbfounded ducks. I'm acutely aware of how short my dress is, how tight it is across my chest, how wild my hair is, how red my lips are. I might die. I want to wrap my arms around my body. For the rest of my life, I'm going to leave the femme fatale-ing to other femmes. All I want is to flee, but I don't want them to stare at my butt as I fly into the woods in this tiny piece of fabric masquerading as a dress. Wait a second here—one by one, I take in their idiotic faces. Was Sarah right? Might this work? Could guys be this simple-minded?

Marcus is ebullient. "One hot tamale, John Lennon."

Joe glares at him. "Shut the hell up, Marcus." He has regained his composure and rage. Nope, Joe is definitely not this simple-minded. I know immediately this was a bad, bad move.

"What's wrong with you two?" he says to Toby and me, throwing up his arms in a perfect mimicry of his father's dervishness.

He pushes past his brothers and Toby, jumps off the stoop, comes up to me, so close that I can smell his fury. "Don't you get it? What you did? It's done, Lennie, we're done." Joe's beautiful lips, the ones that kissed me and whispered in my hair, they are twisting and contorting around words I hate. The ground beneath me begins to tilt. People don't really faint, do they? "Get it, because I mean it. It's ruined. *Everything* is."

I'm mortified. I'm going to kill Sarah. And what a total companion-pony move on my part. I knew this wouldn't work. There was no way he was going to toss aside this behemoth betrayal because I squeezed myself into this ridiculously small dress. How could I be so stupid?

And it's just dawned on me that I might be the author of my own story, but so is everyone else the author of their own stories, and sometimes, like now, there's no overlap.

He's walking away from me. I don't care that there are six pairs of eyes and ears on us. He can't leave before I have a chance to say something, have a chance to make him understand what happened, how I feel about him. I grab the bottom of his T-shirt. He snaps around, flings my hand away, meets my eyes. I don't know what he sees in them, but he softens a little.

I watch some of the rage slip off of him as he looks at me. Without it, he looks unnerved and vulnerable, like a small disheartened boy. It makes me ache with tenderness. I want to touch his beautiful face. I look at his hands; they are shaking.

As is all of me.

He's waiting for me to speak. But I realize the perfect thing to say must be in another girl's mind, because it's not in mine. Nothing is in mine.

"I'm sorry," I manage out.

"I don't care," he says, his voice cracking a little. He looks down at the ground. I follow his gaze, see his bare feet sticking out of jeans; they are long and thin and monkey-toed. I've never seen his feet out of shoes and socks before. They're perfectly simian—toes so long he could play the piano with them.

"Your feet," I say, before I realize it. "I've never seen them before."

My moronic words drum in the air between us, and for a split second, I know he wants to laugh, wants to reach out and pull me to him, wants to tease me about saying something so ridiculous when he's about to murder me. I can see this in his face as if his thoughts were scribbled across it. But then all that gets wiped away as quickly as it came, and what's left is the unwieldy hurt in his unbatting eyes, his grinless mouth. He will never forgive me.

I took the joy out of the most joyful person on planet Earth.

"I'm so sorry," I say. "I—"

"God, stop saying that." His hands swoop around me like lunatic bats. I've reignited his rage. "It doesn't matter to me that you're sorry. You just don't get it." He whips around and bolts into the house before I can say another word.

Marcus shakes his head and sighs, then follows his brother inside with DougFred in tow.

I stand there with Joe's words still scorching my skin, thinking what a terrible idea it was to come up here, in this tiny dress, these skyscraping heels. I wipe the siren song off my lips. I'm disgusted with myself. I didn't ask for his forgiveness, didn't explain a thing, didn't tell him that he is the most amazing thing that's ever happened to me, that I love him, that he's the only one for me. Instead, I talked about his feet. *His feet.*

Talk about choking under pressure. And then I remember *Hey Rachel,* which explodes a Molotov cocktail of jealousy into my misery, completing the dismal picture.

I want to kick the postcard-perfect sky.

I'm so absorbed in my self-flagellation, I forget Toby's there until he says, "Emotional guy."

I look up. He's sitting on the stoop now, leaning back on his arms, his legs kicked out. He must have come straight from work; he's out of his usual skate rat rags and has on mud-splattered jeans and boots and button-down shirt and is only missing the Stetson to complete the Marlboro Man picture. He looks like he did the day he whisked my sister's heart away: Bailey's Revolutionary.

"He almost attacked me with his guitar yesterday. I think we're making progress," he adds.

"Toby, what're you doing here?"

"What are you doing hiding in trees?" he asks back, nodding at the willow behind me.

"Trying to make amends," I say.

"Me too," he says quickly, jumping to his feet. "But to you. Been trying to tell him what's what." His words surprise me.

"I'll take you home," he says.

We both get into his truck. I can't seem to curb the nausea overwhelming me as a result of the hands-down worst seduction in love's history. Ugh. And on top of it, I'm sure Joe is watching us from a window, all his suspicions seething in his hot head as I drive off with Toby.

"So, what'd you say to him?" I ask when we've cleared Fontaine territory.

"Well, the three words I got to say yesterday and the ten I got in today added up to pretty much telling him he should give you a second chance, that there's nothing going on with us, that we were just wrecked . . ."

"Wow, that was nice. Busybody as all get out, but nice."

He looks over at me for a moment before returning his eyes to the road. "I watched you guys that night in the rain. I saw it, how you feel."

His voice is full of emotion that I can't decipher and probably don't want to. "Thanks," I say quietly, touched that he did this despite everything, because of everything.

He doesn't respond, just looks straight ahead into the sun, which is obliterating everything in our path with unruly splendor. The truck blasts through the trees and I stick my hand out the window, trying to catch the wind in my palm like Bails used to, missing her, missing the girl I used to be around her, missing who we all used to be. We will never be those people again. She took them all with her.

I notice Toby's tapping his fingers nervously on the wheel. He keeps doing it. Tap. Tap. Tap.

"What is it?" I ask.

He grips the wheel tight with both hands.

"I really love her," he says, his voice breaking. "More than anything."

"Oh, Toby, I know that." That's the only thing I do understand about this whole mess: that somehow what happened between us happened because there's too much love for Bailey between us, not too little.

"I know," I repeat.

He nods.

Something occurs to me then: Bailey loved both Toby and me so much—he and I almost make up her whole heart, and maybe that's it, what we were trying to do by being together, maybe we were trying to put her heart back together again.

He stops the truck in front of the house. The sun streams into the cab, bathing us in light. I look out my window, can see Bails rushing out of the house, flying off the porch, to jump into this very truck I am sitting in. It's so strange. I spent forever resenting Toby for taking my sister away from me, and now it seems like I count on him to bring her back.

I open the door, put one of my platforms onto the ground.

"Len?"

I turn around.

"You'll wear him down." His smile is warm and genuine. He rests the side of his head on the steering wheel. "I'm going to leave you alone for a bit, but if you need me . . . for anything, okay?"

"Same," I say, my throat knotting up.

Our conjoined love for Bailey trembles between us; it's like a living thing, as delicate as a small bird, and as breathtaking in its hunger for flight. My heart hurts for both of us.

"Don't do anything stupid on that board," I say.

"Nope."

"Okay." Then I slide out, close the door, and head into the house.

chapter 29

Sometimes, I'd see Sarah and her mom
share a look across a room
and I'd want
to heave my life over like a table.
I'd tell myself not to feel that way,
that I was lucky:
I had Bailey,
I had Gram and Big,
I had my clarinet, books, a river, the sky.
I'd tell myself that I had a mother too,
just not one anyone else could see
but Bailey and me.

(Found scribbled on the want ads in The Clover Gazette *under the bench outside Maria's Deli)*

SARAH'S AT STATE, since the symposium is this afternoon, so I have no one on whom to blame the *Hey Rachel* seduction fiasco but myself. I leave her a message telling her I've been totally mortified like a good saint because of her *jouissance* and am now seeking a last-resort miracle.

The house is quiet. Gram must have gone out, which is too bad because for the first time in ages, I'd like nothing more than to sit at the kitchen table with her and drink tea.

I go up to The Sanctum to brood about Joe, but once there, my eyes keep settling on the boxes I packed the other night. I can't stand looking at them, so after I change out of my ridiculous outfit, I take them up to the attic.

I haven't been up here in years. I don't like the tombishness, the burned smell of the trapped heat, the lack of air. It always seems so sad too, full of everything abandoned and forgotten. I look around at the lifeless clutter, feel deflated at the idea of bringing Bailey's things up here. This is what I've been avoiding for months now. I take a deep breath, look around. There's only one window, so I decide, despite the fact that the area around it is packed in with boxes and mountains of bric-a-brac, that Bailey's things should go where the sun will at least seep in each day.

I make my way over there through an obstacle course of broken furniture, boxes, and old canvases. I move a few cartons immediately so I can crack open the window and hear the river. Hints of rose and jasmine blow in on the afternoon breeze. I open it wider, climb up on an old desk so I can lean out. The sky is still spectacular and I hope Joe is gazing up at it. No matter where I look inside myself, I come across more love for him, for everything about him, his anger as much as his tenderness—he's so alive, he makes me feel like I could take a bite out of the whole earth. If only words hadn't eluded me today, if only I yelled back at him: *I do get it! I get that as long as you live no one will ever love you as much as I do—I have a heart so I can give it to you alone!* That's exactly the way I feel—but unfortunately, people don't talk like that outside of Victorian novels.

I take my head out of the sky and bring it back into the stuffy attic. I wait for my eyes to readjust, and when they do, I'm still convinced this is the only possible spot for Bailey's things. I start moving all the junk that's already there to the shelves on the back wall. After many trips back and forth, I finally reach down to pick up the last of it, which is a shoebox, and the top flips open. It's full of letters, all addressed to Big, probably love letters. I peek at one postcard from an Edie. I decide against snooping further; my karma is about as bad as it's ever been right now. I slip the lid back on, place it on one of the lower shelves where there's still some space. Just behind it, I notice an old letter box, its wood polished and shiny. I wonder what an antique like this is doing up here instead of downstairs with all Gram's other treasures. It looks like a showcase piece too. I slide it out; the wood is mahogany and there's a ring of galloping horses engraved into the top. Why isn't it covered in dust like everything else on these shelves? I lift the lid, see that it's full of folded notes on Gram's mint-green stationery, so many of them, and lots of letters as well. I'm about to put it back when I see written on the outside of an envelope in Gram's careful script the name *Paige*. I flip through the other envelopes. Each and every one says *Paige* with the year next to her name. Gram writes letters to Mom? Every year? All the envelopes are sealed. I know that I should put the box back, that this is private, but I can't. Karma be damned. I open one of the folded notes. It says:

Darling,

The second the lilacs are in full bloom, I have to write you. I know I tell you this every year, but they haven't blossomed the same since you left. They're so stingy now. Maybe it's because no one comes close to loving them like you did—how could they? Each spring I wonder if I'm going to find the girls sleeping in the garden, like I'd find you, morning after morning. Did you know how I loved that, walking outside and seeing you asleep with my lilacs and roses all around you—I've never even tried to paint the image. I never will. I wouldn't want to ruin it for myself.

Mom

Wow—my mother loves lilacs, *really* loves them. Yes, yes, it's true, most people love lilacs, but my mother is so gaga about them that she used to sleep in Gram's garden, night after night, all spring long, so gaga she couldn't bear to be inside knowing all those flowers were raising hell outside her window. Did she bring her blankets out with her? A sleeping bag? Nothing? Did she sneak out when everyone else was asleep? Did she do this when she was my age? Did she like looking up at the sky as much as I do? I want to know more. I feel jittery and lightheaded, like I'm meeting her for the first time. I sit down on a box, try to calm down. I can't. I pick up another note. It says:

Remember that pesto you made with walnuts
instead of pine nuts? Well, I tried pecans, and
you know what? Even better. The recipe:
2 cups packed fresh basil leaves
2/3 cup olive oil
1/2 cup pecans, toasted
1/3 cup freshly grated Parmesan
2 large garlic cloves, mashed
1/2 teaspoon salt

My mother makes pesto with walnuts! This is even better
than sleeping with lilacs. So normal. So *I think I'll whip up some
pasta with pesto for dinner.* My mother bangs around a kitchen.
She puts walnuts and basil and olive oil in a food processor, and
presses blend. She boils water for pasta! I have to tell Bails. I
want to scream out the window at her: *Our mother boils water
for pasta!* I'm going to. I'm going to tell Bailey. I make my way
over to the window, climb back up on the desk, put my head
out, holler up at the sky, and tell my sister everything I've just
learned. I feel dizzy, and yes, a bit out of my tree, when I climb
back into the attic, now hoping no one heard this girl screaming about pasta and lilacs at the top of her lungs. I take a deep
breath. Open another one.

Paige,
I've been wearing the fragrance you wore
for years. The one you thought smelled
like sunshine. I've just found out they've
discontinued it. I feel as though I've lost
you now completely. I can't bear it.
Mom

Oh.

But why didn't Gram tell us our mother wore a perfume that smelled like sunshine? That she slept in the garden in the springtime? That she made pesto with walnuts? Why did she keep this real-life mother from us? But as soon as I ask the question, I know the answer, because suddenly there is not blood pumping in my veins, coursing all throughout my body, but longing for a mother who loves lilacs. Longing like I've never had for the Paige Walker who wanders the world. That Paige Walker never made me feel like a daughter, but a mother who boils water for pasta does. Except don't you need to be claimed to be a daughter? Don't you need to be loved?

And now there's something worse than longing flooding me, because how could a mother who boils water for pasta leave two little girls behind?

How could she?

I close the lid, slide the box back on a shelf, quickly stack Bailey's boxes by the window, and go down the stairs into the empty house.

chapter 30

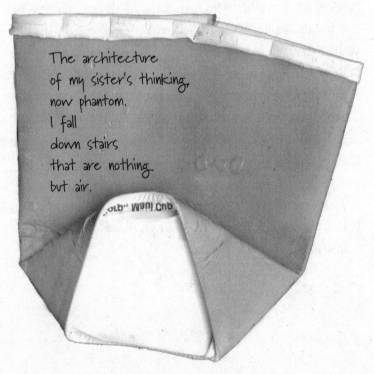

The architecture
of my sister's thinking,
now phantom.
I fall
down stairs
that are nothing
but air.

(Found on a to-go cup by a grove of old growth redwoods)

THE NEXT FEW days inch by miserably. I skip band practice and confine myself to The Sanctum. Joe Fontaine does not stop by, or call, or text, or e-mail, or skywrite, or send Morse code, or telepathically communicate with me. Nothing. I'm quite certain he and *Hey Rachel* have moved to Paris, where they live on chocolate, music, and red wine, while I sit at this window, peering down the road where no one comes bouncing along, guitar in hand, like they used to.

As the days pass, Paige Walker's love of lilacs and ability to boil water have the singular effect of washing sixteen years of myth right off of her. And without it, all that's left is this: Our mother abandoned us. There's no way around it. And what kind of person does that? Rip Van Lennie is right. I've been living in a dream world, totally brainwashed by Gram. My mother's freaking nuts, and I am too, because what kind of ignoramus swallows such a cockamamie story? Those hypothetical families that Big spoke of the other night would've been right not to be kind. My mother is neglectful and irresponsible and probably mentally deficient too. She's not a heroine at all. She's just a selfish woman who couldn't hack it and left two toddlers on her mother's porch and *never came back*. That's who she is. And that's who we are too, two kids, discarded, just left there. I'm glad Bailey never had to see it this way.

I don't go back up to the attic.

It's all right. I'm used to a mother who rides around on a magic carpet. I can get used to this mother too, can't I? But what I can't get used to is that I no longer think Joe, despite my compounding love for him, is ever going to forgive me. How to get used to no one calling you John Lennon? Or making you believe the sky begins at your feet? Or acting like a dork so you'll say *quel dork*? How to get used to being without a boy who turns you into brightness?

217

I can't.

And what's worse is that with each day that passes, The Sanctum gets quieter, even when I'm blasting the stereo, even when I'm talking to Sarah, who's still apologizing for the seduction fiasco, even when I'm practicing Stravinsky, it just gets quieter and quieter, until it is so quiet that what I hear, again and again, is the cranking sound of the casket lowering into the ground.

With each day that passes, there are longer stretches when I don't think I hear Bailey's heels clunking down the hallway, or glimpse her lying on her bed reading, or catch her in my periphery reciting lines into the mirror. I'm becoming accustomed to The Sanctum without her, and I hate it. Hate that when I stand in her closet fumbling from piece to piece, my face pressed into the fabrics, that I can't find one shirt or dress that still has her scent, and it's my fault. They all smell like me now.

Hate that her cell phone finally has been shut down.

With each day that passes, more traces of my sister vanish, not only from the world, but from my very own mind, and there's nothing I can do about it, but sit in the soundless, scentless sanctum and cry.

On the sixth day of this, Sarah declares me a state of emergency and makes me promise to go to the movies with her that night.

She picks me up in Ennui, wearing a black miniskirt, black minier tank top that shows off a lot of tan midriff, three-foot black heels, all topped off with a black ski hat, which I'm supposing is her attempt at practicality, because a chill blew in and it's arctic cold. I'm wearing a brown suede coat, turtleneck, and jeans. We look like we are spliced together from different weather systems.

"Hi!" she says, taking the cigarette out of her mouth to kiss me as I get in. "This movie really is supposed to be good. Not like that last one I made you go to where the woman sat in a chair with her cat for the first half. I admit that one was problematico." Sarah and I have opposite movie-going philosophies. All I want out of celluloid is to sit in the dark with a huge bucket of popcorn. Give me car chases, girl gets boy, underdogs triumphing, let me swoon and scream and weep. Sarah on the other hand can't tolerate such pedestrian fare and complains the whole time about how we're rotting our minds and soon won't be able to think our own thoughts because our brains will be lost to the dominant paradigm. Sarah's preference is The Guild, where they show bleak foreign films where nothing happens, no one talks, everyone loves the one who will never love them back, and then the movie ends. On the program tonight is some stultifyingly boring black-and-white film from Norway.

Her face drops as she studies mine. "You look miserable."

"Sucky week all around."

"It'll be fun tonight, promise." She takes one hand off the wheel and pulls a brown sack out of a backpack. "For the movie." She hands it to me. "Vodka."

"Hmm, then I'll for sure fall asleep in this action-packed, thrill-a-minute, black-and-white, silent movie from Norway."

She rolls her eyes. "It's not silent, Lennie."

While waiting in line, Sarah jumps around trying to keep warm. She's telling me how Luke held up remarkably well at the symposium despite being the only guy there, even made her ask a question about music, but then mid-sentence and mid-jump, her eyes bulge a little. I catch it, even though she's already resumed talking as if nothing has happened. I turn around and there's Joe across the street with Rachel.

They're so lost in conversation they don't even realize the light has changed.

Cross the street, I want to scream. *Cross the street before you fall in love.* Because that's what appears to be happening. I watch Joe lightly tug at her arm while he tells her something or other I'm sure about Paris. I can see the smile, all that radiance pouring over Rachel and I think I might fall like a tree.

"Let's go."

"Yup." Sarah's already walking toward the Jeep, fumbling in her bag for the keys. I follow her, but take one look back and meet Joe's eyes head on. Sarah disappears. Then Rachel. Then all the people waiting in line. Then the cars, the trees, the buildings, the ground, the sky until it is only Joe and me staring across empty space at each other. He does not smile. He anti-smiles. But I can't look away and he can't seem to either. Time has slowed so much that I wonder if when we stop staring at each other we will be old and our whole lives will be over with just a few measly kisses between us. I'm dizzy with missing him, dizzy with seeing him, dizzy with being just yards from him. I want to run across the street, I'm about to—I can feel my heart surge, pushing me toward him, but then he just shakes his head almost to himself and looks away from me and toward Rachel, who now comes back into focus. High-definition focus. Very deliberately, he puts his arm around her and together they cross the street and get in line for the movie. A searing pain claws through me. He doesn't look back, but Rachel does.

She salutes me, a triumphant smile on her face, then flips an insult of blond hair at me as she swings her arm around his waist and turns away.

My heart feels like it's been kicked into a dark corner of my body. *Okay I get it*, I want to holler at the sky. *This is how it feels.* Lesson learned. Comeuppance accepted. I watch them retreat into the theater arm in arm, wishing I had an eraser so I could wipe her out of this picture. Or a vacuum. A vacuum would be better, just suck her up, gone. Out of his arms. Out of my chair. For good.

"C'mon Len, let's get out of here," a familiar voice says. I guess Sarah still exists and she's talking to me, so I must still exist too. I look down, see my legs, realize I'm still standing. I put one foot in front of the other and make my way to Ennui.

There is no moon, no stars, just a brightless, lightless gray bowl over our heads as we drive home.

"I'm going to challenge her for first chair," I say.

"Finally."

"Not because of this—"

"I know. Because you're a racehorse, not some podunk pony." There's no irony in her voice.

I roll down the window and let the cold air slap me silly.

Remember
how it was
when
we
kissed?
Armfuls
and
armfuls
of
light
thrown
right
at
us.
A
rope
dropping
down
from
the
sky.
How
can
the
word
love
the
word
life
even
fit
in
the
mouth?

chapter 31

SARAH AND I are hanging half in, half out my bedroom window, passing the bottle of vodka back and forth.

"We could off her?" Sarah suggests, all her words slurring into one.

"How would we do it?" I ask, swigging a huge gulp of vodka.

"Poison. It's always the best choice, hard to trace."

"Let's poison him too, and all his stupid gorgeous brothers." I can feel the words sticking to the insides of my mouth. "He didn't even wait a week, Sarah."

"That doesn't mean anything. He's hurt."

"God, how can he like her?"

Sarah shakes her head. "I saw the way he looked at you in the street, like a crazy person, really out there, more demented than demented,

(Found on a piece of paper under the big willow)

holy Toledo tigers bonkers. You know what I think? I think he put his arm around her for your benefit."

"What if he has sex with her for my benefit?" Jealousy maddogs through me. Yet, that's not the worst part, neither is the remorse; the worst part is I keep thinking of the afternoon on the forest bed, how vulnerable I'd felt, how much I'd liked it, being that open, that *me,* with him. Had I ever felt so close to anyone?

"Can I have a cigarette?" I ask, taking one before she answers.

She cups a hand around the end of her smoke, lights it with the other, then hands it to me, takes mine, then lights it for herself. I drag on it, cough, don't care, take another and manage not to choke, blowing a gray trail of smoke into the night air.

"Bails would know what to do," I say.

"She would," Sarah agrees.

We smoke together quietly in the moonlight and I realize something I can never say to Sarah. There might've been another reason, a deeper one, why I didn't want to be around her. It's that she's not Bailey, and that's a bit unbearable for me—but I need to bear it. I concentrate on the music of the river, let myself drift along with it as it rushes steadily away.

After a few moments, I say, "You can revoke my free pass."

She tilts her head, smiles at me in a way that floods me with warmth. "Done deal."

She puts out her cigarette on the windowsill and slips back onto the bed. I put mine out too, but stay outside looking over Gram's lustrous garden, breathing it in and practically swooning from the bouquet that wafts up to me on the cool breeze.

And that's when I get the idea. The *brilliant* idea. I have to talk to Joe. I have to at least try to make him understand. But I could use a little help.

"Sarah," I say when I flop back onto the bed. "The roses, they're aphrodisiacal, remember?"

She gets it immediately. "Yes, Lennie! It's the last-resort miracle! Flying figs, yes!"

"Figs?"

"I couldn't think of an animal, I'm too wasted."

I'M ON A mission. I've left Sarah sound asleep in Bailey's bed and I'm tiptoeing my thumping vodka head down the steps and out into the creeping morning light. The fog is thick and sad, the whole world an X-ray of itself. I have my weapon in hand and am about to begin my task. Gram is going to kill me, but this is the price I must pay.

I start at my favorite bush of all, the Magic Lanterns, roses with a symphony of color jammed into each petal. I snip the heads off the most extraordinary ones I can find. Then go to the Opening Nights and snip, snip, snip, merrily along to the Perfect Moments, the Sweet Surrenders, the Black Magics. My heart kicks around in my chest from both fear and excitement. I go from prize bush to bush, from the red velvet Lasting Loves to the pink Fragrant Clouds to the apricot Marilyn Monroes and end at the most beautiful orange-red rose on the planet, appropriately named: the Trumpeter. There I go for broke until I have at my feet a bundle of roses so ravishing that if God got married, there would be no other possible choice for the bouquet. I've cut so many I can't even fit the stems in one hand but have to carry them in both as I head down the road to find a place to stash them until later. I put them beside one of my favorite oaks, totally hidden from the house. Then I worry they'll wilt, so I run back to the house and prepare a basket with wet towels at the bottom and go back to the side of the road and wrap all the stems.

Later that morning, after Sarah leaves, Big goes off to the trees, and Gram retreats into the art room with her green women, I tiptoe out the door. I've convinced myself, despite all reason perhaps, that this is going to work. I keep thinking that Bails would be proud of this harebrained plan. *Extraordinary*, she'd say. In fact, maybe Bails would like that I fell in love with Joe so soon after she died. Maybe it's just the exact inappropriate way my sister would want to be mourned by me.

The flowers are still behind the oak where I left them. When I see them I am struck again by their extraordinary beauty. I've never seen a bouquet of them like this, never seen the explosive color of one bloom right beside another.

I walk up the hill to the Fontaines' in a cloud of exquisite fragrance. Who knows if it's the power of suggestion, or if the roses are truly charmed, but by the time I get to the house, I'm so in love with Joe, I can barely ring the bell. I have serious doubts if I'll be able to form a coherent sentence. If he answers I might just tackle him to the ground till he gives and be done with it.

But no such luck.

The same stylish woman who was in the yard squabbling the other day opens the door. "Don't tell me, you must be Lennie." It's immediately apparent that Fontaine spawn can't come close in the smile department to Mother Fontaine. I should tell Big—her smile has a better shot at reviving bugs than his pyramids.

"I am," I say. "Nice to meet you, Mrs. Fontaine." She's being so friendly that I can't imagine she knows what's happened between her son and me. He probably talks to her about as much as I talk to Gram.

"And will you just look at those roses! I've never seen anything like them in my life. Where'd you pick them? The Garden of Eden?" Like mother, like son. I remember Joe said the same that first day.

"Something like that," I say. "My grandmother has a way with flowers. They're for Joe. Is he home?" All of a sudden, I'm nervous. Really nervous. My stomach seems to be hosting a symposium of bees.

"And the aroma! My God, what an aroma!" she cries. I think the flowers have hypnotized her. Wow. Maybe they do work. "Lucky Joe, what a gift, but I'm sorry dear, he's not home. He said he'd be back soon though. I can put them in water and leave them for him in his room if you like."

I'm too disappointed to answer. I just nod and hand them over to her. I bet he's at Rachel's feeding her family chocolate croissants. I have a dreadful thought—what if the roses actually are love-inducing and Joe comes back here with Rachel and both of them fall under their spell? This was another disastrous idea, but I can't take the roses back now. Actually, I think it would take an automatic weapon to get them back from Mrs. Fontaine, who is leaning farther into the bouquet with each passing second.

226

"Thank you," I say. "For giving them to him." Will she be able to separate herself from these flowers?

"It was very nice to meet you, Lennie. I'd been looking forward to it. I'm sure Joe will *really* appreciate these."

"Lennie," an exasperated voice says from behind me. That symposium in my belly just opened its doors to wasps and hornets too. This is it. I turn around and see Joe making his way up the path. There is no bounce in his walk. It's as if gravity has a hand on his shoulder that it never did before.

"Oh, honey!" Mrs. Fontaine exclaims. "Look what Lennie brought you. Have you ever seen such roses? I sure haven't. My word." Mrs. Fontaine is speaking directly to the roses now, taking in deep aromatic breaths. "Well, I'll just bring these in, find a nice place for them. You kids have fun . . ."

I watch her head disappear completely in the bouquet as the door closes behind her. I want to lunge at her, grab the flowers, shriek, *I need those roses more than you do, lady,* but I have a more pressing concern: Joe's silent fuming beside me.

As soon as the door clicks closed, he says, "You still don't get it, do you?" His voice is full of menace, not quite if a shark could talk, but close. He points at the door behind which dozens of aphrodisiacal roses are filling the air with promise. "You've got to be kidding. You think it's that easy?" His face is getting flushed, his eyes bulgy and wild. "I don't want tiny dresses or stupid fucking magic flowers!" He flails in place like a marionette. "I'm *already* in love with you, Lennie, don't you get it? But I can't be with you. Every time I close my eyes I see you with *him.*"

I stand there dumbstruck—sure, there were some discouraging things just said, but all of them seem to have fallen away. I'm left with six wonderful words: *I'm already in love with you.* Present tense, not past. Rachel Brazile be damned. A skyful of hope knocks into me.

"Let me explain," I say, intent on remembering my lines this time, intent on getting him to understand.

He makes a noise that's part groan, part roar, like *ahhhar-rrrgh,* then says, "Nothing to explain. I *saw* you two. You lied to me over and over again."

"Toby and I were—"

He interrupts. "No way, I don't want to hear it. I told you what happened to me in France and you did this anyway. I can't forgive you. It's just the way I am. You have to leave me alone. I'm sorry."

My legs go weak as it sinks in that his hurt and anger, the sickness of having been deceived and betrayed, has already trumped his love.

He motions down the hill to where Toby and I were that night, and says, "What. Did. You. Expect?" What *did* I expect? One minute he's trying to tell me he loves me and the next he's watching me kiss another guy. Of course he feels this way.

I have to say something, so I say the only thing that makes sense in my mixed-up heart. "I'm so in love with you."

My words knock the wind out of him.

It's as if everything around us stops to see what's going to happen next—the trees lean in, birds hover, flowers hold their petals still. How could he not surrender to this crazy big love we both feel? He couldn't not, right?

I reach my hand out to touch him, but he moves his arm out of my reach.

He shakes his head, looks at the ground. "I can't be with someone who could do that to me." Then he looks right in my eyes, and says, "I can't be with someone who could do that to *her sister*."

The words have guillotine force. I stagger backward, splintering into pieces. His hand flies to his mouth. Maybe he's wishing his words back inside. Maybe he even thinks he went too far, but it doesn't matter. He wanted me to get it and I do.

I do the only thing I can. I turn around and run from him, hoping my trembling legs will keep me up until I can get away. Like Heathcliff and Cathy, I had the Big Bang, once-in-a-lifetime kind of love, and I destroyed it all.

ALL I WANT is to get up to The Sanctum so I can throw the covers over my head and disappear for several hundred years. Out of breath from racing down the hill, I push through the front door of the house. I blow past the kitchen, but backtrack when I glimpse Gram. She's sitting at the kitchen table, her arms folded in front of her chest, her face hard and stern. In front of her on the table are her garden shears and my copy of *Wuthering Heights*.

Uh-oh.

She jumps right in. "You have no idea how close I came to chopping your precious book to bits, but I have some self-control and respect for other people's things." She stands up. When Gram's mad, she practically doubles in size and all twelve feet of her is bulldozing across the kitchen right at me.

"What were you thinking, Lennie? You come like the Grim Reaper and decimate my garden, my *roses*. How could you? You know how I feel about anyone but me touching my flowers. It's the one and only thing I ask. The one and only thing."

She's looming over me. "Well?"

"They'll grow back." I know this is the wrong thing to say, but holler-at-Lennie-day is taking its toll.

She throws her arms up, completely exasperated with me, and it strikes me how closely her expression and arm flailing resemble Joe's. "That is not the point and you know it." She points at me. "You've become very selfish, Lennie Walker."

This I was not expecting. No one's ever called me selfish in my life, least of all Gram—the never-ending fountain of praise and coddling. Are she and Joe testifying at the same trial?

Could this day get any worse?

Isn't the answer to that question always yes?

Gram's hands are on her hips now, face flushed, eyes blazing, double uh-oh—I lean back against the wall, brace myself for the impending assault. She leans in. "Yes, Lennie. You act like you're the only one in this house who has lost somebody. She was like my daughter, do you know what that's like? Do you? My *daughter*. No, you don't because you haven't once asked. Not once have you asked how I'm doing. Did it ever occur to you that *I* might need to talk?" She is yelling now. "I know you're devastated, but Lennie, you're not the only one."

All the air races out of the room, and I race out with it.

chapter 32

Bailey grabs my hand
and pulls me out of the window
into the sky,
pulls music out of my pockets.
"It's time you learned to fly," she says,
and vanishes.

(Found on a candy wrapper on the trail to the Rain River)

I BOLT DOWN the hallway and out the door and jump all four porch steps. I want to run into the woods, veer off the path, find a spot where no one can find me, sit down under an old craggy oak and cry. I want to cry and cry and cry and cry until all the dirt in the whole forest floor has turned to mud. And this is exactly what I'm about to do except that when I hit the path,

I realize I can't. I can't run away from Gram, especially not after everything she just said. Because I know she's right. She and Big have been like background noise to me since Bailey died. I've hardly given any thought to what they're going through. I made Toby my ally in grief, like he and I had an exclusionary right to it, an exclusionary right to Bailey herself. I think of all the times Gram hovered at the door to The Sanctum trying to get me to talk about Bailey, asking me to come down and have a cup of tea, and how I just assumed she wanted to comfort me. It never once occurred to me that she needed to talk herself, that she needed *me*.

How could I have been so careless with her feelings? With Joe's? With everyone's?

I take a deep breath, turn around, and make my way back to the kitchen. I can't make things right with Joe, but at least I can try to make them right with Gram. She's in the same chair at the table. I stand across from her, rest my fingers on the table, wait for her to look up at me. Not one window is open, and the hot stuffy kitchen smells almost rotten.

"I'm sorry," I say. "Really." She nods, looks down at her hands. It occurs to me that I've disappointed or hurt or betrayed everyone I love in the last couple months: Gram, Bailey, Joe, Toby, Sarah, even Big. How did I manage that? Before Bailey died, I don't think I ever really disappointed anyone. Did Bailey just take care of everyone and everything for me? Or did no one expect anything of me before? Or did I just not do anything or want anything before, so I never had to deal with the consequences of my messed-up actions? Or have I become really selfish and self-absorbed? Or all of the above?

I look at the sickly Lennie houseplant on the counter and know that it's not me anymore. It's who I used to be, before, and that's why it's dying. That me is gone.

"I don't know who I am," I say, sitting down. "I can't be who I was, not without her, and who I'm becoming is a total screw-up."

Gram doesn't deny it. She's still mad, not twelve feet of mad, but plenty mad.

"We could go out to lunch in the city next week, spend the whole day together," I add, feeling puny, trying to make up for months of ignoring her with a lunch.

She nods, but that is not what's on her mind. "Just so you know, I don't know who I am without her either."

"Really?"

She shakes her head. "Nope. Every day, after you and Big leave, all I do is stand in front of a blank canvas thinking how much I despise the color green, how every single shade of it disgusts me or disappoints me or breaks my heart." Sadness fills me. I imagine all the green willowy women sliding out of their canvases and slinking their way out the front door.

"I get it," I say quietly.

Gram closes her eyes. Her hands are folded one on top of the other on the table. I reach out and put my hand over hers and she quickly sandwiches it.

"It's horrible," she whispers.

"It is," I say.

The early-afternoon light drains out the windows, zebra-ing the room with long dark shadows. Gram looks old and tired and it makes me feel desolate. Bailey, Uncle Big, and I have been her whole life, except for a few generations of flowers and a lot of green paintings.

"You know what else I hate?" she says. "I hate that everyone keeps telling me that I carry Bailey in my heart. I want to holler at them: *I don't want her there.* I want her in the kitchen with Lennie and me. I want her at the river with Toby and their baby. I want her to be Juliet and Lady Macbeth, you stupid, stupid people. Bailey doesn't want to be trapped in my heart or anyone else's." Gram pounds her fist on the table. I squeeze it with my hands and nod *yes,* and feel *yes,* a giant, pulsing, angry *yes* that passes from her to me. I look down at our hands and catch sight of *Wuthering Heights* lying there silent and helpless and ornery as ever. I think about all the wasted lives, all the wasted love crammed inside it.

"Gram, do it."

"What? Do what?" she asks.

I pick up the book and the shears, hold them out to her. "Just do it, chop it to bits. Here." I slip my fingers and thumb into the handle of the garden shears just like I did this morning, but this time I feel no fear, just that wild, pulsing, pissed-off *yes* coursing through me as I take a cut of a book that I've underlined and annotated, a book that is creased and soiled with years of me, years of river water, and summer sun, and sand from the beach, and sweat from my palms, a book bent to the curves of my waking and sleeping body. I take another cut, slicing through chunks of paper at a time, through all the tiny words, cutting the passionate, hopeless story to pieces, slashing their lives, their impossible love, the whole mess and tragedy of it. I'm attacking it now, enjoying the swish of the blades, the metal scrape after each delicious cut. I cut into Heathcliff, poor, heartsick, embittered Heathcliff and stupid Cathy for her bad choices and unforgivable compromises. And while I'm at it, I take a swipe at Joe's jealousy and anger and judgment, at his *dickhead-him* inability to forgive. I hack away at his ridiculous all-or-nothing-horn-player bullshit, and then I lay into my own duplicity and deceptiveness and confusion and hurt and bad judgment and overwhelming, never-ending grief. I cut and cut and cut at everything I can think of that is keeping Joe and me from having this great big beautiful love while we can.

Gram is wide-eyed, mouth agape. But then I see a faint smile find her lips. She says, "Here, let me have a go." She takes the shears and starts cutting, tentatively at first, but then she gets carried away just as I had, and starts hacking at handfuls and handfuls of pages until words fly all around us like confetti.

Gram's laughing. "Well, that was unexpected." We are both out of breath, spent, and smiling giddily.

"I am related to you, aren't I?" I say.

"Oh, Lennie, I have missed you." She pulls me into her lap like I'm five years old. I think I'm forgiven.

"Sorry I hollered, sweet pea," she says, hugging me into her warmth.

I squeeze her back. "Should I make us some tea?" I ask.

"You better, we have lots of catching up to do. But first things first, you destroyed my whole garden, I have to know if it worked."

I hear again: *I can't be with someone who could do that to her sister,* and my heart squeezes so tight in my chest, I can barely breathe. "Not a chance. It's over."

Gram says quietly, "I saw what happened that night." I tense up even more, slide out of her lap and go over to fill the tea kettle. I suspected Gram saw Toby and me kiss, but the reality of her witnessing it sends shame shifting around within me. I can't look at her. "Lennie?" Her voice isn't incriminating. I relax a little. "Listen to me."

I turn around slowly and face her.

She waves her hand around her head like she's shooing a fly. "I won't say it didn't render me speechless for a minute or two." She smiles. "But crazy things like that happen when people are this shocked and grief-stricken. I'm surprised we're all still standing."

I can't believe how readily Gram is pushing this aside, absolving me. I want to fall to her feet in gratitude. She definitely did not confer with Joe on the matter, but it makes his words sting less, and it gives me the courage to ask, "Do you think she'd ever forgive me?"

"Oh, sweet pea, trust me on this one, she already has."

Gram wags her finger at me. "Now, Joe is another story. He'll need some time . . ."

"Like thirty years," I say.

"Woohoo—poor boy, that was an eyeful, Lennie Walker." Gram looks at me mischievously. She has snapped back into her sassy self. "Yes, Len, when you and Joe Fontaine are forty-seven—" She laughs. "We'll plan a beautiful, beautiful wedding—"

She stops mid-sentence because she must notice my face. I

don't want to kill her cheer, so I'm using every muscle in it to hide my heartbreak, but I've lost the battle.

"Lennie." She comes over to me.

"He hates me," I tell her.

"No," she says warmly. "If ever there was a boy in love, sweet pea, it's Joe Fontaine."

Gram made me go to the doctor
to see if there was something wrong
with my heart.
After a bunch of tests, the doctor said:
Lennie, you lucked out.
I wanted to punch him in the face,
but instead I started to cry
in a drowning kind of way.
I couldn't believe
I had a lucky heart
when what I wanted
was the same kind of heart
as Bailey.
I didn't hear Gram come in,
or come up behind me,
just felt her arms slip around my shaking frame,
then the press of both of her hands hard
against my chest, holding it all in,
holding me together.
Thank God, she whispered,
before the doctor or I
could utter a word.
How could she possibly have known
that I'd gotten good news?

(Found on the back of an envelope on the trail to the forest bedroom)

When she does, her voice is strained, tight. "I thought I was protecting you girls, but now I'm pretty sure I was just protecting myself. It's so hard for me to speak about her. I told myself the better you girls knew her, the more it would hurt." She sweeps some of the book to herself. "I focused on the restlessness, so you girls wouldn't feel so abandoned, wouldn't blame her, or worse, blame yourselves. I wanted you to admire her. That's it."

That's it? Heat rushes up my body. Gram reaches her hand to mine. I slip it away from her.

I say, "You just made up a story so we wouldn't feel abandoned . . ." I raise my eyes to hers, continue despite the pain in her face. "But we *were* abandoned, Gram, and we didn't know why, don't know anything about her except some crazy story." I feel like scooping up a fistful of *Wuthering Heights* and hurling it at her. "Why not just tell us she's crazy if she is? Why not tell the truth, whatever it is? Wouldn't that have been better?"

She grabs my wrist, harder than I think she intended. "But there's not just one truth, Lennie, there never is. What I told you wasn't some story I made up." She's trying to be calm, but I can tell she's moments away from doubling in size. "Yes, it's true that Paige wasn't a stable girl. I mean, who in their proper tree leaves two little girls and doesn't come back?" She lets go of my wrist now that she has my full attention. She looks wildly around the room as if the words she needs might be on the walls. After a moment, she says, "Your mother was an irresponsible tornado of a girl and I'm sure she's an irresponsible tornado of a woman. But it's also true that she's not the first tornado to blast through this family, not the first one who's disappeared like this either. Sylvie swung back into town in that beat-up yellow Cadillac after twenty years drifting around. Twenty years!" She bangs her fist on the table, hard, the piles of *Wuthering Heights* jump with the impact. "Yes, maybe some doctor could give it a name, a diagnosis, but what difference does it make what we call it, it still is what it is, we call it the restless gene, so what? It's as true as anything else."

She takes a sip of her tea, burns her tongue. "Ow," she exclaims uncharacteristically, fanning her mouth.

"Big thinks you have it too," I say. "The restless gene." I'm rearranging words into new sentences on the table. I peek up at her, afraid by her silence that this admission might not have gone over very well.

Her brow's furrowed. "He said that?" Gram's joined me in mixing the words around on the table. I see she's put *under that benign sky* next to *so eternally secluded*.

"He thinks you just bottle it up," I say.

She's stopped shuffling words. There's something very un-Gram in her face, something darting and skittish. She won't meet my eyes, and then I recognize what it is because I've become quite familiar with it myself recently—it's shame.

"What, Gram?"

She's pressing her lips together so tightly, they've gone white; it's like she's trying to seal them, to make sure no words come out.

"What?"

She gets up, walks over to the counter, cradles up against it, looks out the window at a passing kingdom of clouds. I watch her back and wait. "I've been hiding inside that story, Lennie, and I made you girls, and Big, for that matter, hide in it with me."

"But you just said—"

"I know—it's not that it isn't true, but it's also true that blaming things on destiny and genes is a helluva lot easier than blaming them on myself."

"On yourself?"

She nods, doesn't say anything else, just continues to stare out the window.

I feel a chill creep up my spine. "Gram?"

She's turned away from me so I can't see the expression on her face. I don't know why, but I feel afraid of her, like she's slipped into the skin of someone else. Even the way she's holding her body is different, crumpled almost. When she finally speaks, her voice is too deep and calm. "I remember everything about that night . . ." she says, then pauses, and I think about running out of the room, away from this crumpled Gram who talks like she's in a trance. "I remember how cold it was, unseasonably so, how the kitchen was full of lilacs—I'd filled all the vases earlier in the day because she was coming." I can tell by Gram's voice she's smiling now and I relax a little. "She was wearing this long green dress, more like a giant scarf really, totally inappropriate, which was Paige—it's like she had her own weather around her always." I've never heard any of this about my mother, never heard about anything as real as a green dress, a kitchen full of flowers. But then Gram's tone changes again. "She was so upset that night, pacing around the kitchen, no not pacing, billowing back and forth in that scarf. I remember thinking she's like a trapped wind, a wild gale

242

imprisoned in this kitchen with me, like if I opened a window she'd be gone."

Gram turns toward me as if finally remembering I'm in the room. "Your mother was at the end of her rope and she never was someone with a lot of rope on hand. She'd come for the weekend so I could see you girls. At least that's why I'd thought she'd come, until she began asking me what I'd do if she left. 'Left?' I said to her, 'Where? For how long?' which is when I found out she had a plane ticket to God knows where, she wouldn't say, and planned on using it, a one-way ticket. She told me she couldn't do it, that she didn't have it right inside to be a mother. I told her that her insides were right enough, that she couldn't leave, that you girls were her responsibility. I told her that she had to buck up like every other mother on this earth. I told her that you could all live here, that I'd help her, but she couldn't just up and go like those others in this crazy family, I wouldn't have it. 'But if I did leave,' she kept insisting, 'what would you do?' Over and over she asked it. I remember I kept trying to hold her by her arms, to get her to snap out of it, like I'd do when she was young and would get wound up, but she kept slipping out of my grasp like she was made of air." Gram takes a deep breath. "At this point, I was very upset myself, and you know how I get when I blow. I started shouting. I do have my share of the tornado inside, that's for sure, especially when I was younger, Big's right." She sighs. "I lost it, really lost it. 'What do you think I'd do if you left?' I hollered. 'They're my granddaughters, but Paige, if you leave you can never come back. Never. You'll be dead to them, dead in their hearts, and dead to me. Dead. To all of us.' My exact despicable words. Then I locked myself in my art room for the rest of the night. The next morning—she was gone."

I've fallen back into my chair, boneless. Gram stands across the room in a prison of shadows. "I told your mother to never come back."

She'll be back, girls.

A prayer, never a promise.

Her voice is barely above a whisper. "I'm sorry."

Her words have moved through me like fast-moving storm clouds, transforming the landscape. I look around at her framed green ladies, three of them in the kitchen alone, women caught somewhere between here and there—each one Paige, all of them Paige in a billowy green dress, I'm sure of it now. I think about the ways Gram made sure our mother never died in our hearts, made sure Paige Walker never bore any blame for leaving her children. I think about how, unbeknownst to us, Gram culled that blame for herself.

And I remember the ugly thing I'd thought that night at the top of the stairs when I overheard her apologizing to The Half Mom. I'd blamed her too. For things even the almighty Gram can't control.

"It's not your fault," I say, with a certainty in my voice I've never heard before. "It never was, Gram. *She* left. *She* didn't come back—her choice, not yours, no matter what you said to her."

Gram exhales like she's been holding her breath for sixteen years.

"Oh Lennie," she cries. "I think you just opened the window"—she touches her chest—"and let her out."

I rise from my chair and walk over to her, realizing for the first time that she's lost two daughters—I don't know how she bears it. I realize something else too. I don't share this double grief. I have a mother and I'm standing so close to her, I can see the years weighing down her skin, can smell her tea-scented breath. I wonder if Bailey's search for Mom would have led her here too, right back to Gram. I hope so. I gently put my hand on her arm wondering how such a huge love for someone can fit in my tiny body. "Bailey and I are so lucky we got you," I say. "We scored."

She closes her eyes for a moment, and then the next thing I know I'm in her arms and she's squeezing me so as to crush every bone. "I'm the one who lucked out," she says into my hair. "And now I think we need to drink our tea. Enough of this."

As I make my way back to the table, something becomes clear: Life's a freaking mess. In fact, I'm going to tell Sarah we need to start a new philosophical movement: messessentialism instead of existentialism: For those who revel in the essential mess that is life. Because Gram's right, there's not one truth ever, just a whole bunch of stories, all going on at once, in our heads, in our hearts, all getting in the way of each other. It's all a beautiful calamitous mess. It's like the day Mr. James took us into the woods and cried triumphantly, "That's it! That's it!" to the dizzying cacophony of soloing instruments trying to make music together. That is it.

I look down at the piles of words that used to be my favorite book. I want to put the story back together again so Cathy and Heathcliff can make different choices, can stop getting in the way of themselves at every turn, can follow their raging, volcanic hearts right into each other's arms. But I can't. I go to the sink, pull out the trash can, and sweep Cathy and Heathcliff and the rest of their unhappy lot into it.

LATER THAT EVENING, I'm playing Joe's melody over and over on the porch, trying to think of books where love actually triumphs in the end. There's Lizzie Bennet and Mr. Darcy, and Jane Eyre ends up with Mr. Rochester, that's good, but he had that wife locked up for a while, which freaks me out. There's Florentino Aziza in *Love in the Time of Cholera*, but he had to wait over fifty years for Fermina, only for them to end up on a ship going nowhere. Ugh. I'd say there's slim literary pickings on this front, which depresses me; how could true love so infrequently prevail in the classics? And more importantly, how can I make it prevail for Joe and me? If only I could convert him to messessentialism . . . *If only I had wheels on my ass, I'd be a trolley cart.* After all that he said today, I think that about covers my chances.

I'm playing his song for probably the fiftieth time when I realize Gram's in the doorway listening to me. I thought she was locked away in the art room recovering from the emotional tumult of our afternoon. I stop mid-note, suddenly self-conscious. She opens the door, strides out with the mahogany box from the attic in her hands. "What a lovely melody. Bet I could play it myself at this point," she says, rolling her eyes as she puts the box on the table and drops into the love seat. "Though it's very nice to hear you playing again."

I decide to tell her. "I'm going to try for first chair again this fall."

"Oh, sweet pea," she sings. Literally. "Music to my tin ears."

I smile, but inside, my stomach is roiling. I'm planning on telling Rachel next practice. It'd be so much easier if I could just pour a bucket of water on her like the Wicked Witch of the West.

"Come sit down." Gram taps the cushion next to her. I join her, resting my clarinet across my knees. She puts her hand on the box. "Everything in here is yours to read. Open all the envelopes. Read my notes, the letters. Just be prepared, it's not all pretty, especially the earlier letters."

I nod. "Thank you."

"All right." She removes her hand from the box. "I'm going to take a walk to town, meet Big at The Saloon. I need a stiff drink." She ruffles my hair, then leaves the box and me to ourselves.

After putting my clarinet away, I sit with the box on my lap, trailing circles around the ring of galloping horses with my fingers. Around and around. I want to open it, and I also don't want to. It's probably the closest I'll ever get to knowing my mother, whoever she is—adventurer or wack job, heroine or villain, probably just a very troubled, complicated woman. I look out at the gang of oaks across the road, at the Spanish moss hanging over their stooped shoulders like decrepit shawls, the gray, gnarled lot of them like a band of wise old men pondering a verdict—

The door squeaks. I turn to see that Gram has put on a bright pink floral no-clue-what—a coat? A cape? A shower curtain?— over an even brighter purple flowered frock. Her hair is down and wild; it looks like it conducts electricity. She has makeup on, an eggplant-color lipstick, cowboy boots to house her Big Foot feet. She looks beautiful and insane. It's the first time she's gone out at night since Bailey died. She waves at me, winks, then heads down the steps. I watch her stroll across the yard.

Right as she hits the road, she turns back, holds her hair so the breeze doesn't blow it back into her eyes.

"Hey, I give Big one month, you?"

"Are you kidding? Two weeks, tops."

"It's your turn to be best man."

"That's fine," I say, smiling.

She smiles back at me, humor peeking out of her queenly face. Even though we pretend otherwise, nothing quite raises Walker spirits like the thought of another wedding for Uncle Big.

"Be okay, sweet pea," she says. "You know where we are . . ."

"I'll be fine," I say, feeling the weight of the box on my legs.

As soon as she's gone, I open the lid. I'm ready. All these notes, all these letters, sixteen years' worth. I think about Gram jotting down a recipe, a thought, a silly or not-so-pretty something she wanted to share with her daughter, or just remember herself, maybe stuffing it in her pocket all day, and then sneaking up to the attic before bed, to put it in this box, this mailbox with no pickup, year after year, not knowing if her daughter would ever read them, not knowing if anyone would—

I gasp, because isn't that just exactly what I've been doing too: writing poems and scattering them to the winds with the same hope as Gram that someone, someday, somewhere might understand who I am, who my sister was, and what happened to us.

I take out the envelopes, count them—fifteen, all with the name *Paige* and the year. I find the first one, written sixteen years ago by Gram to her daughter. Slipping my finger under the seal, I imagine Bailey sitting beside me. *Okay,* I tell her, taking out the letter, *Let's meet our mother.*

Okay to everything. I'm a messessentialist—okay to it all.

chapter 34

THE SHAW RANCH presides over Clover. Its acreage rolls in green and gold majesty from the ridge all the way down to town. I walk through the iron gate and make my way to the stables, where I find Toby inside talking to a beautiful black mare as he takes her saddle off.

"Don't mean to interrupt," I say, walking over to him.

He turns around. "Wow, Lennie."

We're smiling at each other like idiots. I thought it might be weird to see him, but we both seem to be acting pretty much thrilled. It embarrasses me, so I drop my gaze to the mare between us and stroke her warm moist coat. Heat radiates off her body.

Toby flicks the end of the reins lightly across my hand. "I've missed you."

"Me too, you." But I realize with some relief that my stomach isn't fluttering, even with our eyes locked as they now are. Not even a twitter. Is the spell broken? The horse snorts—perfect: Thanks, Black Beauty—

"Want to go for a ride?" he asks. "We could go up on the ridge. I was just up there. There's a massive herd of elk roaming."

"Actually, Toby . . . I thought maybe we could visit Bailey."

"Okay," he says, without thinking, like I asked him to get an ice cream. Strange.

I told myself I would never go back to the cemetery. No one talks about decaying flesh and maggots and skeletons, but how can you not think of those things? I've done everything in my power to keep those thoughts out of my mind, and staying away from Bailey's grave has been crucial to that end. But last night, I was fingering all the things on her dresser like I always do before I go to sleep, and I realized that she wouldn't want me clinging to the black hair webbed in her hairbrush or the rank laundry I still refuse to wash. She'd think it was totally gross: Lady-Havisham-and-her-wedding-dress gross and dismal. I got an image of her then sitting on the hill at the Clover cemetery with its ancient oaks, firs, and redwoods like a queen holding court, and I knew it was time.

Even though the cemetery is close enough to walk, when Toby's finished, we jump in his truck. He puts the key in the ignition, but doesn't turn it. He stares straight through the windshield at the golden meadows, tapping on the wheel with two fingers in a staccato rhythm. I can tell he's revving up to say something. I rest my head on the passenger window and look out at the fields, imagining his life here, how solitary it must be. A minute or two later, he starts talking in his low lulling bass. "I've always hated being an only child. Used to envy you guys. You were just so tight."

250

He grips his hands on the wheel, stares straight ahead. "I was so psyched to marry Bails, to have this baby . . . I was psyched to be part of your family. It's going to sound so lame now, but I thought I could help you through this. I wanted to. I know Bailey would've wanted me to." He shakes his head. "Sure screwed it all up. I just . . . I don't know. You understood . . . It's like you were the only one who did. I started to feel so close to you, too close. It got all mixed up in my head—"

"But you did help me," I interrupt. "You were the only one who could even find me. I felt that same closeness even if I didn't understand it. I don't know what I would have done without you."

He turns to me. "Yeah?"

"Yeah, Toby."

He smiles his squintiest, sweetest smile. "Well, I'm pretty sure I can keep my hands off you now. I don't know about your frisky self though . . ." He raises his eyebrows, gives me a look, then laughs an unburdened free laugh. I punch his arm. He goes on, "So, maybe we'll be able to hang out a little—I don't think I can keep saying no to Gram's dinner invitations without her sending out the National Guard."

"I can't believe you just made two jokes in one sentence. Amazing."

"I'm not a total doorknob, you know?"

"Guess not. There must have been some reason my sister wanted to spend the rest of her life with you!" And just like that, it feels right between us, finally.

"Well," he says, starting the truck. "Shall we cheer ourselves up with a trip to the cemetery?"

"Three jokes, unbelievable."

However, that was probably Toby's word allotment for the year, I'm thinking as we drive along now in silence. A silence that is full of jitters. Mine. I'm nervous. I'm not sure what I'm afraid of really. I keep telling myself, it's just a stone, it's just a pretty piece of land with gorgeous stately trees overlooking the falls. It's just a place where my beautiful sister's body is in a box decaying in a sexy black dress and sandals. Ugh. I can't help it. Everything I haven't allowed myself to imagine rushes me: I think about airless empty lungs. Lipstick on her unmoving mouth. The silver bracelet that Toby had given her on her pulseless wrist. Her belly ring. Hair and nails growing in the dark. Her body with no thoughts in it. No time in it. No love in it. Six feet of earth crushing down on her. I think about the phone ringing in the kitchen, the thump of Gram collapsing, then the inhuman sound sirening out of her, through the floorboards, up to our room.

I look over at Toby. He doesn't look nervous at all. Something occurs to me.

"Have you been?" I ask.

"Course," he answers. "Almost every day."

"Really?"

He looks over at me, the realization dawning on him. "You mean you haven't been since?"

"No." I look out the window. I'm a terrible sister. Good sisters visit graves despite gruesome thoughts.

"Gram goes," he says. "She planted a few rosebushes, a bunch of other flowers too. The grounds people told her she had to get rid of them, but every time they pulled out her plants, she just replanted more. They finally gave up." I can't believe everyone's been going to Bailey's grave but me. I can't believe how left out it makes me feel.

"What about Big?" I ask.

"I find roaches from his joints a lot. We hung out there a couple times." He looks over at me, studies my face for what feels like forever. "It'll be okay, Len. Easier than you think. I was really scared the first time I went."

Something occurs to me then. "Toby," I say, tentatively, mustering my nerve. "You must be pretty used to being an only child . . ." My voice starts to shake. "But I'm really new at it." I look out the window. "Maybe we . . ." I feel too shy all of a sudden to finish my thought, but he knows what I'm getting at.

"I've always wanted a sister," he says as he swerves into a spot in the tiny parking lot.

"Good," I say, every inch of me relieved. I lean over and give him the world's most sexless peck on the cheek. "C'mon," I say. "Let's go tell her we're sorry."

There once was a girl who found herself dead.
She spent her days peering
over the ledge of heaven,
her chin in her palm.
She was bored as brick,
hadn't adjusted yet
to the slower pace of heavenly life.
Her sister would look up at her
and wave,
and the dead girl would wave back
but she was too far away
for her sister to see.
The dead girl thought her sister
might be writing her notes,
but it was too long a trip to make
for a few scattered words here and there
so she let them be.
And then, one day, her earthbound sister finally realized
she could hear music up there in heaven,
so after that, everything her sister
needed to tell her
she did through her clarinet
and each time she played, the dead girl
jumped up (no matter what else she was doing),
and danced.

(Found on a piece of paper in the stacks, B section, Clover Public Library)

chapter 35

I HAVE A plan. I'm going to write Joe a poem, but first things first.

When I walk into the music room, I see that Rachel's already there unpacking her instrument. This is it. My hand is so clammy I'm afraid the handle on my case will slip out of it as I cross the room and stand in front of her.

"If it isn't John Lennon," she says without looking up. Could she be so awful as to rub Joe's nickname in my face? Obviously, yes. Well, good, because fury seems to calm my nerves. Race on.

"I'm challenging you for first chair," I say, and wild applause bursts from a spontaneous standing ovation in my brain. Never have words felt so good coming out of my mouth! Hmm. Even if Rachel doesn't appear to have heard them. She's still messing with her reed and ligature like the bell didn't go off, like the starting gate didn't just swing open.

I'm about to repeat myself, when she says, "There's nothing there, Lennie." She spits my name on the floor like it disgusts her. "He's so hung up on you. Who knows why?"

Could this moment get any better? No! I try to keep my cool. "This has nothing to do with him," I say, and nothing could be more true. It has nothing to do with her either, not really, though I don't say that. It's about me and my clarinet.

"Yeah, right," she says. "You're just doing this because you saw me with him."

"No." My voice surprises me again with its certainty. "I want the solos, Rachel." At that she stops fiddling with her clarinet, rests it on the stand, and looks up at me. "And I'm starting up again with Marguerite." This I decided on the way to rehearsal. I have her undivided totally freaked-out attention now. "I'm going to try for All-State too," I tell her. This, however, is news to me.

We stare at each other and for the first time I wonder if she's known all year that I threw the audition. I wonder if that's why she's been so horrible. Maybe she thought she could intimidate me into not challenging her. Maybe she thought that was the only way to keep her chair.

She bites her lip. "How about if I split the solos with you. And you can—"

I shake my head. I almost feel sorry for her. Almost.

"Come September," I say. "May the best clarinetist win."

NOT JUST MY ass, but every inch of me is in the wind as I fly out of the music room, away from school, and into the woods to go home and write the poem to Joe. Beside me, step for step, breath for breath, is the unbearable fact that I have a future and Bailey doesn't.

This is when I know it.

My sister will die over and over again for the rest of my life. Grief is forever. It doesn't go away; it becomes part of you, step for step, breath for breath. I will never stop grieving Bailey because I will never stop loving her. That's just how it is. Grief and love are conjoined, you don't get one without the other. All I can do is love her, and love the world, emulate her by living with daring and spirit and joy.

Without thinking, I veer onto the trail to the forest bedroom. All around me, the woods are in an uproar of beauty. Sunlight cascades through the trees, making the fern-covered floor look jeweled and incandescent. Rhododendron bushes sweep past me right and left like women in fabulous dresses. I want to wrap my arms around all of it.

When I get to the forest bedroom, I hop onto the bed and make myself comfortable. I'm going to take my time with this poem, not like all the others I scribbled and scattered. I take the pen out of my pocket, a piece of blank sheet music out of my bag, and start writing.

I tell him everything—everything he means to me, everything I felt with him that I never felt before, everything I hear in his music. I want him to trust me so I bare all. I tell him I belong to him, that my heart is his, and even if he never forgives me it will still be the case.

It's my story, after all, and this is how I choose to tell it.

When I'm done, I scoot off the bed and as I do, I notice a blue guitar pick lying on the white comforter. I must have been sitting on it all afternoon. I lean over and pick it up, and recognize it right away as Joe's. He must've come here to play—a good sign. I decide to leave the poem here for him instead of

chapter 36

I'M TOO MORTIFIED to sleep. What was I thinking? I keep imagining Joe reading my ridiculous poem to his brothers, and worse to Rachel, all of them laughing at poor lovelorn Lennie, who knows nothing about romance except what she learned from Emily Brontë. I told him: *I belong to him.* I told him: *My heart is his.* I told him: *I hear his soul in his music.* I'm going to jump off of a building. Who says things like this in the twenty-first century? No one! How is it possible that something can seem like such a brilliant idea one day and such a bonehead one the next?

As soon as there's enough light, I throw a sweatshirt over my pajamas, put on some sneakers, and run through the dawn to the forest bedroom to retrieve the note, but when I get there, it's gone. I tell myself that the wind blew it away like all the other poems. I mean, how likely is it that Joe showed up yesterday afternoon after I left? Not likely at all.

SARAH IS KEEPING me company, providing humiliation support while I make lasagnas.

She can't stop squealing. "You're going to be first clarinet, Lennie. For sure."

"We'll see."

"It'll really help you get into a conservatory. Juilliard even."

I take a deep breath. How like an imposter I'd felt every time Marguerite mentioned it, how like a traitor, conspiring to steal my sister's dream, just as it got swiped from her. Why didn't it occur to me then I could dream alongside her? Why wasn't I brave enough to have a dream at all?

"I'd love to go to Juilliard," I tell Sarah. There. Finally. "But any good conservatory would be okay." I just want to study music: what life, what living itself sounds like.

"We could go together," Sarah's saying, while shoveling into her mouth each slice of mozzarella as I cut it. I slap her hand. She continues, "Get an apartment together in New York City." I think Sarah might rocket into outer space at the idea—me too, though, I, pathetically, keep thinking: What about Joe? "Or Berklee in Boston," she says, her big blue eyes boinging out of her head. "Don't forget Berklee. Either way, we could drive there in Ennui, zigzag our way across. Hang out at the Grand Canyon, go to New Orleans, maybe—"

"Ughhhhhhhhhhhhhhhhh," I groan.

"Not the poem again. What could be a better distraction than the divine goddesses Juilliard and Berklee. Sheesh. Unfreakingbelievable . . ."

"You have no idea how dildonic it was."

"*Nice* word, Len." She's flipping through a magazine someone left on the counter.

"*Lame* isn't lame enough of a word for this poem," I mutter. "Sarah, I told a guy that *I belong to him.*"

"That's what happens when you read *Wuthering Heights* eighteen times."

"Twenty-three."

I'm layering away: sauce, noodles, *I belong to you,* cheese, sauce, *my heart is yours,* noodles, cheese, *I hear your soul in your music,* cheese, cheese, CHEESE . . .

She's smiling at me. "You know, it might be okay, he seems kind of the same way."

"What way?"

"You know, like you."

Bails?

Yeah.

Can you believe Cathy married Edgar Linton?

No.

I mean would you ever do something so stupid?

No.

I mean what she had with Heathcliff, how could she have just thrown it away?

I don't know. What is it, Len?

What's what?

What's with you and that book already?

I don't know.

Yes you do. Tell me.

It's cornball.

C'mon, Len.

I guess I want it.

What?

To feel that kind of love.

You will.

How do you know?

Just do.

The toes knows?

The toes knows.

But if I find it, I don't want to screw it all up like they did.

You won't. The toes knows that too.

Night, Bails.

Len, I was just thinking something . . .

What?

In the end, Cathy and Heathcliff are together, love is stronger than anything, even death.

Hmm . . .

Night, Len.

(Found on a scrap of staff paper in the parking lot, Clover High)

chapter 37

I TELL MYSELF it's ridiculous to go all the way back to the forest bedroom, that there's no way in the world he's going to be there, that no New Age meets Victorian Age poem is going to make him trust me, that I'm sure he still hates me, and now thinks I'm dildonic on top of it.

But here I am, and of course, here he's not. I flop onto my back on the bed. I look up at the patches of blue sky through the trees, and adhering to the regularly scheduled programming, I think some more about Joe. There's so much I don't know about him. I don't know if he believes in God, or likes macaroni and cheese, or what sign he is, or if he dreams in English or French, or what it would feel like—uh-oh. I'm headed from G to XXX because, oh God, I really wish Joe didn't hate me so much, because I want to do *everything* with him. I'm so fed up with my virginity. It's like the whole world is in on this ecstatic secret but me—

I hear something then: a strange, mournful, decidedly unforest-like sound. I pick my head up and rest on my elbows so I can listen harder and try to isolate the sound from the rustling leaves and the distant river roar and the birds chattering all around me. The sound trickles through the trees, getting louder by the minute, closer. I keep listening, and then I recognize what it is, the notes, clear and perfect now, winding and wending their way to me—the melody from Joe's duet. I close my eyes and hope I'm really hearing a clarinet and it's not just some auditory hallucination inside my lovesick head. It's not, because now I hear steps shuffling through the brush and within a couple minutes the music stops and then the steps.

I'm afraid to open my eyes, but I do, and he's standing at the edge of the bed looking down at me—an army of ninja-cupids who must have all been hiding out in the canopy draw their bows and release—arrows fly at me from every which way.

"I thought you might be here." I can't read his expression. Nervous? Angry? His face seems restless like it doesn't know what to emote. "I got your poem . . ."

I can hear the blood rumbling through my body, drumming in my ears. What's he going to say? I got your poem and I'm sorry, I just can't ever forgive you. I got your poem and I feel the same way—*my heart is yours, John Lennon*. I got your poem and I've already called the psych ward—I have a straitjacket in this backpack. Strange. I've never seen Joe wear a backpack.

He's biting his lip, tapping his clarinet on his leg. Definitely nervous. This can't be good.

"Lennie, I got *all* your poems." What's he talking about? What does he mean *all* my poems? He slides the clarinet between his thighs to hold it and takes off his backpack, unzips it. Then he takes a deep breath, pulls out a box, hands it to me. "Well, probably not all of them, but these."

I open the lid. Inside are scraps of paper, napkins, to-go cups, all with my words on them. The bits and pieces of Bailey and me that I scattered and buried and hid. This is not possible.

"How?" I ask, bewildered, and starting to get uneasy thinking about Joe reading everything in this box. All these private desperate moments. This is worse than having someone read your journal. This is like having someone read the journal that you thought you'd burned. And how did he get them all? Has he been following me around? That would be perfect. I finally fall in love with someone and he's a total freaking maniac.

I look at him. He's smirking a little and I see the faintest: bat. bat. bat. "I know what you're thinking," he says. "That I'm the creepy stalker dude."

Bingo.

He's amused. "I'm not, Len. It just kept happening. At first I kept finding them, and then, well, I started looking. I just couldn't help it. It became like this weird-ass treasure hunt. Remember that first day in the tree?"

I nod. But something even more amazing than Joe being a crazy stalker and finding my poems has just occurred to me— he's not angry anymore. Was it the dildonic poem? Whatever it was I'm caught in such a ferocious uprising of joy I'm not even listening to him as he tries to explain how in the world these poems ended up in this shoebox and not in some trash heap or blowing through Death Valley on a gust of wind.

I try to tune in to what he's saying. "Remember in the tree

I told you that I'd seen you up at The Great Meadow? I told you that I'd watched you writing a note, watched you drop it as you walked away. But I didn't tell you that after you left, I went over and found the piece of paper caught in the fence. It was a poem about Bailey. I guess I shouldn't have kept it. I was going to give it back to you that day in the tree, I had it in my pocket, but then I thought you'd think it was strange that I took it in the first place, so I just kept it." He's biting his lip. I remember him telling me that day he saw me drop something I'd written, but it never occurred to me he would go *find* it and *read* it. He continues, "And then, while we were in the tree, I saw words scrawled on the branches, thought maybe you'd written something else, but I felt weird asking, so I went back another time and wrote it down in a notebook."

I can't believe this. I sit up, fish through the box, looking more closely this time. There are some scraps in his weirdo Unabomber handwriting—probably transcribed from walls or sides of barns or some of the other practical writing surfaces that I found. I'm not sure how to feel. He knows everything—I'm inside out.

His face is caught between worry and excitement, but excitement seems to be winning out. He's pretty much bursting to go on. "That first time I was at your house, I saw one sticking out from under a stone in Gram's garden, and then another one on the sole of your shoe, and then that day when we moved all the stuff, man . . . it's like your words were everywhere I looked. I went a little crazy, found myself looking for them all the time . . ." He shakes his head. "Even kept it up when I was so pissed at you. But the strangest part is that I'd found a couple before I'd even met you, the first was just a few words on the back of a candy wrapper, found it on the trail to the river, had no idea who wrote it, well, until later . . ."

He's staring at me, tapping the clarinet on his leg. He looks nervous again. "Okay, say something. Don't feel weird. They just made me fall more in love with you." And then he smiles, and in all the places around the globe where it's night, day breaks. "Aren't you at least going to say *quel dork?*"

I would say a lot of things right now if I could get any words past the smile that has taken over my face. There it is again, his *I'm in love with you* obliterating all else that comes out of his mouth with it.

He points to the box. "They helped me. I'm kind of an unforgiving doltwad, if you haven't noticed. I'd read them—read them over and over after you came that day with the roses—trying to understand what happened, why you were with him, and I think maybe I do now. I don't know, reading all the poems together, I started to *really* imagine what you've been going through, how horrible it must be . . ." He swallows, looks down, shuffles his foot in the pine needles. "For him too. I guess I can see how it happened."

How can it be I was writing to Joe all these months without knowing it? When he looks up, he's smiling. "And then yesterday . . ." He tosses the clarinet onto the bed. "Found out you belong to me." He points at me. "I own your ass."

I smile. "Making fun of me?"

"Yeah, but it doesn't matter because you own my ass too." He shakes his head and his hair flops into his eyes so that I might die. "Totally."

A flock of hysterically happy birds busts out of my chest and into the world. I'm glad he read the poems. I want him to know all the inside things about me. I want him to know my sister, and now, in some way, he does. Now he knows before as well as after.

He sits down on the edge of the bed, picks up a stick and draws on the ground with it, then tosses it, looks off into the trees. "I'm sorry," he says.

"Don't be. I'm glad—"

He turns around to face me. "No, not about the poems. I'm sorry, what I said that day, about Bailey. From reading all these, I knew how much it would hurt you—"

I put my finger over his lips. "It's okay."

He takes my hand, holds it to his mouth, kisses it. I close my eyes, feel shivers run through me—it's been so long since we've touched. He rests my hand back down. I open my eyes. His are on me, questioning. He smiles, but the vulnerability and hurt still in his face tears into me. "You're not going to do it to me again, are you?" he asks.

"Never," I blurt out. "I want to be with you forever!" Okay, lesson learned twice in as many days: You can chop the Victorian novel to shreds with garden shears but you can't take it out of the girl.

He beams at me. "You're crazier than me."

We stare at each other for a long moment and inside that moment I feel like we are kissing more passionately than we ever have even though we aren't touching.

I reach out and brush my fingers across his arm. "Can't help it. I'm in love."

"First time," he says. "For me."

"I thought in France—"

He shakes his head. "No way, nothing like this." He touches my cheek in that tender way that he does that makes me believe in God and Buddha and Mohammed and Ganesh and Mary, et al. "No one's like you, for me," he whispers.

"Same," I say, right as our lips meet. He lowers me back onto the bed, aligns himself on top of me so we are legs to legs, hips to hips, stomach to stomach. I can feel the weight of him pressing into every inch of me. I rake my fingers through his dark silky curls.

"I missed you," he murmurs into my ears, my neck and hair, and each time he does I say, "Me too," and then we are kissing again and I can't believe there is anything in this uncertain world that can feel this right and real and true.

Later, after we've come up for oxygen, I reach for the box, and start flipping through the scraps. There are a lot of them, but not near as many as I wrote. I'm glad there are some still out there, tucked away between rocks, in trash bins, on walls, in the margins of books, some washed away by rain, erased by the sun, transported by the wind, some never to be found, some to be found in years to come.

"Hey, where's the one from yesterday?" I ask, letting my residual embarrassment get the better of me, thinking I might still be able to accidentally rip it up, now that it's done its job.

"Not in there. That one's mine." Oh well. He's lazily brushing his hand across my neck and down my back. I feel like a tuning fork, my whole body humming.

"You're not going to believe this," he says. "But I think the roses worked. On my parents—I swear, they can't keep their hands off each other. It's disgusting. Marcus and Fred have been going down to your place at night and stealing roses to give to girls so they'll sleep with them." Gram is going to love this. It's a good thing she's so smitten with the Fontaine boys.

I put down the box, scoot around so I'm facing him. "I don't think *any* of you guys need Gram's roses for that."

"John Lennon?"

Bat. Bat. Bat.

I run my finger over his lips, say, "I want to do everything with you too."

"Oh man," he says, pulling me down to him, and then we are kissing so far into the sky I don't think we're ever coming back.

If anyone asks where we are, just tell them to look up.

chapter 38

Bails?

Yeah?

Is it so dull being dead?

It was, not anymore.

What changed?

I stopped peering over the ledge . . .

What do you do now?

It's hard to explain—it's like swimming, but not in water, in light.

Who do you swim with?

Mostly you and Toby, Gram, Big, with Mom too, sometimes.

How come I don't know it?

But you do, don't you?

I guess, like all those days we spent at Flying Man's?

Exactly, only brighter.

(Written in Lennie's journal)

GRAM AND I are baking the day away in preparation for Big's wedding. All the windows and doors are open and we can hear the river and smell the roses and feel the heat of the sun streaming in. We're chirping about the kitchen like sparrows.

We do this every wedding, only this is the first time we're doing it without Bailey. Yet, oddly, I feel her presence more today in the kitchen with Gram than I have since she died. When I roll the dough out, she comes up to me and sticks her hand in the flour and flicks it into my face. When Gram and I lean against the counter and sip our tea, she storms into the kitchen and pours herself a cup. She sits in every chair, blows in and out the doors, whisks in between Gram and me humming under her breath and dipping her finger into our batters. She's in every thought I think, every word I say, and I let her be. I let her enchant me as I roll the dough and think my thoughts and say my words, as we bake and bake—both of us having finally dissuaded Joe of the necessity of an exploding wedding cake—and talk about inanities like what Gram is going to wear for the big party. She is quite concerned with her outfit.

"Maybe I'll wear pants for a change." The earth has just slid off its axis. Gram has a floral frock for every occasion. I've never seen her out of one. "And I might straighten my hair." Okay, the earth has slid off its axis and is now hurtling toward a different galaxy. Imagine Medusa with a blow-dryer. Straight hair is an impossibility for Gram or any Walker, even with thirty hours to go until party time.

"What gives?" I ask.

"I just want to look nice, no crime in that, is there? You know, sweet pea, it's not like I've lost my sex appeal." I can't believe Gram just said sex appeal. "Just a bit of a dry spell is all," she mutters under her breath. I turn to look at her. She's sugaring the raspberries and strawberries and flushing as crimson as they are.

"Oh my God, Gram! You have a crush."

"God no!"

"You're lying. I can see it."

Then she giggles in a wild cackley way. "I am lying! Well, what do you expect? With you so loopy all the time about Joe, and now Big and Dorothy . . . maybe I caught a little of it. Love is contagious, everyone knows that, Lennie."

She grins.

"So, who is it? Did you meet him at The Saloon that night?" That's the only time she's been out socializing in months. Gram is not the Internet dating type. At least I don't think she is.

I put my hands on my hips. "If you don't tell me, I'm just going to ask Maria tomorrow. There's nothing in Clover she doesn't know."

Gram squeals, "Mum's me, sweet pea."

No matter how I prod through hours more of pies, cakes, and even a few batches of berry pudding, her smiling lips remain sealed.

AFTER WE'RE DONE, I get my backpack, which I loaded up earlier, and take off for the cemetery. When I hit the trailhead, I start running. The sun is breaking through the canopy in isolated blocks, so I fly through light and dark and dark and light, through the blazing unapologetic sunlight, into the ghostliest loneliest shade, and back again, back and forth, from one to the next, and through the places where it all blends together into a leafy-lit emerald dream. I run and run and as I do the fabric of death that has clung to me for months begins to loosen and slip away. I run fast and free, suspended in a moment of private raucous happiness, my feet barely touching the ground as I fly forward to the next second, minute, hour, day, week, year of my life.

I break out of the woods on the road to the cemetery. The hot afternoon sunlight is lazing over everything, meandering through the trees, casting long shadows. It's warm and the scent of eucalyptus and pine is thick, overpowering. I walk the footpath that winds through the graves listening to the rush of the falls, remembering how important it was for me, despite all reason, that Bailey's grave be where she could see and hear and even smell the river.

I'm the only person in the small hilltop cemetery and I'm glad. I drop my backpack and sit down beside the gravestone, rest my head against it, wrap my hands and arms around it like I'm playing a cello. The stone is so warm against my body. We chose this one because it had a little cabinet in it, a kind of reliquary, with a metal door that has an engraving of a bird on it. It sits under the chiseled words. I run my fingers across my sister's name, her nineteen years, then across the words I wrote on a piece of paper months ago and handed to Gram in the funeral parlor: *The Color of Extraordinary*.

I reach for my pack, pull a small notebook out of it. I transcribed all the letters Gram wrote to our mom over the last sixteen years. I want Bailey to have those words. I want her to know that there will never be a story that she won't be a part of, that she's everywhere like sky. I open the door and slide the book in the little cabinet, and as I do, I hear something scrape. I reach in and pull out a ring. My stomach drops. It's gorgeous, an orange topaz, big as an acorn. Perfect for Bailey. Toby must have had it made especially for her. I hold it in my palm and the certainty that she never got to see it pierces me. I bet the ring is what they were waiting for to finally tell us about their marriage, the baby. How Bails would've showed it off when they made the grand announcements. I rest it on the edge of the stone where it catches a glint of sun and throws amber prismatic light over all the engraved words.

I try to fend off the oceanic sadness, but I can't. It's such a colossal effort not to be haunted by what's lost, but to be enchanted by what was.

I miss you, I tell her, *I can't stand that you're going to miss so much*.

I don't know how the heart withstands it.

I kiss the ring, put it back into the cabinet next to the notebook, and close the door with the bird on it. Then I reach into my pack and take out the houseplant. It's so decrepit, just a few blackened leaves left. I walk over to the edge of the cliff, so I'm right over the falls. I take the plant out of its pot, shake the dirt off the roots, get a good grip, reach my arm back, take one deep breath before I pitch my arm forward, and let go.

epilogue

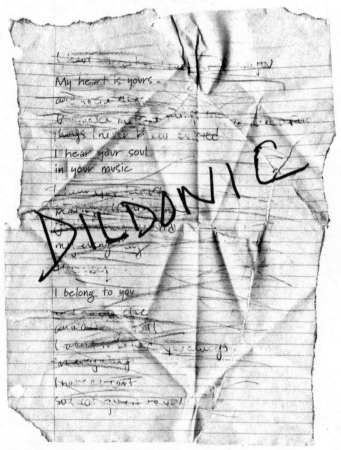

(Found on the bed, in the forest bedroom)
(Found again in the bombroom, in the trash can, ripped into pieces by Lennie)
(Found again on Joe's desk, taped together, with the word dildonic written over it)
(Found framed under glass in Joe's dresser drawer, where it still is)

acknowledgments

In loving memory of Barbie Stein,
who is everywhere like sky

I'D LIKE TO THANK:

First and foremost, my parents, all four of them, for their boundless love and support: my awesome father and Carol, my huge-hearted mother and Ken. My whole family for their rollicking humor and steadfastness: my brothers Bruce, Bobby, and Andy, my sisters-in-law Patricia and Monica, my niece and nephews Adam, Lena, and Jake, my grandparents, particularly the inimitable Cele.

Mark Routhier for so much joy, belief, love.

My amazing friends, my other family, for every day, in every way: Ami Hooker, Anne Rosenthal, Becky MacDonald, Emily Rubin, Jeremy Quittner, Larry Dwyer, Maggie Jones, Sarah Michelson, Julie Regan, Stacy Doris, Maritza Perez, David Booth, Alexander Stadler, Rick Heredia, Patricia Irvine, James

Faerron, Lisa Steindler, and James Assatly, who is so missed, also my extended families: the Routhier, Green, and Block clans... and many others, too many to name.

Patricia Nelson for around the clock laughs and legal expertise, Paul Feuerwerker for glorious eccentricity, revelry, and invaluable insights into the band room, Mark H. for sublime musicality, first love.

The faculty, staff, and student body of Vermont College of Fine Arts, particularly my miracle-working mentors: Deborah Wiles, Brent Hartinger, Julie Larios, Tim Wynne-Jones, Margaret Bechard, and visiting faculty Jane Yolen. And my classmates: the Cliff-hangers, especially Jill Santopolo, Carol Lynch Williams, Erik Talkin, and Mari Jorgensen. Also, the San Francisco VCFA crew. And Marianna Baer—angel at the end of my keyboard.

My other incredible teachers and professors: Regina Wiegand, Bruce Boston, Will Erickson, Archie Ammons, Ken McClane, Phyllis Janowitz, C.D. Wright, among many others.

To those listed above who spirit in and out of this book—a special thank you.

Deepest appreciation and gratitude go to:

My clients at Manus & Associates Literary Agency, as well as my extraordinary colleagues: Stephanie Lee, Dena Fischer, Penny Nelson, Theresa van Eeghen, Janet and Justin Manus, and most especially, Jillian Manus, who doesn't walk, but dances on water.

Alisha Niehaus, my remarkable editor, for her ebullience, profundity, insight, kindness, sense of humor, and for making every part of the process a celebration. Everyone at Dial and

Penguin Books for Young Readers for astounding me each jubilant step of the way.

Emily van Beek of Pippin Properties for being the best literary agent on earth! I am forever mesmerized by her joyfulness, brilliance, ferocity and grace. Holly McGhee for her enthusiasm, humor, savvy and soulfulness. Elena Mechlin for her behind-the-scenes magic and cheer. The Pippin Ladies are without peer. And Jason Dravis at Monteiro Rose Dravis Agency for his vision and dazzling know-how.

And finally, an extra heartfelt double-whammy out-of-the-freaking-park thank you to my brother Bobby: True Believer.

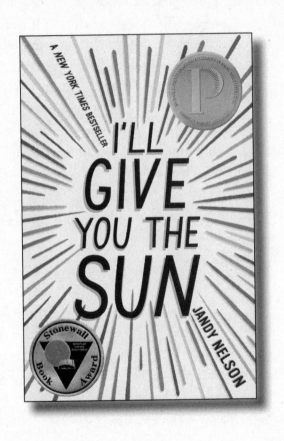

Noah

This is how it all begins.

With Zephyr and Fry—reigning neighborhood sociopaths—torpedoing after me and the whole forest floor shaking under my feet as I blast through air, trees, this white-hot panic.

"You're going over, you pussy!" Fry shouts.

Then Zephyr's on me, has one, both of my arms behind my back, and Fry's grabbed my sketchpad. I lunge for it but I'm armless, helpless. I try to wriggle out of Zephyr's grasp. Can't. Try to blink them into moths. No. They're still themselves: fifteen-foot-tall, tenth-grade asshats who toss living, breathing thirteen-year-old people like me over cliffs for kicks.

Zephyr's got me in a headlock from behind and his chest's heaving into my back, my back into his chest. We're swimming in sweat. Fry starts leafing through the pad. "Whatcha been drawing, Bubble?" I imagine him getting run over by a truck. He holds up a page of sketches. "Zeph, look at all these naked dudes."

The blood in my body stops moving.

"They're not dudes. They're *David,*" I get out, praying I won't sound like a gerbil, praying he won't turn to later drawings in the pad, drawings done today, when I was spying, drawings of *them,* rising out of the water, with their surfboards under arm, no wetsuits, no nothing, totally glistening, and, uh: holding hands. I might have taken some artistic license. So they're going to think . . . They're going to kill me even before they kill me is what they're going to do.

The world starts somersaulting. I fling words at Fry: "You know? Michel-angelo? Ever heard of him?" I'm not going to act like me. *Act tough and you are tough,* as Dad has said and said and said—like I'm some kind of broken umbrella.

"Yeah, I've heard of him," Fry says out of the big bulgy mouth that clumps with the rest of his big bulgy features under the world's most massive forehead, making it very easy to mistake him for a hippopotamus. He rips the page out of the sketchpad. "Heard he was *gay.*"

He *was*—my mom wrote a whole book about it—not that Fry knows. He calls everyone gay when he's not calling them homo and pussy. And me: homo and pussy *and* Bubble.

Zephyr laughs a dark demon laugh. It vibrates through me.

Fry holds up the next sketch. More *David.* The bottom half of him. A study in detail. I go cold.

They're both laughing now. It's echoing through the forest. It's coming out of birds.

Again, I try to break free of the lock Zephyr has me in so I can snatch the pad out of Fry's hands, but it only tightens Zephyr's hold. Zephyr, who's freaking Thor. One of his arms is choked around my neck, the other braced across my torso like a seat belt. He's bare-chested, straight off the beach, and the heat of him is seeping through my T-shirt. His coconut suntan lotion's filling my nose, my whole head—the strong smell of the ocean too, like he's carrying it on his back . . . Zephyr dragging the tide along like a blanket be-hind him . . . That would be good, that would be *it* (PORTRAIT: *The Boy Who Walked Off with the Sea*)—but not now, Noah, *so* not the time to mind-paint this cretin. I snap back, taste the salt on my lips, remind myself I'm about to die—

Zephyr's long seaweedy hair is wet and dripping down my neck and shoul-ders. I notice we're breathing in synch, heavy, bulky breaths. I try to unsynch with him. I try to unsynch with the law of gravity and float up. Can't do either. Can't do anything. The wind's whipping pieces of my drawings—mostly fam-ily portraits now—out of Fry's hands as he tears up one, then another. He rips one of Jude and me down the middle, cuts me right out of it.

I watch myself blow away.

I watch him getting closer and closer to the drawings that are going to get me murdered.

My pulse is thundering in my ears.

Then Zephyr says, "Don't rip 'em up, Fry. His sister says he's good." Because he likes Jude? They mostly all do now because she can surf harder than any of them, likes to jump off cliffs, and isn't afraid of anything, not even great white sharks or Dad. And because of her hair—I use up all my yellows drawing it. It's hundreds of miles long and everyone in Northern California has to worry about getting tangled up in it, especially little kids and poodles and now asshat surfers.

There's also the boobs, which arrived overnight delivery, I swear.

Unbelievably, Fry listens to Zephyr and drops the pad.

Jude peers up at me from it, sunny, knowing. *Thank you,* I tell her in my mind. She's always rescuing me, which usually is embarrassing, but not now. That was righteous.

(PORTRAIT, SELF-PORTRAIT: *Twins: Noah Looking in a Mirror, Jude out of It*)

"You know what we're going to do to you, don't you?" Zephyr rasps in my ear, back to the regularly scheduled homicidal programming. There's too much of him on his breath. There's too much of him on me.

"Please, you guys," I beg.

"Please, you guys," Fry mimics in a squeaky girly voice.

My stomach rolls. Devil's Drop, the second-highest jump on the hill, which they aim to throw me over, has the name for a reason. Beneath it is a jagged gang of rocks and a wicked whirlpool that pulls your dead bones down to the underworld.

I try to break Zephyr's hold again. And again.

"Get his legs, Fry!"

All six-thousand hippopotamus pounds of Fry dive for my ankles. Sorry, this is not happening. It just isn't. I hate the water, prone as I am to drowning and drifting to Asia. I need my skull in one piece. Crushing it would be like taking a wrecking ball to some secret museum before anyone ever got to see what's inside it.

So I grow. And grow, and grow, until I head-butt the sky. Then I count to three and go freaking *berserk,* thanking Dad in my mind for all the wrestling he's forced me to do on the deck, to-the-death matches where he could only use one arm and I could use everything and he'd still pin me because he's thirty feet tall and made of truck parts.

But I'm his son, his *gargantuan* son. I'm a whirling, ass-kicking Goliath, a typhoon wrapped in skin, and then I'm writhing and thrashing and trying to break free and they're wrestling me back down, laughing and saying things like "what a crazy mother." And I think I hear respect even in Zephyr's voice as he says, "I can't pin him, he's like a frickin' eel," and that makes me fight harder—I love eels, they're *electric*—imagining myself a live wire now, fully loaded with my own private voltage, as I whip this way and that, feeling their bodies twisting around mine, warm and slick, both of them pinning me again and again, and me breaking their holds, all our limbs entwined and now Zephyr's head's pressed into my chest and Fry's behind me with a hundred hands it feels like and it's just motion and confusion and I am lost in it, lost, lost, lost, when I begin to suspect . . . when I realize—I have a hard-on, a supernaturally hard hard-on, and it's jammed into Zephyr's stomach. High-octane dread courses through me. I call up the bloodiest most hella gross machete massacre—my most effective boner-buster—but it's too late. Zephyr goes momentarily still, then jumps off me. "What the—?"

Fry rolls up onto his knees. "What happened?" he wheezes out in Zephyr's direction.

I've reeled away, landed in a sitting position, my knees to my chest. I can't stand up yet for fear of a tent, so I put all my effort in trying not to cry. A sickly ferret feeling is burrowing itself into every corner of my body as I pant my last breaths. And even if they don't kill me here and now, by tonight everyone on the hill will know what just happened. I might as well swallow a lit stick of dynamite and hurl my own self off Devil's Drop. This is worse, so much worse, than them seeing some stupid drawings.

(Self-portrait: *Funeral in the Forest*)

But Zephyr's not saying anything, he's just standing there, looking like his

Viking self, except all weird and mute. Why?

Did I disable him with my mind?

No. He gestures in the direction of the ocean, says to Fry, "Hell with this. Let's grab the slabs and head out."

Relief swallows me whole. Is it possible he didn't feel it? No, it isn't—it was steel and he jumped away totally freaked out. He's still freaked out. So why isn't he pussyhomoBubbling me? Is it because he likes Jude?

Fry twirls a finger by his ear as he says to Zephyr, "Someone's Frisbee is seriously on the roof, bro." Then to me: "When you least expect it, Bubble." He mimes my free-fall off Devil's Drop with his mitt of a hand.

It's over. They're headed back toward the beach.

Before they change their Neanderthal minds, I hustle over to my pad, slip it under my arm, and then, without looking back, I speed-walk into the trees like someone whose heart isn't shaking, whose eyes aren't filling up, someone who doesn't feel so newly minted as a human.

When I'm in the clear, I blast out of my skin like a cheetah—they go from zero to seventy-five mph in three seconds flat and I can too practically. I'm the fourth-fastest in the seventh grade. I can unzip the air and disappear inside it, and that's what I do until I'm far away from them and what happened. At least I'm not a mayfly. Male mayflies have two dicks to worry about. I already spend half my life in the shower because of my one, thinking about things I can't stop thinking about no matter how hard I try because I really, really, *really* like thinking about them. Man, I do.

At the creek, I jump rocks until I find a good cave where I can watch the sun swimming inside the rushing water for the next hundred years. There should be a horn or gong or something to wake God. Because I'd like to have a word with him. Three words actually:

WHAT THE FUCK?!

After a while, having gotten no response as usual, I take out the charcoals from my back pocket. They somehow survived the ordeal intact. I sit down and open my sketchbook. I black out a whole blank page, then another, and another. I press so hard, I break stick after stick, using each one down to the very nub, so it's like the blackness is coming out of my finger, out of me, and onto the page. I fill up the whole rest of the pad. It takes hours.

(A SERIES: *Boy Inside a Box of Darkness*)

The next night at dinner, Mom announces that Grandma Sweetwine joined her for a ride in the car that afternoon with a message for Jude and me.

Only, Grandma's dead.

"Finally!" Jude exclaims, falling back in her chair. "She promised me!"

What Grandma promised Jude, right before she died in her sleep three months ago, is that if Jude ever really needed her, she'd be there in a flash. Jude was her favorite.

Mom smiles at Jude and puts her hands on the table. I put mine on the table too, then realize I'm being a Mom-mirror and hide my hands in my lap. Mom's contagious.

And a blow-in—some people just aren't from here and she's one of them. I've been accumulating evidence for years. More on this later.

But now: Her face is all lit up and flickery as she sets the stage, telling us how first the car filled with Grandma's perfume. "You know how the scent used to walk into the room before she did?" Mom breathes in dramatically as if the kitchen's filling with Grandma's thick flowery smell. I breathe in dramatically. Jude breathes in dramatically. Everyone in California, the United States, on Earth, breathes in dramatically.

Except Dad. He clears his throat.

He's not buying it. Because he's an artichoke. This, according to his own mother, Grandma Sweetwine, who never understood how she birthed and raised such a thistle-head. Me neither.

A thistle-head who studies *parasites*—no comment.

I glance at him with his lifeguard-like tan and muscles, with his glow-in-the-dark teeth, with all his glow-in-the-dark normal, and feel the curdling—because what would happen if he knew?

So far Zephyr hasn't blabbed a word. You probably don't know this, because I'm like the only one in the world who does, but a dork is the official name for a whale dick. And a blue whale's dork? Eight feet long. I repeat: EIGHT FEET LOOOOOOOONG! This is how I've felt since it happened yesterday:

(SELF-PORTRAIT: *The Concrete Dork*)

Yeah.

But sometimes I think Dad suspects. Sometimes I think the toaster suspects.

Jude jostles my leg under the table with her foot to get my attention back from the saltshaker I realize I've been staring down. She nods toward Mom, whose eyes are now closed and whose hands are crossed over her heart. Then toward Dad, who's looking at Mom like her eyebrows have crawled down to her chin. We bulge our eyes at each other. I bite my cheek not to laugh. Jude does too—she and me, we share a laugh switch. Our feet press together under the table.

(FAMILY PORTRAIT: *Mom Communes with the Dead at Dinner*)

"Well?" Jude prods. "The message?"

Mom opens her eyes, winks at us, then closes them and continues in a séance-y woo-woo voice. "So, I breathed in the flowery air and there was a kind of shimmering . . ." She swirls her arms like scarves, milking the moment. This is why she gets the professor of the year award so much—everyone always wants to be in her movie with her. We lean in for her next words, for The Message from Upstairs, but then Dad interrupts, throwing a whole load of boring on the moment.

He's never gotten the professor of the year award. Not once. No comment.

"It's important to let the kids know you mean all this metaphorically, honey," he says, sitting straight up so that his head busts through the ceiling. In most of my drawings, he's so big, I can't fit all of him on the page, so I leave off the head.

Mom lifts her eyes, the amusement wiped off her face. "Except I don't mean it metaphorically, Benjamin." Dad used to make Mom's eyes shine; now he makes her grind her teeth. I don't know why. "What I meant quite literally," she says/grinds, "is that the inimitable Grandma Sweetwine, dead and gone, was in the car, sitting next to me, plain as day." She smiles at Jude. "In fact, she was all dressed up in one of her Floating Dresses, looking *spectacular*." The Floating Dress was Grandma's dress line.

"Oh! Which one? The blue?" The way Jude asks this makes my chest pang for her.

"No, the one with the little orange flowers."

"Of course," Jude replies. "Perfect ghost-wear. We discussed what her afterlife attire would be." It occurs to me that Mom's making all this up because Jude can't stop missing Grandma. She hardly left her bedside at the end. When Mom found them that final morning, one asleep, one dead, they were holding hands. I thought this was supremely creepy but kept it to myself. "So . . ." Jude raises an eyebrow. "The message?"

"You know what I'd love?" Dad says, huffing and puffing himself back into the conversation so that we're never going to find out what the freaking message is. "What I'd love is if we could finally declare The Reign of Ridiculous over." This, again. The Reign he's referring to began when Grandma moved in. Dad, "a man of science," told us to take every bit of superstitious hogwash that came out of his mother's mouth with a grain of salt. Grandma told us not to listen to her artichoke of a son and to take those grains of salt and throw them right over our left shoulders to blind the devil.

Then she took out her "bible"—an enormous leather-bound book stuffed with batshit ideas (aka: hogwash)—and started to preach the gospel. Mostly to Jude.

Dad lifts a slice of pizza off his plate. Cheese dives over the edges. He looks at me. "How about this, huh, Noah? Who's a little relieved we're not having one of Grandma's luck-infused stews?"

I remain mum. Sorry, Charlie. I *love* pizza, meaning: Even when I'm in the middle of eating pizza, I wish I were eating pizza, but I wouldn't jump on Dad's train even if Michelangelo were on it. He and I don't get on, though he tends to forget. I never forget. When I hear his big banging voice coming after me to watch the 49ers or some movie where everything gets blown up or to listen to jazz that makes me feel like my body's on backward, I open my bedroom window, jump out, and head for the trees.

Occasionally when no one's home, I go into his office and break his pencils. Once, after a particularly toilet-licking Noah the Broken Umbrella Talk, when he laughed and said if Jude weren't my twin he'd be sure I'd come about from parthenogenesis (looked it up: conception without a father), I snuck into the garage while everyone was sleeping and keyed his car.

Because I can see people's souls sometimes when I draw them, I know the following: Mom has a massive sunflower for a soul so big there's hardly any room in her for organs. Jude and me have one soul between us that we have to share: a tree with its leaves on fire. And Dad has a plate of maggots for his.

Jude says to him, "Do you think Grandma didn't just hear you insult her cooking?"

"That would be a resounding no," Dad replies, then hoovers into the slice. The grease makes his whole mouth gleam.

Jude stands. Her hair hangs all around her head like lightcicles. She looks up at the ceiling and declares, "*I* always loved your cooking, Grandma."

Mom reaches over and squeezes her hand, then says to the ceiling, "Me too, Cassandra."

Jude smiles from the inside out.

Dad finger-shoots himself in the head.

Mom frowns—it makes her look a hundred years old. "Embrace the mystery, Professor," she says. She's always telling Dad this, but she used to say it different. She used to say it like she was opening a door for him to walk through, not closing one in his face.

"I married the mystery, Professor," he answers like always, but it used to sound like a compliment.

We all eat pizza. It's not fun. Mom's and Dad's thoughts are turning the air black. I'm listening to myself chew, when Jude's foot finds mine under the table again. I press back.

"The message from Grandma?" she interjects into the tension, smiling hopefully.

Dad looks at her and his eyes go soft. She's his favorite too. Mom doesn't have a favorite, though, which means the spot is up for grabs.

"As I was saying." This time Mom's using her normal voice, husky, like a cave's talking to you. "I was driving by CSA, the fine arts high school, this afternoon and that's when Grandma swooped in to say what an absolutely perfect fit it would be for you two." She shakes her head, brightening and becoming her usual age again. "And it really is. I can't believe it never occurred to me. I keep thinking of that quote by Picasso: 'Every child is an artist. The problem is how to remain an artist once one grows up.'" She has the bananas look on her face that happens in museums, like she's going to steal the art. "But this. This is a chance of a lifetime, guys. I don't want your spirits to get all tamped down like . . ." She doesn't finish, combs a hand through her hair—black and bombed-out like mine—turns to Dad. "I really want this for them, Benjamin. I know it'll be expensive, but what an oppor—"

"That's it?" Jude interrupts. "That's all Grandma said? That was the message *from the afterlife*? It was about some *school*?" She looks like she might start crying.

Not me. Art school? I never imagined such a thing, never imagined I wouldn't have to go to Roosevelt, to Asshat High with everyone else. I'm pretty sure the blood just started glowing inside my body.

(SELF-PORTRAIT: *A Window Flies Open in My Chest*)

Mom has the bananas look again. "Not just any school, Jude. A school that will let you shout from the rooftops every single day for four years. Don't you two want to shout from the rooftops?"

"Shout what?" Jude asks.

This makes Dad chuckle under his breath in a thistly way. "I don't know, Di," he says. "It's so focused. You forget that for the rest of us, art's just art, not religion." Mom picks up a knife and thrusts it into his gut, twists. Dad forges on, oblivious. "Anyway, they're in seventh grade. High school's still a ways away."

"I want to go!" I explode. "I don't want a tamped-down spirit!" I realize these are the first words I've uttered outside my head this entire meal. Mom beams at me. He can't talk her out of this. There are no surftards there, I know it. Probably only kids whose blood glows. Only revolutionaries.

Mom says to Dad, "It'll take them the year to prepare. It's one of the best fine arts high schools in the country, with topnotch academics as well, no problem there. And it's right in our backyard!" Her excitement is revving me even more. I might start flapping my arms. "Really difficult to get in. But you two have it. Natural ability and you already know so much." She smiles at us with so much pride it's like the sun's rising over the table. It's true. Other kids had picture books, we had art books. "We'll start museum and gallery visits this weekend. It'll be great. You two can have drawing contests."

Jude barfs bright blue fluorescent barf all over the table, but I'm the only one who notices. She can draw okay, but it's different. For me, school only stopped being eight hours of daily stomach surgery when I realized everyone wanted me to sketch them more than they wanted to talk to me or bash my face in. No one ever wanted to bash Jude's face in. She's shiny and funny and normal—not a revolutionary—and talks to everybody. I talk to me. And Jude, of course, though mostly silently because that's how we do it. And Mom because she's a blow-in. (Quickly, the evidence: So far she hasn't walked through a wall or picked up the house with her mind or stopped time or anything totally off-the-hook, but there've been things. One morning recently, for instance, she was out on the deck like usual drinking her tea and when I got closer I saw that she'd floated up into the air. At least that's how it looked to me. And the clincher: She doesn't have parents. She's a foundling! She was just left in some church in Reno, Nevada, as a baby. Hello? Left by *them*.) Oh, and I also talk to Rascal next door, who, for all intents and purposes, is a horse, but yeah right.

Hence, Bubble.

Really, most of the time, I feel like a hostage.

Dad puts his elbows on the table. "Dianna, take a few steps back. I really think you're projecting. Old dreams die—"

Mom doesn't let him say another word. The teeth are grinding like mad. She looks like she's holding in a dictionary of bad words or a nuclear war. "NoahandJude, take your plates and go into the den. I need to talk to your father."

We don't move. "NoahandJude, now."

"Jude, Noah," Dad says.

I grab my plate and I'm glued to Jude's heels out of there. She reaches a hand back for me and I take it. I notice then that her dress is as colorful as a clownfish. Grandma taught her to make her clothes. Oh! I hear our neighbor's new parrot, Prophet, through the open window. "Where the hell is Ralph?" he squawks. "Where the hell is Ralph?" It's the only thing he says, and he says it 24/7. No one knows who, forget where, Ralph is.

"Goddamn stupid parrot!" Dad shouts with so much force all our hair blows back.

"He doesn't mean it," I say to Prophet in my head only to realize I've said it out loud. Sometimes words fly out of my mouth like warty frogs. I begin to explain to Dad that I was talking to the bird but stop because that won't go over well, and instead, out of my mouth comes a weird bleating sound, which makes everyone except Jude look at me funny. We spring for the door.

A moment later we're on the couch. We don't turn on the TV, so we can eavesdrop, but they're speaking in angry whispers, impossible to decipher. After sharing my slice bite for bite because Jude forgot her plate, she says, "I thought Grandma would tell us something awesome in her message. Like if heaven has an ocean, you know?"

I lean back into the couch, relieved to be just with Jude. I never feel like I've been taken hostage when it's just us. "Oh yeah it does, most definitely it has an ocean, only it's purple, and the sand is blue and the sky is hella green."

She smiles, thinks for a moment, then says, "And when you're tired, you crawl into your flower and go to sleep. During the day, everyone talks in colors instead of sounds. It's so quiet." She closes her eyes, says slowly, "When people fall in love, they burst into flames." Jude loves that one—it was one of Grandma's favorites. We used to play this with her when we were little. "Take me away!" she'd say, or sometimes, "Get me the hell out of here, kids!"

When Jude opens her eyes, all the magic is gone from her face. She sighs.

"What?" I ask.

"I'm not going to that school. Only aliens go there."

"Aliens?"

"Yeah, freaks. California School of the Aliens, that's what people call it."

Oh man, oh man, thank you, Grandma. Dad has to cave. I have to get in. Freaks who make art! I'm so happy, I feel like I'm jumping on a trampoline, just boinging around inside myself.

Not Jude. She's all gloomy now. To make her feel better I say, "Maybe Grandma saw your flying women and that's why she wants us to go." Three coves down, Jude's been making them out of the wet sand. The same ones she's always doing out of mashed potatoes or Dad's shaving cream or whatever when she thinks no one's looking. She even does the flying poses herself—in secret, but I've seen it—like she's one of them. From the bluff, I've been watching her build these bigger sand versions and know she's trying to talk to Grandma. I can always tell what's in Jude's head. It's not as easy for her to tell what's in mine, though, because I have shutters and I close them whenever I have to. Like lately.

(SELF-PORTRAIT: *The Boy Hiding Inside the Boy Hiding Inside the Boy*)

"I don't think those are art. Those are . . ." She doesn't finish. "It's because of you, Noah. And you should stop following me down the beach. What if I were kissing someone?"

"Who?" I'm only two hours thirty-seven minutes and thirteen seconds younger than Jude, but she always makes me feel like I'm her little brother. I hate it. "Who would you be kissing? Did you kiss someone?"

"I'll tell you if you tell me what happened yesterday. I know something did and that's why we couldn't walk to school the normal way this morning." I didn't want to see Zephyr or Fry. The high school is next to the middle school. I don't ever want to see them again. Jude touches my arm. "If someone did something to you or said something, tell me."

She's trying to get in my mind, so I close the shutters. Fast, slam them right down with me on one side, her on the other. This isn't like the other horror shows: The time she punched the boulder-come-to-life Michael Stein in the face last year during a soccer game for calling me a retard just because I got distracted by a supremely cool anthill. Or the time I got caught in a rip and she and Dad had to drag me out of the ocean in front of a whole beach of surftards. This is different. This secret is like having hot burning coals under my bare feet all the time. I rise up from the couch to get away from any potential telepathy—when the yelling reaches us.

It's loud, like the house might break in two. Same as the other times lately.

I sink back down. Jude looks at me. Her eyes are the lightest glacier blue; I use mostly white when I draw them. Normally they make you feel floaty and think of puffy clouds and hear harps, but right now they look just plain scared. Everything else has been forgotten.

(PORTRAIT: *Mom and Dad with Screeching Tea Kettles for Heads*)

When Jude speaks, she sounds like she did when she was little, her voice made of tinsel. "Do you really think that's why Grandma wants us to go to that school? Because she saw my flying sand women?"

"I do," I say, lying. I think she was right the first time. I think it's because of me.

She scoots over so we're shoulder to shoulder. This is us. Our pose. The smush. It's even how we are in the ultrasound photo they took of us inside Mom and how I had us in the picture Fry ripped up yesterday. Unlike most everyone else on earth, from the very first cells of us, we were together, we came here together. This is why no one hardly notices that Jude does most of the talking for both of us, why we can only play piano with all four of our hands on the keyboard and not at all alone, why we can never do Rochambeau because not once in thirteen years have we chosen differently. It's always: two rocks, two papers, two scissors. When I don't draw us like this, I draw us as half-people.

The calm of the smush floods me. She breathes in and I join her. Maybe we're too old to still do this, but whatever. I can see her smiling even though I'm looking straight ahead. We exhale together, then inhale together, exhale, inhale, in and out, out and in, until not even the trees remember what happened in the woods yesterday, until Mom's and Dad's voices turn from mad to music, until we're not only one age, but one complete and whole person.

Turn the page for
a discussion guide to

the

sky

is

everywhere

1. A major theme of this book is Lennie's discovery of her sexuality. Do you think this is depicted realistically? Do you think this is tied to her grief or do you think the two are unrelated?

2. Throughout the novel, Lennie writes on anything and everything and leaves these poems scattered around the town. Do you think this is an effective way of showing the reader Lennie and Bailey's relationship? How do these poems ultimately bring Joe and Lennie together? What is the significance of Lennie's scattering these poems?

3. Writing can be a form of therapy for some people. Do you think these poems are Lennie's way of finding an outlet for her grief? If so, what makes you think it works? Doesn't work?

4. When Sarah hears about Lennie and Toby's relationship, she's upset by their actions. Do you agree with Sarah's reaction or should she have reacted differently, knowing Lennie and Toby's situation? What is your opinion on Lennie and Toby's relationship? Do you find it forgivable or heartless?

5. During one of her encounters with Toby, Lennie realizes, "I'm sure a shrink would love this, all of it." (pgs. 146–147) What does she mean by that? Do you agree with this assessment? Discuss whether you believe Lennie's actions in wearing Bailey's clothes and hooking up with her boyfriend are an act to keep Bailey close or to gain the life her sister had.

6. Lennie and Bailey were extremely close sisters. Do you really believe no competition existed between them? Why or why not?

7. Bailey and Lennie's absent mother is a large part of their lives. Ultimately the mystery leads Bailey to search for her. Why do you think she leaves Lennie in the dark about this? Who do you think is a stand-in for Lennie's real mother—Bailey or Gram? Why do you think Lennie decides not to continue with the search? Do you think she'll be content?

8. Lennie's actions hurt Joe very deeply, on account of his relationship history. Do you think his reaction is extreme or understandable? Why do you think he forgives Lennie in the end?

9. Consider the role music plays in the novel. How is this a crucial part of the story? Why does Lennie purposely throw the audition for first chair? How does music help her to heal? Is it just the music that draws Joe to Lennie or something more? How does it shape her relationship with Joe?

10. The novel is saturated with grief. Each person touched by Bailey in the novel—Gram, Big, Lennie, Toby, and Sarah—grieve in distinctly personal ways. Define their grief and how each character learns to move on, if at all. Do you wish any of the characters had worked through his or her grief in a different way? How would you have acted in their situation?

Turn the page
for a Q & A with author

JANDY NELSON

Music plays a large role in Lennie's life. Why did you feel this was an important addition to her character? What made you want to include music in the book in the first place?

Well, the funny thing is I don't feel like I had that much to do with it! Lennie pretty much crashed into my psyche, clarinet in hand. So she was always a musician in my mind and I went from there, believing then that music would be an intrinsic factor in her growth, in the way she coped with her grief, in how she connected in a wordless way with Joe, in how she moved out of Bailey's shadow and into her own light. In the beginning of the story when Lennie's so shut down, she says, to express what she's feeling she'd need "a new alphabet, one made of falling, of tectonic plates shifting, of the deep devouring dark." I think over the course of the story, she realizes that, for her, music is this alphabet. She says, "What if music is what escapes what a heart breaks?" and I think this becomes true for her. More generally, I love music and wanted it to have a curative, aphrodisiacal, celebratory, and transformative role in this story. Like Jack Kerouac said, "The only truth is music." And Shakespeare: "If music be the food of love, play on." I wanted Lennie to play on.

You have an MFA in poetry. Is this why you decided to make Lennie a poet in the novel?

Before writing this book, I'd only written poetry, and *The Sky Is Everywhere* actually started as a novel in verse. I had this image in my mind of a grief-stricken girl scattering her poems all over a town—that was really the inciting image for the whole book and key right from the start to Lennie's character. I kept thinking of her, this bereft girl, who wanted so badly to communicate with someone who was no longer there that she just began writing her words on everything and anything she could, scattering her poems and thoughts and memories to the winds. In my mind, it was a way for Lennie to write her grief on the world, to mark it, to reach out to her sister and at the same time to make sure, in this strange way, that their story was part of everything. So it all began with Lennie's poems, but very early on, like after a couple weeks of writing, it became clear that Lennie's story needed to be told primarily in prose so I dove in and found myself falling in love with writing fiction—it was a total revelation! After that, I wrote both the prose and poems simultaneously, weaving the poems in as I went along.

Why did you want to tell Lennie's story? Did you ever imagine telling Bailey and Lennie's story from another point of view?

No, it was always Lennie's story I wanted to tell and always from her point of view. I wanted the immediacy of first person, to really be able to follow her closely emotionally and psychologically over the course of the story. That image I had of her scattering poems was incredibly persistent; it chased me everywhere until I sat down to write her story. I had lost someone very close to me years earlier and I wanted to write about that kind of catastrophic, transformational life event. I wanted to explore some of the intricacies and complexities of grief, but I wanted to explore them through a love story—or two really. I imagined a story where joy and sorrow cohabitated in really close quarters, where love could be almost as unwieldy as grief. James Baldwin said, "When you're writing you're trying to find out something which you don't know." I think there were things I wanted to explore and discover, and writing Lennie's story helped me do that. She really took me over. What's odd is that despite the subject matter, and even though many days I typed with tears falling onto the keyboard, writing this novel was an incredibly joyful experience, one of the happiest times of my life.

Was setting important to you in writing this story?

Absolutely. I very much wanted the setting to be a "character" in this story interplaying with the other characters. I love California, love writing about it. I'm very inspired by the landscape. The imagined town of Clover, where *The Sky Is Everywhere* takes place, has really dramatic natural elements: roaring rivers, skyscraping redwoods, thick old-growth forests. This landscape is in the DNA of the Walker family, and I wanted it to be instrumental in Lennie's recovery and awakening, as objective correlative, but also as almost a spiritual force in her life.

What do you want readers to take from this story?

It's funny there's a paragraph toward the end of the novel in Chapter 35. Lennie has just told Rachel she's going to challenge her for first chair and she's running through the woods on her way to write the poem for Joe. She's taking steps that will propel her into the future when she's suddenly clobbered (not for the first time) by the realization that she has a future and Bailey doesn't. It's agony for her and it occurs to her that grief is forever, that it will be with her always, step for step, breath for breath, but she also realizes in this moment that this is true because grief and love are conjoined and you can't have one without the other. Grief is always going to be a measure of the love lost. She thinks, "All I can do is love her [Bailey], and love the world, emulate her by living with daring and spirit and joy." Every time I come across this paragraph, I think to myself, Well there it is, the whole book crammed into one paragraph! So for me the ideas in that paragraph kind of ring out, but every reader will take something different from the novel and that's what I want, that's the magic of it all. Reading is such a wonderfully personal and private affair.

What are your favorite parts of the writing process? What were your favorite scenes to write in *The Sky Is Everywhere*?

I have two favorite parts of the whole process. I love the beginning, the first draft, when I'm totally lost inside a story, so immersed that my fictional life overtakes my real one. I love the madness of that, when the story is pouring out and I feel this compulsion to get it down before I lose it. It's fevered, euphoric, like a mad love. And I also adore the later stages of revision, the last draft, when I'm playing with words, fiddling endlessly with this and that. At that point, I kind of just stare zombie-like at my computer screen for days living inside a particular sentence or scene or section trying to make it better, to make it come alive. It's a total blast. I think my favorite scenes to write were the ones where Lennie was falling in love. One of the wonders of writing a love story is you get to swoon right alongside the characters. I love that kind of tumbling rapturous emotion and trying to find language for it. I also loved writing the family scenes with Big and Gram and others around the breakfast table—the two of them were a lot of fun to spend time with, what came out of their mouths always surprised me. And . . . actually I think I have a lot of favorites!

Do you have any tips for aspiring writers?

Yes. Read, read, read. And write, write, write. Also, remember that what makes your voice as a writer unique is the fact that you're you, so don't be afraid to put yourself on the page, to reveal your passions, sorrows, joys, idiosyncrasies, insights, your personal monsters and miracles. Only you can be you and only you can write like you—that's your gift alone. If you have the writing fever, just keep at it—writing takes a ton of practice, patience, and perseverance—make sure to ignore the market and don't let rejection talk you out of your dream. I love this quote by Ray Bradbury: "Yet if I were asked to name the most important items in a writer's make-up, the things that shape his material and rush him along the road to where he wants to go, I could only warn him to look to his zest, see to his gusto."

Have you begun working on your next project? If so, can you give us any hints?

I am currently hard at work on a new YA novel about twins Noah and Jude. It's really two novels in one and it alternates between Noah's story, which takes place when the twins are fourteen, and Jude's, when they're eighteen. It's full of secrets and lies and heartbreak and romance and love and very strong passions. Both narratives revolve around a very charismatic and mysterious sculptor who changes both the twins' lives, and they, his. I'm excited about it—fingers crossed!

For more information, visit
www.theskyiseverywhere.com
or
www.jandynelson.com